EXIT WOUNDS

"A pity you won't help us," Barel said, attaching the wires to the prisoner.

They wanted so little, merely to bring him to trial. Once he admitted who he was they could work on him for months, without pain, without drugs, without pressure. There would even be sympathy, such as exists between interrogator and prisoner.

Dov spoke to the prisoner in German, but he didn't answer. Instead he said, in English:

"This man you say I am—did he do *this* to people?"

EXIT WOUNDS

MICHAEL BALDWIN

AVON BOOKS 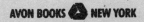 NEW YORK

All characters in this publication are fictitious, and any resemblance to real persons, living or dead, is purely coincidental.

AVON BOOKS
A division of
The Hearst Corporation
105 Madison Avenue
New York, New York 10016

Copyright © 1988 by Michael Baldwin
Published by arrangement with Macdonald & Co. (Publishers) Ltd.
Library of Congress Catalog Card Number: 88-92110
ISBN: 0-380-70657-1

First Avon Books Printing: February 1989

AVON TRADEMARK REG. U.S. PAT. OFF. AND IN OTHER COUNTRIES, MARCA REGISTRADA, HECHO EN U.S.A.

Printed in the U.S.A.

K-R 10 9 8 7 6 5 4 3 2 1

a book for Gill

Coincidence rules to such an extent that the concept of coincidence is itself negated . . . We thus arrive at an image of a world-mosaic or cosmic kaleidoscope which, in spite of constant shufflings and rearrangements, also takes care of bringing like and like together . . .

Paul Kammerer
from *Das Gesetz der Serie*

ONE

1.

He called her his daughter, and continued so till the end. One thing was certain. She couldn't go where he was going.

Victoria Station had made one small concession to modernity even though the trains still ran into it from the nineteenth century. At its eastern end there was a brand-new lavatory for gentlemen. A lavatory with a turnstile. To pass this turnstile, no matter how little else he wanted to pass, a man had to pay. So girls queueing next door for Skytrain tickets or foodstuffs in polythene wraps could smile at the rattle of coins and the jingle of stilebars as in one small corner of England male after male was held to ransom by progress.

Kay was in a hurry. The girl he called his daughter had no such need. She could ignore his rush towards the lavatory, but not his rebuff at the turnstile. She took time to give him a five p piece from her handbag.

"I'll charge interest!" she promised. It sounded like a long-running family joke.

By now there were three men behind him, blocking her view. They took the in-stile in quick succession. Or two did. One vaulted the gate.

The vaulter was reproved by a Sikh with a rubber broom. The place was full of Sikhs with rubber brooms and dark turbans, drenching the tiles with carbolic and water. The cluster of their faces appalled him, as if at an ambush. "Sick," he explained quickly. "Our friend's very ill."

1

Kay heard this, but it was not until the first two had
slammed him into a cubicle and followed him inside that
he realised they were talking about him and not one of
their own number. There is not much room to struggle in
a toilet cubicle, and before he could protest aloud one of
them pinched his nose between forefinger and thumb, then
dug a pistol hard under his chin.

The second man, of all ridiculous moves, unfastened
Kay's trousers and let them drop to his knees.

Kay felt a stab in the backside. A hypodermic syringe
had been jammed round his thigh and into his left buttock,
which was more than flabby, and the discharge was like
an injection of petrol, like snakebite. For ten, twenty seconds he felt sick, very sick indeed, as if a Taipan had
hooked him. He was held up by the pistol at his neck, and
he seemed to hang from it endlessly, tasting it in his throat.
He retched but could not vomit. Then the gagging passed,
and there was only the bruise of the gun. A numbness was
spreading from abdomen to chest, furring his mind.

Hands dragged his trousers up. The men murmured
something in German.

German was a language he refused to understand. He
shook his head dumbly, still choking on the gunmuzzle.

"Get it this way, then"—snapped out in English. "I'm
putting the pistol in my pocket, and we're going to help
you across the station to the Underground. Don't get
fancy—there are three of us, and the gun's still waiting.
And that little needle won't let you run far, I promise. It
needs an antidote. Otherwise you'll die."

They helped him out of the cubicle, where the third man
was waiting, to stagger among Sikhs, black faces grey with
alarm as he wheezed for breath.

They handed over a one-pound note. "He'll feel better
in a little while. We're taking him home."

Mouthing as they joggled past the turnstile: "What about
the girl?"

"In First Aid. Amos bumped her with a parcels trolley."

Kay did not hear this. Or if hear, understand. Outside
in the station, he lurched half-upright, surrounded by their
concern. He glanced for his daughter, inexplicably not
there.

They nagged again in German.

"I wanted the lavatory," he said. "You grabbed me in the lavatory." He started to piss himself.

They clung to him closely, as if to shield him from embarrassment.

"Where's Amos?"

"Skulking back to the Embassy. First he'll alert Yitzak to fix the pretty miss."

"She won't get far. Not in a party frock. Not with a damaged leg."

2.

There was a Metropolitan Police helicopter overheard. Ostensibly it belonged to the Diplomatic Protection Patrol, but in fact it would be full of nosey-parkers with spyglasses, just because he had chosen to give a little party and had some sensitive houseguests. The Ambassador shuddered to think of what else they might have up there—the sort of ridiculous surveillance equipment festooning that *Wonderbird* his children made him watch on T.V., perhaps. If they had, no doubt they would see what they would see. He hoped they made nothing of it.

Meanwhile, the sooner this lot packed their toothbrushes the better.

One was new to his staff, one merely here "for the duration." The Ambassador was annoyed at their public caution every time the helicopter passed over, and the indecent haste they showed ducking back into the marquee. He wanted Amos here to take them off his back. This wasn't Chile or San Salvador. It wasn't as if the Metropolitan Police was about to rain down bombs on them. He wished they would. Once a conspirator, always a conspirator, he supposed. But then he hadn't himself been a member of the Stern Gang or even of the Irgun, let alone all those curious five formations that came later, and sometimes in his middle years made references to his country's secret agents sound like the title of a novel by Enid Blyton, still his children's favourite author. But after all, while all the bad things had been happening to his country he had been at school in England, then college in America.

Neither place had endeared him to the contemporary

scene. He hated transistors, power-drills, motorbikes and helicopters about equally—and he was glad when the one that flickered overhead sheered off at last and left him to his guests. Helicopters were perhaps the worst of all. They whisked up God's miraculous sunshine.

He may have said so. After all, he was left talking to a rabbi . . . no, not quite that: one of those liberal or reformed people who called himself something else, and in consequence left the Ambassador uncertain of what they stood for. Yes, he might have said some such thing, but whatever he said, his mind did not follow his words to the front of his face.

He was brooding on the fact that there are some deeds too hot for accredited personnel to commit.

Such a deed was now being done to the man called Charles Henry Kay on the forecourt of Victoria Station. His embassy served a community which held its host country in almost total contempt; but those of his staff who knew, thought the disposal of Charles Henry Kay might be a little stiff. Better to get away with it than be caught, of course, but it would still look bad. The Ambassador did not like the smell of it at all.

If Kay went missing and was seen to have been Kay, not forever, but just an hour say, on English soil with a British passport, then there would be a stink.

The Ambassador might even be sent home. Such a thing could scarcely be solved by means of a diplomatically acceptable reduction in Embassy staff, a pruning of the B-list. The British Foreign Office might insist on Number Two, Palace Green, being wound up and put in mothballs.

The rabbi, of course, knew nothing of this. What a pity that his tongue also began to run on pain. "I've been sensing a certain unrest," he said. "In the Jewish community, that is. I sense it among the devout, and I sense it even more among the men of substance. They speak with their hands on their wallets, of course. But Israel, they say, is pushing a little far just of late. And those Americans I told you of, they were saying the same thing on my trip there. Israel is tempting trouble, they said. They didn't mean Israel, they meant Begin, I said. The point was lost. They know it is a democratic country that elects the elected, and they also know that trouble means money. It might be

Israel's trouble, but it was always their money, they said. Now where did I ever catch that note before?''

The words were second-hand, but they did nothing for the Ambassador's peace of mind. "They were talking about the settlements?" he asked hopefully.

"They were talking about trouble. They preferred, as a total way of life, to feel that the trouble which counted on their money was not of Israel's own making."

The Keppleman girl joined in the conversation. One moment there was helicopter noise and sunshine, the next this pretty girl was here pushing her pink little face in front of the rabbi's as if she were a drunk at a party.

She wasn't drunk. She was the daughter of one of his oldest friends. "Tell them," she insisted. "Please can't you tell them it does no good for the peoples of the world to look at television and see that poor little nut-faced Sadat make his pilgrimage to Jerusalam against all the odds, only to have certain members of the Knesset laugh in his face? The one Yiddish word the free world knows happens to be *Shalom*. And who makes the peace?"

"*Shalom* isn't Yiddish," the rabbi reproved mildly. He knew the girl too. What was her name? Julia?

The Ambassador signalled for refreshment, but the young are never stilled by diplomatic signs. Or Julia Keppleman wasn't.

"And don't forget to add that as well as being Jews, some of us are eight centuries English, two centuries American. We have Israel engraved on our hearts, but we have our own country too—and if one of them is wrong it must never be Israel."

"I tell them," he said. "I tell them all the time."

He did. He said it in all kinds of contexts on all kinds of occasions. It was not a new idea, however striking it might seem to the wide-eyed girl in front of him.

The waiter he had beckoned at last reached them with a tray.

"No thanks," she said. "I really ought to be going."

It was not always easy to think kindly of one's friends when their children misbehaved so abominably; but August Keppleman came from his infant days in Silesia. Sweet, brash girl. Perhaps she was leaving because she thought, as people of her age always think, that elsewhere

is more important. Perhaps she was miffed that he hadn't
taken more notice of her excited discovery of such a stale
old argument.

Then he noticed the plaster on her leg. As she hurried
away he caught a glimpse of her disfigurement, a lump-
footed walk caused by a wodge of surgical bandage that
thickened her calf and showed pink through the stretched
material of her tights. Perhaps it was the pain that made
her hurry off. He was aware of her limp for the first time,
and also the appropriate blue knitted stockings, before she
was lost in the crowd. Poor Julia. He should have been
kinder to her. Still, she had dealt him a verbal clout or
two; he could hardly be expected to examine people's legs
before he parried the anger that burst out of their faces.

"The young cannot be accused or accursed," he said.
He wondered if he was quoting something.

"And ours is a religion that cannot curse," the rabbi
answered.

If this was reformed, it was liberal indeed.

They were both glad to be on another subject, but her
words stayed with them.

The Ambassador pitied her her youth. She had so much
moral pain, and it must seem to her as if she had to live
with it forever.

Someone at the door would help her find a cab.

3.

Yitzak watched her for a second or two longer, but only
while he rechecked the probabilities. Her leg put the matter beyond reasonable doubt. For a moment he thought
she had stepped from a parked taxi, but then he realised
she must have been walking there all the time. Everything
else was a trick of his rearview mirror.

This must be Kay's woman, the woman he called his
daughter. He slowed, watching for a place to turn the car.

The mirror showed him light hair, a multi-coloured
dress, blue knitted stockings. Everything Kay's daughter
was wearing. There was something hesitant about her
walk, as if she was nursing a recently damaged leg, not
merely wearing a support bandage.

It was twenty-seven minutes since Amos Reitel had

phoned him from the station forecourt, and he had wasted nearly twenty of them in the thick traffic between here and the rendezvous; but the girl would have spent time too, getting her leg dressed.

She hadn't walked far. This end of Buckingham Palace Road was only a step from Victoria—and the far end led back past the side entrance of the station.

He turned the car and began to stalk her, steering wide of the van on a meter and wider again of some uncollected garbage bags.

If she were who she was supposed to be she would be a fool to be here; but the world is full of fools; and twenty-seven minutes meant she was a long chance anyway. But he was an expert in long chances, a descendant of two thousand years of them.

She walked with a pronounced limp. Just as Kay's daughter walked with a limp. Amos or Shlomo had smashed into her leg with a parcels trolley, so she must be supposed to limp if to walk at all.

She wore a plastic tube between knee and high ankle. He could see it through her ridiculous stockings. There was no clinic by the station, but there were first-aid facilities inside it, of course, and if the plastic casing had not come from there, then there was a pharmacy just across the way into Wilton Road. Dressing a leg took time. So it was not such a long chance after all. That was why she was shortly to be dead. She deserved to be dead because any woman who pretended to belong to that man was courting death. She knew it, and deep down would expect it.

She wasn't Kay's daughter. Kay didn't have a daughter, just this inconvenient young woman who so foolishly shared his life. Then Kay wasn't Kay, either. But what's in a name? A name is just an arrangement of letters in a passport. Even faces are changeable—though, to be fair, Kay's face had been curiously immutable down the years. To think that a man with so much money at his disposal for plastic surgery would have neglected that. But it was all in keeping, Shmuel Yitzak thought, tracking her in his car: the little meanness had surfaced like a boil from the poison of the big crime.

He began to pull over.

4.

Julia Keppleman had never seen a gun before. Now she could see nothing else. It enlarged in his hand till it filled her mind entirely, rearranging everything.

She did as it said.

She crouched into the car and slid along the bench seat beside him, while he steadied the pistol over his lap, pushed the changestick into drive and let the pedal up slowly after he had put his left hand back to the wheel. She scarcely noticed any of this. The gun took her. She tried to keep calm as she looked at it, and wondered if it were loaded and the safety-catch off. Somehow she never doubted it would be. If it went off, it would blow a terrible hole just above her right hip. She wondered what it would be like, not so much the hole as the getting it. She suffered the hole in her hip a long long time in her mind.

"Why are you—"

"Bloody wait and see." He didn't like the answer. Was his English idiomatic? "You know why, right enough."

She didn't know. She had been to the garden party. She had taken a taxi from Kensington. Then she had been walking in Buckingham Palace Road, or was it Buckingham Gate? She couldn't remember. Then she had been bullied into a car by a man with a gun. She concluded he meant to rape her. Nothing else made sense. She went back to the wound in her hip. Or the fear of it. Hurting her leg had been bad enough. Then she noticed his smell. Not Acqua di Selva or Aramis. Something much more foreign, a mixture of musk and ash. She wondered if he took dope. She allowed herself to be driven in the trance of his scent as if hypnotised. It was all too improbable for words. The Cortina clawed its way slowly round Hyde Park Corner, then went fast up Park Lane, darting right to avoid Marble Arch and the massed traffic lights of the Edgware Road. Afterwards they snaked northwards by diagonals, and she lost herself entirely.

At a stop-light he turned and stared hard at her, again itemising the description he had been given. Her hair was frosty with fixative, blonde as sunshine on plaster. "Fair like you've never seen before," Amos had said. It was the hair that clinched it for him. It was wrong for her face.

This had the hunted look the women in his own family wore, the legacy of the ghettos and the camps. He knew it was the face of guilt.

There were tower blocks of flats behind Thames Television and Capital Radio, just to the west of Hampstead Road. Here he put the car into a meter slot, parking wide. "Get out and feed it," he said. He pulled the rainmac down from her shoulders and used it to cover his gun hand. As he followed her from the car he looked quite the Continental gentleman, squiring her with her wrap.

"You've parked badly," she said. Her boyfriend would not have let her park like that.

This one grunted.

Inside a glass-framed door across the first court, "We'll take the lift," he said.

"They never work."

It didn't. They climbed five floors, ten half-flights of noisy stone stairs.

"Someone will see us." She spoke as if they were lovers creeping to an assignation. She spoke as to her boyfriend. By now she would have won an advantage over her boyfriend.

"Let me worry about that."

He traced her along a landing-way, then walked her back again, searching for a number. The gun kept her quiet.

The key fitted. They went inside. He handled her towards the telephone, which stood on a cheap tiled mantelpiece the colour of Horlicks.

As he dialled she glanced about her. Everything was so normal: the furniture faceless but durable, a landlady's job lot: congoleum on the floor, four upright chairs in a set with a table in biscuity veneer, two brown armchairs in one of the less effective plastics, with matching settee.

"I've got her," he said into the phone. "Will we want to hang on to this place?" Then he spoke another language, but not into the phone. He pushed her onto the settee.

"Tell us who you are."

She told him.

"Are you a Jew?"

"Yes."

"You let that swine touch you?"

"I've got to get home for tea," she tried. What swine?

"Is English your main language?"

"It's my only language."

"You look German to me!"

He slapped her, not hard. She began to sob, so a rage took him. He went through her bag, remembering details from her diary and address book; but taking nothing.

"Are you the police or something?"

A silly prevarication. This man's woman would be scared witless of the police. As she clearly was. Well, he had read through her possessions: she could be checked out at somebody's leisure, if it was felt to be worthwhile. He glanced at his watch. Her protector, the man called Kay, would be well on his way by now. Yes, he had time. Fear in a woman does things for a man.

Imbecilic professionalism: there must be no marks on his clothing. He faced her into the settee. Once more she was slow to protest.

Dachau, he believed, and Auschwitz. Ravensbruck for women in particular. The names were all let into the ground in that plaque in Jerusalem, the one with two alphabets. Yes, he could remember names. Historically, his own interest flowed from Treblinka.

She knew the job he must do, and why he would do it.

Once, thirty years ago, the man who called himself Kay had done things like this, lots of things.

"You'll tear my bra," she said.

He would tear nothing. He slapped her, not to mark, only to rouse himself. He was finding the beginnings of his own scenario as on some other occasions, even occasions of love.

Ten minutes later she was crying, crying fully and openly and without pretence. Even now he forgot nothing. No marks on his clothing, no blood group in her body. He slipped out of her and fumbled with his discarded trousers to find himself a condom.

Her tooth was broken. She emptied her mouth and said, "Is that meant to make it better?"

He'd teach her for that. He was violent inside her, but kept his right hand clenched on her shoulder, away from her throat.

Afterwards he relaxed for quite some time, then stood up slowly.

"Dress yourself."

She couldn't speak properly because of the blood. He could feel her contempt for him just the same. He was letting her regain her clothes and with them her confidence. Woman abused, but with a social advantage. And that black little gun looked so silly beside the pinkening sag between his legs.

She pulled herself upright and moved away. Then turning her bruised face towards him, she mumbled, "Now what. Now what, Casanova?" The words dribbled.

He liked her spirit. He had done her beauty a lot of damage.

The pistol was heavy, and because of it his own clothing took him that much longer. He glanced round the flat for evidence of his presence. There was none.

As if to answer her question he flipped back the window and stood gazing down into the street. His car was on the corner. There were two little boys playing with its bonnet. She saw him brood down at them, already in her mind the wanted criminal on the run.

What the two little boys remember most clearly is the noise her head made splitting on the pavement, like an apple.

5.

Her face anointed the front page of *The Sun:* LOVE GIRL'S MYSTERY DIVE.

The Mirror put her inside, but with more coverage, including a wide shot of Robert Street, a column-high silhouette of the edge of Maynard Court, with the window ringed, then a precarious reverse angle through an open frame. This last was a masterly piece of photography, with as much vertigo as a tabloid had any right to expect. Technically, it was the picture of the week.

The Mirror had not been content with that. There was also a full-length portrait of Julia from the family shelf, Julia in wraparound straw-coloured pig-tails, a school blouse fastened with a *Finding Out* badge, and her self-conscious schoolgirl hands seeking reassurance on the neck of a cello. The bow hung lifeless from her little finger. A lot of relatives and friends must have been sent that picture, but hardly by Julia, the Ambassador supposed.

The next morning's papers had been brought to him from the station at midnight; it was his custom to anticipate tomorrow. No-one on his staff had noticed that the girl had been on their guest-list, or matched her face with the school photograph published in the press, so the shock was all his own.

Embassies dine on fast news. Julia had died too late and too insignificantly for television: so it was left to the tabloids to pick over the human interest.

Their tone was uncertain, or perhaps it was his reading of it. On holiday once, in the hot lands with his uncle, he had seen birds eat a donkey in the desert. "They're drinking blood," his uncle said in disgust. The boy didn't react to this. He was struck by something else—intrigued by the lop-necked hesitation of the vultures' swallow. Whenever he watched them feeding on carrion he sensed their total lack of conviction: uncertain whether the entrails in their beak were choked up with rubies or running with corruption.

So it was here.

The Mirror write-up was a four-author by-line, and concentrated, in default of anything else, on the family Keppleman, which was at best three, and now tragically two: Papa had been a Belsen survivor, and Olga, his young bride, had nursed him back to health, first in the DP camp where they had met, then in Cyprus, which was another version of the same place, then in England. Their daughter had been the only apple on their tree, and now this tragic mystery had stricken them within a few days of her engagement and only weeks after her discharge from St. Thomas' Hospital after a successful bone-straightening operation on her left leg. A man prides himself on his friends, the Ambassador thought, and yet he knew nothing about them. *The Mirror* did not say it, but somewhere in the biblical rough on the edge of its well-known humanist fairway he detected a bunker with a signboard which read: "Man is born to trouble as the sparks fly upward."

The Ambassador was surprised at how many tears he could manage without weeping aloud and how very damp they made the page. He was not ashamed of them. At some decent hour in the morning, say nine, he would phone August and Olga, and lay his own sorrow next to theirs. First would go the letter.

He reached across his neck for paper and envelope, then stopped. His hand had found the package Amos Reitel had just sent up to him. It was marked INSTANT in red.

TWO

1.

Matson's sexual climate hovered over London like a cloud. He mustn't let his pego get the better of him, particularly now his hands were full of dead girls and newsprint.

His secretary noticed one of his preoccupations and said, "No-one's getting me near no windows."

A stallion in his trouser pocket just where society prefers a gelding. It was scoffing at snaffle and bit, and whinneying for sugar lumps. He slammed a leg on it, then sat behind his desk and gazed out of his office window into a moment so bright that even the girl traffic wardens seemed pretty.

Thank God none of his assorted diplomats and trade-delegates had done anything newsworthy.

If they had, then they remained undetected in the Street of Shame.

Ornamental hands were sliding carbons across his blotter, then soothing away the headlines.

He looked at her, he hoped not with interest.

A stallion about twenty hands high, or did he mean fingers?

" 'Nine inches will please a lady,' " he quoted, and wondered if Burns was boasting.

Brenda wore a disgusting crockery of fingernails. Too long and too sharp and too red.

"Burns was boasting," she said.

She was beginning to read his mind.

How long had she been here with her Thameside vowels, chewed consonants and fly-swelling fatty appendages?

14

Three months. She was threatening to know more about the job than he did. He wondered if fly-swelling was a true gerund, then said, "Trot those nasty Libyans into Leonard, will you? The names I suggested from the B-list. Better have him vet them."

"I've already shown him the carbon. It's your responsibility what names you find on the B-list, he says. He says you can use a pin for all he cares, especially when it's Libyans."

"That all he says?"

"Leonard told me to tell you to stand on your own two feet."

Matson couldn't, or he would have whacked her one. He had to keep his thighline behind the wareite desk top, to prevent her bursting out in girlish hysterics of South London mirth. "All right," he said. "Make me out a nice little copy to show the Yanks, and do some good-looking forms for the Minister. I'm going to declare them."

" 'Declare'?"

"Recommend they be declared—"

"Kick them out?"

"*Persona non grata* is the Queen's English for it. I've been and lost me pin." He did his fruity Irish yawn and hoped that somewhere someone would throw a bomb at someone, so he could read about it in the newspaper and forget his old cock robin.

Brenda was in no hurry to type the deportation orders. She looked him right through the desk top and smiled at what she saw. She had lovely eyes for that side of the river. "I signed the Official Secrets Act," she said. "I never sleep with the enemy."

"The enemy in this case being?"

"I never sleep with the Boss class."

"I'm not a member of the Boss class."

"You don't have to be. You're a Boss. I never sleep with them."

The phone rang.

Brenda picked it up and set it down, then went off to remake her nails. Several of them always shattered about this time in the morning and had to be reassembled like expensive porcelain. Her desk was already dusty with old emery board.

He wished his job was half as complicated as her finger ends. It was responsible, all right, and it gave him power; but power without authority. Still, he had asked for some such chore when he'd put his guns away.

A small department, its task the security coding of aliens, particularly those with embassy affiliations. He knew that politicians aren't fond of shows like this, because they aren't directly accountable. He left that worry to his boss.

Leonard Fossit was very accountable. He made a point of being seen every day, talking to Junior Ministers, Foreign Correspondents, Senior Civil Servants, providing statistics, answering questions. He was open and above-board and not in the least curious about the activities of politicians, even left-wing politicians, even when they were with coded aliens—or not ostensibly; and there was a comfortably naive and vulnerable side to him, too. It was part of his cunning to court their reassurance. Any ambitious Minister could have him sacked tomorrow; but none of them would. He was much too cosy to have around.

Matson found him benign. So it was with no sense of harrassment that he sagged against his chair behind the wareite desk and picked up the memo-board that Brenda clipped with movement notices. She had included a phone message and his pay-slip.

Just one offprint. Not even with a priority prefix. Timecoded at 6.25 yesterday evening, it told him that Dov Gorodish and Major Shlomo Barel had been among a group of businessmen from Tel Aviv departing from Heathrow on EL AL LY306, London-Ben Gurion.

Two nasty near-eastern thugs out of the way. Not as nasty as their Palestinian counterparts because not so hungry, but better out than in. This pair had obviously been behaving themselves, though. They had been accompanied by a career diplomat, and career diplomats are never anxious to put their heads on the block.

Brenda, fingernails nicely hardened, came back and dropped him another offprint. She also left him a coffee mug. The acceptable face of boredom.

Timecode 8.05 p.m, again Heathrow, Shmuel Shmuel, known to some as Yitzak, had taken Air France's second-from-last evening flight to Paris, through-booked to Barcelona. Strange destination, stranger man, but he too was gone. Someone would have to tip off the French, if they didn't know already. The Spanish could look after themselves.

Matson sipped coffee, amazed at how soon he could come to prefer inaction as a total way of life.

Brenda sensed his mood. "When I said what I said just now."

"What was that?"

"About signing Official Secrets. I didn't mean I wouldn't have dinner."

"I always eat dinner with my old mum."

"I thought your old mother was dead."

He missed her annoyance. What was welling through his indolence was the strange little fact that the same diplomat had been doing an awful lot of to-ing and fro-ing just lately. "Get me the Embassy Log," he said. The man wasn't a messenger. It didn't make sense.

Nor did asking for the log. The suspicion was enough. He waved Brenda away, picked up the telephone and called Heathrow.

"A further shipment of Irish bog erotica?" she asked sweetly, as she replaced the index.

"Minute this," he snapped, "and note the time. I'm talking to Passports." He listened to the phone for a few more moments, then said into it, "I was frightened of some such thing. No, we'll wheel it ourselves. I don't want you spreading it on your roses."

He left the phone to Brenda and barged in to see Leonard.

2.

Fossit's desk wasn't wareite. He sat behind imitation leather with one of Matson's lists in front of him. Brenda's typescript had been overscored in a variety of inks.

"Got to do it all again, Paddy. Apparently there's not a name here that isn't worth at least a hundred million to the Balance of Trade."

"I need to talk about something a bit more radical. Barel and Gorodish have gone. Ditto Mister Yitzak."

"Not even a wave goodbye?" Matson's breach of normal courtesy had got to Fossit's eyebrows.

"I think they took someone with them. On a fake passport. An unusual fake, and a hurried one. I'll come to that later. Those boys are much too thorough to move one of their own lot around on suspect documentation."

"They met an emergency contact." Fossit playing Devil's Advocate.

"He was ill. In a state of collapse. Two El Al people helped with a mobile chair."

"You mean a wheel-chair?" A little frown of semantic distaste. "They've stolen an Arab, then."

"They don't steal Arabs. They kill them with letter-bombs or machine-pistols. Besides, this guy was a pinky."

Again the tiny frown. "A terrorist important enough to fish out and put on trial?"

"We don't know of any. We've weeded out Al Fattah; and we've only just kicked out the Iraqis. Anyone lower than command or consular level they'd bump."

Fossit winced at "bump." He was strictly *Surrey Comet*.

"You ever heard of a sixty-year-old terrorist?"

"Grivas. Otherwise, point taken. Sixty?"

"Sixty-plus. Could be an athletic seventy. Certainly in his sixties."

"You're thinking venerable Kraut and the longterm revenge bit?"

"It's come really strong since talking it through."

Fossit looked as if he was about to say something exceptionally violent for Fossit, though doubtless the *Surrey Comet* would have printed the word. He waited, then asked, "How did it get to happen?"

"It gets to happen that we don't exactly hinder undesirable aliens from leaving the country. It also gets to happen that we merely record the passport data of their travelling companions if they're on a homogenous passport. We don't run an instant check. It takes a bit of time."

"Only boarding time."

"They boarded at the last minute. Anyway, this one would have been uncrackable. The passport boys were blinded by the fact that the Izzy heavies were on bona fide documentation. Come on, Leonard. They don't waste time detaining people we want to leave, to the inconvenience of the maybe innocent people they're travelling with, unless someone tips them off."

"Someone should have tipped them off. You're not raising eyebrows at me, are you, Paddy?"

"It's not down to our lot, is it, sir?"

Sir as from police-cadet days, or Adjutant, First Battalion the Thugs?

"So when did the passport office scent a rat?"

"They didn't. We did. I asked for any information about Barel's travelling companions. Gorodish was a natural. So was the other one till they told me he was a chair-bound geriatric. We know the *name,* Leonard. The sixty-year-old man was travelling on the private passport of a diplomat we know to be not a day older than thirty, with beamish eyes and an arsehole full of moonshine. Mr. Amos Reitel."

"The Second Secretary?"

"For trade and tractor parts. It had been re-faced and re-fiched, but it was bloody Amos's right through. His name, his number, Israeli address and recent entrance and exit stamps. Only the photograph had been substituted. It's probably on its way back in the diplomatic bag, though of course he'll have his consular documents as well."

"Smacks of haste, doesn't it? But it's eminently sound. It also reinforces the Big Fish theory if a Second Secretary is risking wet ankles. Do we deport the little beast for passport abuse?"

"He'll simply say it was stolen. Besides, it might be best to have one of them here."

"Claiming immunity?"

"Not in my back alley. Not to my deaf friends."

Fossit didn't even lower an eyelid.

Matson decided that the absence of distaste meant he was being congratulated.

"I take it you aren't pressing this piece of good news on me for information merely?"

"It all looks a bit interdepartmental to me. Just like it was last time we got into something like this."

"Last time the Israelis asked us, and I advised no. Do I tell my tame Minister?"

"Before *they* do. I hope he is tame, your Minister."

"Providing I select the right one. It's when we give it to the Foreign Office that Vulcan will start to rumble."

3.

The seat was reclined, the head lolling witless from an airline blanket, the hair spiky with sweat. Features were softening and ageing at an alarming rate.

Dov wondered if he were experiencing shock, and if it were his own or the prisoner's. They had been waiting much too long in Rome with the doors open. He felt stagnant but tense, as if marooned in a hijack.

The doors closed. Europe was another country.

He glanced at Barel and wasn't reassured. "Shall I give him a whack of pick-me-up?"

"After take-off."

"That last injection must have been fierce. He looks half dead."

"He *is* half dead. We've had to dope him hours longer than intended."

The boarding ramps unhooked themselves but did not swing away. The major pulled himself together and patted the blanket. "Looks geriatric. That's not a bad sign. Seen any elderly people die?" He knelt and checked the ankle-chain, then stood up.

Dov shook his head impatiently, his cheeks angry with stubble.

"The point I'm trying to make is they seem younger as they approach death." His smile tried to encourage. "Birth is the hideous one. We pop out as ancient as mandarins, faces wrinkled, older than the oldest man. Older than Abraham. Older than God." He pushed his shoe against the sprawled foot. "Looks disgusting, doesn't he?"

He spoke too loud and too long, still anxious that the doors might be thrown open again.

The ramp swung away, and the aircraft backed out, began to taxi.

The people thronging the first-class compartment sat down. Their uniforms said they were stewards and stewardesses and perhaps they were; but they were here to keep the fare-paying passengers back inside the tourist cabin. Barel did not know who had recruited the cabin crew, nor what they had been told. He was in charge. If they didn't know it now, they would soon find out.

The wheel-brakes came on. The plane stopped, stressing like a railway carriage. A recall from the tower was still a possibility.

He nodded to Dov who went towards the flight deck. This last take-off would not abort.

He had to put the rat inside its box, and then give its new owners the key. There might be one more box, there might be a million. They might stretch in a straight line or be arranged in a four-dimensional labyrinth. But always, at last, the promise of the cheese. And after the cheese?

The plane began to move forward, its engine-note rising like Hollywood's version of love, or its answer to a child's prayer.

4.

"Pinky not feeling so perky?"

Matson stepped from Fossit's room straight into Brenda's seated eyeline.

"Be busy," he told her. "There's been an Israeli Minister staying at 2 Palace Green. Without portfolio but in the usual military company. I'm suspicious of both."

"David Ben-Yosof. Mister Ben-Yosof's on the Embassy visitors list. So's his General Zefat. I've already been busy, you see. They flew away this morning—Ben-Yosof to Athens, Yigael Zefat to Rome."

"Waited till the other lads were clear, then began to voyage home. Barel's hardly a tiddler, and he had Gorodish and presumably Yitzak, so the general and the Minister were here for something big—perhaps to give it the final O.K."

"As I said, I been busy for you." Brenda began to purr. "Now shouldn't we forget it all and let Leonard pass it on. It's not our job."

"My job. You're secretarial assistance. Get me the Met."

"I mean not our department's. Much more Mr. Dixon's."

She was getting too big for her little knickers, as he suspected. "Get me the Met, then get Dixon."

He did his job well, and believed the whole office did. Therefore he felt pretty sure there was no likely target at large for the Israelis. Not a likely sixty-plus European target, anyway. There were no doubt plenty in South America, but not in the United Kingdom. More important, he didn't believe there had been any, yesterday afternoon.

"Missing Persons?"

Missing Persons was missing. While somebody looked for it he niggled to and fro in search of a reasonable scenario.

Surely the snatch, whether mistake or new pattern, must have been in the metropolitan area? So, with luck, there might be more than a merely alarmist report of a missing person. Speed had seemingly been of the essence. Covering their traces much less important.

The phone got lively at last. He was being passed from extension to extension.

"Sorry," a woman's voice said, "but some of my ladies were a bit nonplussed about your security-rating."

"Not good enough for them?"

"Too good, I fancy. I'm giving you Superintendent Gray."

Matson didn't know whether he was being shuffled backwards or sideways. He gave Superintendent Gray to Brenda. Superintendent Gray was male, but didn't have a voice. He had a swallow, as if all the missing persons were stuck end to end down his throat and gargling from Brenda's ear-piece. They were audible all round the office.

The swallow explained that the Met were not usually concerned to agitate themselves over middle-aged to elderly men going walkabout; but a file must be opened and a thousand errant husbands taken out and dusted. "It's the menopause," it echoed.

"The menopause?" Matson was drawn back to his own receiver.

"The male menopause. We get it every spring-time. Do you want someone to back-trace from Heathrow?"

"Who better than the Met?" Matson hung up for the three of them. "Haven't you got me Dixon yet?" he asked Brenda.

She grew very still. Fortunately her phone rang. She

lifted it and grew stiller. "It's Marcus Pomeroy," she whispered in awe. "You know, of the—"

"Hello, Paddy. Leonard tells me an unlikely story. Leave it to us, I say. But he won't have it. He's gone trotting off all by himself to the Home Office."

"He *is* the Home Office."

"He's gone trotting off, just the same. If your nag has been rustled, he'll still need his hay. And you don't want him knackered before you get him back. So treat the matter gently, is my advice to Uncle Fossit."

"Parables."

"I want to chat about something else. Leonard reminds me you were in the Thugs."

"Ta!"

"How can I beef up my Browning?"

"Grande Puissance? You can't. I've got one here in my desk." Something Brenda didn't know. "If you need foot seconds, buy a revolver. I'll show you how to cook it."

"Slow second shot."

"Shouldn't need a second shot. Come out for some pinking on Sunday."

"Isn't trap-shooting with handguns a mite eccentric?"

"I thought we'd try partridge this time."

Pomeroy whistled and hung up. Brenda looked thoughtful.

"You speak to Dixon," Matson said. "Then perhaps he'll get spoken to."

His own phone rang.

"Tell him what we know and ask him what he's got. He was supposed to have that crowd under surveillance. Remind him Barel was restricted to Inner London."

His own phone wasn't going to give up.

It was the charming lady, rank unknown, from Missing Persons. Apparently the swallow had had its summer. She was much easier to listen to.

"We've got someone for you. A Charles Henry Kay, 42 Caves Road, Chislehurst. Aged sixty-seven. A woman went into Gerard Road Police Station, a Miss Ginevra Kay, twenty-five, and said her father had gone missing in mysterious circumstances."

"Missing where?"

"Victoria Station."

Matson noted her name, then said, "Why didn't she go to the railway police or Victoria Station C.I.D?"

"Gerard Road's only a minute or two from Victoria, and it seems she wanted time to make her mind up. She was only reporting a suspicion at the time; it all seemed a bit daft to her . . . you know how it is. Wait a minute . . ." She was attempting to read from something, trying to disentangle the officialese. "The young lady was in physical shock, but seemed calm enough. Said she had been run into by a parcels trolley in the station, she thinks deliberately. When she got out of First Aid the old boy had disappeared."

"Anything else?"

"Circles, mostly. She said it all happened by the Wilton Road entrance, Platforms One and Two. Her father went into the gents there, the one near the V.I.P. Reception Hall. Last seen being followed in rather urgently by a crowd of fellas. Men rush into men's lavatories all the time, of course . . . but while she is thinking these thoughts, crunch comes the parcels trolley. Subsequently there is no Charles Henry Kay, sixty-seven."

"I'd better talk to the desk at Gerard Road."

"I've just done it for you—hence the mumble jumble of my notes. They said she did suggest abduction, but she could offer no sort of reason, and she didn't sound very convinced herself. She and her Dad had theatre tickets. He wasn't at the theatre, nor back home at Chislehurst. She phoned some of this in from the house later when she was a bit calmer."

"What action did Gerard Road take?"

"They logged it. What else could they do?"

That was all. She had no other elderly disappearances, or not male. So it was this one or he had to think again. Matson said his thanks and hung up.

The name was Kay. Charles Henry Kay. And Charles Henry Kay had to be someone with a Levantine background or a Teutonic past.

Why else would Israeli strong-arm men knock off a sixty-seven-year-old man who lived at Caves Road, Chislehurst, and abduct him on a passport that would aggravate the diplomatic repercussions? If they had. If anyone had. Well, at least Mr. Kay had vanished.

Brenda finished phoning and said, "Why does Mr. Dixon call you Thump?"

"Behave and you'll never need to know." Matson pushed his pad over to her. "Better call him back and give him that."

She studied it for a minute. "Victoria Station don't go to Chislehurst." She coloured. "Doesn't."

"Victoria Station don't go anywhere." He showed her his friendly tooth.

Ginevra Kay. Funny name. Far too bizarre to be assumed. It didn't sound in the least made up.

5.

"That hurt."

"I lack the gentle touch," Dov said, repacking the syringe. He was shocked to hear the man's voice, almost for the first time. There had only been those few words on Victoria Station, then sickness and sleep.

"It's an anti-venom, isn't it?"

"Is it?" Dov's hand held a plastic glass, full of white froth.

The prisoner didn't take it.

Barel left the seat where he had been crouched during take-off, and came back to them, stepping splay-footed. The nose-camber of the first-class compartment was distorted by the angle of climb. "So you're awake. Drink it and you'll feel better. It's vitamin C."

"Not specific for a neurotoxin."

Barel glanced at Dov, who shook his head.

"So you recognise the symptoms. Then you'll know the cure. Where we come from, it's oranges with everything."

"I thought it was chicken soup."

Barel relaxed. "It sounds as though you've been expecting us. Well, now you've accepted the worst, you can knock back your vitamins and we'll fix you a drink. We reckon to be civilised. We've even got you some korn."

"I'd like tea, please. Or a glass of soda water. You're making a ridiculous mistake, but for the minute I'm too groggy to care. I'm certainly going to make you all care, though."

They waited for a girl in a stewardess's uniform to open

a can of soda water. She wasn't used to cans of soda water. She took a long time and when she'd poured it the prisoner couldn't close his hands on it.

Barel had to hold it to his lips.

"You've guessed where we're taking you?"

"Only because you all talk too much. Yes, I've guessed where you're taking me. I've made the flight often."

The eyelids drooped, not only from exhaustion. The face was used to talking with its eyes closed, listening to the music of its own mind. "I have some influential friends in Israel. Professor Flexner of Haifa, for example."

"The Nobel prize-winner? He's influential, I agree. It's a pity he's dead."

"Then there's Doctor Tadeus from the Wellcome Laboratories at Tikva. I met him in Geneva last year. No—Berne. He knows what I am."

"But not, perhaps, who."

"I don't think they can be separated. One thing, please. Please. Will you send a message to my daughter as soon as possible?"

Dov searched for a formula and found one that took care of every possibility he could think of. He liked it so much he got ready to repeat it, close against the smug set of the face. "You have no daughter," he said. "Not any more," he wanted to say. "Or not for much longer."

There was no time for the prisoner to digest all this. He went into spasm, his back locking sideways in alarming rictus, his false teeth flipping to his chin, to his chest, to his knee, then to the floor. He frothed and jerked and heaved as any animal does when it dies.

Not a ritual death. More like a sheep with the hook in its brain.

6.

In Barcelona, Yitzak had trouble with Customs, a sure sign the French had passed the word from Orly.

Warned, he bought a bus-ticket. The airport taxi was definitely not for him.

He walked into the bus bay and loaded the three suitcases with their never-worn suits into the hatch at the back of the bus, and hoped he'd kept the tailoring receipts. For

appearances' sake he fussed over them as if they were
full of real valuables. The Customs would know they
weren't, but more experienced eyes, the eyes watching
him now, would expect film, microdot, waterwriting—
anything, providing he seemed determined not to lose it.
As an extra pantomime he retrieved the smallest case and
carried it onto the bus with him. The watchers would not
be puzzled. They would know that Customs had stopped
short of slitting the lining.

At the big traffic lights by Las Arenas, he left the bus
and the case and lost himself.

He remembered seeing a little hotel on the crossover of
Mallorca and Aribau. He was breathless when he got there,
and he had to check in luggageless. "It's been lost up at
Iberia," he said. "Or even back in Paris. You know these
baggage-handlers." His Spanish was florid, but easy. As
he spoke he flicked out his identification documents.

"Leave your passport with me." The man was middle-
aged with a button nose and a button moustache, Hitler-
ish. It was not a big moustache, but as big as he could get
on his top lip. "No luggage? Yes, leave your passport."
Some little Falangist *flic* who thought he was the Risen
Christ? Or the resurrected Franco?

The man's eyes widened when he saw the travel-
spattered Israeli passport. "You move about a lot."

"Yes, and it's taught me to keep hold of my papers. So
I'll retain my passport"—he spoke as if he had never re-
linquished it—"and you may retain my deposit." He
dragged it from the man's fingers and slid a thousand-
peseta note in its place. "If you're a good boy. I'll need
a receipt, of course."

The man watched speechlessly as he filled in his fiche,
then heard him say, "Have you witnessed this? Get on and
check it, then. I don't want you saying I'm cooking your
books." This time the passport was merely wafted under
his nose.

"You'll take pension?"

"Like belly-ache." He never left himself by daylight
close to where he lay at night. He demoralised the man
further by giving him a hundred-peseta tip, two fifty pieces
tossed onto the table. "When my valises arrive, see they're
taken to my room."

"How many, *señor?*"

"There'll be three." Pray God they never caught up with him.

Outside he let three taxis pass, drinking water deliberately from a tap fountain. The fourth was crawling. He never took a slow taxi on principle. He let that go, then walked a little, but across town, out of view of its mirror.

At last he found a taxi that suited his instincts. He had it take him to the Plaza Cataluna, but daftways about, by Montjuic, pretending he wanted some scenery. The taxi had a shrine over the dash, and a radio playing High Mass. "Turn that crap off," he said. He said it in Hebrew. The driver acknowledged his approval by turning it louder.

Irritated, he got off early.

In Calle Xucla he knew a tiny restaurant that had turned itself into a shrine to the memory of a dead bullfighter.

Shmuel Yitzak ducked through its bead curtain and ordered wine and tapas at the bar. The Embassy was going to have someone meet him here.

Nobody came.

He eyed the posters, the chipped pics and bloodstained suit of lights, with the bored gaze of a man who has seen them often. That was how he liked to look.

The bullfighting muck made him sick. He was waiting merely to make sure the street was clear. Even the Embassy mustn't know his next address.

A few doors down there was a shop that kept a suitcase for him. The shop was the suitcase's permanent home. He had such a shop and such a suitcase in half the major cities in Europe.

The suitcase was solid, though dusty. It would have made him look respectable back in his crummy little hotel. But he didn't want the suitcase.

He wanted what was in it, wrapped in clean underpants. He wanted the gun.

THREE

1.

The houses squatted up there like a giant chess set, like
the queens and castles, anyway. Matson saw them swag-
gering against the clouds in obscene parti-cotta, and his
heart quickened. This, surely, was the instinctive choice
of a rich German with something to hide. Gothic and vulgar, certainly, but above all safe.

Death could come out of those imitation shot-windows
much more easily than into them.

Fortunately for his professional future, he was sure no
such German existed in Chislehurst. Nor was there ru-
moured to be a North West Kent branch of the *Kama-
radwerk*. London's sweeter suburbs were a long way from
São Paulo and Rio Grande do Sul.

So he had no inhabitant in mind for such a Mad Hatter's
Castle as one of these.

They came closer, Matson and the rows of angel cake.
His eyes were still foggy with deskwork. Brenda had once
spilled pink stencil fluid onto the office's water biscuits—
light brown stone with dark brown stipples, now soiled
with the blood of the Dwarf Hildebrand. The houses had
been built from these.

Alas: Number 42 was not among them. Number 42 must
be one of those tucked into trees at the bottom of the
street.

A large picture-frame-windowed modernity. Even the
stairway and landing were bare behind glass. It was a
complete share-my-life.

The Common merged with the garden.

A house built for sudden death or swift abduction. Surely no-one with a secret would live here?

He pushed through wild may and rhododendra, an unlikely combination, but both of them a perfect snapshooter's camouflage. Never, on active service, had he had it so good.

A large bird thrashed heavily into flight, curving round twig sprouts and raucousing through a tin-sounding beak. He guessed a blue jay, but didn't turn to check it. He needed to dry his hands on a tissue. The walk from the station had reminded him how unfit he was.

The door opened while he was still rummaging in his pocket.

2.

The girl who stood there was beautiful and freshlooking, but sexless like lettuce. Her face seemed familiar. Prettiness does.

"Miss Kay?"

He didn't hear her answer. He was tasting her chlorophyll.

To protect himself from greenleaf fantasies he produced his identity wallet, together with his card. The photograph showed Patrick Matson in Eastman Colour but with spots on the lens, or perhaps P. Matson had ezcema or acne. *P. Matson, Esq.* The card called him a Security Adviser. *P. Matson, Security Advice.* He had one that said he was an encyclopedia salesman, but that would invoke the wrong kind of caution. He wanted Miss Kay to sense exactly who he was, but to read nothing that said so.

She led him inside. "You've come about Daddy?"

"Bolting stable doors."

"A version of you has just called," she said. "He came in by the back fence, so I stayed on the look-out." She pulled a face at him, showing she came from the suburbs where they breed good teeth. A complexion pale as hers needed good teeth: her hair was so unusually light.

"A version?"

"Yes, he was wearing the same Marks and Sparks shirting."

"So does Prince Philip."

"It doesn't look so bad on Prince Philip. Is he a policeman?"

"A sort of policeman. His name's Dixon."

"Are you a sort of policeman, or merely a sort of Mr. Dixon?"

Her tummy grumbled, making a noise like a cat growling. Matson saw the mauve darkness beneath her eyes, and realised she had probably been up all night with worry.

He tried to relax his aggression. He followed her through a hallway as big as a room and higher than a stairway, all behind glass so the garden peered in, then into a room as big as a cupboard.

"Daddy's den," she said.

He wondered why he didn't feel randy, randy in a quietly controlled way, as always with a beautiful woman. The chlorophyll. No, not that—the aroma of rotting herb garden. When young he'd stayed many times with his elderly schoolteacher Irish aunts in a sealed overheated house which smelled of their breath which smelled, he supposed, of their stomachs, which smelled of their cooking. This house, like theirs, was foggy with dill weed and chives.

Then he saw the snake. It was big, python big. It lay in its fourteen-foot length in a green glass tank that ran the width of the small room, and watched Matson with a still eye. The tank had a pool at one end, a puddle as big as a meat plate. The snake was responsible for the bad air, all the chlorophyll, dill weed and chives. He began to see his aunts in a new light.

"That's Tim," she explained. "His real name is Genesis. I call him Tim."

Tim indeed.

"Daddy's Taipan, you know."

The phone rang.

She answered it, grimacing with annoyance, then turned brusquely to Matson. "It's a Miss Somebody-or-other. For you."

"Miss Simmonds," he said. He hoped the call was important, and that Brenda didn't resonate too much. In her anxiety, the girl hovered close to him.

The voice in his ear said: "Your dishy Mr. Pomeroy's just been on to me."

"Yes?"

"You aren't going to like what he says. And Mr. Dixon's going to like it even less. Flight whatever to Tel Aviv was grounded at London for two hours yesterday evening; then diverted short-haul to Rome where it's been all night."

Explains Zefat's detour, he thought. He felt Ginevra Kay at his elbow. "Is there any explanation for this strange sequence of events?"

"According to your Mr. Pomeroy an engine overheated, then when it went to leave Rome the starter-motor jammed itself forward in the turbine, just like a car. They had to bolt a whole new engine in place, using a fork truck. Marcus Pomeroy says there was a lot of time for us to have thrown a block, if only someone had known."

"Quite."

"Not least in London."

"Tell that to your Mr. Dixon." He hung up, wondering just how high Barel's pulse rate must have climbed in the last few hours.

Not too high, he hoped—for the sake of the girl at his elbow.

"Just routine," he smiled. "We're covering everything we can think of."

It didn't work. Ginevra Kay was obviously near to breaking-point.

"You were talking about your snake," he said. "What did you call it?"

"A Taipan. It's an Australasian snake, Australian really. There are only a few in all Europe. The Australians won't grant export licences, but Daddy caught some of their earliest Taipans so they think he's special."

"When was that?" Daddy was in the Ark, perhaps.

"1942, I think. They literally evaded discovery till then. The Aborigines knew about them, I suppose."

"There was a war on."

"Work of National Importance, or something. He said they were after venom, or serum. Also other medical and pharmacological stuff. It's a very complex poison."

"I see." He looked at the snake. It was limp but alive, much like himself. "Your father makes a habit of going up to Victoria?"

"Twice a week. He goes to his club and to the Herpetological Society."

"And he always takes the same train?"

"Almost invariably."

"Does he walk over to Bickley station?"

"He goes from Bromley."

"Bromley? That's about three miles."

"Yes. But it's a fast line. Only one stop. Daddy loathes wasting time on trains."

"What about wasting time out of trains?"

"The walk, you mean? He likes to walk. Fitness matters to him. He has to go to some pretty unkempt places sometimes; and it's hard for a man of his age to keep fit save by walking. Also, the long-distance trains stop at Bromley. Daddy likes a train with a lavatory."

Lavatories looked like being Daddy's undoing.

"We both encourage him to walk."

"Both?"

"Daddy does, and I do."

Something very prim about her speech, like a nineteenth-century schoolma'am; or a woman whose father was a foreigner and whose childhood had been nurtured on a gradually self-eradicating foreign accent?

Matson didn't think so. Her speech was like her personality, like lettuce. It was her intelligence that was strange. Matson was used to two sorts of woman. Women made of meat, women made of mind. With Ginevra Kay the mind was never in doubt, but there was an exotic seasoning of snake and *fines herbes,* inspiring him to green thoughts and poetry. Sweet transmogrifying Miss Kay. She wasn't foreign at all, just different, like a vegetable. Her breasts fell into his imagination like cos. He smirked and said, "What does your father do if it rains?"

"He either calls a taxi or he takes the car."

"To London?"

"Never. To the multi-storey in Bromley. It's only a step from the station. Or sometimes I drive him." Something arch and progressive seemed to be creeping into her voice, as if she were implying she generally had better things to do. Miss Kay was recovering her composure fast and with it her attractiveness. He felt as if he had known her a long time.

"You say he always catches the same train?"

"Nearly always. He gets the ten thirty-eight in the

mornings, the fifteen fifty-one if he goes up in the afternoons.''

So why hadn't they taken him on the train?

''Yesterday was a bit different. The Coast train stopped—the train from Dover—while we were waiting. It doesn't normally, but if it does—if it's held up by signals or a train on the section ahead—Daddy always hops aboard. There's a bar, you see. So he gets himself a gin.''

''How long to London?''

''All of fourteen minutes.''

A fourteen-minute gin. An amiable cove, Daddy. What with his gullet and his bladder, Matson had quite an image of him. Or he supposed it was his bladder. The old boy went to foreign climes. He might have trouble with amoebas.

The Israelis must have had trouble with his amoebas as well. He'd taken an unscheduled train, far too empty or too crowded. Or they had been baulked by his daughter being with him—something unrehearsed. No need to ponder the matter further, save to say, ''Did many other people catch the train with you?''

''Only a few. It's always only a few. Men mostly. The porters warn everyone to stand back. They know Daddy won't.''

''Women are more obedient?''

''More responsible will do very nicely.''

''Did you recognise any of the men who got on?''

She shook her head.

''Were they the same men who—?''

''Possibly. They were wearing suits. But then you expect men with suits on a London train. Even Daddy puts a crease on.''

Matson steered the conversation towards Victoria. Nothing much interested him until she mentioned the loo.

''Of course I'm bound to put it to you that the parcel trolley was a coincidence—someone horsing about?''

''So where does that leave Daddy?''

''Well, here's something else. I hope you won't be offended. Perhaps your father simply took himself off for a few days without telling you?''

''Not when he'd booked theatre tickets. You don't know Daddy.''

"Perhaps Daddy's in love."

"Daddy has a prolapsed amorata. Sorry—that's school talk. Daddy has an incurably broken heart."

"Someone he might have gone to?"

"A friend of mine. She used to live next door. And now she's a reserved topic, filed but not forgotten. No—he won't have gone to her." She gazed at him with renewed enthusiasm. Thinking of her father in the round had cheered her up. "Daddy's always a bit prefrontal, if you know what I mean, in spite of the rings on his trunk. No Priapus, Daddy, but a bit of a problem to his tailor—rather like you. His interest in young women is natural enough."

Matson said quickly, "I was thinking of it more from the girl's point of view."

"Oh, Daddy's not in the least geriatric, not quite your conventional Poona. My friends used to call him quaggy."

"What does that mean?"

"School tie beating beneath the frayed bush shirt. He chases snakes in the desert, so that keeps him fit. And he looks after himself, and doesn't let himself grow gnarly. He washes the occasional armpit."

Her enthusiasm seemed unhealthy, but Matson had no time to dwell on it. They hadn't sat down—Brenda's phone-call put paid to that—and now the girl grimaced with pain.

Matson hadn't thought about her leg. He didn't think she'd welcome anything fulsome, so half turned to go and said, "There'll be other people coming to see you. Keep that chain on the door till they've shown you some proper identification." He watched her eyes widen, but pressed on remorselessly. "Then ask them to take a little walk while you close the door and phone your local police station." It wouldn't work. His eyes were suddenly too insistent on her swollen left shin, with its lump of plaster bandage and her thick coloured stocking. "Is that where the trolley hit you?"

She nodded.

"Ah," he said. Unnaturally pale skin, unusually fair hair—was this enough to send an *ad hoc* hit-man after the wrong target? He allowed his face to reassume its Camberwell Irish gormlessness, an expression which had been replaced by Camberwell wide-awake, and then educated to no expression at all.

Hardly an overwhelming coincidence, but it needed following up. What a good thing he read vulgar newspapers.

"Not even the chain," he cautioned. "You speak to them through the letterbox. And post yourself behind some brickwork." He would arrange for her to be watched, and fast.

"You mean these men who've got Daddy—"

"Who *might* have got—"

"They'd come here?"

"They're well-known itinerants."

"Like Thuggee—the Thugs?"

"It's an apt image." Having shot his mouth off, Matson was grateful for a misunderstanding.

"What about Daddy?"

The father, historically, they leave alone. He had gone too far, of course, but the girl's leg had thrown him. Much too far but not far enough. He decided to try the sleuth's three-card trick as a parting shot. So he kneed up his hard top briefcase and splayed out some photographs.

A girl seeing a stranger to the door, a stressed girl at that, is hardly a good witness; so his first thought had been to leave the mug shots to more sympathetic operatives.

"No. None of these." First thought was wise.

Matson sagged. He saw a theory collapsing, or at least not standing up.

"That man there. I think it was him. He was one of a bunch that jostled behind Daddy on the way into the loo. What a coincidence!"

"Ta," said Matson.

"But the trolley, no. I've got his face on my mind. He was straining to get it moving, see. Sort of came at me in slow motion, with his mouth etched into lines, if that makes sense. He's not here."

Three went home, Matson thought, but not quite the three that did the snatching. Also they would have needed a coordinator. There was no reason to suppose this hadn't been an Embassy job, especially since little Amos was already in it up to his neck.

Unfortunately Matson's Embassy photographs were clearly labelled. So were his albums of El Al employees and the courier services. They would make the girl aware of his conclusions, and she might acquaint others. He must get some fresh prints taken and confront her with them later. For similar reasons of discretion he needed to find an outside phonebox.

He said an awkward goodbye, opened the front door and pushed between the bushes.

The noisy bird was back again. It wasn't a blue jay, but a small parrot muttering gibberish at him.

"Strange she's let it out," the girl said. "I'll try and catch it for her."

"So you know the little monster? It's not often I meet one that talks a foreign language."

"Especially Yiddish."

It screamed, high in a laburnum, then fidgeted and scolded after him for ages. He remembered it for years.

3.

The House was still sitting from the night before, but there was a sky-blue optimism about the morning, and in the little recesses off Whitehall the birdsong was stubbornly refusing to be drowned out by traffic. Learning by car-phone that the Home Office was momentarily empty of power, if not of brains, Fossit had himself driven to Parliament. Normally he hated the manoeuvre: it made him feel like a tripper. Today he had birdsong and things on his mind.

Fossit's tamest Minister had been re-shuffled. The lady in question had been victimised for her dedication to certain secret departments, with his own Aliens and the B-list prime among them. But it was a branch of Government with more than one Minister, and he had no intention of stopping off to educate the new assistant of State. His message was complex, and might dilute with repetition.

He was led to Quinlan's private office.

It was not a long wait.

Quinlan came out of the Chamber almost at once, his face reddened by debate, his glasses drooping belligerently past the bridge of his nose to squat like antennae just in front of his well-developed cheek-bones.

Hardly a promising beginning. Typically, though, the man soothed his features, relaxed, got his social intelligence working again, even though he knew it would be no social call that would bring a Departmental Head past the screen of junior functionaries, especially when the House was sitting. "Should have phoned," he said. "I'd have baked a cake." He helped them to coffee briefly, from a tray held by a woman in House of Commons uniform, then watched her go.

Coffee not Scotch, Fossit noted, then let his mind touch upon the reference to cake. He never ceased to wonder at the way politics soiled even the most ebullient intelligence. "It wouldn't sound well on a telephone, Terence. I bear confused tidings."

"I've just been sponsoring a confused amendment to the Official Secrets Act—some call it confusing as well. I bet you lot do, eh?" The glasses were tapped back onto his upper nose by now, and the raised eyebrows framed behind them were seeking an answer to the larger question.

"We've had an Israeli strong-arm gang under surveillance for a week or so. Most of them left yesterday afternoon, the rest were supposed to be at an Embassy garden party, so beyond asking why they were here in the first place that would normally have been the end of it."

"I hope you're not suggesting it was to knock off the Iraqi Ambassador? Police have got that girl for tossing the grenade and my gossips are convinced they're right."

"So am I. Especially now I know what they really came for. They took someone with them." Seeing how vacant Quinlan remained, Fossit added, "By took I mean abducted."

The silence would need to be diluted with a little explanation. "Faked the passport of a man who ostensibly needs no faking of documents. Worse, used the documentation of an Embassy secretary. The man was comatose with sickness, so presumably drugged."

"A political kidnapping, you mean?"

"I can't think of a better explanation."

"Age?"

"That's the nasty bit. He's turned sixty-five. Unless there are implications we can't see yet, then they think they've got a Nazi big wig. He's European, not Arab. The old hate looks the likely motive."

"Then it's down to you lot, Leonard." There was a

snap in the voice; the debate must have been a fraying one.

"If they're right, we've been harbouring an undesirable. Granted. But they were wrong two years ago."

"So you assured us all at the time, and they've never let us forget it."

"They were wrong. We let them have access to most of the file. The Americans gave them a similar briefing, probably even better, because they had nothing to be coy about. The Israelis didn't believe either of us. Well, the supposition must be that things have rankled enough for them to go it alone this time. And be wrong alone." Fossit's gaze was level. It was not seeking reassurance. "Normally we could wait until they told us, the fat being spilt on the new tablecloth and all. But it looks as if they've knocked off a British citizen."

" 'Looks'?" Terence Quinlan's voice was as close to a yelp as decency would allow. "I'll want more than that."

"I'll know by mid-afternoon. If they crow before then, it'll mean they're still convinced they're right. If they stay mum, then arguably it's because doubt is creeping in."

"An ex-Nazi who's a Brit Cit?"

"This man opened an account at Lloyds, Chislehurst, in 1932, and has lived there ever since, except for trips abroad. He's a zoologist of some sort. I mean, a collector."

"Trips abroad suggest substitution."

"But not twenty-five years ago. Coming to England then would be frying-pan to fire. I say twenty-five years because he's got a daughter of about that age. Besides, what about the neighbours?"

"How did you get on to this?"

"A very able desk officer of mine set the passport people buzzing, thus detecting the abduction. Then the Met obliged with a Missing Person entry. He got the rest of the information via the man's bank manager, and phoned my car. It's routine for the Met to ask for bank details from relatives of missing persons."

"You'll tie this together by when, Leonard?"

"Say three o'clock. And if the Israelis haven't squeaked by then, it'll put a further dimension on it—unless they're playing a completely new sort of game."

"My gossips'll have to know."

"We told them at once. Their Near East desks are doing what they can."

"Conference at six o'clock, then. You, their nominees, me, anyone else I think of. Special Branch. I suppose the Met—though it's a bit soon for inquests."

"Here?"

"Home Office. I'll want a daily face report, unless it all evaporates. What's the name of this assistant of yours?"

"Patrick Matson."

"And the target?"

"Charles Henry Kay."

Quinlan made a note of both. "Good. Bring Matson. The other name covers me if anything breaks."

Fossit made to leave, but was interrupted briefly in his going.

"I appreciate the speed of this intelligence. Like you, I think the *prima facie* evidence is flimsy—so a lesser man might have sat on it, Leonard." He paused on his congratulations. "Also, like you, I think it sounds ominous. It's got the ring of something quite nasty." He smiled. "Victoria Station. It's the kind of joke that makes me wish I were in Opposition."

"You want to congratulate yourself it's not Waterloo."

4.

The phonebox was hot. So was Matson's temper. He made several further calls while watching a little old lady with a shopping basket on wheels trundle towards him up the street.

He dialled Euston Police Station, identified himself, and asked for whoever was in charge of the Julia Keppleman case. Then another, more urgent, thought struck him. He left the number of the phonebox with the desk sergeant and told them to call him back.

All of this phoning about the landscape reminded him that Ginevra Kay was vulnerable to more than one line of attack. She could be enticed out and sandbagged. She could be played taped demands from her father. There was also the press to consider.

He pulled the local directory round on its swivel. There

it was; Kay, C.H. *in heavy type.* Kay was not only unsecretive, he was an egomaniac, either abnormal or innocent. Almost certainly both.

Ginevra's voice: "Yes?"

"It's Patrick Matson. I've fixed up some protection for you. I hope it doesn't damage your back fence."

"There's no other news?"

"I'll phone you mid-afternoon, when I've—" He broke off in his turn. "Look, Miss Kay—Ginevra—this is why I'm calling. Phone your local exchange now and ask for an immediate new number and insist that it's strictly ex-directory. Available to no-one. But no-one. The local police will uphold the request if there's any delay."

"Daddy may want—"

"We'll relay any message from Daddy, I promise you."

"Where can I call you?"

"I'll call you."

"But I'm to change my number, you said." She was beginning to sound hysterical again.

He gave her the number of his flat. "You can use it as a longstop. I'll be there sometime before midnight." He didn't explain that getting hold of her number was the one thing his department could be absolutely guaranteed to do.

"They won't hurt him, will they?"

5.

She might have been a florist or a nurse. Her white coat was dull with heat and her legs glistened.

The two men looked like gardeners or road-sweepers. They wore denim overalls similar to military fatigues, but without chevrons or insignia.

And in a landscape of guns they carried no guns, unless inside their clothes.

They stood together in the little yard of the Martello and watched the van back in—and, yes, it was a florist's van from that very chic pottery and flowers shop in Dizengoff, its blazon miraged by exhaust fumes.

Its loading door fell open.

Built for flowers, it was much too small for its contents. It bulged with anxious faces, cramped limbs, four men in a hurry to get out, their skins pale with exhaustion.

Four men tugging to bring something out with them in the same quick movement.

A body on a stretcher, its lips set ajar, its eyes jammed open, the whites rolled up like the corpse of a drowned man. Something was spilling from its mouth, something like water.

The girl said, "Help me get him to the respirator and fetch the doctor."

"Doctor Lubrani hasn't been cleared."

"Help me get him to the respirator—no, carry him face down. There's no time for a pump."

The body trailed its mouthful of dribble across dust and into darkness and then into cold white light.

"I'm supposed to be a nurse—not a mortician."

Barel watched her fasten the body to the machine, first the mask, then the electrodes, then the drips, before saying, "You *are* a nurse. You're supposed to be a soldier. Has his heart stopped?"

"His breathing had. The bellows will take care of that. I'll need to give him something for his heart, just the same. Let's hope he can take it."

Barel saw her inject. He saw Dov wipe the man's face, almost tenderly, and thought how ridiculous it was to need him to live.

"He's had some kind of spinal reaction," she explained.

"We were told this would be safe at this concentration."

"The reaction is probably to the antidote," she snapped. She was becoming increasingly in charge of things, the only one with clean hands. "Why didn't we use sodium pentothal?"

"You need breathing tubes for pentothal. Also you need to syringe it slowly into a main vein—you know that."

"A transfusion would help," she said, "since I'm not allowed to use a doctor. Swill out the poison and the antidote. I'll need time to determine his blood group."

"His blood group is A. We have that on record."

"I do hope you've got the right man. Or this is going to do him a lot of damage."

6.

Someone was tapping on the window of the phonebox. The little old lady with the basket on wheels.

"You've had five minutes already." She spoke with a Middle European accent. "I want to report the loss of my parrot. They're very nice boys but they let my parrot out."

"Engineers, lady. This won't be back on stream for an hour or so." He went back to phoning.

Or more properly, to being phoned. It rang in his ear.

"Hallo," he said. "Engineers. Testing."

"My parrot."

"Of course, your parrot." He smiled his cheeky remembered smile. One German Jewish lady he could really grow to like. He loved old European ladies. "I can see your parrot now, ma'am. It's chewing cherries in number forty-two."

"I wouldn't put anything past the people in forty-two," she said, moving quickly down the hill.

Euston Police Station was calling back.

The voice was diffident, if not plain deferential. "Was you wanting to view a deceased, sir? A Miss Keppleman?" Matson could tell it had been foxed by his little pantomime about engineers, and would spend its next teabreak gossiping about the "Secret Service."

"No thanks."

"No wish to view the body. Right, sir." The voice was much more sure of itself now. Some people had no bottle, particularly those in the toffee-nosed jobs. "Was there what else, sir?"

The syntax did not synchromesh. Both caller and called were confused. Matson did not wish to view the body. Bodies, as such, were not his scene. Still less young women's bodies, unless alert, alive, and nubile. Then there was his repugnance for morgue attendants, particularly after reading Fromm and Kraft-Ebbing. There were men he knew who would be into hat and gloves and away to glance reverentially down and work up some hate. Perhaps they were corpse-screwers too, in their creased little minds. Not Matson. Any corpse he had official reason to view meant a failure for his department. His failure. Julia Keppleman had, if his guess was right, been mistakenly silenced by an Israeli gorilla. Israeli gorillas, and guerillas, and lone-wolf diplomats carrying guns, were his responsibility. So was that young girl's death, therefore. He had her blood on his conscience.

"Was you wanting the Inspector, sir?"

"Mmmm?"

"Or the Inspector CID?"

CID Inspectors and Matson got on well. They were roughly equal in rank and, in general, background—what Matson called "cram-educated nondescript," and what Fossit was pleased to call "coming up the hard way." Fossit had come up the easy way, and since he was only Matson's boss, Matson did not think that was very far.

"Mr. Matson? I hear you're interested in Julia Keppleman."

Yes, he could get on. Matson identified his department again. "What can you tell me," he asked, "in very rough terms? When it comes to murder, I'm an idiot." He had, of course, squeezed one or two triggers and watched the faces fall apart, but that was another matter.

"Conflicting signs of violence. But we're calling it murder—witness this morning's papers. She went upstairs with a man, fell from a window, man exits fast. Also there was evidence of sex, what the educated call fucking, in case you think I'm hinting at anything advanced."

"Raped?"

"Yes and no. On evidence, that is. She was probably in old-fashioned terms a virgin."

"Are there any?"

"Quite a lot, judging from the number that end up on slabs after sex attacks. Strange cases of rape, if rape it was. He'd used a condom. All very tender. She had a fiancé, and we got a bit hopeful till we learned the boy is in Hong Kong, touring with his orchestra."

"Not an alibi you'll be checking, I take it. Is that all you've got?"

"Until we get someone we can work on."

"I'll send you a photostrip. Make it urgent. Two of the mugs it won't be. I'll mark those with a cross. One of them it really might be, if my hunch is correct. I know I shouldn't do it, but I'll mark him with a question. Can you do your own offprints?"

The phonebox overbrewed, even with the door open.

He stepped out and saw the little old lady was talking to Ginevra Kay in her front garden. It didn't look as if Miss Kay was going to prove responsive to his attempts to protect her. He could only hope others would be more successful.

Just then Matson noticed the brotherhood of man in position, three at the front of the house doing kerbside chores on a steamed-up car, two further up meditating on a drain-hatch. Their lack of industry was so spontaneous and unforced it could have qualified immediately for a Trade Union award.

FOUR

1.

The Interrogation Centre was in the Old Town, and stood above a cave scraped out by nomads before the town began. At different times its tunnels, its arches, its *ghorfa* had been used to store goats, wine, mussel shells, nets, embalming oils and possibly the dead. On days like this, Barel could smell them all.

Deciding it was too near the sea, the Romans had secured and vaulted its galleries and set stone ramparts above them. Someone, probably the Crusaders, had turned these to ruin; and someone else had taken the rubble and built a Martello before Martellos were invented. Then, quite recently, a rich man had converted its tower into a dwelling; and the Government immediately suggested he sell it to Barel.

What the world saw was the Martello overshadowing a square. What was interesting happened where it had always happened, in the cave.

There was a natural fissure in the ground, and from this the cave had been started. Here, furthest from the Roman stairwell, Barel had his private quarters.

He stood undressing quickly, looking into the fissure through a reinforced window. This was his garden, a small court without sunshine, and quite unreachable. He stripped off his soiled suit, and the silk shirt he wore on active service so it wouldn't snag his gun.

He didn't need to shave. He was one of those olive-skinned men with thick dark hair that ended in natural sideburns but refused to grow on his face.

46

He was naked when the girl knocked on his door. She may even have entered without knocking, but now she stood outside and knocked again insistently. "The general's on the line, sir."

"Perhaps he'll give us some sense at last."

He saw no need to hurry from where he stood. Here was where he came at the end of each mission. There was no word in Hebrew for his emotions about it. In English it was his sanctuary. In Arabic, which he also spoke fluently, it was his *horm*. From here he took his time.

He put on pants, socks, a bush-shirt with his major's chevrons, khaki drill trousers and mahogany-coloured shoes, then opened the door fully. He waited until he had her full attention, then picked up his hat. Only then did he walk along the corridor to the office phone and wait for her to hold it towards him.

She had taken off her hospital coat. She wasn't wearing a uniform, but her buff blouse and skirt looked like a uniform. As he took the phone he said to her, "Wear your uniform tomorrow, Corporal Tamir."

General Zefat's voice said, "Congratulations. Any snags, Shlomo?"

"It was a clean job, so far as our bit went." He didn't mention the prisoner's female companion.

"So why haven't you delivered him?"

"Orders, sir. Your orders, and—I believe—the Minister's. Dead we don't deliver. Dead or unconscious."

"How bad is he?"

"As you already know, a scheduled five-hour flight took us nineteen hours. We had to use the pharmacology necessary to keep him quiet during the delay and then for the stop-over. Why aren't you here, sir?"

"I had Ben-Yosof down my neck."

"Who else, sir?"

"He'd brought some of his acolytes, yes."

"Did he tell them why?"

"Not in my hearing. He was confident we had the goods, Shlomo, of course he was. But a politician knows when to hold his tongue."

"I guessed he'd bring some Press. I told the pilot to land us on that club strip at Herzliyya."

"He wouldn't?"

"Even with my gun in his ear. Said the runway's too short by a kilometre. As it was, I daren't let him taxi up in front of your little rescue party."

"All for the best. It's made David Ben-Yosof angry. But it's all for the best. Now what do I tell him, my Minister?"

"I'll know once you clear me to call in a doctor."

"It was the stop in Rome frightened them all. You know what politicians are like: they get cold feet from watching people walk in the snow."

"Yes, sir. What about the doctor?" He had to cut through Zefat's euphoria.

"What is it they all say? A week's a long time in politics? That's when they're squatting on their arses, doing nothing. When they're actually doing something, or while they're sitting on their hands and sweating while someone else is doing it for them, well, even a minute makes them nervous."

"Meanwhile, sir?"

"Use as few people as possible, and certainly no-one who isn't billeted on post."

"Doctor Lubrani has a town practice. I can't coop him up here."

"He's no good to us, then. You must have some sort of medic?"

"I've got an Army nurse. Or more exactly, one of my team used to nurse. She's good"—he was watching her all the time he spoke—"very good. But she'll need to consult someone."

"The poison is self-stabilising, unless he's simply had too much of it." Something in Zefat's voice implied he had had too much of something himself. "We went into all that at the briefing. If he dies, keep him on ice, Shlomo. If he mumbles anything interesting get it on tape. Get everything on tape, including his death-rattle. Whatever happens, whatever the pressures from wherever they come, don't produce a corpse except on my orders. Dead he's no problem, providing there's no corpse."

2.

Matson was not a leg man, but he sometimes shook a leg. Strained, as his ex-corporal would say, his greens. The Bromley train returning him to Victoria Station pulled in at Platform Four, a step from the new *Gentlemen* and its turnstile that even a bursting bladder could accomplish.

Once that was all under and done with and nicely tucked inside, he washed his hands, but only as a hygienic prelude to taking out a card. Another card. It said *Home Office Enquiry*. He must remember to get Fossit to have them issued with something that said *Police*. Much more impressive.

With his card in his hand he sought out the Asian responsible for good order in the place.

By the cut of his turban, the old man was a Sikh. He could not read, but was affable. He surrounded himself with several more Sikhs, all armed with brooms. These were young and less affable, but could read.

The senior Sikh pretended to be impressed with Matson's card.

"Yesterday," Matson guessed, "a man was taken sick. It's a matter of tracing the source of his illness. It could be contagious."

"Like the buboes?"

"Very definitely like the buboes."

"Fortunately here there is much carbolic. Against the natural events of the body."

"Also that geezer didn't get sick." One of the young ones speaking, with evident contempt, his accent pure Peckham. "He come in here to sprinkle, and while he was in the sprinkle he give himself a fix."

"Daj nicked his syringe."

"I haven't got the damn' syringe." Daj looked furious, until he saw the note in Matson's hand, a tattered-looking fiver. "You mean—?"

"Daj, he means the needle."

"Go and get the needle."

"And you won't needle me?" Matson smiled with a smile reserved for love at the moment of surrender.

Daj brought him a plastic syringe.

Dropping the syringe into his case, Matson decided to try his photographs.

The identification was positive for Barel and Gorodish. He pressed on with some more from the flap, the ones he hadn't dared show Ginevra.

The old man's hand stopped on one of them. "That man," he said. "That man jumped the barrier."

"Naughty," said Matson. "Jumped the turnstile?"

"No. The central gate there, between the In and the Out." The old man spoke as if to jump neither the In nor the Out meant that he had infringed something much more terrible than either, as if he had vaulted into an awful moral limbo. "Jumped it both ways," he added.

Matson nodded in deep sympathy, then marked the photograph. On the back it said Amos Reitel. Well, well, well. So Amos was in for more than a passport and a postage stamp. Doubtless the little prick would claim diplomatic immunity, as Leonard said.

A pity he hadn't dared to show a labelled picture to Ginevra Kay. Spring-heeled Amos must have been the lad who had hit her with the trolley.

3.

Matson didn't want to be involved any more, not up the sharp end. It was a job for diplomacy or a job for guns. The first was never his to command, and as for the other he was sweating at the thought of it. He felt as he did when he was daft enough to check the City pages in the *Financial Times*. He knew what to do, but no longer had anything in the bank to invest.

He returned to the office in a sour mood.

Brenda was playing bleak. "I had Pomeroy up the phone again, and Dixon *ad nausea*," she said.

"Wanting what?"

"Wanting you. Then that boy Roger from the path lab. Ditto."

"I dropped a syringe in for him to sniff."

"You should have been here," she said crossly. "You always say leg-work isn't down to this office."

"Let's function as a team." He sank into his chair. "I'll be the brains, you be the brawn."

"That's not even funny. I had anorexia."

"Perhaps I'll give you dinner after all."

"What pigs like you don't realise is women are people. I said girls are people, you know."

"You read some very advanced literature, Miss Simmonds."

He answered the phone himself with a flourish. She had quite cheered him up.

"About the syringe." It was Roger from the lab.

"You've been quick."

"Standard enough job. It's a venom."

"Venom?"

"Snake venom. Cobra, most likely. Identifying which snake of a whole bloody tribe may take us several days, but my guess is cobra if the guy's been injected."

"Then the victim will be dead?" He felt too dazed to think. Were they jumping too soon? Had the nasty little bastards merely pulled a murder? In which case it should have been all stitched up before going upstairs.

"Not necessarily. It's a good abduction drug. You can dilute it enough to be unlethal, and the cobra-type venoms aren't tissue-destroying. Indian hippies are using direct snakebite to get themselves high, as a matter of fact. Tiny little teeth. Of course, they see the cobra's glands are well milked first."

"Irony is: the victim keeps snakes. He's an expert on the things."

"Good mark to the abductors. They can tell him what they've done, and then he'll calculate just how much he's got to behave. With this sort of venom they could even alternate a near lethal dose and follow it with an antidote if he said he'd be a good boy. In fact they could go on alternating the treatment for a damned long time. And polish him off quietly with a hot-shot of the undiluted stuff if he got stroppy, or once they'd got what they wanted. He would die quite peacefully, within certain limits. And there wouldn't be all that bleeding you'd get from say a fer-de-lance or a bushmaster bite. Cobra makes a very nice corpse."

"Thanks."

The phone rang again. External this time.

It was the CID Inspector from Euston. "We've drawn a lucky card on that picture you marked for us."

"Shmuel Yitzak?"

"Where can I pick him up?"

"On the way to Barcelona. Or through Barcelona. But that's last night's report, and it could have been a blind."

"Hard little lumps!"

"He's one of them. Also you can't pick him up, and you can't tell Interpol. Write your report, then get your Station Superintendent to tie in with the Commissioner. When the Sunday papers get their D Notice Clearance you'll find you're a part of the story of the century. I can't tell you now, but I'll fill you in over a drink sometime. Shmuel Yitzak is an Israeli hit man, employed by one of their secret departments to tidy things up. What we'd call a 'top-and-tail' but they call a Wand of God."

"Is he Embassy?"

"No. A one-man roving blitz, but this time part of a blitz team. The others have gone on too."

"I appreciate your telling me this."

Matson felt better when the truth had rung off. He had Israeli friends, military friends, none of them like Yitzak. It was the hawks he was after, the hawks and the thugs. Perhaps he just meant their secret services. All secret departments have a thug.

Even his department had a thug.

Not any more. He was a desk officer.

Brenda had been listening on the other phone. " 'I appreciate you telling me this,' " she mimicked.

"You listen and you learn. I'll fill you in over a drink sometime."

"We were talking dinner."

"You'll need to work late, then."

"Providing it's not beefburger." She waited for the importance of her acceptance to sink in, then asked, "Your Chislehurst bird. They going to hurt her old dad?"

4.

Barel relaxed on his bed hoping for a few hours' sleep. In London it had been beyond him. He could never sleep on a raid. He had meant to repay himself yesterday, but last night had been spent in the grounded plane with a prisoner to keep alive. Real passengers had been able to disembark to doze in the bars and complain, while engineers took out the nacelle. Only Dov had stayed with him and Dov had grown hairs in his sleep. He felt so tired it hurt.

The phone bell could be ignored but not the knock on the door.

It was the efficient, too-moral Tamir. The prisoner had come round, was complaining, had levered himself upright and was demanding to see his consul. Dov had sent her to report.

Beyond asking whether the tape was running, Barel moved slowly. There were things to arrange, and once he came into the cell and saw the pinkening colour of the man's skin he was angry. He was enough of an old soldier to resent seeing his general's complacency vindicated so easily. Still, he'd known all along that the operation would either turn out to be his failure or Zefat's success.

He heard himself explaining the prisoner's position to his own satisfaction and the man's evident contempt, then said, "If this tires you, I want you to lie down. We're in no hurry, and the procedures are well established." He smiled urbanely. "We don't tend to see many of your kind, but various European agencies do."

"It should be apparent to you by now—"

Dov had been toying with a metal cigarette case. He snapped it against the prisoner's nose, pinching his nostril, pulling out hairs. "You listen," he said. "We'll do the interrupting. For the moment your role is simply to listen."

Barel smiled again, reprovingly, encouragingly, knowingly. He was going to be the nice one. He would lead the interrogation, it had been decided, but he was always the nice guy. His smile deprecated the necessity for Dov's aggression, but suggested nonetheless that it was all the unfortunate product of the prisoner's ill-manners.

Everyone has read about such techniques, but Kay found it hard to think about them. There were tears in his eye, not because of rage or weakness, but because of the unmanning little blood-drop forming on his nose. He had an image of himself as a bloodied, moist-eyed rabbit, like the ones he had shot in Petts Wood.

"The procedure is this. In a minute we shall ask you to unfasten your left sleeve."

Dov flicked the cigarette case again, less maliciously. "If you don't, we'll slice your arm off," he grinned.

"What will that tell you? I was never an inmate of a concentration camp."

"So you know about that?"

"Yes, he knows all about that."

"The Jews have taught the world about it. Even though they weren't the only inmates, not by a long—"

Dov struck him.

Barel went on as if he was prepared to overlook such an unfortunate incident, but only this once. Next time he would be compelled to reprove the prisoner for being struck. "You were a member of the SS. Therefore, under your left armpit we expect to find a tattoo of your blood-group."

The prisoner's laughter welled up and threatened hysteria.

Barel waited impatiently for Dov to halt it. "More importantly you were a member of the Vril."

The prisoner was curious, infuriatingly eager to learn.

"A restricted, aristocratic secret society."

"You flatter me."

"Hitler was a member. Its members bear what they call the Bloodmark, a small emblem of their superiority pricked out on their forearm. When you unfasten your sleeve we shall find one of three things: those marks, a bad attempt to cauterise them, or skin grafts replacing either the marks or the cauterisation. The grafts may be good. In your case they are probably excellent. But close examination will always detect them."

"Hairs," Dov grunted. "Even a Hun's arse doesn't have enough hairs on it to look convincing on a monkey's forearm."

The amused look had returned, in spite of the prisoner's evident sickness. "The *left* forearm?" He sniggered.

They tore at his sleeve. They tore off his sleeve.

"A bit careless with the caustic," Dov said after a long minute.

The flesh under Barel's fingers was interlaced, flowing over and under itself, wormlike and dead, damascened, with a strange dull colour like spilled metal polish. Most of all it resembled strips of packet cheese that had been melted then hardened.

"What happened there?"

"The protein has been digested. Puff adder."

"That's snake bite. You can't tell us that. We've just hit you with—"

"Whatever you did to me was a different story altogether. This is haemotoxic. Untreated, it rots the flesh."

"On the left forearm. How very convenient."

"I've been damaged on a number of occasions. You'll find comparable lesions on my left calf and my right thigh. May I see my consul, please?"

"When do you claim these things happened?"

"In the nineteen-thirties, while I was learning my trade. Nowadays there wouldn't be the tissue damage, the sloughing of flesh, even with a rattlesnake. The antivenoms are better, and of course there's Linus Pauling with his intravenous Vitamin C. He's another man who could vouch for me, by the way."

5.

The spectacles registered, so did an untrimmed sandy-coloured hair in the left nostril, but nothing else. Otherwise Matson was losing sight of Terence Quinlan. He felt so alienated from everything except the spectacles and the nose-hair that he might well have been drinking all afternoon.

It was a help to detect the same air of dazed constraint about the persons of several others present, particularly the uniformed figure of an Assistant Commissioner of Police. The man was apparently speaking, spurting out half-formed words. Strangury of the mouth, Matson concluded, coupled with total constipation of the ego. It was the boss-gob complex. My message spatters downwards. Upwards it dare not splash.

The Assistant Commissioner was delivering his only information to date on the developing kidnap. This was that the Metropolitan Police Commissioner was on holiday, now, at this moment, at this point of time. With, as it happened, his wife.

Matson sought to grow wise with him, to match the boggle of his face to the boondoggle of his mind, and thus digest his paraphrase of the slowly moving face.

However, as of now, from this moment, at some rapidly approaching point of time, to wit the noon flight tomorrow, it being the soonest, the Commissioner of Metropolitan Police would be returning forthwith. He, together with his Force, was most particularly outraged that a bunch of foreigners could do this, not only to a card-carrying Brit Cit but an English Gentleman by birth Brit Cit. And not only on UK soil, but in London, which was his patch. Not only that, but Victoria Station to boot.

"Thank you, Assistant Commissioner."

You won't be coming back again, Matson thought. Something to tell the wife and kids about over late tea, eh?

Then it was Fossit's turn.

Fossit spoke well. He did the full *Surrey Comet* on everything and got everyone calmed down. Each detail he offered had been briefed into his eye and ear by one Patrick Matson, and being Fossit he said so. "Patrick has one more thing," he added.

Would Matson's voice sound straitened? "Shmuel Yitzak attempted to kill Kay's daughter."

"She's being watched over?"

The nods bristled.

Matson produced a copy of *The Mirror*. "Trouble is, he tried it last night, before his Paris flit. Mistaken identity." He explained his reasoning briefly. "Euston C.I.D. phoned me just before I came to this meeting. We were able to furnish a photograph and they had it toted round. They got three positive identifications."

Quinlan made a noise with his fingernails like a mouse galloping.

The Assistant Commissioner heated slowly to crimson, but evidently decided not to talk about channels of communication.

"So," said Terence Quinlan at last. "One in the meat waggon and one in the penalty box. So how do you account for the foul?"

"Easy," said Pomeroy. "They've pulled a couple of wrong 'uns."

"Two too many. Gentlemen, gentlemen—how can this be?"

Matson, Fossit and Dixon all spoke at once. Matson blundered forward. "We spend our time watching over the right ones, sir. We really can't be expected to anticipate violence making a mistake and blowing off target. We've got the targets covered."

"You talk to the Terror Squad," Dixon growled. "It's the Israelis themselves they're protecting. We can't cover every Englishman against random Israeli screwballs at the same time."

Matson and Dixon and the Branch man basked in each other's approval. In everybody's approval except for Pomeroy's.

"Depends which end of the equation we start with," Quinlan said heavily. "Violence itself is worth surveillance, for its own sake."

"Ah."

"Well done, Patrick, nonetheless. If it weren't for you the Israelis could be telling us first, or simply dropping him into the sea. Since they haven't uttered a bleep, I rather fancy it's what they'd prefer to do. The problem is, when do *we* tell *them*? Not my decision, thank God. It'll have to go to Cabinet. Where've they got him?"

"Tel Aviv. Or, to be more precise, on the edge of the Old Town at Jaffo."

"How do we know?"

Pomeroy spread his hands, as if acknowledging help from God.

"Will they be brutal?"

"They've a great need to be urgent."

"I think we can spare ourselves the details. Anything else?"

The Branch man was still learning how to talk. "Last night they came up with some hand guns at Heathrow. Two pistols. Cleaners. In the lavatory bins."

"If they were carrying guns, they'd have needed to get rid of them before they went through the screening devices," Dixon observed. "*If* they were carrying guns. Speaking for myself, I'd be more interested to know who fed them Kay's hand luggage—and presumably their own."

"The Met are looking for Yitzak's car," Matson added.

"Hire car," the Branch man explained. "Very likely it's—"

"Don't let's write a detective story," Quinlan growled. "All I care to know is, the man's abductors obliged us by not carting him off inside some piece of freight or other. Our critics are growing tired of that one, and so are some of my friends. If I have to make a statement, I'll tell the House he was induced. No guns. No syringes. No wheelchairs. Induced."

Like an abortion, Matson thought.

"Meanwhile, let's turn his past inside out so we can hand them a convincing dossier."

They all shuffled upright, but he would go first. "One more thing." He looked hard at Pomeroy. "Some of you are not mine. You are here on request merely. But of course the Foreign Secretary knows. He is as anxious in his sphere as I am"—the gaze shifted—"that there shall be no attempt at reprisals." He searched for the definitive *mot*. "The horse has been rustled, but he still needs his hay. And we don't want him knackered before he's sent back."

Marcus Pomeroy's quotations were contagious, even at this altitude.

Quinlan aimed at nothing with one eye, as if speaking entirely to himself. "Reprisals jeopardize our chance of getting Charles Henry Kay released quietly." Still the one eye, like a carpenter truing a jack-plane. "If such he proves to be. And even then it is going to require tact to persuade them they ought to act on their best knowledge. Tact and diplomacy."

"Doesn't that dead girl add a new dimension to all this?"

"Those are my instructions."

Nobody moved for some time. There was a terrible inertia once Quinlan had left. Here was where it would all be decided, here but certainly not now.

Dixon leant towards Matson. "Thump," he said, "I spoke to that Chislehurst cracker. She—"

Pomeroy put his back in the way. His back seemed practised at being there. "Could I try some of that pinking you offered me?"

"Sunday," Matson said. "But not with your Browning. Buy a—"

"Not Sunday, Paddy. Now. There's no time to wait for Woolworth's to open. Tell her you'll be late, there's a lad."

6.

A soldier with a worry keeps it to himself. But once he has a little bit of success to report?

Barel sent Judi Tamir off-duty and dialled the General. Zefat's voice was furry with sleep.

"He did his best to die, sir. But I'm happy to tell you—"

"So the poison burnt itself out?"

"Or the antidote stabilised. We gave him a—"

"Good. The venom burnt itself out. I'll report to the Minister, who'll report to Cabinet. Meanwhile we'll send someone to take him off your hands."

"Then what?"

"We'll wheel him in front of the Press."

"He's not ready for that sort of thing."

'Not ready? I'm not going to treat him like a cooking egg."

"He won't admit to being who he is. He still says his name is Kay. Every other minute he asks for the British Consulate." Barel laughed. "He's really quite aggrieved."

"He's being cheeky?"

"If you like. But he'll be bad news if you give him to the Press. Why don't we wait for the trial?"

"That will take months. The Press must have him now, with an acknowledged identity. Or we'll have a diplomatic storm on our hands."

"We didn't with Eichmann—or not until we hanged him."

"Eichmann agreed to being Eichmann the moment we took him. He co-operated even before we'd started to move him from South America."

"This one's different. He's an angry man, very confident of his cover. You can't put this one in front of a Press conference."

There was a long pause, then the phone said, "This

question of identity cannot be left until the trial. You'll have to make him change his mind before we bring him up to Jerusalem.''

"I'll need experts for that.''

"There's no time for experts. You must be very firm with him.''

"I think we'll need to be more than that.''

"Better you than the experts, then. Experts never like to be firm. They like to be expert. You have my full permission to be firm, Shlomo—do you understand?''

"We've only just managed to resurrect the old boy.''

"Within limits, that is. Moderately firm.''

"As I said, sir. A job for experts. This is an operational unit. I've not even got the beginnings—''

"You're tired, Shlomo. We're all tired.''

"Yes, sir.''

"I mean, bandage your fist. I don't mean don't smack him.''

"And bandage my boot?''

"If you feel like kicking him, just unbandage your fist. I'm not asking you to be fancy. I'm telling you to be quick. There's no need for a confession. That can wait. Just get him to agree to who he is. Break him, major. I'll take responsibility for it. Break him tonight.''

7.

They went up to Albany Street, where Matson's nod secured them guns from stores.

"It was more of a chit-chat I had in mind, Paddy.''

"It'll be in ear muffs, then. You told me you wanted to practise your lethal and swift.''

"The innocence of the intelligent artisan.'' Pomeroy stopped short, surprised to find the Thugs had an indoor clay-shoot.

"Don't worry,'' Matson said. "If you squint just right they won't reach the rafters, or not in one piece. There's sandbags up there somewhere, a bloody mile deep.''

He held his revolver like a rifle, with his left hand along the barrel, his wrist sheathed in a woman's glove to protect it from cylinder-burn. "I prefer my own guns. I've got one of those big Rugers with the overstrapping—ideal for this sort of shooting.'' He had chosen a Smith magnum with too much snout for a production model. His Irish accent was suddenly very prominent, as it must have been when he was with the Regiment. Pomeroy guessed he would talk that way to women, too. Women and weapons—anything to do with passion.

He had seen Matson shoot a pistol before, but not *balle trappe*.

Nobody called.

Two clay plates whirled into the air and splintered before they had time to fly. The double crash of the boosted forty-fours was deafening, even in bins, but Matson fired again. A fragment was still airborne, and splintered in turn. The echoes hurt Pomeroy's teeth, then drilled them again as Matson shattered the splinter of a splinter.

What a magnificent shot the man was, balanced, immediate and deadly. What a magnificent redundancy.

''Come in with us, Paddy. You could be an instructor. It wouldn't mean any loss of loot.''

''Only influence.''

''You don't care about influence, Paddy. You're only interested in your wick.''

''It's been tended by wise as well as foolish.''

Pomeroy put his pistol down on the ledge of the butt. ''Talking of virgins, what's the unexpurgated story on Julia Keppleman?''

''So that's it.'' Matson told him in careful detail. ''The little bastard'll be flown away home by now.''

''I don't see why. They don't even know we're on to the Chislehurst thing. My betting is they won't pull him back until they're satisfied the whole job's over. He's only ninety minutes from London, ostensibly with clean hands. When they find out he's made a mistake, his hands'll look even cleaner—there'll be no line of logic to tie him to the truth.''

Pomeroy's aftershave had been obvious. Now it smelled sour. Matson hadn't realised how much hate there was in him. He listened to Pomeroy trying to fool them both with, ''It's a pity I don't have the desk any more. The chaps there'll tell me not to muss with their dons and dagoes.''

Matson reloaded.

''Of course, we might ask some tacky Levantine to do

us a favour. A lot of people'd give their right arm just to get their mitts on that fella's balls.''

Matson checked the cylinder swivel of both their guns. It seemed as good a distraction as any.

"Your firm would have to put up the money," Pomeroy went on. "I can't play domestic banker—you all know that."

"It's the problem with all these side-loaders. How much?"

"Ten thousand? The lot I've a fancy for will do it for love. Trouble is we're so far away that only money can reach them."

"I can't tell Leonard."

"No need. You're glowing with gold dust today. Are you a betting man, Patrick?"

"Always."

Pomeroy winced through merged detonations as several plates of clay broke in dusky pieces.

"I'll lay you a tenner—"

Six more plates rose into the air and damaged themselves among the rafters.

"I'll lay you a tenner they get to Kay's daughter."

"They flew those buggers for you, Pomeroy." Life had been simpler in the Thugs. It had taken a desk job to teach him first hand that women too can be targets.

8.

No secret service sets up its officers. Contact agents, yes; contract agents often. Principals sometimes. Staff never.

And in his own case everything always ran like clockwork. Barel made the General see to that, and to every little cog in the whole operation.

Yitzak still hadn't heard anything by suppertime; but he was here where he wanted to be, and the better for Catalan sausage and Basque hare. He would look by again at noon tomorrow, and then if necessary at six. He doubted if it would be necessary, but in a job like this waiting was an art form.

He pushed the table away from his chair, and realised that an afternoon sipping wine had exaggerated his gestures. He steadied himself with coffee at the counter, and when he knew he looked unobtrusive again he started strolling towards the harbour, where the girls are. The Ramblas were bulging with people. He waded against shoulders and elbows, young toothlight jarring his eyes.

If he didn't find a girl before the statue, he'd duck into a club. The statue was too close to the harbour for comfort, and commemorated poor melancholy Columbus looking furtive about America and the pox.

Suddenly there was no-one. The pavements were empty. Only distant footsteps like blown leaves.

He heard dogs howling—no, wolves, like a pang from childhood. Throats on the hills beyond the wire. Muzzles uplifted to the neon stars.

Then English voices. He was sober, fast.

The crowd had vanished merely to concentrate. He looked towards an area his drunkenness had called shadow, and saw a hundred, two hundred people in a tight throng.

They were watching a girl auction herself from the roof of a taxi. She was surrounded by headless figures, sailors, negro sailors in American summer uniforms.

He pushed among them. She was slim and painted and beautiful.

"Jesus, man. Three thousand for that!"

She wore a silly gold belt, it was true.

"All those pennies for a hosepipe full of herpes!"

Nobody laughed. It was somebody's habitual chorus.

Yitzak wanted her, but not enough to fight. He turned away, but did not leave.

A black girl as tall as an ostrich was dancing tight turns on a pair of roller skates. She was wearing cut-away green pants the size of a small leaf, and two tiny knotted handkerchieves.

Columbus jarred, or perhaps it was *herpes simplex*. Then her body got the better of him, and he moved towards her.

Someone was already buying her. He swore softly and made for the clubs.

He called in only briefly, hoping to see a young group of gigglers, a little party of college girls, say, Julia Kepplemans on the loose. He found gangs of English holidaymakers; and even if he didn't like English girls he'd come to prize a certain quality of reserve between their legs. But none of them would talk to him.

The next bar was blue, its women nearly naked as dansettes, all moving their limbs agogo in its numb blue light.

And a chat girl, just for him, at the counter.

The drink cost five thousand pesetas for the pair of them.

"Do you work here?"

"I drop in for a drink."

"To be bought a drink?"

"When I'm lucky."

"At that price I hope you get commission."

"No," she said. "But I always bank any compliments."

"Are you a whore?"

"You must be a poet," she said. "We've got too many of those in Spain."

FIVE

1.

"A pity you won't help us. And too bad for you your teeth are not your own. We'll just have to start somewhere else."

Kay had a jubilee clip tightened at the base of his penis. From this a jump lead ran to a concealed magneto. There was a brass-lined cork in his backside and a wire connection curling to the waterpipe. It was all positive impulse, just like a car-starter, so the earth was really a refinement. But then the earth always is. The earth, the real earth, God's earth, seemed a million miles away.

Dov listened to Barel, then added, "A filled tooth we can work with. You'd be surprised at the buzz."

So far, Kay had said nothing of significance, and they hated him for his steadiness of will. They wanted so little, merely to bring him self-confidently to trial. Once he agreed who he was they could work on him for months, work with sensitive and sophisticated refinement, without pain, without drugs, without pressure. There would even be sympathy, such as exists between interrogator and prisoner. There could even be love. But they needed him to offer his identity. They already had reports of comings and goings in London. A message from the El Al offices in Regent Street had said that Fossit had been to see Quinlan. Major Shlomo Barel knew exactly what Quinlan was. He knew all about Leonard Fossit. He had twice discussed killing him in the last seven years.

He settled the clip and said, "Don't twitch or you'll tear it off." He tried everything first in German, but again not a flicker.

"I don't understand German."

"But you know it *is* German?"

Kay didn't answer. He watched what was happening to him, then said, "This man you say I am—did he do this?"

They looked at him, appalled at his self-deceit.

"A rabbi didn't give you that one," Shlomo grunted. He still wasn't ready. He tightened the jubilee some more, as gently as he could. "It will limit the damage," he explained. "Not that the International Panel of Jurists are going to take evidence on this." This was one magneto burn they wouldn't get to see. "You may as well tell us what we want," he said. "You'll break under this. Everyone does. No exceptions. We know who you are. Why not save a bad ride and confess it?"

The men grouped around grunted agreement. There may have been women. Kay was too dazzled to see.

"I'm Charles Kay, and I'm English. I'm a British citizen of some international standing. My people will protest to your government, and you'll all be in trouble." He had nerved himself for the shock, but it did not come.

Instead Barel said, "They don't know we've got you."

"They'll know soon enough."

"Not until we choose to tell them. And when we tell them who you are they'll be too embarrassed to open their mouths on the subject again." Barel paused. "As I say, you'll break under this. So why not let it out. You can do it the easy way, a bit at a time. Since you've been concealing your identity, you could begin by telling us where and when, in what surgery, what obliging doctor pickled that arm and that leg in caustic. Start by stripping away the camouflage."

The prisoner glanced down at himself, then closed his eyes, once again secure. "It wasn't caustic," he lectured. "I've not been scalded. My leg's been digested." He smiled, to correct himself slightly. "Pre-digested. As I explained before—"

The man who called himself Kay lifted off the bedframe. He was strapped to it, but he still lifted off it. His skull had been smashed from inside. The pain was too terrible to feel, so the pain in a sense was negligible. It wasn't the pain that opened his mouth. It was feeling the spine stretch apart, and the hip-joints gape, then hammer

together, leaving the memory eternally ajar. It was hearing
a girl who was himself screaming in the next room, or did
they have his daughter? It was this and this again before
he was ready and knowing there was no way to make
himself ready. The voices came to him in German. He
wished he spoke German, just to answer in German.

But he didn't speak German, so he couldn't.

He screamed in a million languages. He had the gift of
tongues.

2.

Matson dropped Pomeroy off at the Savage, then had the
still scented cab carry on to the office. Brenda was typing
his daily summary and would want him to check it.

Brenda was in a bad temper. She seemed to have damaged a finger-end.

"Why've we got manuals? Play havoc with my nails.
We're the only office that's got manuals."

"Ask the Ministry of Defence."

"We're not under the M.O.D."

"You're learning. Try typing with your toes."

"Wish we were under the M.O.D."

"You'd get yourself screwed. I used to screw little girls
when I worked for Defence."

She yawned.

Matson yawned back.

She had better teeth than he had.

"All right," he conceded. "Dinner. If you insist on
taking me out. I've got to make a phone-call first."

"To your old mum?"

"Kay's daughter in Chislehurst. My mum's still dead."

Brenda played lumpish notes on the typewriter with her
undamaged hand while he charmed Ginevra's number from
the Monitoring Unit.

He needn't have bothered. Her number was still the one
in the book. He said so as soon as she answered the phone.

"It's not being changed until I'm persuaded it's necessary. Any news about Daddy?"

"Only what I couldn't tell you earlier. He's in Israel,
and he's the victim of a rather bizarre case of mistaken
identity."

"You mean they think he's a Nazi like that natty Mr. Hitler?" She sounded relieved. "I wonder which one?"

"We'll know when they tell us. We're demanding his immediate release, of course." He heard himself being brusque, a sure sign he fancied her.

"I'd quite made my mind up it would be a ransom demand. Not that Lloyds would tell me how much he's got in the piggy. All the manager volunteered was that *that* Mr. Dixon with your and Prince Philip's shirt told him it would be a ransom demand."

"That was me, Miss Kay. I always lie to bank managers. Please have your number changed. I assure you it's essential." He put the phone down and smiled encouragingly at Brenda. "Dinner," he repeated.

"You fancy that Chislehurst bird," she said.

3.

Corporal Tamir was in uniform, as ordered. She was also wearing eye make-up. It was not quite bold enough to conceal her lack of sleep.

She listened to Barel come out of the Interrogation Room, then called to stop him hurrying past the office door.

"The General phoned," she said. She pretended to consult her pad. "That was at 22.50. He said the Minister was pressing for a progress report. When I told him you'd left no message, he said I wasn't to disturb you. At 23.05, the Cabinet Secretary phoned."

"He shouldn't have access to this exchange. Have the number scrubbed and all of our calls re-routed."

"Shall I inform General Zefat when it's done?"

"No. The General can contact me along the corridor. The Cabinet people must have bullied the number out of his office. Not from him, that's for sure, but from someone." He came in, and sat down and shivered. "Let him find out who it was and sack him. Then we can reopen a command link." His shivering disturbed him. He told himself it was the airconditioning but he knew it was fatigue. An interrogator had less adrenalin to call on than his subject, he supposed. He had intended to walk briefly from this icebox into his refrigerated flat and have a nice hot shower and get himself ready for his prisoner again. Instead he gestured for coffee and then towards the drinking fountain. "What did you tell him, the Cabinet Secretary?"

"I said you were busy."

"And?" He grabbed a coffee cup in his right hand and a water-beaker in his left and sipped hot and cold in turn. The prisoner had too much energy. He must be defending a gigantic guilt. "So what did he say to that?"

"He tried to insist he speak to you. I said you had left orders that you were not to be disturbed. He got very cross, then asked for my name. I said I had no authority to give my name to anybody."

Barel grinned and went to toss away his empty water-beaker. Something in her expression stopped him.

"Isn't it risky to be using the magneto on a man of that age?"

His grin hardened. "If you're worried about his medical condition, forget it. It's no longer your responsibility. We've been briefed by experts."

"I don't suppose Yigael Zefat is an expert on ventricular fibrillation."

Barel did not offer any opinion on the General, nor did he condescend to argue. He knew he was some sort of relative of hers, an uncle by marriage.

She took his silence for anger. "What I meant was— well, if we're working against the clock, why not simply confront him with his identity? Just name him to his face."

"Evidence," he said slowly. "I don't mean in law, because we are applying pressure. If we can get him to own up to a name of his own providing—well, I take that to be a proper confession, whatever the lawyers say. But if we force an agreement to an identity we've already dangled in front of him, then that's no more than brainwashing. I want the prisoner to tell me who he is. I need to be sure."

"Aren't we already sure? The Cabinet is sure."

"I've never known a politician stay steadfast in anything. They scramble after power, then use it to sit still. This is a briefing, Corporal Tamir, not a confessional. We've not really roughed him up, I can assure you; but he's bruised enough, and shocked enough, and thirsty enough, to start feeling sorry for himself. So we mayn't

have to start again. If we do, it'll be hard questioning
followed by the magneto. You clearly don't like the idea.
I hope it won't be necessary.'' He gave her his cup to
refill. ''If it is necessary, I'll want you in there to monitor
his pulse and his heartbeat. And if you start feeling com-
passionate, because he's such a nice pink-headed old man,
just remind yourself what he was doing in nineteen forty-
one and nineteen forty-two and nineteen forty-three and
nineteen forty-four when he was not so old and not so
nice. And remember who he was doing it to. Us.''

''And we all want to be sure, don't we, sir?''

4.

A room just behind that sex-cinema near Columbus. They
had not even started the block when he was last here.
Something in the place brought him to a stinking unease.
It was over-furnished and too fluffy for a Spanish interior. He had never bought a whore in Barcelona before,
and didn't know the style of it.

Sometime or other he would have to get undressed,
and then where would he put his gun?

''Where's the bathroom?''

''Shy are we?''

''Can I have a towel?'' He would wrap his little gun
in the towel, then retrieve it when he left. Or before he
left. He didn't overlook the distant possibility that she
had been planted on him.

On his way to the lavatory he made sure that the outer
door was locked, and that he could reach his gun before
anyone could get to him.

Then he glanced round the rest of the apartment. It
was only a long yesterday ago that he had been with
another girl in another apartment. Was it the wine and
the night club firewater that kept bringing her back? Or
was he growing soft? He had done nasty things to women
before. The last one was a little Arab.

No need as yet to be violent with this one. In spite of
the saint in the corner and some demonic posters for the
Opera and El Liceo he was having no trouble at all, except in what was once called the soul. God blew on dust

and turned it into man. Woman blows on man and turns him into God.

She brought him white wine, excellently iced, then added some powder to the jug.

"What's that?"

"Cocaine. A weeny pinch." That strange husked voice, husked rather than husky, as if somewhere in the throat there was European corn blackening into summer. A sexy voice, but localised and appropriate. It was a voice made for Iberia, the peninsula of man-throated women. "You're not getting paranoid about a little coco, are you? As I say, a weeny pinch and we'll become the slightest bit high. We'll be tired else."

She poured them wine from the jug, and drank some herself, then began to undress both of them, keeping her gloves on.

He helped her undress, keen to see what he had bought.

She was beautiful but bizarre, like a painting by Tchelitchew. It must be the effect on him of the coke, or even the wine, he thought, but she seemed to have eccentric tendons, long and glistening like unripe rhubarb, and a tracery on the buttocks like the leaves of rhubarb, too. The image was ridiculous. She was a damask girl, or did he mean damascened?

"Is that really coco? Or is it Spanish Fly?"

"A boy like you doesn't need catharides. From everything I feel you take vitamins every day."

Her thighs were coyly formed, the lips prim and gritty. She increased their interest with some scented lubricant.

They were snugger than Julia Keppleman's, tighter yet less protesting.

"Do you want me to use a condom?"

"Do condoms turn you on? They mean nothing at all to me. Do anything you want."

He wanted for fifty minutes, timed by her apartment's little clock. Its splayed modernismo hands wandered about its face from pimple to molten pimple, as he meandered languorous and slow, sipping the misted junk in its long dilution of wine, dunking in decadence. He got rid of the weeks of planning, of the times he had waited to kill, and then of his last dead girl, who he had now again and again.

He got rid of his lonely panic. Only his lust for survival, that was all that remained.

"Ouf. You keep on going, don't you?"

Some whores come, some just pretend to come, and some do not come at all.

"You did, didn't you?"

"Did I?"

Getting dressed while he was still sipping, she seemed to think some further revelation was called for. The junk was now turning nauseous. He becked at her owlishly, but listened to the lady. When it came to women's needs he was always glad to learn. Satisfying women went with the job. What was she saying?

"I'm glad you think they made a nice cut. They fixed me up properly. Not out in Morocco, where, granted, they do a neat thing. But over in Canada, in Toronto. They've got surgeons there who are very sympathetic. They can skin your little plantain, then pull it inside out."

He did not think he quite understood.

"I started life as a boy, my hunky dear. Didn't you even guess?"

He felt sick now, properly.

"Anyway, my sweet, you weren't fucking plastic. You were doing it in my tulip turned wrong ways about. It's really very sensitive to what another boy's got."

"Is that why—"

"I let you off a condom? Of course not, darling. It's because I'm a Catholic. Have another drink."

"Really no thanks." He had to be going. There was something in Leviticus. It was like pouring his seed into the grave. And then there was Onan and the Cities of the Plain.

"Will I get to see you?"

"Yes, you'll get to see me." He nearly forgot his gun.

5.

"Will toffy Mr. Pomeroy get the old bloke back?"

"Just how would he manage that?"

"Borrow the pop-gun you keep up your desk." She wasn't trying to be hurtful. He'd seen it all before. It was the same with all the girls of that bunny-bummed deb-set the office used for secretaries. They compared notes about him picking his teeth and cracking crude Irish jokes, but ultimately the sheer sexual tension wore them down. They had to shag him or die. Very few died.

Brenda, alas, was not a member of the bunny class. Unfortunately for his immediate plans. He needed something to distract him from Charles Henry Kay. A desk officer could not afford to be obsessed with the dramas of the job.

He signalled for another bottle of wine and tried not to listen to his own thickening voice. "My flat's only just round the corner," he remarked, as if he had just made a brilliant discovery.

She was building something stupid with a napkin. "I'm right across town," she said. "I'll have to get a taxi."

He waited until the wine came, then said, "You know what you're here for?"

"Am I?"

He began, or heard his mouth begin, a long and involved story about something he was finding it increasingly difficult to remember. The kidnap had rearranged his thinking. He retraced to say hurriedly, "I put that badly just now. What I meant was: you seem to have a good idea of what our little job is all about."

"I've spent quite a few months studying you, Patrick."

"We could go there for coffee," he said quickly.

"Perhaps. Depends on the taxis. You worried about that old codger?"

"As a matter of fact—yes." Everything was very clear again. "I identify with him, anyway."

"Why? I mean: how? You're half his age—almost a spring chicken."

"Yes. Yes, I'm chicken all right." He paused, wondering how confidential to be, but knowing that the wine had won. "Being chicken is something I know about—perhaps that's why so much of my mind's inside that Interrogation Centre." He added what he thought was already obvious. "I've been done over myself, you see."

"Interrogated?"

"That? Oh yes."

"When?"

"In the old days." There were limits to the looseness of the tongue.

"Leonard and Marcus Pomeroy both say you've been in the Thugs. Tortured, you mean?"

"Heavy interrogation is the word." She'd shouted she wanted to be treated as a person. Unfortunately he wasn't sure what sort of person a woman could turn out to be. "It makes you feel soiled. Even a young man feels soiled. Kay's quite an old man. Still, Miss Kay says he's tough enough."

"They won't damage him, Patrick. They'll use experts."

"Torture's a bit like rape. I don't like making the comparison, but that's what the shrinks say. It doesn't matter how brief it is, how unfussy, how *considerate* even. You're just not the same again afterwards, not ever."

Brenda was clearly in need of a profundity. Instead she giggled, then stopped, embarrassed at herself. "That old bloke the Israelis have got," she said. "He is who he is, you know. He's Charles Henry Kay. He's not that cuddly little daughter of his in her Daddy's trousers. Or out of them, come to that. So you can stop fussing."

6.

Shlomo Barel signalled Corporal Tamir to follow him, then walked back along the corridor, thinking, why do I do it, why the hell do I do it? There are men who want revenge, and men who want to rise above it. Revenge is an out-of-date emotion, too discardably European. A man born into a landscape of little kings must suffer the emotions of little kings, wear the masks of their ridiculous passions. I am not such a man.

The little kings had their triumphs, of course, but none of them as bitter as this one, the captive armoured only in motley, his face a howling jigsaw.

In the Interrogation Room the extractors were full on, sucking tangible tornadoes of updraught through the vortex holes in the ceiling. Otherwise the room was a room which smelled slyly of vomit or was it diarrhoea?

"The swine's fouled himself."

Barel didn't look at his subordinates, but at the face on

the iron bed. The jigsaw with the shat pants. He was beyond communing with anything else. He could only talk with this motley. He followed the terminal into the open fly. Man as the ultimate marionette. They were father and child, he and Kay. And which was father and which was child? And who was Kay?

Just a half whirr at low spasm, like a disc-jockey testing the public address system. Kay became briefly amplified. Judi Tamir failed to assist.

There was also a new sort of revenge. Revenge for the two thousand years of withheld national identity. Revenge for a lack of confidence. Revenge for self-disgust. Ah, but revenge upon whom? Upon poor screamless Kay, voiced like a crouped chicken? Revenge for a cowed father, a cowed grandfather? Neither the father nor the grandfather felt cowed, for they had seen what they had seen and been where they had been, and that they said was Hell; but the son felt they were cowed and—yes—cowards. They had let a nation perish. They had let it perish two thousand years after it had ceased to exist, but that did not absolve them in the eyes of the son. Something precariously preserved by Moses and Abraham and uncorrupted by Solomon had been allowed to be squandered in Dauchau and Auschwitz. Two thousand years of tribulation passed unseen. All History is a telescope to such sons. And now, remote as in a lens, he had his forefathers' testicles in his hand. So what was their truth's milk?

He leant across the prisoner and spoke to him gently. He did not address his eyes, which were shut tight. He talked to himself, to the terminal in the fly. "The Mossad isn't enamoured of torture." He talked to himself, but he was speaking to Judi Tamir. "Among intelligent people—and most of our enemies are intelligent—torture is counterproductive. But when we use it"—this to the little corporal most of all—"don't let us be mealymouthed about it, we use it hard. We go immediately for quick results."

The prisoner blinked his lids awake. He kept his gaze very still.

Barel did not like what he saw—a fierceness far from extinguished. Was this the collective fanaticism of the SS, or something more personal?

''Men have their eyes,'' he said. ''They have their balls. Normally they get a glimmering of reason through one or the other.''

Kay turned his head and faced him. ''Someone said you were going to produce me for the Press?''

''We're going to hang you in front of the Press,'' Dov corrected.

''Before then, at some time soon, someone from some consulate will have to see me.''

''But which consulate will you agree to?''

''You will soon have to decide on one of them yourselves,'' the prisoner said slowly. ''And whichever consulate it is, you will then have to let that consulate decide in its turn.''

''Hell has no consulate.'' Judi Tamir looked surprised to find herself hating him so completely.

''You're quite right,'' Barel said gently. ''We are about to show you to the world. We make no secret of it. We are going to bring you publicly to trial, and therefore I must make you this promise. We shall leave you your eyes. We shall leave you your hands. We will not sprain even a little finger of them. What's available to sunshine is yours. But what normally resides inside your suit—that's ours. We'll start where it hurts, where the truth is. We'll exercise the franchise of the torturer. It grants us ninety-five per cent of your surface to operate on.'' He waited for his words to sink in, then added quietly, ''And all of your interior, of course.''

''My body has survived harder things than you can throw at it. Likewise my mind.''

''How interesting,'' Barel murmured. ''You're not asking for justice anymore—only strength. Well, I can tell you that whatever resilience you have, we shall overcome it with the magneto. It may take us five minutes; you may have five hours. You won't have any longer.''

''I intend to be strong enough to report you to my consul. You forget I have lived rough.''

''You don't look like a man who's been in the desert,'' Dov said. ''Any desert.''

Kay swirled upwards, gusting through his bonds like a duststorm, and hit him. Then tripped headlong on his ankle chain.

"You take my point?" Dov asked. He was bleeding from a damaged tooth, but he had not felt the blow. It was like being struck by tumbleweed. "You're weak wristed, like a woman."

"Like a torturer," Barel agreed with him. "Desert— what desert?"

"In the desert I'd have killed you."

"I wonder how you killed Kay. Not by hitting him."

They retied him with wire to the iron bedframe. They plugged him in.

7.

Brenda blinked at his lounge. It had austere oak furniture. A wooden standard lamp was sited in the middle of the room so its base could disguise a rainbow-tinted oilstain on the parquet. There were books everywhere, books and a stack of hardwood boxes. She squinted at a mahogany lid and read: PYTHON 357.

"Reptiles?" she asked in alarm.

His hands were busy with her clothes. "I'll protect you," they insisted.

"So this is your Camden 'Higher Rented,' " she wondered. "So called not because the rental is in any way higher but because—"

"It's rented to a 'Higher Sort of Person,' " he quoted.

She broke away and made for the kitchen. It was huge, and elaborate, but its labour-saving work-surfaces were laden with mechanical presses and so many bits of machinery it looked like a garage workshop.

"I'm not stopping here," she said.

"Not good enough for you?"

"I live in a council flat myself. This is a sodding torture chamber. What's that? And that?"

"A swaging block," he recited with pride. "A mechanical crimping tool, a calibrated reamer, a hand-chocking primer reamer, a cast-trimmer."

"Like I said—a torture chamber."

They were back in the lounge and then the bedroom, herself standing with nothing on.

"Where do you think you are?" he demanded. "The Sixties?"

''The Tribe of Dan,'' she yawned. ''It's stirring beneath your greengage kilt.''

The phone rang for some time before Matson could remember where he'd left it.

''It's Ginevra Kay. I'm sorry it's so late, but you said to phone.''

''No more news, I'm afraid, Miss Kay.''

''They won't hurt Daddy, will they? I know you think I go on, but—''

''They're not going to be rough, Ginevra. Please let me promise you they've no reason to harm him in any way.''

8.

The music was loud. Made of pressure made of flame.

Someone with a chisel prised back the fontanelles, then let them recompress till the skull slammed shut.

''*Could he in fact be—*''

The lamplight a grindstone where the bone edge scarred, the shoulderblades splintered:

Could he be—?

No. He was Charles Henry Kay.

Bombed open between the legs, leaking hot fragments, dribbling bits of light.

Then he fainted backwards, leaving go the sharp bits like a climber on a cliff face, but they screamed him back up again on one scald of wire.

Could he, again could he be—

Was Charles Henry Kay—

Another bomb of pain. He felt his balls shatter, the spine go needles.

Kay Kay Kay

It happened again to the body reconnected.

As the body reconnected.

I am Kay. Surely I am Kay?

But who is Kay?

What, save for skull burst and cathode burn in the scrotum, is Charles Henry Kay?

The mouth in the lampshade came closer:

Charles Henry Kay or

Henry Charles Kay or

A Man Called Kay or

A Man who called himself Kay
or
Now in a dream remembering his daughter. He had sired Ginevra Was-it-Kay. She had come from the loins that the race who decorate the loins had now burnt raw. A mouthing tribe of generations, a nation of families. Well, brick, glass and child had all grown out of him. Brick, glass, child and dangerous snakes: a whole world in Chislehurst, there and the Outback.
And now the burning bush.
"You ought to see what your lot did to my grandmother," said Shlomo Barel.
Said the mouth in the lampshade.
With his balls burnt out he entered the bush.
And began to scream then. To scream and to scream.
They were working into his private horror.
And his horror was his guilt.

Terrible truths began to burst from the prisoner's mouth on that iron bed. Every man has his secret, if you squeeze him long enough.

So they switched off the magneto. When they let him speak, he spoke. He spoke of that time in Australia that nobody knew about. Not even his wife, who knew him all. Not even his daughter.

His eyes were still shut, his nostrils fastidious at the smell of his own burning. It was hardly apocalypse he uttered, but a life's reserve of meanness, each word settling into their collective disgust like a meatfly on a bone.

9.

Sand running to swampland. The area was not big, or the area of vision not big. The sun close as an arc-lamp. The heat like a weight on the head.

Himself and Bosie Elderkin, that best of Australian snake-handlers. Not, on the evidence of this foray, snake-catchers, not either of them. But find Bosie a snake to handle and he would handle it.

So far, it had been death-adders, several king snakes, and one Tiger snake on the wrong side of the continent. The Tiger had come at them in the water, just where they are fastest and most dangerous. Bosie had waited as calm

as soaked cucumber and lifted it out of the drink by the
neck, waiting till it was a cock's length off and just about
to whip at him. Then held it between forefinger and thumb
where it hung like a wet rope and didn't even complain.
Not even when he dropped it *tail first* into a bag, all four
feet of it. Kay had never seen a snake bagged like that
before, particularly one their serum wouldn't touch: but
he said nothing. Bosie wasn't called Bosie lightly. He was
a wrong 'un. Even an experienced snake found itself baf-
fled by him. Perhaps it felt that going tail first into Bosie's
bag was preferable to going tail first into his mouth.

"Jeez," said Bosie, wiping his brow with snake water.
"I thought I was back home in the Hope River for a minute."

Kay noticed he hadn't tied the bag properly, but still the
Tiger didn't come out and protest.

"Do you always handle snakes like that?"

"No. But he was so far off-course I figured his compass
was wrong. I got an instinct what I'll get away with."

"What about the snake's instinct?"

"Snakes reason like I do. Only a fool's going to pick
'em up wrong, and a fool won't be fast enough to pick
'em up in the first place. The snake ain't going to take
chances. Jesus, I might be a God. You ask the Abbos.
Snakes have got a big respect for religion. Got to have. A
lot of the world's religions give them big publicity."

To be fair, Bosie had climbed out of the river very fast.

"What's your worry now, Elderkin?"

"The Great Australian Crocodile. One of them wouldn't
have to be so far off-course, and I don't know nothing
about them, not from the arse of a drongo."

"I thought crocodiles were Gods as well."

"Yes, mister, but they give you the Great Australian
Bite. You heard of the Great Australian Bite? It's on all
the kid maps."

Bosie didn't believe in maps, nor in compasses either.
"Why carry a compass when you got a little Abbo? Those
guys know the North from the way their balls hang. And
they can do things with a piece of bark, I mean a scored
piece of bark with no orientation, no scale, no relation
between one point and another save each point's got a

name, that you can't do with maps. 'Sides, there are no maps for up here."

"There's the Aerial Survey."

"You wait till they give an Abbo some wings. Then I'll start believing the Aerial Survey of these parts."

Once out of the water and dried, they found they were lost. Not that Elderkin would admit it. "I'm puzzled," he said. "That's all. I've been puzzled for days, but that don't mean I'm lost. We've been found by the river, haven't we? And a river always goes somewhere. It's a First Rule of Nature. Now a river *is* a God!"

"And what's this God called?"

"He's got several names, I daresay."

"There are several rivers to choose from, you mean."

"Trust the Abbos."

10.

The Abbos were with them to lead them to Taipans. The Abbos were called Big Neiiji and Willi Kukulu, but Elderkin was not one to bother with names, and he was right with this also; for no sooner had Kay memorised them and learned a little tongue and tried to get talking, than Neiiji and Kuku deserted.

He woke up next morning, this morning, to find a night log smouldering, but the Aborigines gone.

"They ain't gone deserting," Bosie explained. "They only gone walkabout."

"When will they be back?"

"Maybe three months, maybe a year. I ain't painting you roses. I'm drawing you a picture of their state of mind."

"On a scored bit of bark."

Bosie had his dignity, so they finished breakfast in silence.

"See it this way," said Bosie. "They contracted to bring us where the Big Snakes are."

"To find us some Taipans."

"They don't call 'em Taipans. They call them the Rainbow Serpent. They think they're the World Spirit left over from the Dream Time. They think they're related to the circle where the land meets the sky. They think the Great Circle is a snake with its tail in its mouth.''

"Must be a monster snake.''

"The Taipan is a big snake. I ain't seen one, but you can take it from me, it's big.''

"Well, Big Neiiji and Kukulu have welched on their contract.''

"Not the way they see it. Maybe there are Taipans right here. After their walkabout they'll come back to see.''

They puffed up the fire a bit, to burn off their utensils, what Bosie called their tuck tins. Then they kicked it out. The heat was getting up, and things began moving.

Then they saw their Taipan.

"Jesus,'' said Bosie. "They led us right to it.''

It was big as a python, bigger than an Australian python, and in their moment of awe growing bigger and bigger.

The ground was difficult, and they fevered to sort out their tackle without alarming the snake. They had pitched last night by a bank, but it was basically a place where the earth had fissured open into big scars, like a labyrinth of dead streams. Rains had silted the base of these hollows, and the sun had baked them hard. They were at the dry end of one of them, against the lip. The snake was at the other, where there was a drift of dry grass, then scrub lifting over the top. They must have been very close to it last evening when they'd gone combing for wood.

They both watched and worked. Whatever happened now, it wouldn't move far. Snakes are not very itinerant, and a big snake likes to lord it over its own terrain.

"Don't forget they've got a reputation,'' Kay muttered. He didn't know why he was being so quiet. Snakes are deaf, but it would have smelled them and before that sensed their vibration.

"Balls.''

It was fully in view, coming from shadow back to sun, adjusting for heat. The sun would be much too hot, the shadow a fair bit too cold until the air warmed up. In these circumstances even a big snake had to move around to stay alive. Only when the temperature was a slowly rising constant would it be able to lie up.

"Big enough for you?''

"We need the Abbos.''

"They'd only be in the way. You ready?"

"Let's get it then."

Snake catching is not complicated by theory. Broadly it consists of catching snakes. A little deftness allied to a lot of know-how. Not much daring. Not much special equipment, except for very special snakes.

Kay and Elderkin had all of the qualities, even if their styles didn't mix.

They were both experts, knowing more about snakes than snakes themselves. They had seen many more snakes than any mere snake had.

In this case there was no special equipment because there was no special know-how. Nothing much was known about the Taipan then, save a number of zoos were beginning to put an encouraging price on it.

And the North Eastern Aborigines thought it was a God.

Or that was how it seemed to Kay, looking back with the flame in his head.

11.

Yitzak walked the cobbled pavings of the Calle de Aribau just as dawn was breaking. He no longer felt drunk, but his groin was a melancholy ache, sadder than moonlight.

Well, the birds were singing in the plane trees, and somewhere in his misery there was a kind of elation. He couldn't dine out on it: but sometimes he had done murder, and he couldn't dine out on murder, either.

He had demanded a night key. His key hand was shaky.

Inside the courtyard someone was talking.

His host was still up, sitting at his desk in Reception and using the telephone. His host was wearing, of all things, a nightcap. He wondered at the nightcap, as if the world was turning queer in his dreams. Then he remembered the man's hair oil. Somewhere in his life there would be a woman to complain about the pillows.

The man saw him and became agitated. He inflated his little moustache and began to beckon towards him, shouting into the phone, "No, señor. He is here now. He is arrived."

Yitzak made to go past. His own people would never

call him like this; didn't, in any event, know where he was.

"No, *señor*. He is at this moment back from the city, and will assuredly talk to you."

It would be pleasing to smack him over the nightcap with the barrel of his gun. Instead, Yitzak took the phone from the man's fingers. They were dull and dry. Perhaps he rolled tobacco or took snuff. A curious odour came from him. Yitzak hoped it wasn't fear.

"Is that Shmuel, called Yitzak, from the land of the Ancient Hebrews?"

He nearly put the phone down, but the man was already in English, and he wanted to know what he knew.

"Shmuel Shmuel, Her Majesty wants Her goods back."

"I've no instructions to trade."

"Someone must talk to someone. It's really in all our interests."

"So what is it you suggest?"

"Why not a daylight meeting, somewhere proper and public? I suggest the bar at the Yacht Club. We can sign you on at the Yacht Club if your allowance will run to a tie."

"Where's that?"

"On the wall of the main harbour. You walk along the eastern mole."

"I'm allergic to salt water. And as I said very clearly before, I've no instructions to trade."

"Not got the goods in your holdall? Look, I've been asked to make contact, to see if there's any way forward. You have our unreserved assurance."

"The terrace bar of the Oriente, then. The one smack in the middle of the Ramblas. At some decent hour tomorrow. I don't think you'll try anything there."

"After lunch, at three then. When decent folks are abed, and you'll be ready for breakfast. Believe me when I say we've got orders to stay off you. Your side are holding the pack."

"How will I recognise you?"

"We know who you are." The voice became aloof, and blurred with disconnection noises on the wire. The call might have come from Paris, say, or London. It might mean they had tied him to the girl's death as well, but he doubted they were smart enough for that. And even if they had, he must remember they weren't Israelis. Blood was not blood to them.

He checked the Registrations Book, elbowing Hitler contemptuously aside.

"Nobody new," the man muttered. His guts were rumbling.

"You got a woman up there?"

"What's it to you?"

"Bring me some wine. If you've got yourself a woman, you won't need to find yourself a glass."

"I'll take one cup, just to give you good day and to rinse my mouth."

"Bring a good bottle and a jug of water."

He watched the man shuffle off. He was wearing slippers, and they or the feet inside them were responsible for the curious odour. If he had a woman up there, she wouldn't like that.

Yitzak slipped quickly upstairs to check his room. Nothing. Just the same, he would sleep in a chair in the courtyard where he could watch the door. It was cooler downstairs; there was a palm tree and a gravity fountain. Better sleep beside a fountain than beside a woman, the Arab proverb says.

Hitler was waiting downstairs, so Yitzak grinned and pulled an imaginary chain in the air.

"It's a sign of good health," the man agreed. "Even in the night."

They sipped Banda Azul together and tried to look appreciative. Hitler slipped his footwear off, for a moment destroying the sweetness of the palm. Then a cat came and began to lick between his toes, pink-tongued, fastidious.

Things got better. Yitzak looked for talk, but his host needed sleep.

I'll talk to the bottle, he thought, moodily alone. Then took one more drink. The bottle was best, better than talk, better than woman. Better sleep beside a bottle than sleep beside a fountain.

12.

It was dark when Matson awoke, midsummer fiery, crackling with dreams. The room smoked with faces. He answered them back till they faded. Terence Quinlan first, then the Assistant Commissioner and Fossit, till all their lamps were out. All except Yitzak and Pomeroy who kept themselves quiet behind Matson's eyelids. Still, it was a proper dark at last, a seasonable dark that laid its comfort everywhere except inside his skull.

He rolled towards the bedside table looking for water, but found himself wrapped in flesh, somebody's flesh, somebody else's warm arms and legs that tangled with his own and had always been there, save he was too numb to notice.

He had been drunk. The body in bed was part of the evidence.

There had been a girl the night before. But the night before was before, a whole night before. He had gone to the office since then. He had unmasked a cunning Israeli plot. He had met important people and been important.

The phone began to ring, as the phone always will at such moments.

"Who are you?" he asked. His hand missed the water jar then clawed along the bedhead wall, which lay at angles in quite the wrong place. If it weren't for that dip in the plaster he might be anywhere; but he knew where he was. There's only one Hell. "Who are you?" To put the light on would be foolish, experience taught. It would also be churlish. "Who am I kipping with?" The girl from his dreams who'd proved Mummy wrong with her soothing fingers? He didn't think so. Possibly a tart. He'd had to do with tarts when his heart was hard up and his paddy even harder. Tarts never answer the phone. "Bloody who are you?"

"Your Christmas stocking," the voice said, its note arch from drinking, its tone familiar.

He pressed his hands to his eyelids and thought of Ginevra Kay.

The girl felt him over, finding nothing.

"I don't keep pockets in my skin."

"Christ knows why. It's a loose enough fit."

She pulled down his hands from his eyes. He was blind. He had tortures and torture chambers printed on his retina.

He felt her in turn, looking for a clue in braille. Then someone switched the sun on.

"Don't do that," he said.

She had leant across to pull the blind, and handed him the phone in his sleep.

The phone was horribly full of cheerful Pomeroy. "Not too early for you, is it, Paddy?"

"I've just been jogging."

"Can you get your bottom over here for lunch? Not your whole bottom, Patrick—no need for you to do any thinking. Just a half buttock, say, and your departmental paybook."

"Where?"

"That little bistro where Leonard takes you and you took your lady last night." The phone went dead.

Matson addressed the room. "You let me oversleep," he said. "What have you cooked for breakfast?" He still didn't know who he was talking to.

13.

The Taipan was aware of them, had settled to static. From where Kay stood, it was a lot of snake.

They moved round it quickly, confusing its escape. Each had a handling pole, and they'd shuffled up a basket. They would bag the basket, once the snake was in it, rather than try to bag the snake and put a bagged snake in the basket. A snake like that would weigh a hundredweight.

A taper-headed monster, sloping from the neck.

It was, he decided, beautifully marked. When God created the Serpent, all his Artforms came together.

The snake didn't particularly watch them as basking snakes will if they're reluctant to be disturbed. Or retreat, as most snakes do.

It gave them a yard or two.

They moved up cautiously.

It came straight at them in a flattened down slurry, and no longer at *them,* because Bosie was past it. It came at Kay, who looked down the pink black tube of its mouth and saw its fangs, very small fangs for the size of it. Or did he mean thin? He sidestepped and snapped on his cramp then twisted its pole.

The snake kept on coming through the clamp, lunged at him rather than struck; then turned right round and pushed into Bosie's midriff, bumping up from the soil. The dirt was scale hard, but the snake cracked it open with the snap of its turn then whipped up and down like a severed hawser.

Kay tightened on the clamp, but the thing had too much muscle for its weight, and too much weight for his muscle. For a second it was all around both of them, do what he could, like a cable accident, played in slow motion; but this was fast; and it kept on butting at Bosie, butting and biting. It didn't strike. It fell on and chewed like a mamba or a cobra, but faster than a cobra. Bosie didn't have a chance. His clothes were torn and there was juice on his trousers from its sacs, the snake with the biggest sacs in the world; and he got the lot. Kay wrestled and swore, hearing its breath like a gale in a drainpipe, or perhaps it was Bosie grunting as it hit him, then screaming aloud.

"My balls," he was saying or Kay was dreaming. "It's got my balls."

The snake was in a frenzy, with a grapple on board, but towing away. It went threshing and floundering off, but not too far, say thirty feet, with the clamp-pole flagging round in the trees, the tongs tearing out meat and working it up into a whirlwind of tooth.

Bosie merely frothing now, frothing and writhing.

"His balls," thought Kay. "I'll have to cut them off." He felt himself going demented, nightmare demented. He tore down Bosie's trousers.

Elderkin was beyond speech. The Taipan, as he said, had hooked him in the scrotum. He was bleeding from punctures in the sack and in the dick. His bleeding was blood but also it was venom, and the blood was changing hue, the platelets all dyed out and the lymph dripping separate. He wasn't bleeding blood but frothed-up like frogs-spawn.

Kay had his knife out. You pull out your knife to excise a wound, to liberate the blood or to . . .

But everywhere he looked was more froth than blood; and there was something very nasty not just down there but in the slime of the eyeballs which were quite turned up.

Bosie Elderkin's stomach was shaking underneath his hand. Kay pulled up his bushshirt and found the other chewmarks. All those bloody bites, part neurotoxic, part haemotoxic, from the biggest poison sac of any reptile in the world.

Bosie was curdling. His arteries were strangled. His bowels and lungs were bleeding as the linings broke down. He looked what he was, a pre-digested mess.

There was only one mercy. The spasms started weak, and went weaker. He was clinically dead within a minute of the biting. The venom blanks the brain then burns out the heartbeat.

Then the snake scythed back at them, its meat torn in patches. One second it was flogging through its clamp, the next coming straight at Kay.

He turned and ran.

SIX

1.

Today the little restaurant looked grubby. It needed a girl-friend and candleflame. There was even a television, switched on, on a high corner shelf. Matson had never noticed it before. Now his hangover was aware of nothing else. He stood among a wilderness of tables and said, "This place. The chips are always cold."

"*Pommes frites*, Patrick." Pomeroy was already seated, and halfway down a glass that smelled like mouthwash, but if Pomeroy was drinking it, then it was clearly *de rigueur*. "You should eat in your own gaff. Get yourself a cat." He smiled as if he was offering to play pussy himself. "It's well known that spooks only eat in three restaurants. You certainly can't afford the other two."

"Where do you eat?"

"I'm not a spook. Ah—here's my other guest."

"Tell him to take his hat off."

A tall Arab, in a brown western suit, but with his head-cloth worn in the Palestinian manner, was approaching the table.

They stood to greet him.

"Patrick Matson—Doctor Ibrahim Nuseibeh."

"Mr. Mat*son* knows who I am. He had his secretary type my name on a list as recently as yesterday." Dr. Nuseibeh should have been embarrassed to make such an undiplomatic disclosure. Instead he added, "With almost total disregard for my immediate wellbeing."

"Yesterday was yesterday. You should be on a plane somewhere by now."

The Arab sat and spread his hands, which were so much cleaner than Matson's. ''Ah, but where to, my dear Mat*son? Where?* Some of us can only be deported to a hole in the ground. Do you ever think of that?''

''I just make the list.''

''And the list digs the hole. 'The hand that signs the paper fells a city'—isn't that what your great English poet said?''

''He was Welsh.''

A small piece of spinach glinted in the man's tooth. Matson watched it with distaste before he realised it wasn't spinach at all, but a gem in a filling. Nuseibeh touched it proudly with his tongue and said, ''It is almost the only line of English in which an Arab can detect any meaning, Mr. Mat*son.*''

''I'm glad you two are getting on so well,'' Pomeroy smiled. ''I'm just off to rinse my fingers.'' He stood up and did something unusually imprecise and silly for Pomeroy, making a nervous little bow and showing a bald spot on his head before moving towards the cloakroom.

Nuseibeh watched his back for a second, then said, ''Speaking to me is going to do you no good at all.'' He glanced about him. ''Wherever I go there's always some little Jew in attendance.''

''Israeli?''

''No, not an Israeli. Not this time. There aren't enough Israelis to keep an eye on me. Just a dirty little Jew.''

''That sort of talk makes me feel very uneasy, Dr. Nuseibeh.''

''So it should, Mr. Mat*son.* It was intended to. I like my friends to be uneasy. I want you to be alert and stay alive. You are going to owe me several favours, you see.''

''Me or Pomeroy?''

''A man like Pomeroy never owes favours.''

''And I don't treat with members of your organisation—I kick them out.''

''Libyans. Yesterday your target was the Libyan Embassy, I believe. Gadaffi's men. I am not one of Gadaffi's men, though what have you got against Libya? Good things come to you from Libya.''

''Name one.''

''Mister Mat*son.*''

"One. Or I'll trot you out of here to the nearest policeman. You're *persona non grata,* and in contravention of an expulsion order."

"Where shall I go? I cannot go to Israel, nor to my own Left Bank."

"Tough cheese. You should learn to behave yourself."

"Not even to Barcelona. Barcelona, Mr. Mat*son,* the cradle of anarchy—even there it is going to become a trifle warm for me very soon."

A coldness began to trickle. Matson felt damp behind the knee as he did when the plane throttled back before a jump. At last he said, wondering at his own naivety, "It's not you we're going to owe for that, is it?"

Pomeroy came back from the bathroom, all smiles. He had rearranged some hair over his bald patch and now sat with ease.

Nuseibeh ignored him and gave his green smile to Matson. "You mustn't worry about the chemistry of it. What goes on inside the alembic is our business, not yours. People like the object under discussion have stolen other men's land." Again the gangrene in the tooth. "Some of those men's sons have enough spunk to want it back."

Pomeroy yawned. Matson felt the irritation that always comes when a foreigner tries to be over-colloquial in English. He said to him, "You will not have to expel Dr. Nuseibeh. Technically he is in default. But in fact I shall make a recommendation tomorrow that the exclusion order be rescinded, and his diplomatic immunity extended for six months."

"Indefinitely, surely?"

"Six months will do for starters. In recognition of a certain accommodation he has been able to arrive at."

Nuseibeh had already stood up to leave. He was watching his "little Jew" beckoning frantically for a bill, the green smile still on his face. Then he heard what Matson was saying. "One?" he hissed. *"One* accommodation? Soon there is to be another favour. I thought you knew that? I shall need an indefinite extension then." He became calm again, businesslike, and held out two little typewritten cards. "Mr. Mat*son*'s ten K will please go to this number at C. Hoare and Company at Waterloo Place. And my bonus, Mr. Pomeroy, will not be added to my usual account but will be paid to this one at Messrs. Coutts in Sloane Street.'' He smiled. ''Thank you, Mr. Matson, and please be careful. After all, you are merely going to enjoy a bargain. For Mr. Pomeroy I have arranged the sale of the century.''

Matson wasn't up to this conversation. For a second he wasn't up to anything.

Pomeroy waited until Nuseibeh had left the restaurant, together with his shadow, and then said dreamily, ''You mustn't wear it on the bone, Patrick. Ours is an imprecise art.''

''Providing we protect the odd British life or two?''

''British lives are a bit outside our brief. Gone is the day when we'd send a gunboat to demand reparation for a tweaked handlebar moustache. British lives come relatively cheap, Paddy. It's British interests that command my office's attention.''

''Leaving Kay where?''

''Relative to the exact location of the appropriate British interest.''

''And who determines where that is?''

''In that part of the world, and for quite a few thousand map squares, me.''

''You'll seek authority?''

''I'm not a Catholic.''

''I was thinking of the Cabinet Office.''

''The cabinet is composed of mere men, Patrick. In my small way I am a God.''

2.

There was a bed and it was wooden. It had blankets and sheets and a striped cotton pillow. Kay knew there was a mattress, and that the mattress was soft. Inside the bed it was softer than childhood.

The room was too cold. Its air was too clean. The walls were painted ice. He heard his teeth chatter as if his mouth were a typewriter. The chatter wasn't coming from his head. His teeth no longer functioned in his head. They were an ache inside his thoughts, which were cold. He hunched against the cold, and envied his body lying in the bed where it was comfortable and warm.

His body was asleep. His body was stuck with tubes and asleep; but out here in the corner his mouth was swollen dry and his teeth gibbered.

He felt a coward crouching in the corner. And though he was afraid, terribly afraid, he decided to move out and face the door.

The door was like the walls, made of ice, and like the walls painted white.

There was no catch or handle on the door. There was no hinge or hole for a key.

The door looked like lines drawn on the wall, but he knew it was a door.

Outside the door he had spent half his lifetime in another room. They had done terrible things to his body in that room, and something even worse had happened to the rest of him.

He wanted to drink some water to ease his swollen mouth, and he wanted to relieve himself.

They hadn't let him drink and they had told him not to urinate.

They hadn't left him any water, and his teeth wouldn't stop chattering and aching long enough to let him drink.

He wanted to relieve himself behind the door, but he couldn't find his penis.

A night and a day and a night.

He wondered what time it was.

It must be dark outside because the electric light was on. He looked towards the window. There was no window. He looked but he couldn't find the door. He looked into the lightbulb and it seemed to drip with ice. His teeth went on chattering in an office miles away, and a phone began to ring.

The door stayed locked until it swung open.

It was Barel who came in, Major Barel with the blurred face.

Here he was, totally dehydrated, couldn't pee, couldn't spit; and yet the great teardrops formed their distorting lenses, then shattered and scattered themselves all the way down his cheek. His nice striped pyjama top was getting quite wet.

"Did you sleep all right? We're going to need to ask you a few more questions."

Matron with the boy who'd wet the bed.

"Here?"

"No. Along the corridor."

"Where I was?"

"Yes, where you were." The major sounded thoughtful, as if "here" were a sanctuary he might decide to withdraw.

"I need a glass of water."

"It's not advisable."

Kay's mouth began to shake, his jaw to tremble. "There's cobra venom in my veins. I must have water."

"You still pretend to know about snakes."

"I know I must have water."

"Later. You'll come to no harm. You've had the antidote. We injected glucose. We've left you on saline and yet more glucose." He nodded towards the drip bottles, the tubes in Kay's arms. "And, of course, K and C."

"For how long?"

"What do you mean?"

"I want to know what day it is."

"Time is for us, not you." Barel seemed to grow, to become much taller, and Kay realised he had been crouching by the bed and was now standing. "I wouldn't worry about the juice in your blood. We've given you a pretty total transfusion. Jewish blood, I'm afraid."

It wasn't a jibe he could answer.

The major turned for the door, then swung back and said, "The nurse will be in to disconnect your drip. I'll see you in an hour."

He tapped on the door and it was opened. He went out and it was closed.

An hour. His life was becoming orderly.

There wasn't a clock on the wall.

3.

Yitzak was glad he hadn't slept in his room. It was full of traffic noise, and the water in the sink stank of petrol.

He used it to scrub the collar of his shirt and rinse its armpits. The damp patches dried as he walked downstairs.

The fountain had been switched off, and there was a woman behind the desk across the courtyard.

He greeted her with the deference of a man who has kept her husband up drinking. Somehow she would know he was going out to buy a newspaper, find a cup of coffee, perhaps write a postcard or two. His face said so. It didn't say he daren't come back to pay the bill.

He had a tinny taste in his mouth. Not disgust for last night nor remorse for the day before. Fear.

Barel would expect him to meet the British, just in case there was something to learn. But after that, he would have to get lost; and this time it would be hard.

He bought himself some spearmint and a foldex, then went through his usual juggle with the taxis. Habit, not necessity. No-one would follow him. Not yet.

The inside of his cab smelled like a wet boot. Someone had been washing the leather.

The driver began to gabble about the Catalan Independence celebrations.

Yitzak did not answer.

"You do not understand me?"

"Not a word. I have no Spanish and less Catalan."

"Are you English?" The driver spoke in English. "I like the English."

English seemed a good thing to be.

"If you're English you should grant the Irish their freedom, then lock up your football fans. That way you'll stop them being sick in the back of my car. It wouldn't happen in Franco's day." He went up the gears. "Franco believed in the garrotte." He came down the gears. "One thing about the garrotte. It keeps people from being sick in cars."

Yitzak stopped the taxi. He did not feel English enough to be shamed into leaving a tip. He felt lonely again, as lonely as if he were still a little boy.

He walked a block, two blocks, trying to calm his nerves. He couldn't. The streets were full of women. They had a bad effect on him. He watched them scolding on doorsteps, lugging home their shopping, doing busy things, and he hated them for their self-assurance. They made him feel so much apart, such an unnecessary object.

Their minds only touched on him if he fucked them or killed them. Even when he tore their lives into tatters he felt he'd got to nothing.

A girl in blue stockings had been wearing that self-same expression one second before he threw her from the window. Loneliness does not let you look like that, nor does fear. Not the loneliness he felt now, which was full of Julia Keppleman.

4.

She was dressed in an Army uniform without a tunic. She wore a white lab coat a long way open. The nurse, the civilian and the soldier all shared one Gorgon's face. He must be going mad.

She removed the adhesive blocks from his arms, then the pads and dressings. She prised out glass claws and dropped them on cotton in a dish. His arms were too numb to hurt. Tiny craters gaped open and dribbled full of blood as if he had been sucked by leeches. He examined each wound with interest, like a hurt child. He saw his forearms were bruised, the veins skeined with poison. He began to ache with life.

She took his left hand, then right, bathed the wounds and dressed them.

"I'm going to have to give you an enema."

He heard himself say, "I've been humiliated enough."

"It's advisable after—after certain procedures."

"You need to keep me alive, that's all."

"We don't want you getting yourself into difficulties." Her accent, if anything, was American. "Much more important, I'll need to catheterise you. That may be painful. I'll promise to do my best."

"Must you?"

"It's imperative. I'd better do that first, then leave you alone for the other. There's a bucket in the corner. You can freshen up at the sink."

He put his hand to his face. The stubble was long enough to be soft, and his skin was flaking. "Where did you put my clothes?"

"We'll get someone to shave you," she said. She had the brisk no-nonsense tone of nurses and warders the wide world over. She turned down the blankets and was unfastening his pyjamas.

Her hands grew much too still. "Let's leave the enema

till later,'' she said. ''And as for the rest, I think I'd better get a doctor to see to you.''

She left the door wide open. He could have got up and run, if it weren't for the prison pyjamas.

He didn't. He knew where the corridor led. He didn't know what it came from.

He heard approaching footsteps, low voices, then a fruity professional laugh.

The doctor was brisk and fat. He had an unhygienic moustache.

The nurse stood beside him with a kidney dish and swabs while he did the necessary cleaning. Then she helped with the tube.

''It's too damned warm outside,'' the doctor said, as if this were a salaried visit. ''Too warm and ten degrees too humid.'' His mouth was nicely shaded by bristle. ''Are you hurting?''

Kay didn't answer.

''Well, you won't be able to scrape any carrots with it. Not for a day or two. What are you here for, anyway? You're not an Arab.''

5.

The office atmosphere was terrible. It was like marriage. Matson got in at two fifteen, immediately after lunch, to a level eyeful of Brenda's disapproval. He wasn't going to tell her he had gone back to bed after she had left; so she probably thought he had done something frivolous, like visiting Chislehurst.

''Marcus Pomeroy's been on your phone all day,'' she said.

''I've just this moment had lunch with him.''

''There's no gun in your desk like you told him there was, either.''

''Not for the cleaners to find.'' He opened the top right hand drawer and eased the Browning from its clip up against the underside of the wareite, then snugged it back again. ''Never had to hide any love-letters?''

''Never known anyone literate enough to write any.''

''Well, keep your mitts out of my drawers, Miss Simmonds.''

"That wasn't what you were saying last night."

It was then he noticed some of the handwriting in the in-tray. His drawers weren't the only place she'd been. "You've soddingwell opened my mail."

"I open it every morning," she said primly.

"My mail from home."

"I brought it in with me to make sure you'd get here."

Loving Brenda had all been a silly mistake, hadn't it, especially now she had her smile back? He waited until one of her fingernails took her out of the office and phoned Ginevra Kay.

She didn't sound at all impressed to hear him.

"Look," he lied. "I've got to go out this evening on a job. I wondered if you'd like to come on to dinner afterwards, sort of provide some colour? I can bring you up to date with the news while we're at it."

"A job to do with Daddy?"

"To do with the Irish, actually."

"You're from the Celtic realms yourself, aren't you? Don't you think Daddy's a big enough job already? And what sort of news are you going to give me? Nothing about Daddy, that's for sure. I've bought every newspaper today, listened to everything, and there's nothing."

"That's because we want to give them every diplomatic—"

"What about his tablets? All there is about Israel is that we're blaming one of their diplomats for that window girl—"

Good for Quinlan.

"So she's to be the ration, is she? I must say she gives *The Sun* a golden opportunity to wrinkle its smut."

Brenda came back in with the foreign newspaper tray, and he decided it was high time to be stern and important and shut Miss Kay up. The newspapers are only telling half of it, Ginevra. She was killed by an associate of the men who took your father. She was killed because someone thought she was you."

The phone gasped, then went on gasping. Perhaps she was crying. He'd like that. It would mean that something had got through to her. "We've had you watched, of course. But if you feel scared, we can have someone actually stay in the house. But our best hope now is the time factor. It always was. Two days is a considerable interval: we're not really expecting they'll try again.''

We're not; but Pomeroy has a tenner on it.

He put the phone down, and heard Brenda mimicking, '' 'If you feel scared we can have someone actually stay in the house.' Like WPC Patricia Matson for one!'' She smirked and added, ''Well, they've leaked it, Patrick.'' She pointed to the foreign newspaper tray. ''Not his name, just that they've got someone. These aren't from the news-stand. They're today's from the airport.''

''I want the stuff here on my desk, not cluttering up your little noddle.''

''And I thought I was being bright and early.''

''They're three hours ahead of us in the Eastern Med.'' Matson picked out the papers written in English and German, and pushed the Hebrew ones back to her. ''Get those translated for me, please.''

''Have to get ourself into work earlier, won't we?''

''It won't be difficult if you're all there is to sleep with.''

The cheeky bitch had anchored the newsprint to his desk with the office's copy of Collins' German Dictionary.

She was right, of course. They didn't name names, even in Gothic.

The external phone buzzer went. It was Pomeroy. ''Something I couldn't mention in front of the burnous'd Levantine: I spoke to that little tick last night.''

''Who?''

''Don't be a prune. Our Barcelona boy. The dagoes put a tail on him from the starting gate and obliged one of our friendly dons with the name of his kennel—forefinger beside the nose, of course. It's a clear argument for your police state.''

'' 'Spoke to him'?''

''By STD, just like I'm chatting to you. I wouldn't put any more money on him, Paddy. Not even each way. Particularly after your generous help with the starting price.''

The phone became silent.

Matson put it down and eyed it carefully.

''A mystery, is it?'' Brenda being perceptive again. ''Your job is all mysteries, Patrick. You should learn not to be so furtive about them.''

It was the pain of it that made him look sly. As a boy he had even looked sly with the toothache.

6.

An hour, a whole hour of himself, though the time had nearly run.

Barel sat in his underpants sipping iced coffee.

He was interrupted by an insistent ringing. His hand reached for the phone, then he realised it was the doorbell.

He padded across and opened it.

Lubrani, the centre doctor, stood there. "You look awful," he said, after due inspection.

"Just tired. What do you want?" Barel grunted and went back to his chair.

"Somewhere decent to wash my hands. Your prisoner's got my sink."

"Have some coffee and help yourself." He waved towards the bathroom.

The doctor didn't move.

"This chap of yours—what is he?"

Barel refilled his cup, seeing how slowly he could pour.

"Well, whatever his name is, your little nurse called me to him. She's not much of a nurse, either."

"It's not her major function," Barel agreed. He decided he could listen better in his shirt and trousers. He got up and the doctor took his chair.

"I gather you're not destroying his genitals for fun?"

He let his breath out and growled, "Seriously, Lubrani, you must know I've got better things to do."

The doctor didn't speak for a moment. Then he said, "He's got blood pressure and what sounds like a dicky heart."

"He's led an active life and Corporal Tamir's been monitoring him."

"We agreed she's not much of a nurse."

"How dicky?"

"You're going to need a bit more than she is if you're going to carry on roughing him up."

"Electricity flusters the heart. Surely that's what you can hear?"

"I'm not an expert, thank God. I doubt if there are

experts. I don't even know of any literature. An electric pulse—or a random shock—can throw the heart into spasm, yes. Either it stops, or else it returns pretty rapidly to normal. If it doesn't, then I'd say there's some kind of damage, an infarction.''

"What's an infarction?''

"Damage. I'll do some reading up for you when I get home. If I can find anything to read. He's sweating too. In spite of manifest dehydration. A touch of geriatric diabetes, perhaps.''

"Dehydration's a specific after electricity.''

"So they tell me. He's been on a drip, of course. And a transfusion. There may be a stronger than normal platelet rejection. Why did you give him plasma?''

"He's been bitten by a snake.''

"Bitten?''

"In a manner of speaking.''

"What snake?''

"A snake with a neurotoxic mouth. Wouldn't that make his heart murmur a bit?''

"It might. I'm not an encyclopedia.''

"You're a doctor.''

"Yes. And I'm warning you.'' He gave Barel his chair back and made for the door. "Well, you've given me some reading to catch up with. Tell you one thing: he looks in better shape than you do.''

He closed the door, which rang again.

Barel finished buttoning his shirt, picked up his beret and opened the door.

It was still Doctor Lubrani. "One thing I learned at medical school—there's no such thing as a totally neurotoxic snake. Some tissue always suffers. I'm not a histologist, but nerve cells aren't made of air, you know. Even Nurse Tamir knows that much.''

7.

There was a bar on the Plaza, facing down the Ramblas. Yitzak sat on a cane and chromium chair at an outside table and decided he was a clown in a very black comedy. He must be. He was becoming obsessed with a dead woman.

He clapped for a waiter, but nobody came.

He had tried to bury a girl in a girl, and instead found himself in bed with a man. No, not quite that. With a woman made by a surgeon.

He sat in a landscape of deaf waiters, and then he noticed the boy-girl walking towards him up the Ramblas.

For a moment he felt pleasure, several moments.

He forced the pleasure away from him. He mistrusted the coincidence. Shlomo had taught him there was no such thing as coincidence, only covert calculation or acute mischance.

Smiling, he rose to greet her.

She had not expected to see him. There was too much surprise on her face.

"What are you doing here?"

"Shopping for breakfast. Want to join me?"

God thinks in very big numbers, Shlomo had stressed. So when you find one next to one you must always expect them to add up to three.

She hesitated.

"If you could bear to walk back down to the Oriente, that is. There's no service here, and I've got an appointment there later." He searched her face quietly.

She turned to walk with him, then said, "I've always had hormonal problems, you know. What I mean is you're examining my skin as if you're looking for eight o'clock shadow. I've never grown any kind of fuzz, and certainly not whiskers."

How could he tell her he was searching her face for lies?

"I was always a girl. I even had the necessary gonads. All wrapped up in the wrong appendages."

"Last night you were talking about unnecessary gonads."

"I had those as well. I'm a better woman than a woman is, just the same. I get more sensation. I can even menstruate after a fashion. I'm an extreme case. Though why I'm telling you all this . . ."

"I hope because you trust me."

"I've had lots of fun since the Wizard of Toronto tailored me into Superwoman. I have to have something to compensate me for all the shit I've been through." She pointed to some tables under an awning. "The Oriente. This isn't your town, is it? Where are you from?"

"The Lebanon." Before she could ask anything more, he said, "Children?"

"Don't be silly. Blood on the apron doesn't mean there's lamb's meat in the oven."

Nor did all these confidences mean she hadn't been planted on him last night.

They sat down and a pale-faced waiter in a white uniform stood beside them. He had the patrician pallor of dark-skinned men who keep out of the sun.

They ordered two breakfasts.

Yitzak waited for his companion to stop admiring the waiter, then said, "Tell me your name."

"I was wondering when you'd get to that."

"Breakfast is the usual time to ask."

"Pedra."

Rock, he thought. She was like drilling rock.

He had enjoyed sex with her. Plastic sex. But he had enjoyed sex before. Sex was his continuum. He smiled at her warmly. In a few days he would have her in perspective. And the next girl. And the last girl.

A shadow pushed its way onto their table. Someone was sitting close. Too close. Nobody ought to sit near lovers in an empty bar.

Yitzak turned and saw the American sailor. He was all smiles and anxiety. He looked like bad luck.

8.

Quinlan looked a little pinker today—flushed with calm, Fossit would call it.

He fluffed a pile of print-outs and said, "We now know who it is they think they've got. Ernst Halder. Not a Bormann, not an Eichmann—no-one whose name originally appeared on the lists of the highly proscribed. And yet— well, it's a name we've all come to know down the years. Sightings in Egypt, sightings in Paraguay. A positive in Brazil. A grade one five-page colour supplement villain. Destroyer of Slavs, Communists, queers, and—of course— lots and lots of Jews. Ernst Halder. Living in Chislehurst since the war. Is that any more possible than it was yesterday?''

''No.'' An instant groundswell from Matson, the Commander from Special Branch and Dixon. Everyone except Pomeroy.

Dixon got the go-ahead.

''I'd say the stuff Matson dug out originally is good enough to knock that. The bank details, the address, the normal birth and wedding certification. We've deepened it all since then, of course. School records, parents' births, marriage and deaths; building society details, land registration. All we were faced with putting paid to was the substitution theory. Beyond the fact it *smells* wrong—for a foreigner to pretend to be English and to show no traces of foreignness, I mean—I can't think of a more unlikely place to try it. It would be easier in the States where there's a background of European immigration, though in my view it's as impossible there as here—easier to try it in Israel, for God's sake! Beyond all that, we have the pre-war marriage. Wife lasted long enough after the war to give birth to the present daughter, years since the substitution is supposed to have happened. How was the late lamented Mrs. Kay persuaded, bribed or coerced to accept a surrogate husband? We have witnesses—not many, but enough—to say not only that *he* was always the same Kay, but that *she* was always the same Mrs. Kay.''

''But compare these photographs.'' Quinlan playing Devil's Advocate.

''They're photographs of Halder then and Kay now,'' Matson said. ''In his home there are all kinds of album pictures of Kay in the forties, and he was much more stringy then, much more dark; he was living a pretty hard kind of . . .''

''That argument circles on itself,'' Quinlan commented. ''If Halder then were Kay now, one might expect . . .''

''Not if we consider the whole sequence,'' Matson interrupted, feeling the flush on his cheeks. ''I'm talking of pictures in the late forties and early fifties. Kay has grown towards looking like the way this man Halder did *then*. God knows what Halder looks like now.''

''We're convinced they're wrong. They are convinced

they're right," Quinlan observed. "We've got enough to suggest his innocence in any reasonable court of law. They'll say their courts are more than reasonable. I have to thank you all, gentlemen, and to say that this concludes our business together." He paused, perhaps seeing Matson's lips part. Perhaps hearing everyone growl with frustration. "This is a business solely for the Foreign Office now. I shall forward to them the minutes of these meetings, together with any other documentation your various departments can let me have. They'll need every scrap of evidence to present at diplomatic level, and of course if it *is* to come to a Court of Law . . ."

"For God's sake!" Matson's voice in a strangled little echo, everyone else trying not to look appalled.

"Sorry, Patrick. As I say, it's a Foreign Office matter now. Though as to what they'll do . . ."

Pomeroy came to life in the corner. "We won't try to rescue him in a gunboat—that's for sure." He waited till Quinlan had left the room, before saying to Matson: "If you don't think this sort of life's a giggle, Paddy, you'd better stop living it and go back to your pop-guns."

Matson's mind had moved on. He was thinking he had nothing to tell the girl in the salad room, and nothing to tell the snake.

9.

Kay hadn't seen him before. He was in full uniform, tunic, web-belt, the lot; but his tunic was too long and the crease in his trousers was twisted, making him look knock-kneed.

His round face smiled without showing a line. He was obviously a recruit, not just to the Army but to life itself.

"Come with me, sir."

"I need my clothes."

"The major said you're all right as you are." His voice sounded just like a talking clock.

They were robbing him of time, just as they had robbed him of identity.

"You speak excellent English."

"I have a business in London. London and Tel Aviv."

"You're a soldier."

"Everyone's a soldier here."

"I'll see you're arrested when you're next in London."

"What for, sir? I've not done any harm."

"You're keeping me prisoner here."

"Sir, you *are* a prisoner."

"What business are you in?"

"The same as in Tel Aviv. This is the door, sir."

Only Kay went in.

The girl was alone in there.

The girl and the bedframe and a smell of disinfectant. She was not dressed as a nurse any more.

"You've got to lie down for me to fasten your hands. The major says you can have a blanket when I've fastened you."

He wanted to run. First an innocent and now just the woman. They were treating him with contempt.

"There's nowhere to run," she said. "Believe me, there isn't."

He lay on the bed and watched her cuff his wrists. He could move all the limbs of his mind, but his arms were still.

"I'm sorry about this. In spite of what you've done."

"I don't know what it is I've done."

"Just to do it is enough. You don't have to know it. Why don't you make it easy for yourself?"

"You mean easy for you."

10.

Fossit sat in the Savile Club and moistened his lips with a Johnny Walker. He disliked Johnny Walkers so the Savile Club was his idea of a good place to drink them in. It was only a spit from the American Embassy.

His guest was wearing a lightweight tweed suit, so immaculate it looked like man-made fibre. He had the sort of figure, without fatness and without angle, on which suits look new for years, though he had probably picked this one up from his tailor this morning.

His accent was just American. His voice had been filled out by a number of European languages. His vowels were round and deliberate, his consonants whole. He sipped and grimaced and pushed his own Johnny Walker away as he said, "This fellow you call Kay and they say is Halder, we'll run him through the computer. That much I'll promise you."

Fossit had been hoping for something less canny. Instead he had to listen to a sermon from on top of the fence.

"He still might match someone we know they know—but I wasn't thinking of that. We've got scenario profiles, not of individual cases and actions, but of the type: how they thought; more important, how they bunked for cover. We might have a clue curled up among the software."

"We've found people who knew this man in Chislehurst during the 1930s. Does your profile suggest the existence of any Nazis who prepared their escape that early?"

"I don't know till I've asked."

"With respect, your answer defies common sense."

"Let's wait for the computer. You tell me the Englishman was out of the country in 1942?"

"The date hardly signifies. Halder was being active in Silesia in those days. We log him late into 1944. We have copies of his SS documentation from Bonn, and some additional notes from the Nazi Bureau in Vienna. There is no record of him knowing English or England."

"I wouldn't put anything past the bastard. It's a pity no-one can turn up his fingerprints."

"He would have needed to discover and research *in wartime* a man who was his exact double, and then contrive a substitution either in wartime or during the chaos at the end of the war."

"I wouldn't rule out anything."

"I just don't believe what I'm hearing. Is your drink all right?"

"It's the wrong label."

"You said Johnny Walker."

"I drink the black one. As I say, let's wait for the computer. You invited the transatlantic view. That is the transatlantic view."

"Let's slow everything down a moment. The Israelis think they've found a war criminal. We say they've got his double. Their case is perfectly reasonable unless we can authenticate the double. That is exactly what we have done. We have authenticated the double. Halder could have lived in Chislehurst, agreed. But not as Kay. Kay has his own life and it goes too far back. Don't you see the simplicity of our logic?''

''And theirs.''

''But they only allow for one supposition. I hope someone can take this argument further with your people.''

''I doubt if even the President is going to overrule that computer. Look. You and Israel are our two good friends. You can't both be right. So one of you is wrong. Israel began by behaving improperly. Now it's behaving properly. It will bring the man to trial. They assure us of that. Surely you don't object to taking it to court?''

''They're not taking 'it' to court. They're taking our man to court. And meantime they'll have held him and worked on him a very long while. Do you really suppose that court will be concerned with the identity of its prisoner? It will be intent on establishing—reasonably, openly and legally—the guilt of a Nazi called Ernst Halder, a bully we all want to see hang. Well, we don't want our man to hang. So you can feed your computer that little fact. And your President.'' Rage wasn't Fossit's custom, whatever the frustration. He decided he was suffering from Matsonitis.

''Do you know Marcus Pomeroy?''

''Yes,'' said Fossit tiredly. ''Yes, I do.''

''He's a very sound man, Leonard. Thanks for the drink.''

11.

Strategies founder on deviant tactics. Tactics trip under ridiculous error. He had been remembering that day with his platoon in Sinai when the tank had rolled backwards; and now here it was, the totally unprovided for:

''Ernst!''

Barel hissed at Dov. It was surely Dov and not himself who had let the name go in rage and fatigue or simple absentmindedness.

He did not lose control of himself. What was the purpose? Besides, there was the effect on the prisoner to be noted and dwelt upon. He had glimpsed a clenching of the jaw, a blot of tension on the cheek. The milk had been spilt, but perhaps to good effect.

"Yes," said Barel, "he called you by your own true name. It *is* Ernst, isn't it—the name your mother gave you? Ernst Halder?"

The man did not condescend to answer. Or was even too stunned?

Yet, if he were Ernst Halder, he would have been waiting for this, surely.

"Ernst—why don't you answer to Ernst?"

"It isn't my name."

"Yet you flinched when the lieutenant called you by it. I think flinch is the word. Why was that?"

"I don't remember."

"We shall certainly help you."

"Perhaps it was being addressed by a foreign name. Perhaps—"

"Yes?"

"You hissed, major. That's it. I remember now. You hissed and it alarmed me."

"Come, Ernst. A man's mouth makes many noises."

"This time you spoke like a snake. I looked for the snake behind you."

"Come along, Ernst. You pretend to be an expert on snakes. A man cannot possibly sound like a snake."

"I fail to see how you would know, Major Barel. Besides, I am no longer hearing very well. I am sick." He cast for a further explanation. "You made an exclamation of alarm. I was alarmed. I am, after all, just a little frightened."

"You have reason to be," Dov said.

"Let me assure you I am. Not always, Lieutenant Gorodish. And never by you. You are just a bully, and I've met plenty of those. But in general, from time to time, I *am* frightened." The eyes did their superior droop, once more abashed at their own profundity. "The major does induce a certain awe." He coughed and then laughed. "Especially at the range of his English."

"You are wise to be fearful of me," Barel whispered. "But not when I hiss and you pretend it reminds you of a snake."

"Snakes don't frighten you—remember?"

"One snake did. You all know that."

12.

So here they were feeding him to his name.

"Ernst!"

"Hal . . . Harry . . . Henry . . . Charles . . ."

"Ernst!"

Once more the metronomic thump of tears, the pulse-like drip as if his blood was beating on the outside of his face.

The major wasn't finished with the magneto. First the shouting, then the pain. Then the lack of sleep, lack of food, lack of water. Then the cool clean bed in the sick-bay.

Halder would be childlike and soft now, might respond to pain, having lost his last armour, his sense of human outrage. Yes, he might respond.

Perhaps not to pain, but to the idea of pain.

If not to the magneto, to the threat of the magneto.

The magneto, after all, was only an idea. Just a little coil, like a snake in a box.

"You're a rapist, aren't you? You raped our women in the camps."

No time to answer. Just the hammer in the brain.

"Strange how rapists always fail in love."

"I never . . ."

"Never is a very big word."

"I have loved. I have loved my wife. I have loved . . ."

The pain was so acute he could see it. He knew very little about such matters, yet he knew they had gone too far. He saw his ribs and his pelvis burn, then solder together, a cage full of birds: he saw his spine wriggle off. But yes, his ribs were a cage and in it the songbirds continued to beat.

Barel was trying to bring him to his mind. Barel was reading aloud from a paper.

"Your 'own little girl'—what a silly expression."

"I loved her. Her name is . . ."

"We know what her name is. Tell us about the woman you live with."

"Woman? I don't live with . . ."

"We have watched you at home, and she was there. On

Victoria Station she was there. Our informants tell us she is always there.''

''That's not a woman. That's my daughter.''

The faces mocked him, asking him to explain himself.

''I don't think of her as a woman. She's scarcely grown up.''

''You used to like them younger once upon a time. Where did you find her?''

''She's my daughter, my wife's child.''

''What wife?''

''She died.''

''Kay's wife died, did she?''

''She died in 1951.''

''How convenient for you.''

Wives and daughters were gentle. Women were gentle. They changed your tubes and your dressings.

He began to cry once again, but there was something new in his tears. There was rage. The interrogation was a pretence, his whole predicament a farce. He knew who he was, and yet, in spite of it all, he was prepared to grant his captors their point of view. They couldn't help their mistake any more than he could. It was a divine error they were making.

But when they scoffed at the existence of his wife, they muddled all sense of reality.

Then they spoke of his daughter as if she was his whore and threw him into a black fury.

He was, he supposed, an old-fashioned man. Not Gentleman: Man. Women, all women, were far too good to be included in a thing like this. Certainly his women were.

He watched them eyeing his tears and it angered him even more to see they thought they were getting somewhere.

SEVEN

1.

Fossit's face was full of excellent features—the sort girls fall in love with. Unfortunately none of them fitted his head.

Men knew what he was at once. He was a clown. And a perceptive girl like Brenda, collecting yet another version of yet another Libyan list from a room that smelled only of cleanness, not of smoke, not of soap, not of aftershave: what did she think?

Beyond the fact that he was her boss's boss?

She thought that he was very nice, but distinctly epicene.

Why not be honest about it and say pouffy?

Matson was different. Matson was a bastard. He had left the office without saying a word, even after chatting her up so heavily the night before. Even after everything.

She hated herself for having such a good excuse to call him. "I've typed the Log," she said.

"It'll be news when you don't type it. You're very efficient, Miss Simmonds." His voice sounded insolent, or was it just the telephone?

"I'm calling because Leonard says Quinlan wants some more names."

"Quinlan never wants names. Amos Reitel—there's a name."

"No-one diplomatic, he says. And no-one from El Al. The kick must land where it hurts, he says."

"He means their Trade Delegation. I've pencilled some suggestions on the jotter."

''I think Leonard would like to feel they'd been mulled. Someone who's selling, he says. Not someone who's buying. He spoke about the goose that lays the golden calf. He says he wishes you hadn't dropped that Nuseibeh creep from the Libyan list, either. Want me to pop round with my little pen and pad?''

''If it's what Leonard wants.''

In the taxi she thought, sod letting myself get caught between the two of them like this. Leonard was a wrong 'un, and Matson? Well, he wasn't like Leonard, was he? His face was all right, she supposed, except for the teeth. It was only his manners that hung out. He was someone who had been misused in youth and partially healed by manhood. She must be careful to behave more like the iodine and less like the lint.

Camden Higher Rented looked even less appealing by daylight. There was dust and plaster gritting the concrete stairs. A fuse box was open, and the wires were pulled aside and left untidy.

His door waited open for her, and a tape was playing some piece of orchestral pop.

''Bloody electricity company left a mess on the stairs.''

''That's the sort of thing that wives say.''

He sat in his factory of a kitchen, smelling of gun oil, with bits and pieces all over the table.

He smiled the smile of a man who knows secrets, then assembled and loaded the pistols he had been cleaning.

It struck her then, with fear, that he didn't need to take his eyes from her face. His fingers knew what they were doing.

''As they used to say in Sing Sing,'' he said, ''never trust an electrician.'' He stood up and went out of the kitchen, across the lounge and out of the flat.

The music wasn't loud but it bothered her.

A moment later he came back and stuck the screwdriver in an orange. The gun had disappeared.

He went outside again with a dustpan and brush. Coming back and closing the door, he said, ''I have a lot of trouble with cats.''

She pulled the screwdriver from the orange. ''Is that supposed to improve the flavour?''

''No—improve the screwdriver. Lemons are better.''

"Why are you sitting here listening to Rachmaninov?"

"Without music the world would end."

"Why him? Why not sodding Bartok for instance?"

"I know a torturer who listens to Bartok."

"We're doing Bartok at our evening group down the South London Poly."

"He's a lecturer at the South London Poly."

"Bartok?"

"No, the torturer. If you will insist on doing night work for Leonard I suppose I'd better take you somewhere to eat."

His condescension was horrid, but she couldn't keep the gratitude out of her eyes.

"I'd better go home and pack some clean knickers."

"You don't have to change your knickers to see an Irishman."

"No, but I might meet someone on the way." Her first dab of iodine.

He let her go and went into the bathroom to clean the swarf from his hands. As he washed he noticed a broken piece of red fingernail like a wizened peony on what his Old Mum used to call the Vanity Set.

The phone rang.

It was Ginevra Kay. "Sorry," she said. "I was a trifle brusque this afternoon. I think I would like to come out. Keep myself sane. I owe it to Daddy."

"I've got various bits and pieces of news," he said cautiously.

"Also, I thought it might be nice to have a man about this evening, in all these teasing circs."

"All right," he said.

"Show some form and put a decent shirt on for a change," the phone instructed him. "And wear a tie that's deft rather than dapper."

Matson might be half in love with her, but she was pushing a bit far, even for a spiritual orphan. He told her he'd pick her up at home, then took a bright red shirt from its cellophane. It was so hideous he had never dared wear it before.

He left Brenda a key and a note telling her where to find the Chinese Takeaway. Charles Henry Kay was much

more important. He could spend all night on Brenda and
the B-list.

2.

"Where were you in 1941?"

"I don't remember."

"You remembered last time. You remembered very
clearly."

"I think in England to start with, and then—"

"You see? You can remember. You can remember the
little fiction you told us before. But it's getting harder and
harder to hold on to it, isn't it? Where were you in 1942?"

"Australia."

"No, Halder: not in 1942."

"My name is Kay."

"Not in 1942 it wasn't. Where were you in 1945?"

"In England, I think. Yes, I was working at—"

"You were in Australia, Halder."

"Kay. My name's Kay."

"You were in Australia for the first time, preparing for
your new life. You impersonated a man named Elderkin
and met a man called Kay. What do you say to that?"

"I want to see someone from the consulate."

"The German Consulate? They won't like your sort of
rodent there. The rats were all leaving them in 1945,
weren't they, Reichmarshall Halder?"

"I'm not a Reichmarshall."

"Look, there's a photograph of you. Don't you recognise yourself?"

"That's not me."

"It's like you, isn't it?"

"Yes."

"Very like you."

"I suppose so."

"As like as two pencils?"

"I wasn't a Reichmarshall."

"Of course not, Halder. We know that. Now tell us
what your real rank was."

"Kay. Kay. Kay. I'm Charles Henry Kay, and I want
the British—"

"Henry Charles Kay wants the consulate."

"Charles Henry Kay. I'm not this man Halder, whoever he is. That is not my picture. Nor is that. No, nor that. I have never dressed up in those sorts of clothes. I have never worn a uniform in my life."

"You've never worn Halder's uniform? Not just once? Not for fun? At a party, say? Not at one of those little torch parties in the Third Reich?"

"No."

"Not once?"

"No."

"Not even for fun? Not even borrowed it for fun?"

"No."

"You've worn his ears, though. And his eyes. Look: you're wearing them there. Look at that. Look at that. And his mouth. His nose. Haven't you, Halder? Answer me please. Look at his ears. You've still got his ears. Ears don't lie."

"It isn't me."

"It's your ears, though."

"It isn't me. I haven't got his ears."

"Oh yes you have, Halder. There's only one thing of his you haven't got. You haven't got his prick, have you? Not any more."

The man who called himself Kay began to cry. The man they called Halder felt the wet tears run. His name didn't matter. The man began to cry.

The major moved Dov Gorodish aside. He did so very gently, with just a pat on the shoulder. Dov had had enough. Interrogators must take turn and turn about. And turn and turn. Interrogators mustn't break.

When he spoke, he only had one little thing to say. "Kay," he said. "Mr. Kay."

The man recognised his name only slowly; but he heard it and looked up.

"Just now you used the name Halder—do you remember?"

"I don't answer to that name."

"No, you don't. By and large you don't; I'll give you that. But just now you said something that seemed to me quite remarkable. You said, 'Halder, whoever he is.' " Barel gestured for the notes, to be absolutely sure. "You said, 'I am not this man Halder, whoever he is.' I do find it remarkable that you have absolutely no knowledge of this man Halder.''

''I have never heard of him.''

''Outside, even the little children have heard of him. Now why haven't you heard of him?''

''I wasn't brought up in Israel.''

''You have willed yourself to forget where you were brought up—isn't that what you mean?''

''I grew up in Kent. I went to school at Dulwich College and—''

''No, Halder. Not you. This Kay, he went to school in those places. We know all about poor Kay. But Kay died, didn't he, Halder? And then Ernst Halder took over his identity.''

The man began to cry again. It wasn't the first time, nor would it be the last.

Barel held out a tissue and waited. Suddenly he'd had enough. He motioned for someone else to take his place.

Before leaving to get some sleep he said, ''Tell us some more about the snakes. 1942 or 1945, we won't argue over the date. Just tell us the rest of it.''

The prisoner's hand opened slowly, the wet tissue clinging to its palm. He said, ''I don't want to talk about the snake. The snake means nothing. I want to talk about her daughter.''

The prisoner was quite mad.

The prisoner started to hum.

Barel hesitated on his way out. ''When you make a man break you have to be very patient with the fragments. This is the second great rule of interrogation.'' He was whispering to them all, instructing them to the last.

Kay was in some other world, dribbling like a child, hearing nothing.

''The first great rule is don't make him break unless time is against you.''

3.

Kay nibbled little cakes and hungered for the girl, little Jewish cakes the shape of hard nipples. He hadn't wanted anyone so much since he'd loved Ginevra's mother. And he'd only had her to the backbone. He wanted this one into the soul.

"Try another cake, Harry."

His wife had called him Charlie. Well, a man has two names: one of them for Heaven, or so the Aborigines said.

All this time, the old woman said nothing. They were supposed to be neighbours, but she was watching him like a cobra. Not hooding low as it watches a rat, but puffed right up as it watched a man. There was something Indian about her. India, of course, was the home of certain of the more damnably feminine religions. Meanwhile there she was, goitered throat inflated, watching his intention come closer, left eye, right eye, monocular little head right over that swollen neck, rearing up, rearing up, aspidistra-topped and unbeautiful, waiting to strike.

"Have another cake?"

"They're like honey in the desert. I'm making a pig of myself."

"Have you seen many deserts?" The old woman spoke at last, but he knew that she already hated his answer.

"My life is all desert. I hunt desert snakes."

"And have you seen the pigs in the desert, Mr. Kay?"

"I hope not, Coloma. Herpetologists don't like to encounter pigs. They're bad for snakes. It's a very rare snake that can kill a pig; its skin is too thick. Pigs eat snakes, or at least their young. A pig feeds on anything. Had there been a wild pig in Eden our lives would have been different."

"Even as far as the Diaspora, Mr. Kay?"

"Not Mr. Kay," he said to the old woman, who was younger than he was. "Harry, please. Even as far as the Holocaust, Coloma."

He looked at his plate but he saw the round pond with the midges and the courting couples. His little girl was behaving as if nothing old-fashioned had happened there. Though it struck him below hooded eyelids as he placed another little nipple cake somewhere beneath his eyes and he hoped under his nose that a modern young thing like she was would probably be surprised to encounter the quick finger at the back of a starlit pond. They were used to cushions on the floor and cups of coffee, and all kinds of civilised extras. His was the last real generation of horny

open-air lovers, the last of the genuine cave men. He'd
have to watch his step. Once might pass as romantic. Twice
as inconsiderate to her back. Unless things were different
in Central Europe. Though in fact she had come here in
swaddling clothes, and knew nothing of her boring past.
She didn't even speak Polish or that other damned tongue.
Her English was impeccable: she belonged to Ginevra's
tennis club. This last thought was followed with a terrible
wave of guilt.

In a silence full of nothing much but chewing, and Ginevra's resourceful English chat, his guilt bleared quickly.
Ginevra herself was all of . . . well, now what was she?
She was just the same age as his own little girl. And now
here was his own little girl with a dirty old man who had
given her a bunk up, prematrimonially. So what did Ginevra do? I mean: did she do it? Perish the incestuous
jealousy. You don't bring a girl up all by yourself to have
some nasty fellow just like yourself do nasty that to her.
So much was certain.

Coloma, the old woman, was still watching him, but
she had clearly made her mind up about something, something that gave her satisfaction.

Now he was getting on like a house on fire. Ginevra
relaxed as he warmed to his theme. His little girl savoured
her catch. He was old, no doubt, but stuffed full of wisdom. And he was told that they prized that sort of thing
over there, unlike England where everything is youth and
ignorance.

But still she watched him with the proudly lifted head.
Still like a cobra. Cobra strike is the most boring strike in
the world, of course, herpetologically speaking. The
deadly little rat-catcher doesn't throw itself, spray itself,
pump itself into action, merely falls forward, gravity
heavy, then chew-chew-chews with short little unsophis-
ticated teeth.

"You interest me about the desert, Coloma. There's
some great theory of a European dust bowl, made by the
Devil disguised as a goat. A lot of myths come out of it.
But not, I think, the interesting ones, like the Fenris Wolf
or the Dragon."

A little while later: "You're keeping quiet," he said.
Whichever snake got him, it wouldn't be a cobra.

Coloma drooped into more total silence. She was having trouble with her top set. But then, Treblinka victims were like that. A few months there minus'd them of so many I.U.s of each and every vitamin that their gums receded permanently. And they didn't get to chew any meat.

His own little girl had told him all about it. The bone rails of her poor Mummy's face kept on chipping back into the gums, and one day in Coloma's case the skull would crack too, rotting apart as if even God had given up on her.

4.

Something struck his cheek and the light began to open and to open and to open.

"Kay. Mr. Kay."

You don't as a rule find a door in the bush; so it came as a shock to discover a door in this great white desert they had found inside his head.

"Halder, wake up!"

Only once had he attended a synagogue, and for the meanest of reasons he hated every second of it.

For the meanest and most personal.

"She fills you with guilt, Mr. Kay?"

"Halder, we are talking to you. This old Jewish woman fills you with guilt?"

"No, not guilt."

"You mean you can't relate to Jews? They get up your nose?"

"He hates Jews."

Why couldn't they see? "I mean I'm in love with her daughter."

She married, didn't she?

The question was difficult to answer.

"She married, didn't she, Halder?"

"Yes, she married!"

"Why didn't you answer till we called you Halder?"

"I was thinking of the wreckage of it all." Very blubber mouthed. "Please may I drink? I've got to rest."

His tormentors changed round. A fresh team of shades, another shift of lamps.

"Not till you tell us about the snake, Mr. Kay."

"Halder, what about the snake?"

"I can't go on."

"We're going to give you a little injection."

"No more cobra-juice. I know about that. The anti-venom nearly killed me last time."

At some stage they'd given him clean trousers, to cover his memory. They must have done that before they gave him his bed.

So he took this jab in the arm. It hurt like fire.

"Not venom, Kay."

"Scopolamine, Halder. Your tongue will run on clock-work. So try and pay attention."

The magneto caused him no more pain now, but he was in pain enough.

"Tell us about Elderkin?"

"Isn't it a fact that his real name was Kay?"

"Tell us about the snake."

"Tell us about Elderkin."

"Tell us about the Taipan."

"What's its scale count?"

"Is it an elapid or a colubrine?"

"You're not Kay."

"Perhaps you're Ernst Halder."

"Were you ever Elderkin?"

"Halder was a snake."

"Tell us about the snake."

Kay said nothing. He wanted a drink of water. His burns had been cleanly dressed, but he needed a drink of water.

"Tell us about the snake."

"Why don't you talk in German?"

"Why don't you talk in snake?"

He spoke four or five words of North Eastern Aborigine. Then his mouth rasped dry. Only air came out. He was talking snake.

5.

Matson parked beneath a lamp and got out to stand beside his car long enough to be recognised by whoever was on watch. Then he slipped back into the driving seat and eased the handbrake off, letting it drift the few remaining yards downhill.

Ginevra let him in quickly, showing her teeth the way a dog does. It was meant to be a smile, but dogs can't smile either.

"I'm not coming out," she said. "The phone keeps ringing."

"I suggested you changed the number. Who is it?"

"Men," she said.

"Saying what?"

"They ask me my name and then they ring off."

"Our people checking up on you." It didn't sound like our people at all. "So why not come out for a change of scene?"

"Daddy might ring. If *they* can, Daddy can."

"That's not very logical, is it?"

"No," she said. "It's not very logical. It's axiomatic. When Daddy rings I shall be here, manning the stockade."

"Where's the nearest off-licence? I'll go and get some wine."

"Daddy's got lots of wine. Lots of white wine, anyway." She went into the kitchen and came back with a bottle and an opener and two unmatched glasses. For some reason they were sitting with the snake again. Matson wished it would go to sleep. It never slept.

He noticed his hands on the bottle. The nails were still dull with gun oil, in spite of the swarfega and the lanolin.

He wished he'd thought to put a gun in his pocket. Then you don't wear a gun to take a girl out to dinner, even if Pomeroy does have money on her as a target. Sitting here behind uncurtained windows was a different thing altogether.

"Are you a fully paid-up Communist?" she asked. "That shirt is a social aberration."

"How's the parrot?"

"I don't know. My neighbour has gone away on holiday. Someone seems to come in and feed it, though."

"Parrots get lonely."

"We all get lonely. It seems happy enough. I hear it talking."

"To itself? I didn't know they did."

"This one does."

Kay's wine wasn't white, it was yellow as ancient urine.

''The evening papers are saying that Daddy is being tortured.''

''The evening papers say lots of things that are simply not true. Are your doors locked?''

''Why?''

''I'll just take a breath of air—have a look round for you.''

She had a straight nose, a wide face, and something that was slightly nearer to being a smile. ''I suppose you're frightfully good at that sort of thing,'' she said. ''You know—the amateur dramatics. I see you as Bosola. No not Bosola. De Flores.''

''I don't have enough boils and warts.''

''Your manners are bumpy enough.''

He let himself into the front garden, and eased his way sideways through the rhododendra until he came to the neighbour's wall. She was the old woman he'd met at the phonebox, he remembered. There was something else he was trying to remember as well.

He padded down the side of the house until he found a window. The curtain wasn't drawn. He could see into and through a room that was the rough equivalent of Kay's big hallway.

The parrot cage was silhouetted against a distant window, and it wasn't covered. That would explain its chatting.

He peered into the darkness of the room, and felt it peer back at him.

He stood it as long as he could and then he started to go back to Ginevra.

6.

The major's head was ringing. He needed aspirin but he wanted to think. He daren't let himself fall asleep.

Will is a fragile thing—Barel knew that. Or his was. Fragile and illogical. He could not will himself to will.

And this collapse of will he sensed to be taking place in the man called Kay—was it any more than one of those glimmerings of guilt such as all men share? There could be no doubt that Kay was guilty, but guilty of what? Guilty of being Halder? All men are guilty. Guilty of being themselves, guilty to wanting or not wanting to be someone else. Perhaps—only this was the illogic of his lack of sleep—all men can be guilty of being Halder. Or not all, but any man. This man. Give him too much protein, too little water, too much electricity . . .

Aspirin. Coffee. The imbecile's conjunction. His brain still buzzed.

Also he liked Kay, if not Halder. Respected him, at least. So much electricity, so little response. Would he himself be so brave? He did not think so. If Kay was Halder, was he, Barel, saying any more than that he liked the Kay in Halder?

The phone rang. It rang for real, in the room not the head. The voice in his ear was familiar, but changed. It was from London. It was Amos Reitel, but his usual light note was sunk to a bass growl.

"Yitzak is dead."

News like that brings its own silence. Barel leant his ear against it.

"I said they've got to Yitzak."

"Who?"

"The British. Who else in Barcelona? Besides, there are indications. I'm very sorry, Shlomo. What will you do?"

"I shall need a bit of time to evaluate this. I shall have to tell the general, of course. Is it worth another smack at the girl?"

"I don't think the Ambassador would welcome a second mess for the newspapers."

"If you do set something up for her, or if you're ordered to make any kind of move from your own people, will you take care to leave my own plans in place? I may need to use my reserves on my own account. Or on Yitzak's."

"I've got resources, Shlomo, without borrowing yours. Yitzak will be revenged, when I know who to aim at. Tonight I'll probably concentrate on cracking a few heads."

"Whose?"

"Some of those gentlemen in the Aliens Department. We've been told they're up to something."

"Matson and Fossit?"

"Something like that."

"Amos, if you come up with any really hard talk, please

let me know. I shall want more than broken bones on this
one. He belonged to the Unit. He was my blood.''

7.

Matson felt the panic of his pulse. He knocked on Ginevra's door and waited a long time for her to let him in. He
didn't think there was anything around to make him nervous, not in any animal sense. It must be social unease,
or even good old-fashioned sexual guilt. Of course he
wasn't going to get anywhere with this one, or do anything
his old mum would once have disapproved of. But he had
left Brenda high and dry at home, and that was naughty.

The door came open slowly and wobbled. Her father's
wine had been good for Ginevra.

"Next door's very secure," he said. "It's just that I
remembered Dixon saying he couldn't get permission to
billet anyone there.''

"Well he wouldn't, would he? Not from a parrot. Do
you carry a gun?''

"Only as a hobby." He showed her his hands. "I'm a
part-time gunsmith." He sensed her disappointment as she
chained the door, so added, "I used to carry a Kalashni-
kov in the Eastern Mediterranean—the girls expected it.
They wouldn't give you a dance without one.''

"What were you doing in the Eastern Mediterranean?''

"What the girls expected.''

Back in the salad room, she said, "I've opened another
bottle of Daddy's plonk.''

"Gosh," he said.

"Will they really do something for Daddy? HMG, I
mean. Will you think about it for me?''

He sat with the Taipan watching him and pretended to
consider. They have the necessary power. Fossit and I
merely have the knowledge. Surely their power will enable
them to do something for her not inconsiderable parent?

His eyes took in the snake, the comfortable chairs, the
books, the *privilege*. Then his mind really worked. He
thought: what have governments *ever* done? People still
die in the streets, get themselves born under railway arches
and on scraps of waste ground.

Surely he hadn't said any of this? Yet she said, "You're

not the first man to have more knowledge than influence. Look at Leonardo. He invented but he couldn't build. He had dreams that could not be realised.''

''He had the Sistine Chapel, even so.''

''You're thinking of Michelangelo. Kiss me,'' she said. ''Please.''

''Where would that leave your father?'' Matson waited a few more minutes for the extra wine to take effect, and then he got on with what needed to be said. ''What they are going to say—what the Israeli papers are saying now— is that your father is a man called Ernst Halder. Ernst Halder was a pretty nasty thug. An SS Executioner.''

''That's impossible because . . .''

''They know all the becauses. They are going to say that this man who became your father—''

''Is. Is. Is my father. It's all too feudal.''

''They are going to suggest that Halder killed Kay, or arranged for Kay's demise; so—according to your age and how they make their case—either your real father or your surrogate father will be presented to you as an ordinary domestic murderer, on top of every other claim they make.''

Some time or other the real tears, the long tears, would need to come. They didn't. Why did he think she would show them to him? He smiled at her encouragingly. ''They may even claim he killed Kay's wife—your mother.''

''I've heard all this before,'' she said. ''Some gnomic little stereotype from the Foreign Office has already rehearsed me.''

''I'm sorry.''

''At least he wore a decent shirt, though. And he didn't tie his tie in a Windsor knot.''

''Nor do I,'' Matson almost squeaked.

''How does it get so ham-shouldered, then?''

The phone rang.

He tried to take it, but he wouldn't always be there to take it, would he? He mightn't even be here for another five minutes.

She listened to the phone and began to shudder.

He really must insist she change the number.

She turned to him, with the phone against her chest, but

he took it from her and placed it under a cushion on her chair. "Bone conduction," he explained.

"It's a journalist. He says he can take me to Daddy. Providing I tell no-one." She had told him, and now she was going to get hysterical.

"A journalist from which paper?"

"He said I could contact him at the Israeli Embassy. He said his name was Reiter."

"Reitel." Matson took the phone from under the cushion and placed it back on its cradle. "That's why I advised you to change your number." He didn't bother to tell her that her line was being listened to, and that if she'd gone hurrying out after receiving such a call, a car-load of friendly ladies and gentlemen would have taken her into protection somewhere. Such advice might make her more evasive—more evasive and even more manic. "If you go to the Israeli Embassy," he said, "or to any other embassy, or to any place that such a man might suggest, yes, they'll take you to your father all right. They'll take you to him done up in a nice plastic bag. They don't think of you as his daughter. They think of you as some piece of rubbish it would punish him to eradicate. That girl we spoke about, the sweet little Jewish cello-player with the busted leg, she was killed because they thought she was you. Now is a bad time to forget it. How about making us some coffee?"

"You bastard."

"How's your leg, anyway?" He forced her to sit down.

He crouched with her in that pondweedy little room with the Taipan, waiting for coffee to happen. It didn't. Matson was the man she was going to cry with, after all; blotting paper in a red shirt.

She leant against him. She didn't cling and he didn't cling back. He held her with one arm, watching the snake in its big cage, feeling her sob. Or he supposed sob. The snake was a distraction. He wanted to hug her, send his hands about her, feel her; but all he felt were her tears on his shirt front.

He said, "Is there anything the office can do to help? Anything at all?"

"Yes," she said. "Timmy."

"Timmy?" Oh, Timmy the Taipan, he remembered. He and the snake still watched each other.

"I don't know how to feed him."

Prickles ran up and down his spine. Toad prickles. She wanted him to feed the snake.

"Well," he said. "From what I can gather . . ."

"I mean: will you find out? A man like you must have access to all kinds of expert advice."

"Of course," he said, relieved and put down at the same time.

She began to cling a little harder, so he decided to be a man for both of them, there on her father's green settee.

She didn't seem to notice. Only the Taipan noticed.

Once, right at the end, she opened her wet eyes and looked at him with absolute loathing.

8.

All day long Barel had no will at all for the prisoner. Now, after Yitzak's death, he returned to the interrogation with renewed interest.

He didn't like what he saw. You can beat a man too hard, torture him overlong until he drifts towards a trance which has elements of ecstasy. The process is easily reversible, but if you do not reverse it then it is the beginning of death.

The prisoner must not be allowed to drift, especially not now. His was the body from which the truth must be delivered like a newborn child. Without this howl of truth where would be the meaning of Yitzak's passing?

Barel laid his hand on the magneto. It was still warm. He struggled to clutch it against his chest, to lift it like a cask until it was level with the prisoner's face. "This is still here for you, Halder. In a little while you can be reunited, but I think you are growing overfond of each other." He set the coil down again. "A bit like the pains of an old marriage, eh, Ernst?" He dusted his hands above the prisoner's face, forcing him to blink his eyes away from the rusty flakes of iron. "Well, there are more sorts of juice than one, Ernst. Corporal Tamir?"

She stirred, white-lipped against the wall.

"Take this gentleman along the corridor, will you? To

the sick room. He is, after all, feeling very very sorry for himself. Give him a nice fat drink, Corporal. Not from the tap, from the medicine cupboard. Give him some Scotch.'' Barel's little fit was over. He brought his voice down to its normal professional level. ''Give him all the Scotch he wants. And if he doesn't want Scotch, simply tip it in.''

9.

Kay knew what the Scotch was for. It was to increase the dehydration and the frenzy.

On the way it would kill a little time. When he came in from the bush he used to get drunk. He did not bother about the hangover while he was getting drunk.

He smiled as she unlocked the cupboard and uncapped the bottle, and smiled some more to think they were giving it to him on the reasonable assumption it would make him lose control of himself.

So it would. So it would. But there would be nothing of value in his indiscretions. ''Thank you for dressing me earlier,'' he said. ''Thank you for ameliorating your barbarities.''

She poured him half a tumbler of Scotch.

''Water would be kinder. What's your name?''

''You wouldn't expect us to give you our names.''

''It's Tamir, isn't it? Corporal Tamir, the major said. The other one calls you Judi.'' She was older than his own little girl had been, though he supposed as old as his little girl was now, as old as Ginevra.

He wanted to hate her, but he couldn't. Wanting to hate is a real emotion, he decided. Hate isn't, or not always. Hate is chemistry.

Or to lust after her, to feel the old animal rising, at least in his mind so he could put her down. But they'd taken care of that. A few days ago, in London, sixty-seven had seemed young, still covered in blossom. He had been planning an expedition, charming funds from people. They had turned him into an old man in a few days, into Gerontion. It had only taken a couple of pieces of electric wire and a car battery.

All this time she had been holding him the whisky, but he still hadn't taken it.

"You're beautiful," he said. "Truly beautiful." He spoke as that soldier in the film spoke to the butterfly before they shot him.

She leant over him, being careful with the Scotch and struck him on the mouth very hard. Then she drew back, appalled at her own violence.

"Don't be shocked," he said. "Don't be frightened of yourself. The birds do it all the time. You'll have seen chickens. They always peck the damaged one."

The corporal had turned away, was almost crying. He was getting a little of his own back.

He looked at her half-averted face and the door. He knew he lacked the strength and the will. He didn't have the knowledge. He was too weak for murder, too old.

There was always suicide to consider. He reached out for Barel's Scotch with interest.

10.

Matson came lumpishly up the half-flight of stairs from the porch. There was a slight smell of drains on the landing. So much for Camden Higher Rented Accommodation.

He just had his key in the Chubb when the truth hit him; several truths, several times. Men who wait on violence, such men get to smell.

They were waiting for him in the small hallway. Three of them, with wraps on their faces.

Matson did as he had been taught to do. He went straight in behind a side flip of the boot, knowing as he did so that his training would be the death of him.

He felt a leg-bone thud, perhaps break. Perhaps it was his own. There were too many of them. Two would be too many. Three was two too many again. He put up a good fight for six or seven seconds, landing a chop, setting himself for a chin-jab. But they had too many hands. Hands, Matson thought, there are too many hands. Then he was down among too many feet, seeing his own front door burst open and a naked girl, Brenda, shout and flail about with a book.

He managed to drag himself upright. Then he was hit by something heavy and short-handled, like a cobbler's last.

"I didn't mean cobbler's last . . ."

11.

"I meant cobbler's hammer."

The nurse was grave-faced and pretty as a full moon. Or perhaps his eye confused her with the overhead lamp.

His eye. He only had one open, and when it focussed again it found Brenda. She was dressed in something he hadn't seen before, and she didn't give him time to notice it.

"You bloody Irish thug," she said. "You keep talking in your sleep. It's bad enough the medical staff hearing it, but Leonard'll be here in a minute."

"He's listened to the occasional four letters, even in Surbiton."

"He hasn't heard you saying over and over again like a bloody cuckoo clock that you owe your mouldy life to my ginger pubic hair."

"Your eyebrows don't match your sticking plaster."

"One of those sods hit me."

When he woke up, he would thank her. If he remembered.

12.

Leonard had him wakened. "What the office help doing here?"

"She gently interposed her body between me and the nasty men, Leonard."

"That's not the point."

"She offered to come round to help with Expulsions from the B-list. I had to go out, so I left my key and a Chinese takeaway."

"Out? Out where."

"To ask Miss Kay a few more questions."

"You keep your brains in a funny part of your trousers, Patrick. And?"

"When I got back they were waiting for me. Three of

them. They must have been waiting some time. The place stank of fear.''

''Who were they?''

''They kept pretty quiet about that. One of them swore in English.''

''A contract spanking?''

''I suppose so.''

''It's the Israelis, then.''

''I don't see why.''

''Yitzak is dead.''

Matson still felt dazed, but he thought the explanation over carefully. ''The office had nothing to do with Yitzak. Did it?''

''I certainly hope not. But the Israelis have good Intelligence and they may think otherwise. They've had time to sniff around and find out that you were the man who spotted the connection between that girl's death and the abduction. They'll think Yitzak's death just a bit much of a coincidence. And it is one hell of a coincidence, isn't it?''

''All I do is dig my way through the world's Press, Leonard.''

''So do they.''

''We wouldn't have had time to set anything up, would we?''

''They evidently have a higher opinion of us than we have of ourselves. And they move quickly too. They're so damned prickly about revenge. Amateurs, you see. A nation of amateurs. Good amateurs, I grant you. Better than most professionals. But there are some things you can trust a professional for. Quite a lot you can trust the Russians for, as an example.''

Matson shifted his buckled face. The interview was drawing on.

''You can trust the Russians to leave you alone, or kill you, for one thing. Can't see them handing out spankings, can you? Let's see what you've got . . .'' He read Matson's card for the first time. ''Compression fracture of the left orbit, multiple contusions, three cracked ribs. A spanking, as I say.'' He brightened. ''I'll run Miss Whatsit home. I've told the nurses to be nice to you. You can have a day or two off. But if you take time off work you'll have to take time off Miss Kay as well.'' He grinned and turned away.

Matson's lips were sore, his ribs were sore, his legs were sore and his balls ached. He couldn't think of Ginevra at all. He wanted to say something to Brenda, but Leonard had asked her to stay outside.

Someone was pushing his shoulder.

He opened his eyes. It was still Leonard.

''I don't rate this little do. If they blame us for Yitzak, then this was a hurried response, set up from this end by someone close to the Embassy. Someone like Amos Reitel. If Barel gets angry with us, or any of his crowd—well, it'll take them a day or two, but I doubt if it'll be this simple.''

Matson wasn't listening. Matson was finally asleep. In his sleep he muttered, ''That's Marcus Pomeroy's opinion, too.''

''What the hell have you got to do with Pomeroy?''

''Nothing. I just teach him how to shoot.''

''He's never been known to do his own shooting, Patrick. And your card hasn't been marked for any more dirty business.''

EIGHT

1.

Neon is the colour of tiredness.

Barel looked at his watch. It was dawn outside. The fruit bats would be settling again, fidgeting beneath their perches under the leaves. As a child he used to watch them in their not-quite sleep, their mouths stained with juice, their fur spattered with an extra pelt of faeces.

The prisoner had not been sick again. He was still drunk, but this time could only heave on air. His veins wanted all they could get from the Scotch.

He smelled awful, especially with your face against his ear. Barel wished he could forget the fruit bats. If only he hadn't brought the image up at such a time.

All night long he had been zipping in and out of the interrogation, confusing prisoner and gaolers alike with his bewildering images and unfocussed proposals; now here he was hanging with his mouth close against the prisoner's ear, snuffling blood. He could write a book about Halder's ear, but that would have to wait until he had found his own two feet again. His world had been turned upside down by Yitzak's death, so all he could do was hang in close. "Ernst," he said, looking for inspiration. "Why don't we have a party? Yes, that's what we're going to do. We're going to have a party. You've drunk enough for us all, and it's good of you. But now we're all going to join in." He brightened, and added, "We're going to toast Adolf Hitler, Herman Goering, Heinrich Himmler and any other pimply little pal of yours from the Third Reich you care to mention." He leant his weight on the prisoner's stomach. "But principally our tipple will be for our favourite Nazi, none other than you, you, you." He pumped up and down. The fruit bat became exultant. "Yes, you. We're going to share your mind, Ernst."

The prisoner's reply did not reach as far as words, but they all understood him to complain of a headache.

Barel bleared around for support and then shouted, "So we're all going to take a little drink. And then we're going to listen while you tell us what it was like with Adolf and darling Herman and Heinrich and dear little wing-eared Goebbels—now what was his name? Was it Joseph? That's right."

"Tell us, Obersturmführer." They were giving him his correct rank this time. Dov filled a glass and joined the madness. "You must be proud of it all. Of course you must. You must be proud of bearing an insignia that once had its talons in the entire civilised world. I should have been proud myself."

Kay moved his head like a tortoise on its back.

"Be careful he doesn't suffocate," Judi Tamir murmured. "If he vomits he'll choke."

"It's ages since we've seen anyone choke. Here—have another drink," Dov said. He inverted the bottle in the prisoner's mouth and, yes, the prisoner choked. He choked for some time.

Judi Tamir wiped his lips, which were scalded from his stomach.

"Kill me," they whispered.

"Tell us what it was like, Ernst."

"You could let the little corporal feed me back to the snake. She could do it with her needle."

"Tell us what it was like, Ernst. Don't you wish you were there? With your death's heads and the torchlight and all that gear?"

"Yes, I wish I were there."

They all gathered closer now, Barel triumphant in his batty inspiration.

"If I were there, if I *had* been there"—the damnable ambiguity of these English tenses!—"if I had been there, you would merely be getting ready to hang me. You would be treating me decently, not doing this." One eye came fully on, like a lamp scorching everyone except Barel, who still hung by his ear as if only here could apocalypse bite. ''Besides''—it was a lamp with a red bulb, one only: the other was bruised shut by a weal that ran upwards from the mouth where Dov or Judi Tamir had hit him; the plum bruises easily, the fruit bat thought—''besides, if I had been there I should have had the opportunity to be revenged on some of your fathers.''

''Oh, but you were revenged, Ernst. Even so, the survivors are here. We are here.''

''And mothers. I'd have screwed your little corporal, for one.''

Barel protected the obscene face with his hand. ''Yes, you liked little girls, didn't you? Before the electricity took away your taste for them.'' He began to see a way forward again. ''So many little girls when little girls were easy. But now little girls are hard. You lost one of them, didn't you?''

''Yes. I lost her.''

''And now you've only the one left. We might even manage to lose her for you as well. Or find her, if you like. We might even strike a little bargain.''

''I don't know what you mean.''

''I was thinking of Ginevra—isn't that her name?''

''Ginevra is my daughter. I've told you about her. You know she's my daughter.''

Barel motioned for Judi Tamir to note the reading on the tape, before saying, ''Yes, Obersturmführer, we might be able to have ourselves a bargain. You might like to see her. Well, that could be arranged, if the circumstances were right. Tell us what we need and we can fix almost anything in that direction.''

The eye stayed unhopeful.

''A nice civilised encounter somewhere cool and clean. You in new clothes, smelling like a baby. And Ginevra, well, Ginevra just like she is. Make you feel a man again.''

The prisoner did not speak.

''Equally, you might decide to tell us nothing. In which case I could bring her right here and strap her to the next cot. I bet you'd soon talk to us then.''

''You'd tell us almost anything to keep that one's skin unbroken,'' Dov prompted.

The interrogation reached a crisis of silence.

It was the prisoner who spoiled things. "How can such people think they've right on their side?" he wondered.

Barel had to justify himself. "Halder," he said, "they killed one of my men." As he spoke he realised that no-one else in the room knew that Yitzak was dead. "One of my best men."

"One of the men on the station?"

"No-one you know, Halder. No-one you know." The rest of them would guess who it was in the context of such an operation.

The prisoner heaved himself upright, his face wincing with alcohol, unable to find words to say.

Barel watched him dribble and struggle and felt a return of compassion. After all, the confessor becomes a kind of father in the end. And when you've burned a man's cock you have the thing between you. When you've burned it and forged a new umbilicus and turned him into a marionette you've taught to dance into its dream time. Now, especially, when the puppet can't speak.

"If one of your chaps is dead, let me tell you sincerely—let me tell you how truly glad I am, Major." He seemed to wait for someone to strike him, before adding, "I do wish you could all be dead. Let me tell you why." His voice became high and babyish, like a goat bleating for its mother. "I have come to think badly of all kinds of people because of you: Jews because of you—and I have never thought badly of Jews before. Germans because of you, Israelis especially, because of you. Women because of this one. Soldiers because of what you are, doctors and nurses because of what you pretend to be—all people who once had my liking or admiration. Through you I have come to hate the world, and that is something I shall never—"

His voice ran out of syllables, because Dov had begun to cluck at him. Others clucked also, clucking like the hens in an Arab's yard.

Barel didn't demean himself. He was saved from further madness by the phone in the office. Judi Tamir went to answer it and came back to beckon him, just as he was wondering whether to let their communal wrath obliterate the red eye on the bed.

2.

"I'm sorry, Shlomo." It was the General's voice. "About Shmuel Shmuel. He was a good man. Do we have anyone else for them to vent their spite on?"

"Perhaps."

"Bring them out softly. One dark night when the wind's not blowing."

"There could still be some jobs for them to do."

"This won't look good. You told me everything was tidy."

"Hoovering up useful documentation for example, sir. We still can't tell what the legal people will want."

"We don't need paper to set that rat on fire. How is he?"

"Broken," said Major Barel. The telephone sweated. It had been a long break, and now there was Yitzak. "Broken but still uncooperative."

"So how can this be?"

"Breaking is not giving in. It's not giving up. It's running out of reality. I thought you knew that, sir. Breaking is having nothing more to fall back on. You have a reflection in the mirror and the mirror shatters. Then what you've got are the little bits of glass. These little bits of glass keep insisting they're part of something called Kay."

"And what do you think?"

"I think he's not Kay. I think he's who you say. But I think it's buried deep. When a man breaks, he may say nothing. There's been a lot of nothing. But there's also been something. What that something might be is really a job for the head-shrinkers. We've done more than we should and we've done it badly."

"Can I show him to the Press?"

"Not as he is. He needs hospitalisation. Tell them the truth. Tell them he's an old man, broken by his capture. The guilts of fifty years—we all know the script."

"Do I tell David Ben-Yosof the same truth—that you've got the Cabinet nothing?"

"I got his bloody end off."

"And add that you are growing insubordinate?"

"And add that they're wasting my men. We do it as they say. We do it when they say. We do it why they say.

Even when they say it wrong. If the prisoner is broken and exhausted, you can bet his interrogators are. We live on his emotions. You're just a voice on the telephone.''

"Calm down, Shlomo.''

"By the way, he's drunk. I hope you don't mind that little extra. We got the parcel for you. We've been holding it for days. Now you want the Cabinet to keep their hands clean till it's been emptied and rewrapped.''

"Shlomo—''

"I'll tell you what I've got, and I'm only saying this because of all that's missing from your homework.''

"There's nothing missing. You've seen the file against him. There are three hundred depositions.''

"Against Ernst Halder. Not against a man called Kay. I have the man. All you have are the pieces of paper. I congratulate you on your confidence in them. You have as much as you always had. Enough for a very convincing trial. Let me tell you what I've got. Material for the substitution theory. It isn't very much, but it's there. Something very strange happened to him in Australia, and it's all blowing loose and in tatters. Your experts will have to walk around it carefully before it falls back into his head.''

"But you're convinced they'll prove us right? You're certain he is our man?''

"Yes.''

"Intuition?''

"Something much safer than that. Simple mathematics: call it the law of coincidence. His cover is too pat. It's all so completely good that it's got to be cover. If he had a clean arm, without bloodmark, scar or graft, then I think we would say he is innocent, in spite of all you've got. But to have explainable *traumatic* erasure like that, and in all the right places—it's too good to be true.''

"You don't think it's just true enough to be true? He has some superfluous scarring as well.''

"These men *prepared* their cover. If one of them decided to live in the West, rather than in the Third World, he would select an occupation that would provide him with suitable scarring.''

"Industrial lesions, surgical lesions, perhaps. But come on, Shlomo! Could *you* have thought of snakebite?''

"No, General Zefat. But then I'm not a poet. Someone

in the SS Intelligence was, and he was paid to think up these uncrackable little solutions.''

"I thought you said you weren't an expert. You must be one. You haven't spoken a damned word I can understand, still less pass on. I may have to ask you to do it for me.''

"What does that mean, sir?''

"Up here in Jerusalem.'' The phone chuckled. The phone couldn't see his face. "Get someone to put some spit and polish on your second-best belt. The best one will keep for the funeral. I'm going to see Yitzak gets a decent send-off.''

Barel still had the phone and the prisoner. He smashed the phone first.

3.

Dawn was breaking as the taxi drew up. Matson tried to read the meter, but his head hurt, and he saw each number two, three and four times at different distances in space. What had Leonard said—''Compression fracture of the left orbit?'' His fingers were thick and unhandy too. In the end he found a five. It wouldn't be this much.

"Let's hope she's sweet and forgiving,'' his cabby said. "I've read about them being like that. I've never seen one.''

Matson blinked and watched him drive off. There was yellow everywhere: yellow cab signs, yellow street lamps, yellow puddles, yellow paving, yellow dawn, yellow dark. Someone had been kicking his liver with deliberate boots, but that was hours ago, in a fog of analgesic. All he felt now was the dirt of his bruises and, somewhere round the edges, the guilt.

He lifted his head to glance towards his flat. His bones could scarcely articulate. He should have stayed where they'd told him to stay.

He felt fear, quick between the shoulderblades, before his brain told him what frightened him.

His windows were lit up.

It only needed a blunder like last night's to let the panic back in.

Perhaps Brenda had left them burning.

One went off, then another. Only one stayed bright. Chilly fingers were touching his switches.

He was bruised; he wasn't handy any more. He turned towards the phonebox to call the police, then stopped. This was Camden. It would be vandalised. That wasn't the reason, either. There was the sullen smoulder of revenge.

He took out his key-ring and stepped into the lower hallway. The place still stank of old fart. Last night he really should have been warned.

Under the concrete stairs was the junction box. LEB thought that only they and the caretaker had the key. Matson unlocked it, and pulled the oilskin package from behind the plate.

The American Officers' Combat Colt sweated tiny droplets of oil, but it felt very good in his damaged fist.

A reliable gun for an automatic. He wouldn't bet a million pounds it would always fire when he pulled the trigger, but he was ready to stake his life on it this time. After all, he had cleaned and reloaded it just those few hours ago.

He went up the first half-flight and the second half-flight and inspected his front door. It showed no sign of being forced or . . .

It opened in his face. He saw the darkness and then the girl.

"It's Lazarus come back from the tomb," she said.

He wasn't holding the pistol very steadily and Brenda took it away from him with no effort at all.

4.

Barel had been with the politicians in Jerusalem before this thing could get off the ground. He didn't want to quarrel with Ben-Yosof and the phantoms of the Cabinet again.

If he had to unpick the bundle by himself he would unpick it. Better tear it apart on his own behalf and rend it to rags and tatters, than leave himself exposed to that lot.

He went back to the Interrogation Room like a man possessed—no, not that. As he said to himself, he went back like a civil servant.

"We've got the bundle for you. Now you want it re-wrapped."

The bundle was a piece of squeaking flesh, smaller than an ox, bigger than a goat.

The bundle by now was nothing like a man. Sooner or later you have what all prisoners become, a piece of intelligent vomit. The vomit deserves your violence; the intelligence does not deflect it.

You cannot go back now. Everything beseeches you to go on. Everything insists.

The man's penis and scrotum were much too damaged to be of further use to them.

They looked inside his mouth. They had considered his mouth at the beginning, then until now they had forgotten it.

Now they remembered it was his mouth's arrogance that obsessed them.

His mouth, of course, meant his teeth, but he had so few that were his own.

All he had were the anchors of his endlessly expensive dentures.

Three pegs at the top and four at the bottom, lifeless as the trees in Polygon Wood. The dentist had lopped them and filed them and filled them to stand security for his top and bottom set.

Barel fastened the generator back into the magneto and Dov set them flaring like old-fashioned cinema organs, some completely whole around the nerve, some filled with metallic amalgam, some plugged with ceramic, or cored with paste into the roots, each playing a different tune.

"This is worse than the dentist," Dov said. "Still, I wish we had Lubrani here with his brace and bit to make the comparison."

"Your lot drilled teeth, didn't they? The Gestapo, I mean. As a tongue-loosener." Barel didn't know why he said it—for Judi Tamir, perhaps.

Then it was the roving probe on the spine, then the callipers again.

Then something cold and indigenous searching to prise apart his sphincters before switching on, pretending to enter him entire like a miraculous serpent, but mostly playing on his backbone key by key. It must have been the nurse in Judi Tamir that did not look amused. Barel hoped it wasn't the warrior.

"Why is he chained so tightly? I'm worried about the constriction."

"Electricity makes the skeleton want to curl like a foetus," Dov said.

"No, it's just like cyanide. It throws the other way."

Barel tried to reassure, but his face was vulpine. "The chains lock him open, like a man." Changing into English. "There's no cosy womb for you now, is there, Ernst? When we take you from this bed we'll have to dig a circle for your grave."

"They'll have to hang you bent," Dov scoffed. "Bent as a European question-mark."

Once more the prisoner had lost the will to live. They abused him with banalities so he could not summon up a calm in which to die.

He heard the girl screaming again, screaming with the family voice.

What they were doing to Ginevra was impossible to bear. He had to find something to protect that shape on the other bed.

He saw the young woman scream. He saw the young woman fail to scream, strapped to a parallelogram of iron.

He watched her burn under desert sun, bleached by neon. He saw her grow old.

He watched the old woman on the other bed, the old woman who was his daughter and his love and his wife and his mother. He watched her being tortured to death.

Then he saw there was no other bed. He was watching himself. Watching and listening entirely without pain.

"Why are you doing all this?" he asked, as lucidly and manically awake as a patient undergoing brain surgery.

"To stop myself going to Jerusalem," Barel answered. He owed the world his honesty after this.

5.

Matson hadn't been tucked up before—or not since his old mum last did it.

His bed was too narrow for cracked ribs, so he waited

until Brenda had strewn herself some cushions on the carpet before saying, "How the hell did you get in?"

"You gave me the key, remember?"

"Leonard said he was driving you home."

"Very prim and proper. I packed a case and took a taxi. He gave me a couple of days off. Thinks I'm in shock. I was expecting time to give this slum a clear up before you got back."

"Do it while I'm out."

"You're staying in bed."

"This matrimonial bullying has got to stop. I shall nod into the office, very battered and heroic, just in time for lunch. After lunch, overcome with fatigue and pain, I shall toddle back home to a sprung clung flat."

" 'Sprung clung'?"

"Scrub the flat and leave my bloody Irish alone."

"Who bashed you?"

"Someone gave a couple of lads sixpence to slap me. Someone I shall slap back in my own good time."

"Leonard seemed to think the Israelis?"

"Not with their hearts in it."

"Will your heart be in it?"

"It'd cause a diplomatic incident. They were just saying 'Naughty!' "

"Why you? Why not Leonard?"

"I've got our Near East desk. They know that. Leonard tells me one of their men was killed."

"Killed where?"

"In a lot of Spanish newspapers."

"You're talking about Shmuel Yitzak, aren't you?"

He didn't answer.

"So they blame you?" She had left the floor and was in bed beside him now, a slim piece of weightless sympathy.

"They know who goes to the meetings."

"We're *that* leaky?"

"About eight, ten people at a meeting with Quinlan. Those people's assistants will know. In some cases their whole departments will know. Then there's the Jewish dimension."

"You old fascist."

"I'm from the Tribe of Dan. Jews talk like other people

talk, perhaps a bit less. Historically to be a Jew is to be a
member of a secret society, so if anything a Jew is less
talkative, less likely to betray than the rest of us. A lot of
our best agents are Jews. That being said, if a Jew talks
there's a possibility that someone he talks to will be talking in turn to an Israeli. Not betraying his country of res-
idence, not selling out. Just talking. Intelligence gatherers
don't depend on traitors; they depend on ordinary gossip.
I know who my Israeli opposite numbers are, and sometimes I know what they're thinking. I'd be foolish to expect that they don't know the same about me, probably a
bit more.''

Brenda became heavy. He nudged her awake. ''You
saved me a couple of ribs, perhaps worse.''

''It's not ginger.''

When he woke in his turn, she was pussyfooting about
the place, now naked, now dressed in his shirt.

''What's for breakfast, Patrick?''

''Bacon and eggs, and suchlike. You cook it. I can't do
everything.''

He still ached, but his humdrum maisonette became
giddy with the aroma of showerbathing woman and cooking pig. He felt better in time to enjoy both of them.

6.

*When the prisoner suffers a crisis, it is likely that the in-
terrogator will be in crisis too . . .* Barel knew the training
manual well enough: he had written most of it . . . *Therefore it follows that a crisis in the interrogator is an indi-
cation not to be ignored. Indeed, by precipitating a crisis
in himself the interrogator may well . . .*

''Can I speak to you outside, sir—away from the prisoner?''

Corporal Tamir sounded edgy, but Barel was glad
enough to follow her. He needed a change of air. He had
been quite mad for the last few hours—he recognised it
now. He had lost control of the soldier in himself. He had
hissed at his little corporal. He had shouted obscenities
into the appalling caverns of the prisoner's ear. He had
even cheeked General Zefat.

The girl walked quickly, so quickly that Barel hoped he

had managed to convey dignified agreement. He would hate to feel that a subordinate was willing him through the door by force of an assumed moral superiority.

They stood in the office, but not together. She was giving herself room to register a complaint.

"I've read up on the magneto, sir. According to the medical papers, it's at its most effective when one terminal is applied to the base of the spine, say the coccyx, and the other higher than the ninth vertebra. That way the current articulates the backbone and—"

"There are no papers—medical or otherwise."

"Yesterday you fastened a terminal to his penis. Doctor Lubrani was appalled at the damage. Today, all day long, you have been concentrating on his teeth, his tongue, his—"

"His invisibilities. That's not my term. It's Amnesty International's."

"I think we're being unnecessarily sadistic."

"It's what the Nazis did to us." It was what the Arabs did, likewise whole regiments of South American secret police. For all he knew it was what the Russians do. The fact that it was what the Nazis did, that was enough. He kept his rage within bounds—after all, it wasn't rage at the girl—and said, "I wouldn't underestimate the persuasive powers of sadism, Corporal. The Germans used psychopaths for that very reason. A sadist is too absolute to be outwitted."

"You are not a psychopath, Major Barel."

"I don't intend to be outwitted, either. You'd better go back to grinding coffee, if you can't put up with the rest of it."

The smell of scorched flesh and burning hair had not tasted well with roast coffee. Given time she would say so.

"Why did you sign on, Corporal Tamir?"

"To protect the State. The old cliché. But we're not protecting the State. We're protecting the Cabinet Office, and behind them the politicians. There's something else, sir. It's an odd kind of State that needs to be protected against the past. When he was doing what our schoolchildren are taught to accuse him of, our State didn't even exist."

''We did. Not me, not you, Corporal. Us. We've always existed.'' He knew the answer to that one.

''It's today we should be on guard against,'' she persisted. ''Today and tomorrow and tomorrow. It's the future that will be the end of us, not the men who wronged our ancestors. Surely you agree with me? You're not as old as Ben-Yosof or even Uncle Zefat. Tell me what you think.''

''I think I signed on to do as I was told.''

''I've eaten suppers with David Ben-Yosof and Yigael Zefat.''

''Indigestion is a terrible thing, Corporal Tamir.''

''You may joke—I don't. None of my generation would keep the Old Hate going if we hadn't been forcibly fed it. Just to think of Uncle Zefat is enough to make one contemptuous of his version of history. Time is an old sausage skin that he continues to stuff with stale meat.'' She shuddered, so that Barel wondered if there might be something sexual in her revulsion. ''He chews too long. And he's making us chew, sir. I understand you when you say you get no pleasure from hurting and humiliating that old man. Suppose the prisoner were a young man or a girl, what then?''

''I wouldn't torture a girl or a young man, not like this.''

''Then your answer is my question.''

''My prisoner could not be a young man or girl because he is who he is.''

''Stale meat in the sausage skin?''

''I'm tired, Judi Tamir. Tired and growing old before my time. My problem with the general is that he is a general and a good one. Not that he's your uncle. Your problems are not my problems, or not until you become a problem yourself, and I see no sign of that. With regard to the prisoner''—he yawned, and he had hoped not to yawn—''with regard to the prisoner, we've got miles and miles of tape, and there's bound to be an obliging knot in it somewhere. So if you're worried about the magneto—''

The girl's eyes looked bruised. Barel had an embarrassing instinct to kiss her. He said quickly, ''There's one thing about that little device, used as I have used it. Electricity inhibits the secretion of testosterones. Without his testosterones a man runs low on courage. You see, I have a reason for everything. Don't be such an old woman, Judi.''

''Perhaps the prisoner's an old woman too. Women don't fuel themselves with testosterones, and yet they have courage enough.'' Bruised and very close to tears; yet nothing could blur her disapproval.

Barel began to glimpse history and her uncle in a new light, so he finished very firmly indeed. ''I'd like you to give the prisoner a little time, say long enough for you to make us some coffee. Then go and tell him I've a surprise for him. It may be today. It may come tomorrow.'' He enjoyed her tiny spasm of rage as he added, ''No, Corporal Tamir. You needn't know what it is. Then he won't get to know either!''

NINE

1.

Fossit looked up and inspected Matson's face, which was largely stitches and iodine wincing behind sun-glasses. "Scarcely scratched you. That'll be Amos Reitel, as I said last night. The English end. You needn't have come in, Paddy."

"Any news of Kay?"

"Only what you got for me yesterday. The minutes of your Home Office meeting are on my desk, and I thank you."

"What are your conclusions, Leonard?"

"He's got bollocks, hasn't he?"

"I don't recognise the quotation."

"He's got bollocks, so his enemies can squeeze them."

"Shakespeare?"

"Robespierre. The media got a bit of it during the evening, just when you were having your chin biffed. Some of our agencies ran Israel's claim yesterday. Today our Press, and so far the American East Coast, has the counter that their Halder is in fact our Mr. Kay. After all, that is the real story. Some of the latter also push Israel's thing very strongly. You'd expect that. No-one, but no-one, connects Julia Keppleman with anything except a random Israeli diplomat. I mean, some of them can sniff, and some of them have enough thumbs to recognise the laws of coincidence, but the D notices are out and every ferret in Fleet Street is lying with more rocks on his chest than a Celtic bard. We've protested about her to the Israelis, but in private, so they know she's tucked up the diplomatic sleeve, and there's a bargaining counter, so to speak.''

Matson's bruised brain was already on other matters.

"Can I go to the trial?''

"Which trial?''

"The one we don't look like preventing them holding in Jerusalem.''

"Don't be an ass, Paddy. There is no way I could get you past the Israelis' vetting machinery, even if you were acceptable from our own point of view. And of course you are not.''

"Even though I laid the thing out in the first place?''

"You're speaking like a teenager, dear boy. If you don't mind my saying so. By the by, there's a little chitty on my desk says you charged rather a fistful to petty cash yesterday. Taking dancing lessons?''

"I'm salting the chars in an embassy.''

"Ten thousand buys a lot of salt. I do hope it's not going Pomeranian. They tell me the Foreign Secretary is putting the cuffs on that lad.''

Matson got ready to sulk, but Fossit wasn't having any. He said, "Please don't think I'm being patronising, but work sometimes takes on too much of a glitter. I don't mean the sexual thing, even though this one does have Whatsit's daughter in the middle of it. Once in a while a job comes up that seems to call to some buried nerve of excitement. This job has been that way to you.''

"Ta, Leonard. Ta very much.''

"There's last night's episode to consider. It's not just the careless nooky. It's the whole darned scenario. Little girls, Patrick. The neighbourhood vets tell me you know too many little girls.''

"Big girls,'' Matson growled. "Big bloody girls.'' So this was to be it.

"Even worse. Big girls talk to people with a more developed vocabulary. By and large—it's a sad fact—by and large the Department likes chaps who steer clear of double beds altogether. A clean-living wife or two with cellotape round her gob and only one trip a week to the supermarket—now that's a different matter.''

"What am I supposed to do—wank?''

"Someone might take a photograph.''

"I know you've already thought the worst, Leonard, but I was going to recommend Miss Simmonds for some sort of promotion."

"That one. She's your office girl, Patrick. Much too valuable for promotion. You should go to the Zoo more often. All the species separate and labelled. Out here there are no labels, but office girls are office girls, just the same. Even at their best they are part of genus Woman. You can't promote a woman, not at our end of the cage. Tell her a secret and she starts looking mum and furtive about it."

"I can't see what's wrong with that." Especially since Brenda had said much the same thing about him.

"Some ruffian comes along and shags her—that's what's the matter. Stick to being a ruffian, Paddy. Fancy some lunch?"

"Do you know a good book on snakes, Leonard?"

"I'm buying, by the way." Fossit stood up and said, "Genesis, Chapter One. It's quite the best on everything with a tail on it. As from now that Chislehurst thing belongs to the Foreign Office. We've both had Quinlan's nod on that one. He's looked at his atlas and so has he pronounced. Chislehurst's in Kent, for goodness sake. That includes the Virgin and her Fig, and certainly the Wreathed Serpent."

Matson followed him to the door. "The Foreign Office is Pomeroy. You don't expect him to keep Kay's daughter out of harm's way?"

"Hardly. He never does what is decent, merely what is proper. You should take some lessons from him." Outside he added, "I thought we'd try the new one, where you feed your Miss Thinggummy."

2.

"Where's the prisoner?"

"Finding nightmares in the crook of his arm. Asleep and fighting with his dream. She's good, that little corporal. She's jarred his anticipation with some new trick or other you are going to be trying on him in the morning."

Dov was smoking. Barel hated cigarettes, but had no friend who did not smoke.

"Morning is when we make it." It was only mid-afternoon, but they were in a cellar of windowless rooms, and he had tasks to perform, decisions to make in the blood. Besides, they all needed rest. In training lectures he always said: *Pace yourself, not your prisoner.*

"So Judi Tamir was useful? She doesn't do much for my peace of mind."

"She questions her orders, but she certainly carries them out." Dov ground out his cigarette, but somehow retained a lungful of smoke to blow about the room. "Even so, we've still got nothing much before 1942."

"The year of the snake?"

"Exactly."

"He must have had a harmonious childhood. How old was he then?"

"Halder was thirty. Kay a year or two older."

"Forget Kay."

"He won't."

"How can he? He's lived as Kay ever since. He's been Kay for thirty years. Kay's been half his life, the peaceable half. These interrogation techniques are meant to prise out current information. You can use crude methods of persuasion to smash a way past recent duplicity. How to force a man to dig beneath half a lifetime—that's our problem." He chuckled. "When I was a kid my grandmother used to cook uneatable puddings. She'd heap a basin with meat and vegetables, then pile suet dough on top, just like God made the world, she said. Suet pudding I called it. She called it meat pudding. I loathed suet and I never did seem to get through the crust as far as the meat. The rest of the family loved it. In Halder's case, we're not going to get through the crust either. He's made up his mind to be Kay and he's determined we won't find the gravy. As I say, we're used to dealing with agents. An agent may have a lot of willpower, but time has only baked a very thin crust on him."

"None of that sounds very kosher."

"Nor was the pudding. But it's instructive. Do you know what my Granny used to do when I complained about her crust? She used to put some more meat on top. That's what we're going to do before our man comes to trial. We can't find the meat underneath, so we'll add it on top."

"You mean that if Kay can't remember enough Halder we'll have to teach him some?"

"What wonderful assistants I have," Barel mocked. But he meant it. He even lit Dov's cigarette for him.

"What drugs do we use?"

"It won't be down to us. Or it shouldn't be. If it is to be, I wouldn't mind continuing with high protein and alcohol. It brings quick results. Especially in his case: the electricity must have left him like a dried-up water course."

"If we are going to lead him back to the desert, I suppose we must expect the odd mirage or two. Is that what you had the little corporal warn him about, Shlomo?"

"No, Lieutenant Gorodish, it wasn't. What I had in mind for tomorrow is much more sweet."

"So what about Yitzak?"

"You didn't like him, did you?"

"I didn't love him, if that's what you mean. He was a good member of the team. He did a good job. So what about him?"

"I'm working on it. Just as I would if it were any of the rest of you."

3.

Matson left the wine to Leonard. Leonard didn't hesitate. He ordered the same rubbish that Matson had given Brenda, and had it served in an ice-bucket. And let the waiter pour it for him. Then he wiped his lips and delivered himself of the death sentence:

"They're going to hang him, you know, just like Eichmann. It'll be a classic case of mistaken identity, but they'll do it. There's too much riding on it. The defence'll bring two dozen foreign witnesses to prove he is who he is, and the prosecution'll produce two hundred home-grown ones to prove he is who he ain't. They'll break his neck with the sheer mathematics of it."

"They're humane people." Matson was trying hard to forget the bumps on his face.

"That's what they like to say. But they've been modified by inhuman wrongs."

"They must have their doubts. Suppose the real Halder turns up?"

"Who's going to turn him up? When Kay's neck goes, the case'll be closed. No Israeli agency is going to search any more, and we never lost him in the first place. Besides, the real Halder is wearing a new face somewhere—either that or an old coffin." Leonard speared a fresh sardine. "This is a disgusting little restaurant, even down to the television set. Quite appropriate for what I've got to do next." He slid a buff piece of paper across the table. "Mind the gravy. It's your Annual Report." He pronounced the capital letters without enthusiasm.

"So you're really telling me it's not just our department that's washing its hands of him?"

"When you have agreed it, I'll initial your signature."

"What I never get to see is the bit you add in long hand. Is there really nothing we can do, Leonard? We *were* talking of closing down Number Two Palace Green and kicking them all back to the kibbutz."

"At least three dozen members of the prattle parlour have spoken to me, all saying they hoped we wouldn't do anything so rash."

"This is really enormously flattering, Leonard."

"They want you to be flattered, Quinlan especially."

"And shut up?"

"What I told them all was that it was up to the Foreign Office to decide. It always is when it comes to embassies. We propose: they dispose. I told them that, all separately, all clearly, over a lot of gin and a lot more tonic."

"The Zionist lobby?"

"A surprising lot of Arabs, too. You'll probably get a mention in the Honours List, Patrick. We both will. You'll begin. I'll go up one. Meanwhile, I want you to take some leave."

Matson ate fish.

"Take a couple of weeks off. I'll look after your desk."

The fish was too lumpy to swallow.

"You're very close to the middle of this thing, Paddy. There can only be pain in it for you. You know how it is. When a chap gets keen, he's no bloody good at it. This isn't the Army any more."

Fossit began to wave an arm, rather more elaborately

than he would for a waiter, and Matson turned his sore neck to see Dixon making for their table.

"Here you are, Leonard. They told me you'd been doing some dangerous knitting, Paddy."

Dixon was obviously here by arrangement. He waited while Fossit pocketed the buff sheet of paper, signed something the manager held out to him and left the restaurant, before saying, "Exit Thump's Minder. That's what we call him where I come from."

"Careful with Leonard's wine. It's two headaches a bottle. I'm sure you didn't come here to swap compliments, Mr. D."

"Absolutely. I came to chat about that Chislehurst cracker."

Matson felt uneasy to hear Ginevra spoken of like this—almost as if Dixon were going to make some profession of involvement with her.

Dixon wasn't. He took a tart mouthful of headache and said, "Is she safe?"

"Pomeroy doesn't think so."

"What do you think?"

"Someone from the Embassy—presumably Reitel—tried to talk her out last night."

"I'd better check with the monitoring unit." Dixon radiated uncertainty. "What about Leonard?"

"Hands off is his motto."

"He's Quinlan's good boy. Still, he can't be all bad. He's encouraged this meeting, for one, so he may be about to turn a blind periscope." Dixon's voice sank to a level that did him no credit at all, before confiding, "My bosses are pushing Miss Kay's safety very much to the edge of the plate. Trust the diplomats, they tell me. The Israelis wouldn't dare."

"They've already had one crack. She must be an awful problem to them, Dixon, especially if the defence call her in her daddy's trial. Obviously they won't want some little prick with an Uzi building a two-car garage in her head"—he felt himself wince to say it—"anything so gross would be counter-productive. But what about dead in her bath, or from an overdose, a shock with the electric iron—all those things that professionals specialise in? It's reasonable to assume she's stressed. It need only look half like a suicide for it to be taken that way. Or so they'll reason. You think there's a stay-behind party in place somewhere?''

"Yes, Thump. Yes and no. Yes because there's got to be. No because I can't find it.''

"Pomeroy's more intelligent observation was that Yitzak was the stay-behind.''

"Not so daft, but bloody uncomfortable. I'm a simple soul and I prefer to look for trouble a bit closer in. Talking of which, Leonard wants us to post some muscle at your bed's foot, or at least in an adjacent dustbin.''

"I had nothing to do with Yitzak.''

"That's what Leonard assures us. It's his fear, though, that Shlomo Barel has an even more suspicious mind than he has himself.''

Matson gazed at Dixon with the vacant expression of a man attempting to digest a brand-new idea, before saying, "Those Chislehurst chaps—are they yours or Marcus Pomeroy's?''

"Never. If I so much as glimpse any of his little scrubbers I have them arrested for soliciting. They're very thick on the ground at the minute.''

"You don't quite approve of his style?''

"Do you? Too much chicken and egg in his dealings.''

"I don't think I understand you.''

"I don't always follow myself. All I know is the Pomeranian egg is always on someone else's tie, Thump. Then there's his tinsy trick of knowing everything light years in advance of it happening.''

"It's just his generally snooty air of omniscience.''

"Or his aftershave. To hear him talk to Quinlan, he might have planned the bloody abduction himself.''

Dixon finished his wine and tried to look amused at it. "You're a glandular lad by all accounts, Patrick, so couldn't you spend more time down at Chislehurst? It was good to see the manly frame on parade last night.''

Matson wondered how slack his drill had seemed.

"It would help me concentrate my resources, you see. I know you've got some pussy in your own family mansion—but can't you leave her some whiskas? I'd volunteer myself, but Anne's a bit funny that way.''

"Miss Kay isn't looking for a man. She's looking for someone to feed her daddy's snake."

"Feed it, dear Paddy. Feed it, my Thump. Gorge the bloody serpent day and night. We must have someone there when the gasmen call."

This was too bleak for Matson. He signalled for the bill.

As they stood up to go, he had a moment of hope. "Suppose we get her old man out?"

"That might confuse their thuggish ambition, I agree. But who's going to do that for us, Thump? Not Marcus Pomeroy, and certainly not you or yours truly."

Outside in the street, Dixon added, "Our best bet is little Amos Reitel."

4.

Brenda's stand-in was demoralisingly good-looking. She examined Matson's busted face with much more amusement than compassion, then dumped an armful of holiday brochures on his desk. "Mr. Fossit asked me to fetch you these. He said I was to be sure to give you them with his compliments."

So Leonard was going to insist. Matson let them lie, just the same.

"See if you can raise the Israeli Embassy for me, there's a good girl. I'd like to speak to a Mr. Reitel there. He's a second secretary, so do it properly."

If he had to take some leave, he'd do as Dixon said and spend it at Chislehurst with Ginevra Kay. He would pack all of his favourite guns and make her a present of a flak-jacket. He had a beguiling image of that briefly glimpsed body wearing nothing else—but it wouldn't do.

First, there was Brenda. Then, in the unlikely event of that morsel of South London intelligence proving to be soluble in a gobful of Irish lies, there was Ginevra herself.

He mumped over a brochure.

Last night he had committed the social error of making love to a distraught and drunken girl before she had allowed herself to become properly introduced. There was only one way to go after that. It was down, and he didn't need any help from a travel-agent to get there.

He dialled home.

Brenda was still in his flat, sticky as marriage. "There's a book about snakes," she said. "Come by special messenger."

"I ordered it at lunchtime. It should be in a package."

"She keeps on phoning. Wants you to feed someone called Timmy for her."

"You've been opening my mail again."

"Keep the sodding telephone in an envelope, do you?"

"Stop being affectionate and fold me some shirts. I've been ordered overseas."

She hung up, so he dialled to find out if Dixon was back from lunch.

"Where does Amos lay his head when it's not at Palace Green?"

"He's an elusive little sod. I mean, I've got his off-campus address and such, but it'll take me a day or two to serve up his tastier secrets. Still, you're hardly fit enough for the return fight, are you, Thump?"

"I'm hoping for this evening, actually."

"Someone resourceful will have to watch your back."

"There's really no need. You mentioned a dirty spoons in Kensington Church Street, right behind their Embassy. Where Mister Yitzak waited for the call to hit Julia Keppleman. I thought I'd meet him there."

"How very clever of you. What we do know is he's knocking a pair of sisters, Paddy. You might use that."

"Seeing one, can't help bumping into the other?"

"Separate addresses. We bugged the bedrooms, the snugs, the phones and the clocks, the whole bloody lot. We even bugged the bidet in one case. Nothing. No state secrets. Just highly articulate body talk. Don't let him get suspicious about the bugs."

Matson hung up and caught the new girl's eye.

"My brother plays rugger, too," she confided. "Oh, I've got you your embassy gentleman. He's been waiting for some time."

The voice in his ear said, "I don't see why we need to meet." The tone was neither edgy nor truculent.

Matson opened his embassy album and studied Reitel's face. It had less to offer than the holiday brochures, but he found it much more intriguing, just the same. "To discuss your continuing accreditation."

"It's not within your power to afford accreditation."

"Absolutely correct, Amos. I'm merely the bloke who unaccredits you. Discredits, if you prefer. One of the U.K.'s amazing little anomalies, ain't it?" That's what came of phoning Brenda.

He didn't catch all of Reitel's answer. Leonard buzzed him, so he showed the new girl what he'd written in his diary and left the arrangements to her.

5.

"He looks a mess," Judi Tamir said.

"He'll clean up. He's still human."

"Just."

"I've seen a lot of death," Barel reflected. "I've even seen birth," he added quickly, to soften her. "They're both worse than this. Wash his face and irrigate his mouth. Don't let him drink. Then give him a shot—some caffeine will do."

There would perhaps be a round or two more, but not too many. The limits were no longer with the prisoner; they were with Barel's need for sleep. He had worked beyond frenzy, he had worked beyond inspiration, yet hours after his man was broken, here he was still probing to discover an appropriate word.

There could be no more violence and not much hurt, Barel was sure of that. There was the trick he had promised via Judi Tamir, and he had one more cruelty up his sleeve if Lubrani would cooperate, say two days more. Three if they made him go to Jerusalem.

If he had to go there, he would travel in the morning or the evening when the traffic was thickest and catch an hour's nap in the back of the car.

Barel felt as if he had been tugging on an iron bar, fevering it to and fro, levering it until it snapped. Well, it hadn't snapped. He was what had snapped.

He scrambled to his feet and stood back from the man on the bed. They had not used the magneto for hours, or was it days? He unfastened it from the generator but left it in view. He was like a schoolmaster propping up his cane in the corner. "Undress him," he said to Dov and

Corporal Tamir. "Strip him off." Having her there would diminish the prisoner even further.

For the moment he had to consider the mathematics of it all.

He had spoken in Hebrew, but as they tugged at trouser-leg and sleeve the man opened his eyes. They had torn his pyjama jacket upwards, and now he blinked at them from his little nest of rag and said, "Do you want to admire what you have done to me?" The girl did not abash him in the least.

"No." Barel returned to English. "I want you to examine what you have done to yourself. I am fed up with swaddling you like an old pudding."

The words did not work and the prisoner scoffed at them. He tried to draw Barel's attention to their lack of idiom but ran out of breath. The sneer settled in the corner of his mouth just the same and stayed there.

They searched his slack face, the eyes wandering and wincing from the bright light more than any other pain. They saw the chapped penis, the raw scrotum. The bruises were not so noticeable now, even the welts on his cheek. They had not healed, so much as lost themselves in the general wreckage. Only his Adam's apple stood out. It throbbed like the throat of a dying chicken.

The scar tissue on the left arm looked newly made. So did the wasted muscle of his right thigh. His injured limbs seemed to have been born at a different time from the rest of his body.

Barel said, "Those bites of yours don't impress me. They're much too convenient."

"You're saying I arranged them this way? Talk to someone who knows about snakes. The trauma would be unbelievable. No man would willingly bring that on himself."

"In the bush, and with the fang, certainly. I'm prepared to believe it would be horrible. But in a surgery, with anaesthesia, and tourniquets, and the doctor perhaps dripping in a little venom at the time with a syringe and some judicious decoration with the knife. Yes, that's how it was, Ernst, I'm sure of it. They settled on your cover—Halder will become Kay the eccentric snake man, they said—and then they camouflaged your various body marks with an extensive, old-fashioned vaccination rash. First it bubbles, then it scabs, and then it makes a lot of convenient new tissue. I've seen this sort of thing before, Ernst. We all have. Every time we sit among elderly ladies on the beach.''

Evidently the prisoner wore his scars with pride. ''The pain would be insupportable, even so. The pain *was* insupportable.''

''So is being hanged. Men go to great lengths to escape being hanged.''

''I almost lost the use of my limbs. Of that arm in particular.''

''That arm *is* particular, Ernst. To have a new skin on that arm must have seemed worth paying any price for, taking any risk.'' It was good to see the prisoner's eyes closing not from rage or conceit, though both were clearly there, but because he obviously had a thundering headache. ''The noose makes us reconsider our premiums. One of the European pirates—not a Nazi this time, I forget which one—one of those other pirates begged his executioners to chop off his arms and his legs rather than conduct him to the gallows. You were in a similar case, Ernst. What do you say to that?''

The prisoner's eyes remained shut. ''Paranoia. I think that's the word. Surely that's what I'm listening to?''

''Perhaps you'd like to listen to the magneto instead?''

''My life has come a long way, Major. And a long way again since meeting you. I am very grateful to you for the last few minutes. You have brought me to remember matters the mind does not willingly recall. The pain of those snake bites, for instance. It is strange how readily we come to forget pain. We remember that pain was, not what it was. It's my leg I remember most—the fire of the bite, the slow agony alone in the desert when it began to curdle. And the smell. I'd forgotten pain's smell. When it comes to the magneto, Major, you must do what you must do. Nothing you can do to me equals the pain I have just remembered.''

Barel realised that the man was speaking whole sentences again; the nightmare had put him together. There was something Teutonic in his tone, too, a lumpish eccentricity of structure. Then he thought: he is speaking English the way I do. That is all. He has caught me, the way we all catch foreigners' bad habits when we try to speak to them in our own language. When it came to English, though, Barel was not that much of a foreigner. A trifle rough, perhaps, but certainly more than ready. Not quite ready enough to tell how rough Kay had sounded before his capture, alas.

"You are going to be given a general anaesthetic, Ernst."

"Good—then I shall sleep."

"You mustn't be impatient. We're bringing you a visitor as well, but all in a day or two. These things take time."

"You've given me lots of time, Major."

6.

Leonard's gaze was on the severe side, for Leonard. No boss quite likes you accepting the leave he's just forced upon you.

"Rhodes is a good idea," he conceded at length. "It's got concrete all round the edges, but the middle's still intact. Also it's sunnier than Chislehurst. I'm afraid this Office will have to forbid you any excursions on the old paddle steamer while you're there."

"Of course."

"Should you step athwart a wind-surfer, Patrick, do make absolutely sure that the fisherman's breeze does not waft you any closer to the rising sun than, shall we say, thirty degrees East."

Matson's face was too buckled to blush.

"All my other embargoes are at Force Ten, by the by."

Obedience is all right in the office. Holidays are for heroes.

"You'll need to pop into that delicatessen across the road—"

"Anything to oblige, Leonard."

"And take a couple of good close-ups of the sliced pastrami. For your passport, you ass."

There must be an answer, if he could dig it out.

"Time for a rest, as I say. Pity I can't let you take Miss Whatsit along to help with the lint and embrocation, but she knows how your filing system works. I expect you'll find something just as good on the beach.''

"Miss Simmonds. I'll build sandcastles.''

"Not with a bucket, Patrick. Too much like Martellos. Stick to windsurfing.''

7.

The oak and glass door was becoming a compulsion. Matson rang its chimes and wondered if he would ever see it again. Roger's hamper was heavy. Its occupants scuffled, sniffed and then stilled, listening with him.

The door opened at last, and she hesitated inside it just long enough to indicate her total lack of enthusiasm before leading him quickly to Daddy's green den.

"I'm here to feed the snake," he said. "Or didn't you remember?''

This time the coffee was ready, and the little table set between them. She had kept him at the door while she erected the obstacles.

"I've got to go away," he said.

"Something to do with Daddy?''

"That's right. I've got to go away from Daddy.''

Was this love's face or merely its mask? As so often at moments of hurt he did not believe it was either.

He watched her pour coffee and felt churlish for status. "This cup's not clean," he said.

The girl blushed in the salad room, her little ears glowing like lobsters, then said, "Your face has been coaxed to resemble a tray of *hors d'oeuvres variés*. I suppose it goes with the job?''

"Yes.''

"I shan't forgive you the other night.''

"God's already punished me.''

"I've got some things to talk about.''

"So's the Office. I'd like to agree an agenda.''

"Mine are rather pressing. Timmy is going to have some babies.''

The snake-talk was starting early today. "I thought Timmy was a boy.''

"So, I think, did Daddy. It's very hard to know about

snakes. Even snakes have difficulty. Now Timmy's gone and solved it by laying some eggs.''

''Doesn't he—doesn't Timmy need to be fertilised to lay eggs?''

''I don't know. Perhaps it's like chickens. I mean: chickens lay eggs whatever their current state of concubinage. If he needs fertilising, I'm sure Daddy would have fertilised him.''

''That would involve . . .''

''I'd like to stay away from any kind of swarf. You said you were going to feed him.''

''When I've finished my coffee.''

''From your dirty cup.''

''If you insist. Look, before we drift apart. Two things. My departmental head is absolutely insistent you only go out with the full cognisance of the security services.''

''So is Mr. Nixon.''

''Mr. Dixon.'' Nice Oxbridge Ralph Dixon. ''So is everyone from the Home Secretary downwards.''

''How far downwards are you, Mr. Matson?''

''There is also, as I said at the beginning, the business of the Press.''

''I've already engaged someone to take care of that. That only leaves you with Timmy to bother about, Mr. Matson.''

''I should have thought Patrick, after what you're never going to forgive me for.''

''Timmy's just behind you.''

Timmy looked different today. Timmy looked slimmer but longer. Timmy had laid a lot of eggs, about three dozen as far as Matson could see. Some were nearly buried, some half-concealed by Timmy's coils.

''Not a very good mother, is it?''

''Your coming in has distracted her.''

''I have that effect on women. Now the first question is: is Timmy *Oxyuranus scutellatus*, in which case he—she—eats lizards, birds, bandicoots, mice and rats. Or is she—he—*Oxyuranus microlepidotus?* In which case the favoured diet is the Plague rat.''

''What have you brought?''

''Rat. Lots of rat. Not Plague rat. Laboratory rat. Rat seems to be the universal item on the herpetological menu.'' He hesitated, then said firmly, ''I can see the safety partition. I will not let Timmy out. I promise you that it is no part of my intention that Timmy should get out.''

''What's this leading up to?''

''A clean cup. Look, why don't you go and put the percolator on again? I have to throw Timmy these squeaking morsels live.'' He touched his foot against the basket he had brought with him.

''I find this sort of demonstration interesting, thanks very much.''

Matson looked at her closely. A quick intelligent girl with a quick intelligent eye, just like Timmy's. He pulled on his glove and took out a rat. He dropped it through the feeding hatch. Timmy thrashed angrily. ''A mother guarding her young,'' he observed. He added two more rats and closed the feeding hatch.

The rats watched Timmy through the safety partition.

Timmy went back to being bored on her eggs.

Matson bolted the feeding hatch and lifted the safety partition.

Timmy moved twice, very quickly.

Two of the rats lay twitching, dribbling, stilled at once.

Timmy took one in her mouth. It jammed for a moment like a duster in a vacuum nozzle. Then it disappeared. Timmy nudged the second rat around and about, getting it just right, but didn't swallow it.

''It's not just herself she has to feed,'' Matson said, quoting his old mum.

The third rat and Timmy watched one another like old friends, and went on watching and watching.

Ginevra kissed Matson on the nose.

''That,'' said Matson, ''should last the lady for a week or two.''

''What Daddy needs is someone to go and visit him.''

''With a file in a birthday cake? I've been instructed to leave that to the Foreign Office.''

8.

Matson was early. He studied the little restaurant as avidly as a small boy on his first visit to the Chamber of Horrors.

Intriguing that a place with at most eight tables should have three public telephones, as well as two on the bar. Dixon said there was a direct line to 2, Palace Green. Probably most embassies had a similar annexe, but it would be easy enough for the Israelis to arrange. Uncle Sam was their big brother. They were friendlies. Come to that, the two addresses were so near that it could all have been done by burying a clandestine wire in the back yard.

Yitzak had taken a call on one of those phones, and then gone out to kill Julia Keppleman.

Matson was only just beginning to grasp why Yitzak had waited here in the first place. He was never meant to back up Barel and Amos on Victoria Station. He was the command link. He was here to provide cover at Heathrow, or at some intermediate underground station. Here to alert the El Al desk by phone to the fact that one of their registered passengers had been taken ill and would need special clearance and facilities. Probably very few, if any, El Al people need be in the know. Ironic that the most security-conscious airline in the world would, in this at least, be the most susceptible. After all, it served a country to which, above all, a sick man would be encouraged home to die in the bosom of his family.

The man who squeezed himself in opposite was wearing the sort of cologne that smells of fabric rather than fabric that stinks of cologne, but there was nothing reticent about his enjoyment of Matson's bruised face.

Matson examined his suit and tie, then said, "I'm told they do some very good spaghetti and meatballs. Home grown and probably kosher."

"I'm a Christian."

"We're both outsiders, Amos."

Reitel waited for the waiter to do things with a bottle and cork before saying, "We know we've got the right man, so there's not really too much to talk about, is there?"

"There's you, for starters. You're quite a big subject. As I said on the phone, the thing about being a diplomat is that you can claim immunity from everything except being kicked out. And no-one likes being kicked out. There's always a man somewhere behind the stuffed shirt, Amos.'' Matson peered at Reitel's delicate polka-dot as if glimpsing something profound. ''You can hardly take both girlies home to Mummy, can you?''

''I've already seen Dixon. I've had several chats with Marcus Pomeroy, and discussed everything appropriate for you to know. I don't see what further leverage you can apply.''

''One murder. One abduction. One grievous bodily harm.''

''That's right. And some of us crucified Jesus too. Try to remember—''

''I'm trying to remember you're not a football. What interests me is your role in the death of a girl called Julia Keppleman.''

Reitel became much more watchful. ''I was at the Embassy.''

''I pluck a death from the air and you have your alibi ready, just like that.''

''One of the papers came close to implying an Israeli was somehow involved, so naturally the Ambassador—''

''Naturally,'' Matson agreed. ''Naturally your Ambassador asked you where you were, and you were prompt to tell him you were smashing into Ginevra Kay with some mobile luggage on Victoria Station, and not Julia Keppleman up in Euston with your prick.''

''So you do admit to making the connection between the two women and—'' He didn't finish but said again, ''Between the two women?''

''Admit? I've made the connection all right, and my knowledge is shared by everyone from Quinlan down.''

''Including the PLO,'' Reitel hissed.

''There you leave me far, far behind.'' But not enough for comfort. ''What we have not allowed into the Press is the fact that the Keppleman girl fell into the street from one of your accommodation addresses. Come on, Amos: we know your role in England. And what we have not even allowed to reach your Ambassador, *yet,* is the degree to which the girl was abused by, as it happens, someone who escaped in a hired car and left your pistol under the seats.''

"*My* pistol?"

"A pistol with your thumb prints on it."

"Give me some credit, Matson." He grinned and added, "You can't print embassy personnel anyway."

Matson's lies were careful ones. "You took a little drink with Ralph Dixon, didn't you? A drink from a nice sticky glass. Just like you're sniffing another one with me. We're not all amateurs, Amos." He allowed time for Reitel to think things over, then said, "If I arrange to show you poor Miss Keppleman on her slab, you might just have time to reflect—"

"On what I'm being framed for?"

"On what your future would be saddled with. Diplomats accused of abusing young women and leaving them boot-soiled are not going to have much more of a career, are they?" He poured himself some more wine and waited.

"Just what do you have in mind?"

"A civilised *quid pro quo*. The lady my department knows as Ginevra Kay—"

"What of her?"

"We want her left alone. We want her left alive. We know that Miss Keppleman was killed in mistake for Miss Kay. We know that you have already tried to talk Miss Kay out. Oh, come on, Amos: I was there when you did it."

Reitel pushed his drink away, hesitated, then contemptuously slid his glass even further in Matson's direction as if offering him some more fingerprints. "Do you seriously suppose I can effect anything, *now?* Or even think I would? Anything that comes of this—*if* it comes—will come from Jerusalem."

"What about Jaffo? The old Wrath of God—isn't that what the unit calls itself?"

"Better men than you have tried to avert the Wrath of God, Matson. They're all dead now."

"Will you speak to Barel for us? All you have to do is lift your little telephone. I'll give you a photograph to send to the major, a morgue photograph."

"Of Julia Keppleman? He won't believe it."

"You've had our eye. We've had your tooth. Tell him he doesn't need our other eye. Our countries are supposed to be friends."

"He's not your sort of man, Matson. He's an Israeli."

As he stood up, he said, "You did know Yitzak is dead, didn't you?"

"I do now. You've just told me."

9.

As it happened, someone was already calling Israel. Someone with an instinct for contact and a well-developed addiction to the telephone.

Even if England were at war he would still try to manipulate his enemy's thinking until all the lines were down.

He had access to most of the numbers that were of interest to him, but even he could do no better than the Defence Ministry's sub-exchange at Tel Aviv.

"I need to contact one of your serving officers. In the Army. I'm speaking from the British Foreign Office in London." He wasn't. He was much too prudent for that. "It is a personal matter, but one of some resonance. I am quite sure he'll want to talk to me."

There was a ten-second pause, long enough for the rest of the conversation to be routed through a tape-deck.

"What rank is he?"

"He was a major in your last list of seniority."

"I'm afraid—"

"Not an ordinary major. Not any major," the caller said loftily. "His name's Barel, Major Shlomo Barel. You will have to seek him out with some discretion, I think."

"You are?"

"I don't think any of you will know me by name."

"We shall certainly need to know you, before any attempt is made at a connection."

"Try the name Matson. It's an ident, of course. But I think the major will respond to Matson." He sensed the duty officer was already projecting his attention elsewhere, so he sipped at his coffee and brandy and said to the faraway tape deck, "If he doesn't like Matson I've got several more."

He knew they would not keep him waiting long.

10.

Barel sat in his quarters and looked at the file in front of him. It bulged with photocopies of news-clippings, prefaced by a digest prefixed in turn by a summary. There was also a substantial-looking sealed envelope he would explore when he had more stomach for it. The general had been quick.

The general was always quick. Barel had beneath his thumb every aspect of Julia Keppleman's death as it unfolded itself in the English Press; and he was not disposed to doubt its essential truth. Yitzak had killed the wrong girl, and before killing her he had beaten and raped her. He did not give a rap to read that she was a Jew. Israel had plenty of enemies who were Jews, both within and without the State. This was overborne by Shmuel's own death. He had trained Shmuel Shmuel. Yitzak and he were friends.

His men and women were special people. They had special needs. They were, in the best sense of the word, amateurs. None more so than Yitzak. Killing was not an abstraction to him. It was always personal, sometimes hot.

He wondered what the unit should do. The just man does not always seek the second eye or the last tooth.

Barel opened a vent onto his inner courtyard, and the heat cancelled everything, even the ducted air; but at least the dryness was real.

He spat into the heat of the vent, then turned to the telephone and asked for the general's aide. He didn't need the general. Just a voice would do.

It took an age to clear the codes.

"Barel," he said. "About my agent. I need to know everything."

11.

Yitzak had turned to notice an American sailor. A chubby, middle-aged matelot in his late thirties, perhaps older. A podgy Germanic body and a syrupy waffle of a face. He was shielding something with his arm, something as big as a gun-dog, which perched beside him on an empty chair. Something with a squeaker in its belly.

It was a huge teddy bear, mauve and synthetic. It looked like a poodle with a blue rinse.

"You two look happy."

Perhaps Pedra was happy. "Yes," Yitzak said.

"I bet you've got lots of kids."

Her tongue ghosted along her lips. She said nothing.

"I'd like you to have this for them. Take it home with you. I've got buddies in town, Spanish buddies." He padded the teddy bear. "I bought this for their little one, but they seem to be out."

"What's up with waiting until they seem to be in?"

"I'm not walking round all day with that thing on my arm. The town's full of Redcaps. One of us'll get arrested, and it won't be the bear."

Pedra took it and fondled it, making it squeak. Yitzak could just picture it in that odd little flat of hers. "What shall we tell them?" He managed to smile. "A present from the Sixth Fleet?"

"Hell no. Just from me. I'm an armaments artificer on the carrier. You want to let me take you both out there some time. You're Jewish, aren't you? There's lots of them in the Fleet, the nice guys especially."

Pedra moved the bear in and out of the silence.

"You got some pictures of the kids?"

"Not with me."

Pedra said she had no photographs either. "Have you?" she asked sweetly.

"No. No pictures. No kids. No wife." He paddled his spoon in his drinking chocolate.

Yitzak couldn't stand him any more. He gazed at the girls loitering on the ornamental paving, at their ankles, then their legs, then their bums.

A white uniform blocked his view. A new waiter stood facing him, waiting for an order. The man seemed uncertain of himself, unhappy at being stared at, perhaps because of the deep scar on his chin.

Yitzak felt Pedra's hand on his sleeve. "Have a drink," he said to the American.

The sailor brightened and pushed away his chocolate. "I'll take a beer."

Yitzak ordered a cognac for himself and raised his eyebrows to Pedra.

''I'd better finish my shopping,'' she smiled. She slid a key across the table and said in Spanish, ''Don't be late for supper.''

He took it. ''See you later,'' he lied.

The sailor watched her leave, then said, ''Your English is so good—and hers—I quite overlooked you're both Spaniards.''

''Catalans,'' he said. Then he noticed she'd forgotten the bear. He'd been left the key and a mauve teddy bear. The American would expect him to take it with him. What did she think they were—married?

The new waiter hurried back. He was dark-skinned and gypsyish: his brown face was very arresting above the white uniform with its gilded epaulettes and buttons. And like a gypsy he was intent on being somewhere else.

Yitzak took the lonely glass of cognac from the platter, and was just about to hiss to the already turning back that he hadn't seen it poured when he realised that the American had not been brought his beer.

Too late. The waiter was hurrying off, clattering his tray on a chair.

Yitzak left his drink on the table and clapped his hand.

The original waiter was there in an instant. He looked puzzled then appalled at the torrent of words that fell from Yitzak. He reappeared very quickly with the sailor's beer, though, and declined to add it to the bill.

''You sure laid into that fellow,'' the sailor said, and raised his glass.

Yitzak smiled tiredly. He still had thirty-five minutes in which to dump the man before the English put in their appearance.

Then he saw Pedra returning towards them. She had remembered the wretched teddy bear.

He relaxed, and lifted his glass to the American. He sipped at the cognac, then tried to cough it back. He was heaving on scalding almonds. He saw them on the sailor's sleeve, heard the tables scatter.

Then his spine flung him up and arched over. He turned and kicked backwards to fall on a hard blue lump of teddy bear whose belly fluff squeaked beneath his spasms, and squeaked and squeaked and squeaked.

12.

"Our agents had to make do with what the police passed on. There's no-one good in Barcelona. We're not strength A, even in Madrid—you know that."

"We've got people there."

"Merely consular. And Amos fixed Yitzak a postman."

"If the police told us, they could just as easily have told someone else. How do we know the British were involved?"

"He was talked out by telephone to keep an appointment downtown. The talk was in English. There's a probability, again according to the Spanish police, that the call came from London."

Barel whistled softly.

"After being talked out, he arrived at an open bar with the girl."

"That's true enough to form."

"The girl left and he bought a drink for an American sailor who had spoken to him and the girl earlier. It was then that he was killed."

"You're sure the Americans aren't implicated?"

"Forget it, Shlomo. The sailor was a fitter from the fleet. No kind of cover for an American agent. The girl we don't know about, and probably never will. What we do know, as you can see, is he killed the wrong woman in England. Very efficient job."

"Very efficient job of detection, too. Too efficient."

"The English Press is full of it. So full that our own embassy has seen fit to protest to the general on its own account."

"Amos?"

"The Ambassador. He's an anglophile, that one. Notice the English keep Yitzak's name from the papers, yet they most certainly got on to the embassy, or old Rumbleguts wouldn't have done his whinge."

"The English don't usually react so strongly."

"Not by themselves. They're too gutless. But the actual job was pretty certainly done by the Palestinians."

"Who?"

"We'll find out. Someone with a deformed chin, but we don't know who was at the back of him. There was a substitute waiter. Witnesses say he was dark-skinned, not negroid. 'Gypsyish' was the word. They can only have found out that Yitzak was there because somebody told them. Somebody in England. Nothing else makes sense. Somebody who does not normally involve himself in such matters but who would pass on information, and perhaps money, in order to close a file. Somebody prissy. Somebody spiteful. Someone above all who knew about that girl's death several days ago, and knew all the dirt that we only know now.''

''I'll think about it.'' Barel rang off. He knew it had gone beyond thinking, but he would think about it.

He picked up the envelope, and tossed it onto his bed. Then he left his quarters and walked back to the office.

Judi Tamir was asleep by the telephone.

He woke her and asked, ''How's the prisoner?''

''Worried, I think. He can't sleep.''

''Well, well, Corporal Tamir. An interrogation centre is hardly a hospital.''

''No, sir.''

''Dov tells me I must be pleased with you. I am pleased with you. You're doing too much. Go off duty now. Go home. The place is swarming with conscripts.''

The phone rang.

She answered it and mouthed something at him.

He took it from her.

''I have a caller from London who is convinced you will talk to him. His codename is Matson.''

''Matson is not a codename.'' His chest thumped with rage. ''Put him on.''

''All right, caller. Go ahead now. Your call is on record.''

''There's no need to play it back to me.'' The voice was insolent. ''Major Barel?''

''Make your point.''

''You realise that HMG is not about to quarrel with the inevitable findings of your House of Justice.''

''I'm waiting.''

''Damage limitation, Shlomo. We'd like things to stop there. The diplomats assure us they will, but people like yourself have a swash-buckling autonomy, wouldn't you say?''

"One of my men is dead."

"Let us just agree that you have acquired a certain article of ours, and that your vanman behaved abominably during its collection. He has been punished for it, so now we are square."

"One of my best men."

"You will hardly seek to make Miss Kay suffer for that."

"Not for that. I have a better solution in mind, believe me."

The caller tutted impatiently, then began to chuckle. He laughed so immoderately that Barel wondered if he had been drinking. "What are you going to do?" he spluttered. "Dive-bomb St. Paul's?"

Barel gave Judi Tamir back the phone and said, "I thought we were re-routing the codes?"

"Somebody wants their thumb on us, sir."

He looked at her thoughtfully. " 'Vanman,' " he quoted. "I'll take a drink, Corporal Tamir. The medicine cupboard will do."

In the scrolls they had written *The sun was not planted yesterday*. His revenge would take time.

He dialled Antwerp. It took several minutes to dictate his targets' names and addresses.

She returned with the huge jar of whisky they had used on the prisoner.

He kept her waiting while his instructions were read back to him.

The decision would take nights and days to mature, but because of it Yitzak would again walk whole in his mind.

He smiled at the girl and took the jar from her hands. As he tugged at its stopper, he had an absurd craving to ask her to stay with him. But he resisted it as inappropriate.

He stood alone in the dark with Shmuel Shmuel and toasted him quietly in torture-room Scotch.

The sun was not planted yesterday, nor will its leaf lend shade.

13.

Brenda was in a mood. "You didn't need to take a break," she said. "Not now. Not when I can't."

"Leonard insisted I have some leave."

"Didn't you ask for some for me? What you think I'm learning Spanish for?"

"I thought it was Bartok."

"I was waiting for someone nice to invite me down the Costas."

"I think you're forgetting a thing or two. Like you're the office help."

"Can I stay in the flat?"

"You can drop in once in a while and feed the cat."

"You don't have a cat."

"Feed it just the same."

"What you getting ready for bed for?"

"Every little gunsmith needs a bit of magic in his life."

After a bit she said, unhappy beside him, "Leonard's not asked you to take little Ginny to Rhodes?"

"She wouldn't come," he said wistfully.

"Nice to know where I am."

"You're here and now."

"Funny name, Ginevra. Know what it means in Espagnol? Gin. I got that up the Spanish class. It also means screwy."

"You don't talk like that in the office."

"I'm relaxing, silly."

He relaxed all over her. "I'll miss you," he said.

She mumbled, ajar. "You're not going on a job?"

"No, I'm not going on a job."

"I'll find out from Leonard."

"Leonard mustn't even suspect your intuition."

"You're going on this job."

"Leonard says no."

"Leonard says no to lots of things, and that includes us."

Several times during the night she said, almost with approval, "You're not even an overgrown schoolboy."

When he'd gone, she went through the kitchen cupboards and made sure his polished hardwood boxes still held their guns. Then she remembered his Browning in the office drawer, but it was easier to go back to bed.

In her sleep, she saw him as she'd seen him the other night, tottering on the stair with a pistol in his hand.

He had guns everywhere. His life was all guns, just as a gambler's is full of cards or dice. Nothing about him was real, she decided. That was why loving him hurt so much.

TEN

1.

The plane smashed through a cloud as menacing as a mountainside, then banked against sunny hills. The aerodrome was the only one on the island, but even the big maps marked it with no more than a thin ring and triangle. Matson knew what that meant. It meant it was a landing-strip with a four-hole lavatory. He took Scotch from a plastic tumbler, wondered if he was truly glad not to be jumping, then felt the reverse thrust come on and heard the squeak of brakes on the tarmac. Someone behind him was sick or perhaps worse. That was the trouble with package tours.

The customs barrier was formidable, but a small Greek walked around it from the outer sunshine and encouraged them to follow him on his return journey. No-one from Immigration challenged Matson. The man was obviously the holiday company's agent, possibly the agent for all the holiday companies in the world. He spoke the kind of English that comes from deploying a hundred and fifty words in brilliant permutations, the sort of English that most people in England use; but it jarred on Matson's Irish expansiveness.

Matson took out his wallet and said, "My name is Patrick Matson and—"

The man consulted a list in a transparent binder, then examined Matson's bruised face and dark glasses with suspicion.

"We have no Matson Pee. You must be Mister Layt-Joyner, sex indeterminate."

''That's me.''

''Mister or Miss Layt-Joyner Room 40, The Grande.''

''I'll check in later. I have an appointment in Rhodos.''

Matson tucked what he hoped was the equivalent of about three pounds into the top pocket of the man's suit and said, ''Will that ensure my cases get to room 40? They are, unfortunately, labelled Matson. I shall have no special requirements for a day or two. No girls are to wake me with breakfast. I shall not eat in the hotel.'' He started towards what might just be a taxi.

''Mr. Joyner—the company has despatched a mini-bus.''

''The flight was late. I must hurry ahead for my appointment. Don't forget that you—and my luggage—will be at the actual hotel before me.''

2.

The taxi driver had a smile like a radiator grill. The smile looked dangerous, particularly in view of the taxi's soft tyres, but it could clearly be offered an inducement.

Matson induced it to drive him at speed towards Rhodos. Three hours delay at Luton had made him dangerously late.

The taxi trailed a dust-plume even on a paved road. Matson watched it change colour in the mirror and concluded it was smoke. He would be safer arriving by twenty-thousand foot freefall with a leg-pack and a Bergen. Even with a primed satchel-charge between his beating heart and his string vest.

The sun was behind the town rim when they reached the harbour. There were sardine-boats and tuna-floats everywhere, already snugging their tackle and testing their floods. Otherwise a motor vessel the size of a small river ferry was coming to life alongside a jetty of floating plank-wood. Mr. Layt-Joyner of Room 40 paid off his taxi driver and bought a pass for Haifa.

The flight had been late. The boat was late. Night was on time. Or just here it was.

The *Paulina* warped out backwards, shed its bow line and got some screws churning in time to avoid Rhodos's biggest disaster since the Colossos got legless in the big earthquake of 227 BC. Several of the sardine boats re-exposed their rear floods in warning, but *Paulina* got a grip on herself, and began to slew broadsides and then half-beam away beyond the rock mole and thump against the slack waves of the open Mediterranean. Matson decided the taxi ride had made him drunk.

He began to thread his way around the boat's planking. He only had a deck ticket, or a deck chair ticket, but he reckoned that most of the next few hours would be spent in the bar.

He once thought there was nothing quite so sordid as a London river boat, but that was before he had examined M.V. *Paulina* of the Nabluth Line as a prelude to examining himself.

When sunset behind a wild coast cannot obliterate someone's face you know you are in love. Here, at the day's drowning, neither the deepening phosphorescence of the sea nor the jostling nastiness of the boat could make him forget Ginevra's eyes, the taste of her tears, her protesting unmeant kisses. And then there was his guilt about Brenda. Well, love and his own grubby little profession had the same sour aftertaste: they were both about duplicity and betrayal. Wet booze-induced thoughts, but this was just the ship to have them on; hell's little cess-hole for lovers would smell just like the *Paulina*'s lee rail, with its witty blend of lavatory and hair-oil.

He was just beginning to analyse his real motives for being here when he recognised the hair-oil.

Or rather, it recognised him.

"Mr. Mat*son*: you really should have stayed in London, I think."

Dr. Ibrahim Nuseibeh was at his elbow, his keffiyeh no longer worn in the Palestinian fashion, his keffiyeh no longer worn at all, his green tooth only to be guessed at, but Dr. Nuseibeh nonetheless, whether by bilge or starlight. A dark youth stood next to him, his face almost invisible except for his chin, which was so deeply cleft with shadow it might have been gouged out by a pickaxe.

"I heard about your face, Mr. Mat*son*. Such a pity. Still, no-one will notice in this kind of climate. If they do, they'll only think you've been philandering." He giggled. "Boys are such quarrelsome little fellows, and they slap hard."

"So what are you doing here?"

The man sneezed, and the scent of his nostrils further saddened the air. "Shall we say I sometimes have to accompany the diplomatic bag, Mr. Mat*son*?"

"Where is it?"

"Here and there." Again he sneezed, like an estuary mist. "You know it's a blanket term—sometimes a pantechnicon, sometimes a portfolio, sometimes a pouch on a dog-collar." He glanced at the young man with the split chin. "Sometimes it's full of matters so damned delicate I have to keep it up my arse." He gazed again towards the young man as if for approval of his wit, but the young man had moved away from him and was looking at his own piece of sea.

"Is he the dog," Matson asked, "or something you keep up your arse?"

The lad with the cleft chin was not there any longer. Matson was aware of someone standing on his other side, of people leaning behind him. Their weight was imperceptible, but not he thought accidental. It forced him, ever so gently, over the water.

Nuseibeh lifted a finger beside his nose, and the pressure was withdrawn.

"Mister Mat*son*: businessmen should not presume on one another's acquaintance. Believe me, you will be far happier inside the saloon. There is a bar, you see."

"I've seen."

"Far more appropriate for one of Her Majesty's Irishmen. You never find followers of the Prophet in a bar, for instance."

3.

The saloon was almost empty, except for tobacco smoke. The only occupant had his back to the door, and his glazed white trousers and cream safari jacket would have let him pass as an oceanic tramp on any film set. It was the bald patch that attracted Matson's attention. He took his miniature Scotch and huge carafe of yellow water across to sit at the man's table.

"Crusader martellos, Paddy? There's only a single example in Jaffo, you know, and that one's pedigree's a mite apocryphal. It won't repay a visit. I'll mark it on your map for you, just the same.'' He reached for Matson's side pocket, and unfolded and examined his map, before saying, ''Good Heavens, you've got one of those Barzuns—excellent value.'' Then he rebundled it and slapped Matson in the chest with it, hard.

''I've taken some leave,'' Matson said.

''Of your senses, dear chap.'' Pomeroy sighed. ''Nuseibeh is no kind of travelling companion.''

''Snap. At least he owes *me* a favour.''

''Ten thousand quid wouldn't even keep that old bandit in a fortnight's sodomy. He might take it upon himself to suppose that were you to plunge beneath the puddle of the moon certain entries in the B-list would founder with you.''

''That's rubbish. You know as well as I do—''

''Ours is a delicate operation, Paddy. Much too finicky for every pimply sixth-form hacker to be able to pop it up on his VDU. I bet you don't even keep a little black book. Many a wicked thought—I need look no further than my own case—many a wicked thought is locked inside the thinker's skull and could certainly be drowned there. Nuseibeh'll take silence instead of secrets anyday.''

''I thought he was one of yours.''

''Nuseibeh is his own man, which is another way of saying he's everybody's.''

''The PLO's?''

''Look at his companions.''

''Who else's?''

''Where the whale spews him up, so will he find himself a passport.''

''The Mossad's?''

''I have grunted my grunt.'' He poured himself a disgusting-looking measure from Matson's carafe, then yawned. ''Who was it said diplomacy is a bit like playing table tennis with a billiard ball? It was me, Paddy. And I'm highly quotable.''

''When, exactly, did you find out that Kay had been abducted?''

''Ah, him. 'Memory fades like a star in daylight.' ''

''Before or after it happened?''

''That comes disagreeably close to being an *oeufish*

question. Let's just say its answer will be something to
tease our biographers. Have you ever thought of going into
politics, Paddy? History will give you a lot more space if
you do. Who we are, *and* what we do—which is often so
much more considerable than the work of any mere president, primate or prime minister—what *I* do, anyway—is
not even afforded a footnote."

Pomeroy stood up, but he wasn't done with his sermon.
"Do you suppose a little chip off the Old Thuggee like
yourself'll even rate an obituary in *Exchange and Mart?*"

Matson got to his feet as well. "Where the hell are you
going?"

Pomeroy consulted his watch, as if it was full of secrets.
"I'm getting off the boat," he confessed.

"We're not there yet."

"I'm always there, Paddy. You never will be."

4.

Dov's head felt heavy. He wanted to finish up and have a
rest, but he waited patiently for Shlomo's little signal before saying, "That girl we saw at your house—"

The prisoner said nothing.

"The young woman who was with you on the station."

The prisoner was more awake than any of them. He
waited until the words had begun to settle before taking
charge of the moment and saying quietly, "My daughter."

"What is she like in bed?"

This time he did not seem to hear.

"You must have had sex with her. There must have been
the occasional little piece of enjoyment. You've agreed
you like them young, Ernst. So why don't you answer us.
Do you fuck with her?"

"I must remind you again that she's my daughter. I
don't know what your domestic habits are in Israel—"

His face sogged with another blow.

"Whatever they are out here, she *is* my daughter; and
there your answer must be."

"Tell us her name, Ernst. Say this daughter's name."

"You know her name."

"Tell us again. We want to see how well your lies are
holding up. Have you forgotten, old man?"

"Ginevra."

"We know you've got a daughter in Germany, and even a grand-daughter. But Ginevra's not *your* daughter, is she? Perhaps she's this Kay's child."

"You keep on coming back to that. It's like one of those wretched loops of music. It's like riding round and round on the Inner Circle in a dream."

Barel spoke from beyond Dov's shoulder. He spoke from a long way away. "You must see how important it is for us to investigate all of the relationships in that house, Ernst. That is why we have to persist with you."

"This Mrs. Kay," Dov tried. "This woman you lived with."

The prisoner made to say her name, then seemed to think better of exposing it. "My wife," he said quietly. His nostrils twitched as if he were sniffing old clothes.

"This surrogate. She was clearly a very odd woman to allow a substitute husband in her bed. Especially a German. Especially her husband's murderer."

The prisoner managed a laugh. It was a modified laugh, but it was the laugh he had come to give them. Only the tape-recorder could remind them how much they had changed its tune in a night and a day and a night. Still, he laughed and they hated him for it.

"I took Caroline Amy Rogers to wife in St. George's Church, Beckenham, in 1938. I married her there. It's in the register. We had Ginevra in—" He shook his head. He couldn't remember. "Ginevra is our daughter."

"Why such a long time afterwards?"

"You're forgetting your homework, Ernst."

"I had to go away, you see. I had to." He made to laugh again, at some memory, but it made him cry instead, with much the same sound.

Dov jerked his head to be away from him, and hissed, "Ginevra Kay is not your daughter."

The man was dry-eyed. His body could make no tears. He stared, then whispered, "You're a damned fool."

"There's no fool like a cuckold."

Barel had spoken from his chair in the corner. He motioned Dov aside and said, "Suppose you are this Kay. Suppose you at least invented him, you and some bureau of the S.S. You can hold on to what idea of yourself you like. We will come back later to the way you and this Kay talk about each other, as if one of you is the other's glove puppet or ventriloquist's dummy. Just for the minute, don't you bother your head with being Kay, Ernst; just you concentrate on being Mrs. Kay's husband. Are you with me?''

Barel and the prisoner could not drag their eyes away from each other. It was as if one of them was in a hypnotic trance.

"There you are with Mrs. Kay's swelling belly, with her cooking, with her laundry, with her waist growing bigger and bigger and getting ready to produce this—what was its name?—this little Ginevra. And before then, there were the times between a man and a woman, you and she in bed, the passion, the sleeping, but mostly those things that even the Christian end of the Western tradition cannot quite bring itself to talk about; yet what does your Apocrypha say—'Her belly like an heap of wheat'? I could read you that poem, Ernst; if only we had the time. Corporal Tamir here could read it for you beautifully. What I am telling you is this: you were not the only one to fondle that belly, Ernst. Whether you are Kay, or Halder, or some creeping Devil, let me assure you that you are *not* this Ginevra's father." He moved his eyes quickly between the prisoner, Dov, then Judi Tamir before saying, "We compared your bloods, Ernst. She is not of your blood. We have typed you both, and she is some other man's daughter. Somebody else was there, in your bed, doing as you did, and doing as you didn't do also, because it was he who fathered your daughter, however much you may have come to be your daughter's father."

"Blood?" The question came after a very long time. "You have Ginevra's blood? Where is she?"

"If the State needs her," Barel said, "she will certainly be brought here. That much I have already promised you. I, or Dov, or someone will go to fetch her."

"Her blood, you said."

"She hurt her leg on a trolley. Or perhaps it wasn't then. Perhaps she met with a further accident."

"You said—"

"Or perhaps she had a nose bleed, or sneezed, or wept into a stranger's handkerchief. Suffice it is, we have her blood-print. Perhaps, if you can bring yourself to think of it, she has even been as wicked as her mother, as wicked and imprudent. Perhaps she left her underclothes somewhere, and since we are everywhere, even a laundry basket will do. We are all around her, Ernst, believe you me. She is, after all, a woman, and menstruates. We have whatever her body produces. And everything it produces, her sweat, her tears, her spit, but most of all her blood, tells us she is not your daughter.''

The silence was total. Barel let it last for as long as the prisoner wanted. It was only when the man licked his lips as if ready to speak that he leant towards him again. ''Well?''

''Where is she?''

''We were talking about your wife, Ernst.''

''I'm not.''

Grief, suspicion, anxiety—they were all on Barel's side. He smiled, then said, ''Corporal Tamir, ask Lubrani to come down to the Centre, please.'' To Dov he whispered, ''They can put him together in Jerusalem. We must just carry on pulling him gently to bits.''

It was then that the prisoner said emphatically, ''My wife is dead. My wife is a private matter.''

5.

It was dark outside the saloon. Matson tripped over flesh, kicked a rucksack, trod on some hair and perhaps a head, then picked his way aft by clinging to the port rail. The upper deck was lit like a bonfire display, so the sleepers had congregated down here. They complained as he trod among them, generally in teenage American.

Pomeroy had passed by without the least disturbance. He had finished his drink, disembarrassed himself of an aphorism or so, and vanished.

Matson searched both decks for him. Pomeroy could be skulking in a lavatory, of course, but the idea was ridiculous. Most ideas were when applied to Pomeroy: the thought of him even using a lavatory, let alone hiding in one, was not to be touched on. Perhaps he had simply got off the boat.

You need a boat to get off a boat. Matson made sure the cutter was inboard and there were no empty davits.

Then he scraped his head under the lifeboats on the blacked-out half-deck, but that was daft.

Whisky had taken his wits, but not his sense of proportion. He had always known he could do nothing for Kay. To help him would take an army and a miracle, and even drunk he hoped for neither.

All he wanted was to say to Ginevra, "I've been there. I know how it is. I've seen the place where they're keeping him. We're going to get him out." He needed to make this terrible aberration of the heart seem controlled and, more than that, official. She had to believe there was no self-will in anything he did for her, that his motives came from Quinlan and Fossit, from the Cabinet Office even, in other words from somewhere deeper in his self-importance than the sordid little maggot called love.

Finding Nuseibeh here had modified that, or finding him sharing a boat with Pomeroy had. Between them, and with Matson's cash, they had murdered Yitzak. For Pomeroy alone, Nuseibeh claimed he was arranging "the sale of the century." Matson wondered just who the bargain was to be, and how soon the hammer would fall.

He heard a noise seaward, an engine-pulse shorter and lighter than the *Paulina*'s. He peered outwards, and for a while saw nothing.

He could smell land, but that didn't mean much. The air was so humid that scents stayed close to the water and carried for miles.

The sea makes a little light, even in total darkness. By this shifting wave-fire or water-glow he detected a flake of shadow disengage itself, enlarge, and float nearer.

The fishing boat was bigger than those at Rhodos, but less well-kept. Its navigation lamps were as dull as ink on milk, and it only exposed a riding lantern at its masthead as a kind of afterthought before sidling up to the *Paulina*'s quarter. Matson watched it make fast at the foot of the pilot ladder.

There was no attempt at concealment. Very likely these vessels were intercepted all along the route by jollyboats, to put aboard passengers and supplies, to take off other passengers and post. Matson was the only traveller who seemed to think it worth a look.

The Mediterranean is a flat sea, a rowers' sea: so the

Paulina was able to stream a boarding flap below the ladder. Black shapes in dark cloth were clambering down to it.

It was the young Arab with the cleft chin he picked out first, his notched face sharp in the light from the fisherman's wheelhouse. Nuseibeh and Pomeroy were with him, but harder to see. There were four other men, perhaps Arabs too. Matson was not very clear about Arabs. He hailed them and started to go down.

He didn't descend the pilot-ladder too tidily.

He set his foot on the platform and then felt foolish. It was like blundering into a room where everyone is talking about you.

It seemed prudent to throw his arms around Pomeroy: "Where's the lucky lad stepping ashore, then?"

Pomeroy did not look disturbed enough for trouble. "Here, I fancy." He shrugged, muttered something in Arabic, then said, "One Greek island is much like another."

"Seen one," Matson agreed, "seen them all."

"With this little difference. This one has a daily airstrip—I *think* that's what the real-estate people call it." He glanced towards Nuseibeh, as if seeking guidance.

The doctor was a wordsmith in all of his languages. "Ours is one dragon your saint will not slay."

Matson didn't understand him.

"The English St. George was born in Israel, you know. Do you understand now?"

"I'm Irish."

"A Queen's Irishman, Mr. Matson. St. Patrick, they tell me, wasn't born at all."

The fishing boat revved its engine, pushing its fenders against the boarding-step, spraying phosphorescence like a dentist's smile. Then it stopped revving and a pause developed.

"I'm sure we'll all have a good trip," Matson suggested.

Pomeroy slapped something hard against his hand.

Matson glanced down. By binnacle light it looked like a consular air-warrant.

"Oh no," he said. "I'm not going back. The secrecy compact holds. Otherwise—"

A hard thump on the back of the neck, perhaps a hand, perhaps a rubber torch, propelled him forward into Pomeroy's grip.

Pomeroy didn't grip him. Matson was held from behind while the ticket was tucked solicitously into his inner pocket.

It had been an expert blow, struck by someone whose intention he had not even guessed at.

He didn't lose consciousness. He thought he didn't. He heard Nuseibeh say, "Her Majesty's Irishman has a beautiful skin. He'd make a lovely white slave, if only he weren't so scraggy."

Everyone laughed.

Nuseibeh added something in his click-tongued Arabic that made them laugh even more.

"He bleeds too easily," a voice said, once more in English. "A man likes to buy something a little more robust."

Matson, to his surprise, was lying in the boat.

6.

Tiredness blurred Barel's beardless face, rendering it epicene. He sat in his quarters and poured coffee with the grace of a man who is used to his limbs obeying him, even in *extremis*.

Not epicene, Lubrani thought: leonine.

"Doctor, you know we've had a prisoner here for some time—you were good enough to look at him for us."

The saucer rattled.

"I didn't realise you were going to hang on to him. I had rather hoped—"

"Lubrani, we had the prisoner on a ventilator."

"I should have been informed of that."

"That was a day or two back, and we're informing you now. You've been cleared to know."

"And who cleared me?" Lubrani was too relaxed a man to be intimidated by silence, so he added, "This is agreeable coffee. Thank you."

"Nothing is free in this place, Lubrani, not even the coffee. Not even your fee."

Doctors don't blush.

"I want you to put him on the ventilator again."

"You don't pay my fee, Shlomo. The State does."

"You keep on talking one sentence behind."

"You put a man on the ventilator when he has breathing difficulties, when his lungs collapse, or during the course of certain anaesthetic procedures—damn it! Why am I telling you what you already know?"

"In an effort to get yourself one sentence ahead. What if you merely *feared* his lungs would collapse?"

"I'd recommend medical procedures."

"Not during surgery, you wouldn't."

"No, Shlomo."

"You're contradicting me?"

"I mean *no*, Shlomo. I'm not going to do this thing. Your prisoner is my patient."

"Ahead of me at last." Barel reached for the doctor's cup and saucer as if he was withdrawing his last inducement. "I'll give you five minutes to think it over, Lubrani. No, I'll be generous: I'll let you have ten. You're going to have to face one of the classic dilemmas of the doctor, aren't you? Just as those bastards up in Jerusalem have asked me to confront one of the classic dilemmas of the soldier. You're going to have to ask yourself whether you're prepared to anaesthetise and ventilate the prisoner, then inject him with some muscle-relaxants so I can wake him up and frighten him out of his wits—"

"The answer is still no."

"Or go home to your wife and your hi-fi and your chess-set, secure in the knowledge that back in the Interrogation Centre you have left poor little Corporal Tamir to do it for you. She too has a conscience. She's an obedient soldier, is Judi Tamir. She's also very closely connected to some of the bastards that are doing this to me."

"They're doing it to the prisoner, Shlomo. And insofar as he's my patient, I must insist that my conscience is where it always was, between myself and Hippocrates."

"They're not doing anything to the prisoner, Lubrani, I wish they were. They're telling me to ask you to do it. And you're pushing that little girl into doing it."

"She's not so little as all that."

"Perhaps. But as you reminded me last time—she's not much of a nurse."

Lubrani took back his cup and reached for the coffee pot. It was empty. "You should keep it on the charcoal," he said. "Like an Arab. I prefer their sugar." He stood up and went into the bathroom, washing noisily with the door open.

Having emphasised his rights, he came back and said, "I thought you lot were experts in whatever's necessary." He didn't sit down again.

"Do you know what an expert is, when it comes to that sort of thing?"

"I can't begin to guess what sort of thing you're talking about."

"The brutish sort. When it comes to that, the expert is always somebody else, Doctor. My general has just cleared me to tell you that you are that somebody." He stood up, pleading, not bullying. "You've seen the man's scrotum and teeth, and you've told me his heart's not much better. It looks as if his lungs are all you've got left."

"Tomorrow, Shlomo."

"We live in a cellar, Lubrani. There is no tomorrow down here."

"You mentioned ten minutes."

"Thank you, Doctor. We'll make a start in ten minutes. Phone your wife and tell her you've got to do a caesar."

7.

He lay in the bottom of the boat feeling distant from his limbs, yet warm and content as one can after injury. A leather coat had been thrown over him, and the leather smelled of its curing—a strange must of fishmeal and cat, presumably camel dung.

There was a numbness in his foot, and he was alert enough to know this defied logic. Then he woke properly; he was alone and he had a headache. The coat had gone, but the stink had seeped into his bones.

It was the second time his high vertebrae had been smacked in how many hours, in how many miles? It couldn't be good for his brain-cells; nor could each bottle of Bushmills.

He concentrated on the ache and tried to force it away. He felt in his pocket for his traveller's pack of aspirin and swallowed three tablets dry; it was like eating hairballs, but the ache would go through with them.

Inside the ache he drank wine with Brenda, and something too yellow and bitter for wine with Ginevra Kay. He began to vomit, but neatly and away from himself, like a professional invalid. He drank wine with the snake.

The headache was distant but hot. He was able to shut himself apart from it in a tobacco-scented phonebox and watch Ginevra's house, until the headache became a blue-green parrot talking all the languages in the world.

The little East European lady stood holding the crook of her basket-on-wheels as if it were a walking-stick, and she spoke to him. She was warning him about something, as people kindly do in dreams. He couldn't hear what she said, because the phonebox was locked against his headache, but he liked her more and more. She was, he decided, a nice old cock. A proper sprig of parsley, as they said in Peckham, worth her weight in sunshine.

He sat bolt upright. The boat was a ship's lifeboat, and it was ballasted with sand. It was otherwise empty and the sand was grey, but at least he wasn't dead. He'd leant his left hand palm down in his sick; you don't have an experience as rich as that when you're dead.

The sky was greyer than the sand. It had a pewter lining and he knocked his head on it. Then it began to unlace itself and God leaned in. The sky was a lifeboat cover.

God's breath was unbelievably clean when it spoke to him: it smelled as a fish must smell after gargling salt all day. It said, "Leonard mustn't know about this—no-one must know."

" 'Know'?"

The fish breath belonged to Pomeroy, and as a result seemed full of ancient anchovy. "Know I was on a boat that you were on." The blue sky above made the face look cloudy. "Still, our conundrum is mutual and it does manifest a certain symmetry. Leonard mustn't know that you were on a boat that I was on either, must he? Or I take it he mustn't."

"I'm feeling a bit sick."

"That unfortunate knock on the nap. Never trust a Cypriot. I told them not to noddle you."

"It's not your bloody thugs that made me puke." If it

was a Greek, I'm an Irishman, he thought; and then he *was* sick. "It's seeing you holding hands with Nuseibeh."

"He's locked into my budget, and I don't always trust him to do what he's paid for."

"I thought you needed to be invisible."

"Only to appear to be invisible."

It was too soon in the day for paradox. "Lifeboats should not be full of sand," he said.

"Out here they should. You wouldn't want to spew in the sort of lavatories they've got in this boat. Why don't you hop out from between the thwarts before the Other Ranks wake up?" Pomeroy's arm was remarkably strong, considering who it was attached to.

Matson let it prise him onto the deck, which was a long way beneath his expectations. Pomeroy had been standing up on the launching skid.

He got down and said, "Stay in the saloon and stick to bottled water. You'll survive till you get back to Rhodos."

The boat was moored in an ancient harbour. Matson gazed at its black-edged, not quite, sea. "This," he said, "is Haifa."

"They'll have your bollocks if you step ashore here. And find ways of making them kosher."

"I'm not the bloody villain of the piece."

"Nor me. A bit player, like you—a sort of flanneled fool in their eyes. They're much too cock-a-hoop to harm a little toddler from the Foreign Office. Besides, I'm here on official business. I can come—and equally certainly go—just as I damn well please."

Matson felt he owed him one, but Pomeroy's cheekbone was harder and more elusive than he anticipated.

When the sleepers on the deck woke up, it was to find the two Britishers punching each other's heads, just as if they were at a football match.

8.

Lubrani looked at the prisoner and the prisoner gazed back at him. The man's face was a mess; but then so is a boxer's. It was his eye that defeated Lubrani. It was completely devoid of hope but not, unfortunately, of trust.

The drip was already blocked against the man's arm and

strapped tight. Lubrani fussed over the tap, then inspected Judi Tamir's work with the tourniquet. He had insisted she wore surgical green and blue, as he did himself. Barel and his lieutenant had white coats open above their uniforms, as if that somehow rendered their uniforms sterile—or as if their commissions meant they were clean.

Lubrani knew he was being fanciful. He spoke to the prisoner reassuringly: "I want to do a few things to your dressings and generally tidy you up. So we're putting you to sleep."

"The vulture cleans its teeth," Dov said in the background.

"It's nice of the major to watch," the prisoner whispered. "Well, you must do what you must do, doctor. Though I think you ought to know I was threatened with something or other that was supposed to happen to me under a general anaesthetic."

"He's going to give you a baby," Dov chuckled. "He told his wife he's here for a caesar."

Lubrani was disturbed at the implication of menace. He looked at the forearm below the tourniquet: the veins were suffusing too slowly—a very bad sign indeed. He said, "This is silly in all the circumstances, but I can't find a vein for the pentathol. It happens sometimes."

Barel hissed behind him, perhaps in warning.

"Well, I said it was silly: what we must do is slap one up."

"I am aware of that procedure, Doctor." The prisoner seemed calm enough. He watched Judi Tamir whip at the underside of his arm with one of the tie-ribbons of her surgical jacket, and then at the back of his hand. He had old man's hands, and she was in her nurse's gear so she slapped him with compassion.

She raised a site behind the middle finger.

Lubrani handed her the syringe of anaesthetic. "Just break it through the top wall of the vein," he instructed.

She smiled. She knew what to do, and the danger of getting it wrong. She injected slowly and Lubrani unwrapped the tourniquet. The prisoner began to snore.

He motioned her towards the mask of oxygen and nitrous oxide.

"Give him the other needle, Doc; and let's have an end of his awful noise," Barel growled.

Judi Tamir's eyes questioned him as he wrenched the man's head closer to the gas trolley.

"You don't need me to do this," Lubrani told Barel. "The papers are full of his name. The court will be sure to find he is guilty."

"Just you keep on crawling ahead, Doctor, and leave running for those who can run. You help us on this one and you'll find we're not ungrateful. We can take you and your family down to Eilat for a week's yachting."

"I'm too old for that sort of heat."

"What aren't you too old for?" Dov asked. He smiled encouragingly at Judi, but she was watching the doctor examine his patient's abdomen.

Barel spoke to the bowed head. He spoke harshly: "It's the old joke, Lubrani. We've established you're prepared to be a prostitute. All we have to haggle about is your price."

"I can give him some myanesin or scoline via the drip if you like. No charge for those."

"No myanesin, I'm sorry." Judi Tamir told him. "And no scoline. "We've got tubarine."

"What's tubarine?" Barel asked.

"It's marketed by the local Burroughs Wellcome," Lubrani said easily. "It's good, if a little old-fashioned. But like the pentathol it's not the best thing for the heart." He watched Judi fit it to the drip rig, but leave the tap closed. "It's made from curare," he explained. "Just like the poison on blowpipe darts."

"Good, so it'll give him a fright round the bellows. What else is in that drip, Doctor?"

"Saline and plasma—"

"No blood?"

"You give him blood, you'll kill him. Nurse Tamir shouldn't have given him blood the other day. His circulation's at risk, not his supply of oxygen. You want to be very careful about blood." It was good watching Judi Tamir blush: her face had all of the blood it needed. "Too many red cells and he'll clog up like an old drain. I've had to use insulin and sugar for his heart as it is."

"Insulin? You said you suspected a middle-age diabetes?"

"The protein diet you're giving him will help with that, but again it's a burden to his heart. Anaesthesia is a balancing act, even at the best of times, a bit like juggling. That's what I think you should realise."

The prisoner snored with a long, palatal vibrato, even inside the mask, and then began to sputter through his lips. The snore began again, hoglike and indestructible.

"Turn on the tap, Doctor."

"I'll remain in charge, if you don't mind, gentlemen. Nurse Tamir, please let him have exactly one thirtieth."

The chest sagged beneath his hand, the belly slackened like a woman after birth, its skin unsupported as an old paper lantern.

The prisoner, his patient, became completely quiet.

"Now wake him up."

The silence became as intolerable as the snoring had been. The prisoner still made sounds, but it took a special ear to detect them. He was sleeping a mechanical sleep, which in a second could be stimulated to agonised lung-collapsed wakefulness.

The doctor became his own nursing assistant. He arranged and rearranged a layette of unnecessary instruments.

"Corporal Tamir!" Barel had almost come to the end. "Corporal Tamir: I don't know what you do in order to do it, but wake the man up."

"Jews of all people must know the consequence of this sort of behaviour." Lubrani fought his rearguard. "What are you saying: we've got the power, so it's our turn now?"

"Yes," Dov raged.

Barel did not answer Lubrani. He spoke to the girl. "I'm saying that now I can do what has to be done."

Judi Tamir slid her fingertips past the prisoner's ears and rested them gently at each angle of the jaw, her palms cupping his temples. It is a trick hunters use to wake a sleeping comrade, but you can't rouse an anaesthetised person that way.

Barel knew she wasn't trying. She had had enough. It was then he realised she wasn't his office girl, still less his nurse or corporal. She was a woman with stripes on her sleeve. And at that moment he understood it wasn't his prisoner she was protecting, but himself.

"I've spent too long as a citizen of the Western liberal tradition," Lubrani said. "Sorry." He offered Barel his compassion. Then he began to clean Kay's loins, separating skin from skin, transforming him tenderly into something that would heal into a man.

9.

Nothing is worse for a leader than to find himself unable to compel good men to do ill. Someone must have said that. Barel hoped it wasn't a philosophy thrown up by his own creaking subconscious. He went to his quarters, exhausted by failure. But then he had been exhausted long before he had allowed failure to creep up on him.

There was a knock on his door. They weren't going to leave him alone in his crisis.

Corporal Tamir stepped inside. She offered a rare salute.

An officer learns the vocabulary of salutes. This one was correct and untruculent.

"I've come to apologise, sir. I was insubordinate and I was disloyal. I am afraid I lack the belief."

"Insubordination is a military matter, Corporal. As such I would rather not be forced to think about it. This unit has been proud of its ability to go beyond the merely soldierly. Our country needs us to be good servants, that's all."

"You were the good servant, Shlomo Barel. You caught the rare fish and now your master does not want it."

"Moreover, it's going rotten. Would you care for some coffee?"

He was drinking Arab tea. She took Arab tea.

"You are wrong to sully loyalty with belief," he said. "Loyalty is an absolute, Judi. To think belief is an absolute is to fetter your mind."

"Who says that?"

"I do. De Vigny offers some amusing instances of it."

"Where?"

"Servitudes et Grandeurs Militaires."

"And what does he say?"

"I can see you're a product of the new education. You want summaries, abstracts, the key phrase, the quintessential truth. Myself, I'm a little too old for messages, still less for slogans. I like to read the whole book."

"You like to follow the argument?"

"Merely to sniff its integrity."

She nodded intently, transformed as she had been the previous time they had argued. He wondered if her protest in the medical room had been like most people's acts of rebellion, a shout for recognition. No: it went deeper than that. She had, as she said, eaten supper with the general and at least one of the Cabinet. She couldn't be bought off with an increase in rank, a bit more power. She needed the consolation of truth, whatever that was.

She began to explain herself, but he wasn't really listening. His eyes were sore and dry, and his tiredness was making noises at the back of his throat, a kind of waking snore which he hoped she couldn't hear. His body was fit, he knew that, fit almost to obscenity; and yet he wondered what damage fatigue was doing to his heart.

He may have put out his hand in apology, or perhaps stretched forward to wake himself. What he knew was she was standing behind him—always the nurse, his little corporal, her thumbs pushing hard into his shoulder muscles, as he had seen her do so often for the prisoner.

He wished he had kept her mind on de Vigny. She was talking, or refusing to talk, about the Greece of the Colonels, her fingers deep in the ganglia of his neck like a punishment, killing fatigue the hard way, torturing out sleep.

"I wish you wouldn't concern yourself for Kay," he grumbled—had "Kay" been a slip?

"I don't, not off duty."

"The jawbone, the penis, the vagina—aren't they the organs with the swiftest rate of healing, Corporal Tamir?"

She knew "corporal" was a mockery. "The quickest healing flesh: there's a difference. The jawbone and vagina, at least. Could I have a transfer from the unit? I mean, could you arrange it without too much difficulty, somewhere not far?"

"A transfer?" She really had brought him round with a vengeance. "I thought—" He thought she had done with all that. "Why, Judi? You're a highly valued member of the team."

"And you run a disciplined unit, Shlomo Barel," smiled the girl who was related to his general. "I should want us to be discreet about this, for your sake. So I think it will be best if I transfer out." She had been using her thumbs and her fingers inside the back of his shirt, and now leant forward to unbutton it. "Even Samson was allowed to rest from the mill," she murmured.

She was making love to him, so it was hardly the time to reprove her for an inappropriate metaphor.

They went together into his bedroom, but they slept much sooner than lovers do. Fatigue was the landscape they shared, and somewhere out there they had their consummation. Sleep was her first gift to him, and if she had been able to share it for long she would have heard him cry out, because even in love he was exhausted and bitter.

It would have been painful to counter his dream, for in its shallowness he began as so often to tally his dead. Some men watch the dead as others count sheep. He checked all their faces as they pitched from their burning tanks, their backs ablaze like resin. The tank might be Syrian, Jordanian, Israeli; and many times the tank was Egyptian. The identity of the tanks did not matter. The tanks might be different, but the dead were all the same. Napalm would make a nonsense of the foreskins of Ga'ath, but nothing burned the faces in the tanks that held Yitzak.

When he woke he was even more tired. But at least he was at peace with his calling. It was hard to live in Israel and not be a soldier of some sort or other.

He wanted the girl again. He dressed and found her at the door.

"The General's waiting to talk to you," she said.

"In the flesh or on the phone?"

The phone was still his thorn.

ELEVEN

1.

The inflatables had been lolloping about for hours. From beach level the horizon was near. At a thousand yards on a flat sea the divers seemed to perch on nothing, or sometimes disappear altogether. They were making too much noise out there.

The beach was noisy too. From time to time the divers would wave towards the beach. People would wave back, then catch themselves feeling foolish.

Three youngsters at the front of the beach didn't mind looking silly. They waved and kept waving, calling words of encouragement, abuse.

"We've got some wine waiting here. Where's our fish?"

"Stuff your fish. I had fish yesterday."

It was generally the man who called. The two girls were quieter, but they clapped and waved; and their behaviour made others shut up. Newcomers would wave, then feel they were interrupting some kind of party. Either the youth and girls on the beach were with the four out there, or knew them as old friends, or had taken up some proprietary stance towards them from which they could not now be dislodged.

"You be careful what you do with that fish. I'm going to tell your wife about it."

"I . . . can't . . . hear . . . you."

"I'm going to tell Josie about that fish."

Everyone agreed it was foolish to be bouncing up and down so far offshore in craft like that.

They also agreed that it was best not to concentrate on

what was being shouted, because it was, well, a bit loud-mouthed for this stretch of beach.

This stretch of beach was going down.

There was, it was true, a better beach just to the north; but this was the bit by the Old Town, and the medieval walls and the bright new shops deserved something better than this sort of loudvoiced lout.

Wasn't it dangerous out there?

Dangerous for skin-divers, that is.

People who had been holidaying on the Red Sea where the sharks were frequent and ferocious said that here wasn't really dangerous even if it wasn't entirely safe.

This wasn't as sensitive a place as Haifa, but sooner or later the Coastguards would become annoyed, then the Shore and Harbour Patrol, and perhaps even the Navy would pitch in and tow them away.

A small motor missile launch could be seen, pulsing up fast from the south, coming from behind the silhouette of the Old Town and towing a big wake.

The three on the shore were amused, not anxious.

"I warned him about that." The young man's Hebrew sounded like a lump in his mouth. It was flawed but bold. Like many others, he was still learning.

One of the girls agreed. Her accent was like silk.

Then they were joined by three other young men, carrying beach umbrellas, enormous sunbathing mats and a hamper.

These young men were quiet.

The girls kissed them all in turn.

The first young man didn't seem at all put-out by the newcomers' arrival. He felt all their luggage with his foot, and even took a look inside their hamper.

2.

The orange-coloured inflatables were shaped like horse-shoes, huge plantains or bananas that had bent too far. They had crossboards for seats and no motors. They were propelled by paddlepower.

It was these squat ungainly paddles that proclaimed the young men's innocence. They would need outboard engines to travel fast or cover any distance.

Three of them sat with their flippers dangling in the water. The head of the fourth broke the surface just as the patrol-boat backed screws and flatbellied off its hydroplane. The wash and ripple of the boat jerked the swimmer's head towards his own inflatable, then rocked both inflatables in their turn.

He pulled his mask up, the water draining through the ungainly groove in his chin. The solo diver helped him aboard so now they sat two and two.

"It's a bit far out for skuba-ing."

The patrol-boat nudged between them, separating them. They had to hand off from its clearboard, but the slow forward drift of the boat sucked them back again.

"Yes."

"So what are you diving for?"

"We'd rather not say." The same man spoke, the one who had just been in the water.

"You're towing underwater hampers. I don't see any fish."

The divers weren't armed, weren't menacing in any way; but it did not escape them that the crewmen on the patrol-boat had their sidearms to hand.

The man who had been in the water looked at his colleagues, each in turn, as if seeking guidance. Then he said, "O.K., we'll tell you. Better still, show you. Carl! Carl, you there?"

The inflatables nudged in and out of sight of one another as they bobbled by the stem of the larger vessel.

"Carl, show him your sack. Let's hope the Navy's not greedy."

The two divers on the far inflatable lifted their hamper from the water. It was heavy, and as it came clear of the sea it rattled like shingle on a beach.

They opened it up.

It was full of wet clay fragments like broken flowerpots.

"Amphora. They look better when dry."

"There's plenty of that inshore, close by the old town."

"Yes, but it's Arabic or at best Crusader. Most of the stuff you pick up back there is not even medieval. See this marking here—and this shard here? Like an indented triangle. That's Phoenician."

"What does that make it worth?"

"Something, I suppose—if we could find or reconstruct a whole jar. We've got some complete handles and necks. But the real interest is historical—that's why we're hoping the Navy can hold its tongue."

"We'll have to make a report, of course. I didn't catch your names."

"Sorry. Buber. I and Carl are from the University of Haifa. I'm an Associate Professor of History there. Our two friends are from the School of Marine Archaeology in Barcelona."

"That's a long way to come. Particularly for an afternoon's frustration. I'm sorry to close you down now, but you'll have to get proper permission from the coastguard: you must have known that. We'll make our report, tell them what we've seen. You should have clearance by tomorrow. Can we tow you in?"

"We'll paddle in, unless you want to foul your propellers. I've got to meet up with some of my students . . ."

Once again the shout reached them from the beach.

"That lot there."

"Make sure you all have clearance when we call by tomorrow."

"Thanks for your help."

The lieutenant signalled. The patrol-boat backwatered to avoid sucking them towards its propellers. Then it pivotted to port, punched up into its hydroplane position and went powering away northwards up the coast.

When he was several cable lengths off, it struck the lieutenant that only one man had spoken. But then he was the professor, the person in charge of things, so it would be natural for him to speak for them all. And two of the men were Spaniards and perhaps hadn't even understood his questions.

Besides, the rubber boats had no outboard motors, just paddles. That's what clinched it for him and stopped him from turning back. The whole venture was obviously the usual underfinanced academic operation they claimed it to be.

He put his glasses on the boats. They were doing as he had told them. They were striking towards the shore.

He couldn't check their speed by any kind of parallax, or he would have seen they were only making about a quarter of a knot, as if both inflatables were towing not baskets of wineshards, but huge underwater anchors.

3.

Matson had been in Haifa before. He felt a compulsion to linger. The most he could hope for was to be allowed to be a tourist, and he ached to walk the curving lanes and bent avenues of Carmel, with the sea turned to breeze and the green leaf for sky. He was beginning to ask himself whether his recent spankings had broken his bottle. Well, his brain had made its mind up, so his gut must take the consequence.

He was standing in a dusty queue behind Arabs in plastic sandals, and Americans, Italians and, yes, he supposed, Israelis and acquiescent Palestinians in a variety of jeans and trainers.

He bought himself a bus ticket to Tel Aviv, and got the only seat on the bus. The queue had to wait for the next one, or some said tomorrow.

"How come we all got our tickets first and you get the seat?"

Matson lifted his eyes above foot level and gazed at the beautiful American. "I paid more."

"What do you suggest we do?"

"In this country it's intelligent to hire a car." He knew she couldn't afford it. Students never can. Nor, at these prices, can people. He could. He could hire a car and fit himself up with her and a few similar pieces of camouflage. But anyone having him watched would conclude he was much less dangerous on a bus.

He showed her some uneven teeth and bruised gums, and hoped she recognised a smile when she saw one. Then he climbed aboard the bus. It was air-conditioned but odorous. It travelled faster than he dared drive a car at this moment.

For the next two hours everything would be out of his hands. He was hurrying towards Kay, or more exactly towards Ginevra Kay's father, but he was not in charge of getting himself there. There was time for the thoughts to crowd in.

It struck him that although it might be usual for jollyboats to rendezvous with the Nabluth steamers, they hardly represented a satisfactory supply-line for a covert operation. He doubted very much if Israeli security waited until the vessel docked in Haifa before it began to operate.

Was that why the ubiquitous Marcus Pomeroy had not departed on the fisherman?

He had no way of knowing where Nuseibeh had gone.

Matson once operated in the Eastern Mediterranean, as he had confessed to Ginevra. When the Greek Islands have been left behind—and Rhodes is the last of them—there are no other islands, certainly not islands big enough for "a daily airstrip." It seemed totally unlikely that Pomeroy or even the lavishly funded Dr. Nuseibeh could persuade the captain and crew of a cruise steamer to sail in a circle.

There was Cyprus, of course. That was on a straight line. But the Israelis were reputed to have an efficient presence there.

The coach slowed down. They had scarcely left the southern suburbs. Matson knew these Egged buses: they were always obliging, and operated almost like taxis.

Then the brakes came on hard, and he saw they were at a roadblock.

There were lots of soldiers, perhaps as many as a platoon of them behind sandbags. It really was strength ten.

The bus-driver was called down into the road, and some agitated talking began. Matson smelled tobacco smoke. The voices calmed down.

Four men climbed on board. A young officer with a holstered pistol and anxious eyes. Two soldiers with their Uzis on shoulder slings, their right hands ostensibly steadying them, their butts collapsed forward and ready for use as machine pistols. A civilian in a dirty blue suit that looked as if it had been cut from cold-weather cloth. The four of them began to search the bus.

They did all of this in brisk slow motion. They looked through the hand-luggage, they opened books and magazines, they made people turn out their pockets and tip up their handbags. Matson saw some other soldiers turfing through the main luggage in the road, emptying cases, rucksacks, animal baskets, unrolling and cracking an expensive inlaid linoleum that someone had gone shopping for. Inside, the officer's holster was unbuttoned, the flap tucked behind the plastic grip of the weapon and—very disturbing—the safety-catch disengaged. Matson *thought* the action was forward but he didn't want to show too much interest.

A female voice raised itself. A tough-looking youth began to swear in the sort of epicene whine that some men acquire when they are very angry. An old Middle-European lady was scolding aloud. Matson felt a protective fondness for old Middle-European ladies or anyone else of any genus that was connected even remotely with Ginevra Kay. They were being body-searched, tap-searched at least, and the fact that it was men who were doing it, feeling under breast and into armpit and crotch, and with such clinical dispassion, only added to their overall sense of outrage.

The road-block and its procedures were clearly *ad hoc,* efficient but improvised, because there weren't the usual female searchers. The security services were reacting to a tip-off, Matson concluded. They knew exactly what they were looking for, and it couldn't be Matson or they wouldn't be groping between that old woman's legs for him. The young officer was using his left hand on everyone with evident embarrassment, while his right tried to remain stern around his pistol.

It was the civilian who was in charge. He was particularly concerned with passports, which he would demand brusquely, then take only a cursory interest in.

He made towards Matson. He gestured for Matson to take off his jacket, and soothe down his own trouserlegs with the palm of his hands pressed tight against ankle and calf. Then he snatched off Matson's sunglasses. His eyes widened at the bruising, and then refused to focus on the face behind it. They shifted from side to side. They evaded the front of Matson's head. They simultaneously studied the lobes of both of his ears. They requested, without speech, that he please cover himself up again.

Matson recognised the look. It was the old-fashioned I-do-not-wish-to-be-seen-to-recognise-you expression. The one priests put on in brothels or that policemen wear when they are arresting friends.

4.

It was only a few steps from the sea, but this was another world, a world without sunlight.

He had been greeted by a major and a lieutenant and by a medic called Lubrani who kept on talking nervously about ''our man'' and ''our man's condition.''

Dr. Tadeus from Tikva was not a doctor of medicine. His degrees related to his own peculiar specialism that hovered midway between zoology and bio-chemistry, ''like a gnat over sour water'' as he called it.

The doctor felt gnatlike himself after his helicopter flight between the brown lands of the snake-farm and the splintering light of the sea. Now, before his eyes had stopped shuttering with the rotors, he was taken down even deeper into dark, and then into neon-lit coolness, as if he was about to be shown a most elusive reptile in its man-made catchment.

His own reptiles were not, of course, prisoners. A snake has few needs, and none of them territorial. You can keep it for years in its box, and providing you grant it a suitable allowance of mice, frogs and baby starlings, it will pop out and bite you with exactly the same enthusiasm as before.

They all went into the Medical Room.

Dr. Tadeus was appalled at the bruised face, the thickened lips, but they gave the man's face a kind of made-up, amorphous look. Also, it is hard to take a person seriously if his speech is thickened from alcohol or a stroke.

The doctor didn't really hear the opening exchanges. He felt as if he was socialising after too much to drink, so that at some moments his attention would be fixed on the prisoner's feet, then his hands, both of which seemed to exist quite separately.

The prisoner was observing all the courtesies. He started with domestic matters. He said he knew all about the milk of the Palestinian and Saw-scaled Vipers, and offered a searching remark or two about the venom enzymes of *Vipera Palestrinae* and *Echis Carinatus*.

Doctor Tadeus had played these kinds of conversational games with amateurs, but he didn't think anyone could be quite so knowledgeable about the concentrations of the endopeptidases in the skulls of those particular vipers, unless he had read certain doctoral theses published only by the University Library in Jerusalem. Or he could have been at the conference at Berne where young Aaronson had delivered that paper. One would have needed to be a pretty rabid venomologist. There hadn't been more than a dozen people in the room . . .

As he posed this to himself, he suddenly recognised the man for who he was. Who he had been. The pain-loosened features set and tanned in his mind's eye. The loose-mouthed traumatic became Doctor Kay, the world-renowned—in herpetological circles—C.H. Kay.

The mouth in front of him was dribbling unpleasantly, and anecdotes were pouring from it.

Doctor Tadeus had never seen any pictures of Ernst Halder; but he believed this could be Halder as well, delivering this contemptuous account of the Aborigine Dream Ritual, with its confused mumbling, no, drooling, about the World Serpent, the Rainbow Snake biting Bosie in the balls. Surely Bosie was a notorious homosexual?

The man became lucid again: "I was comparatively new to it then; and, of course, hardly any professional snake-handler, let alone a scientifically trained herpetologist, had set eyes on a Taipan. I was a virgin, venomologically speaking. He lost blood, you see, and a great amount of lymphous matter. Quite extraordinary for a bite by an elapid—or at least according to the thinking in those days. I remember wondering if his bladder had been punctured—and perhaps it had been: the post-mortem was hardly designed to meet more than the most superficial of forensic needs. Had he been at Wittwatersrand, say, or Nairobi, we could have had an examination that might have advanced science a little."

More cold-blooded calculation from this fossilised remnant of the Master Race?

"I also wondered whether the presence of all that neurotoxin caused an ejaculation of semen. It seems obscene, I know, but I sensed myself in some ways in the presence of a myth. I was bearding an archetype. Such a damned big snake, so aggressive. Also, then as now, I was in a profound state of shock. No, Doctor Tadeus, I was not calm.''

He began to cry. Nazis can cry. Especially at the death of pets. Look at Goebbels.

His tears did not diminish him. ''It was only when I sat down a week or two later and analysed the venom that I realised there was a very high proportion of hyaluronidase in it. And, of course, no-one really knows what a *large dose* of phospholipase-A will do to *living* tissue. I don't count the D-fifty test. What that stuff'll do to recently killed meat is remarkable. It doesn't so much break down the blood vessels as burst them apart with excessive dilation, as you know.''

''You caught the snake, then?''

The man became evasive, confused. He buried his head in his hands, as if this was the greatest guilt of all. After a time, he said, ''No. I killed it. I hadn't ever told that to anyone, not till the other night, when I told the little girl here. Not till after what they did to me the other night.''

''It must have been a difficult brute to kill. What did you do—thump it with your clamp?''

''No. I'd dropped the thing. I'd dropped everything. And, of course, Elderkin was lying on his own extension clamp. There must have been L-sticks, other rods, but the bloody snake was *everywhere* . . . no, I shot it. Even that was no good. I went for a headshot—not very convincing field behaviour for a venomologist—but luckily missed and broke its back just below the neck instead. It didn't die for a damn' long time, but I milked it into a thermos. What method do you use here, the same?''

Tadeus couldn't answer. He felt confused, as if he was being asked to betray something to a spy.

''I've never let anyone know I *shot* the thing—not even *these* bastards!'' He jerked his hand towards Barel and Dov.

Doctor Tadeus stood up to leave. He didn't quite know why. Perhaps the major had thought him onto his feet.

Kay chuckled. ''Do you know how your fellows pinched me?''

''They're not my fellows.''

''They stuck me full of cobra venom.''

''What—Egyptian Cobra?''

"Too risky. Besides, that beast is so near and yet so far. No, dear old *Naja naja*. It's perfect for the job. I'm still quite high on it. I recommend it to you, if you'd like to take a little trip in the interests of science."

They were both appalled by the accidental pun.

Barel opened the door, and there was an odd moment of revelation.

Tadeus searched for a word of comfort in parting and came up with the Yiddish: *"Noyt brekht azyn!"*

"Need breaks iron," Barel translated.

"Tell him he should rather say *'Falshe tseyn tu'en nit vey,'* " Kay said sweetly. It was Yiddish too, and it was possible someone had mocked him with it as they'd tortured his mouth. But who on earth among them could it be?

"I learned that one from Coloma," he said proudly, but they didn't understand him: you can't learn Yiddish from a dove.

They slammed the door shut on him and left him gawping back at it from the far side.

Scoffing that false teeth don't hurt came oddly in Yiddish from a man who so far confessed to speaking only English, North Eastern Aborigine and Snake.

"That's almost low German," Barel chuckled. "The *Plattdeutsch* of Hamburg. Well, Doctor? He's a sadist and a racist."

"So are lots of other scientists. This man knows too much to be anything other than what he says he is. Besides, he has a worldwide reputation as a herpetologist."

"Is that a big world?"

"No. Comparatively small."

"Convenient for him."

"Let me say it again, Major. I'd have to be a witness for the Defence. The man knows too much."

"It's his cover. He's mugged up on it."

"It's not his cover. It's his life."

"It's his life *now*. We're going to hang him for his life *then*. It's *being* a serpent that's going to be the death of him, not studying them. Anyway, Doctor Tadeus, you'll stay for something to eat?"

Tadeus had a bad feeling the moment he accepted the invitation.

5.

So they knew he was here, and doubtless Barel would have the information before the day was very much older.

Matson got off the bus between the railway station and Arlorzorov and found himself a taxi. He was carrying the little duffel bag that only held underclothes, and wearing the slacks and jacket that the man in the blue suit had satisfied himself contained nothing more.

He had the taxi run him towards Jaffo, but taking in the sights. Dizengoff was even more of a tart than he remembered. All the great towns in the world have somewhere like this, a street pulsating and vulgar which nonetheless catches you by the throat. He went on reluctantly, and paid off his taxi by the Grand Mosque. Then he walked a road that curved seawards.

The afternoon was unpleasantly humid. It would be even harder to be a hero here than under Carmel. He walked on through the Old Town, getting near to the sea, the Martello, and Charles Henry Kay.

He had a glimpse of the Andromeda Rock, and felt more uneasy than ever.

They were searching for someone from Haifa, perhaps from his boat. There was nothing to suggest they were looking for Nuseibeh or any of his motley Palestinians, nothing except Matson's overriding dissatisfaction with any other solution. There are many circumstances in the world that are completely unknown to us, but questions and answers gravitate ceaselessly towards each other. It seemed unlikely that this particular pair could be so close and remain unrelated.

He was in a road of little stall-fronted shops selling high-priced bric-a-brac. Everywhere around him the artists were busy, all of them diligent fakers like himself. They were hardworking craftsmen manufacturing trashy artworks of dazzling surface bravura in everything from metal to oils.

He walked through them and into a calm and unpretentious square. On one side there was a synagogue, on the other the Martello. He hurried out of it quickly.

A hundred yards further on he was pleased to find a little coffee shop. It had an awning which it didn't need:

the walls were too steep. The shadow was even older than Ireland.

The table cost him as much as a week's car-rental back home, but the coffee was excellent and woke up his nerve. He was wondering whether to afford a second cup when the shooting started.

6.

Corporal Tamir had changed into civilian clothes for the street. In her green blouse and Bermuda shorts she looked very fetching. Tadeus started to pay her a compliment as he stood blinking in the sunlight by the doorway of the Martello. He didn't. Instead he said, "I know it seems ridiculous, but I don't think I know your name."

Doctor Lubrani chuckled beside him. "With her lot it's best not to ask. When I was a lad we used to have a trick with girls who wouldn't tell us their names."

They turned towards him. Obviously it was going to be a cheery little secret. But his face, already loosened by mirth, seemed to drop outwards as if he had just been punched in the stomach; and even that was only a memory. His body was flung backwards against the Martello door, like an insect swatted in flight. It stuck there briefly, then slid downwards, smearing thick blood.

Tadeus put out a hand, tried to clutch at her, hold on to somebody, but he missed and tumbled.

They were being shot at, not accidentally or at random, but with deliberate, aimed shots.

The door was too far behind her. The door was barred tight. The little square in front of her was rimmed with an ornamental bed full of shrubs and flowering cactus.

Judi Tamir took a diving stride towards the flowerbed, trying to think as she did so.

She was struck in the left knee. It was a little blow, a silly blow, like at school when a playmate kicks you in the fold of the leg from behind and you go sprawling from the softness of his sandal. She tumbled midway through her footstep, and as her face hit the concrete rim of the flowerbed she heard the bone ring. Not her head, but her spine or her knee ached. She tried to get up. She couldn't. Something that made her feel cold but was hot to her hands was sliding through her fingers. Something made of her leg.

She knew the doctor had been shot. She had seen the mist about his skull, heard the splinters. Seen him thrown against the door. If the doctor could be shot, so could she.

Her right leg was good. She pushed herself over. Her left was numb, and the ankle twitched with cold. Her right leg couldn't find it.

Then she saw the girl with the rocket-launcher.

The girl was in beachwear. She was aiming her weapon at the tower door. Not one of the smaller SAMs, more a bomb on a lance: a kind of Bangalore torpedo.

Judi Tamir recognised it as an RPG-7. It would certainly bring down the outer door of the Martello. She got her hand inside her shoulder bag and huddled behind the rim of the flowerbed as she felt for her pistol. Everywhere was wet, and everything was shrinking except for the girl with the rocket launcher.

Somebody was shrieking, somebody else was shooting. She didn't hear the shots, just the bullets overhead. In battle, she remembered, no-one hears the shots, just the shockwaves, like little diving jet planes, louder than the shots.

She could see only the girl with the rocket.

Kneeling in the wet and aiming two-handed she could easily shoot the girl with the rocket.

7.

Barel unpinned a grenade and pulled his chair closer to the bed. He pushed the grenade beneath his foot, jamming its lever with his sole. "You'll have to trust I have good nerves," he said.

Kav did not open his eyes.

Barel pulled the magazine from his pistol, checked that the first bullet was mobile and free of grit, and snapped the gun together again.

"Someone's coming to take you home. We're not going to let them get you, Ernst."

The eyes opened reluctantly.

"I wonder who they think they're after."

"The Lamb in the Thicket." Kay was beginning to understand them now. They wanted a victim, these Jews. They knew they had offended their God, and they accused themselves of having been weak. A sacrifice would help them, they thought. His sacrifice. He mustn't blame them. After all, Abraham was prepared to sacrifice Bosie in the desert.

The firing was very near. Sometimes stone magnifies.

"You've come to hold after false gods, Major."

"What gods are they?"

"Yourselves, I think."

"You are a brave man, Obersturmführer. Then, of course, you've seen it all before."

"I'd like a cup of water, please." Petulant, like an invalid.

A knock on the door.

Barel didn't answer.

A voice came through the heavy woodwork.

"It's Dov."

"Stay outside the door. What's happening?"

"Nothing. No-one's got in. If they should be so lucky, then the sooner they're killed."

"Give me a drink of water."

"Shut up."

Distant firing, like a pneumatic drill ten streets away.

"Water." He was a man with only one imperative.

"If I take my foot off this thing and go to the sink, then you'll certainly be dead. I may be dead, but you'll certainly be dead."

"I'd like that," said Kay. "I'd like that very much."

"All you'll be is bits."

"They'll be my own bits, Major, not like the bits you've got now."

8.

The afternoon lengthened. Footprints that all day long had dimpled the sand deepened to gouges of shadow.

The young bather was by himself now. He picked at his skin. It was blotchy and looked overclean, as if it had been exposed too long to salt water. The soles of his feet were peeling.

He examined his watch and got to his feet. He gathered

up the four scuba-suits and stowed them on the inflatables, then walked round to the inflatables' sterns, which were seaward.

He waited, fingering the great cleft in his chin and standing quietly in the water while a man and woman and their child walked past along the pebbles. Then he held his breath and stooped under the little waves. One of the inflatables bounced a little, and bubbles gushed to the surface. There was a grating sound, like metal on rock.

The young man stood up, waist deep in the sea. The inflatable rode higher now, lighter. He nosed it firmly ashore, took a second big breath and went down behind the other one.

The same bubble and bounce and grating of metal on stone.

He stood up red-faced.

A swimmer was watching him from closer to, squatting on his heels between the beach screens and the sea.

"You trawling for crayfish?"

He listened towards the town, gazed casually at his diver's watch. He was running late. "No," he said in his thick voice. "Not exactly. Come and lend a hand. I'll show you."

The young man joined him in the water and between them they lifted a heavy bundle, bound mummy-tight in black polythene, and dumped it on the rear thwart of one of the inflatables.

"You got a motor there?"

"Maybe."

They smiled together and dived again, bringing up a second bundle.

"It's an outboard, isn't it?"

"Help yourself."

The package was fastened with the sort of tensioned octopus hooks that fix luggage onto the roofs of cars.

"Watch the spring-back or you'll knock an eye out."

There they were, unwrapped, one to each inflatable, a pair of mansize overpowered triple-screw outboards.

"You don't want these," the swimmer said. "They're immense. You could power a launch with these brutes." He stood facing the far inflatable, his hands resting on the rubber laminate, his gaze thoughtful. "One little squirt of throttle and you'll take off and fly."

He heard the water stir behind him and felt a great pain in the lumbar region, just to the right of the spine. He couldn't shout, breathe, move. He didn't lose consciousness, not even come near to fainting. His jaw trembled and his whole body was paralysed on a great sob.

The other had slipped his fishing knife shallowly in and out between pelvis and kidney. A man cannot call or move when you stab him just there. Nor need he die. But this one had to. He was pinned by the elbows and stuffed under the inflatable, which juddered just a little as if his jaw still trembled.

The young bather hinged the first outboard back into its slot and screwed it down. He primed it, and moved towards the second inflatable. This one did not twitch.

A burst of automatic fire, from up in the Old Town.

It seemed muffled, like cloth being torn; but that was the sound that had travelled direct, through rock and cement and adobe and brick; it was immediately obliterated in the larger echo that blasted up between walls and rattled the teeth.

An exchange of fire in the open meant that things were going wrong. There was no way of telling if they had ever gone right.

He started both outboards.

The noise did not drown the whoosh and bang of the rocket launcher. It seemed probable that they hadn't even got in. The two girls might just be creating a diversion, of course.

There was another whoosh and a bang, detonations, a lot more shouting, sustained fire on repetition, screams.

Black smoke began to billow, and crackle like birds' wings. There was flame in the smoke, flame muffled by smoke. Hydrocarbon was burning, petrol or diesel. A vehicle was on fire.

The beach was alerted now. People were swarming, looking. A brave tribe, or afflicted with an overwhelming curiosity? He couldn't tell.

His own manoeuvres were attracting attention.

He reached inside the hamper on his boat and took out a machine pistol with its butt still folded forward, and laid it on the thwart. He placed two electrical impact grenades beside it and checked he could find them with his hand. That was the nearer problem taken care of.

Then he lifted the Armalite, slotted in the magazine, and laid out four more magazines, side by side.

One hundred rounds.

Eighty rounds a minute automatic, forty rounds single shot. Who were they kidding?''

An awful normality returned. He heard birdsong, car-noises, transistors, children's voices.

He drifted out from behind the bathing screens. The world was looking in his direction.

A smoke marker: that would be a good idea. It would confuse fire and he could dodge to and fro behind it.

His hand could not find it. He could not bring himself to tear his eyes from the beach and look inside the hamper. The desire to open throttle and retreat was overpowering.

He saw them running along the road at the top of the beach. Two of them, one of the girls, and a man.

They were being chased by soldiers, police, a whole crowd of civilians.

Away to his right there were some women gathering children together. It would be too far to throw, especially from the boat, but he threw. The grenade nearly reached them too. He threw other bombs straight up the beach.

That way he would distract the pursuers.

The explosions joined together, sowing screams.

He began to fire. He fired just ahead of the pursuers on the road. He held the gun steady and emptied a magazine, waiting for them to run into it.

Too much muzzle velocity. Every shot missed.

He reloaded.

The couple ran on to the beach. He hit a standing sun-bather, then a uniformed figure with a pistol who was run-ning some thirty yards behind them. It was a satisfying shot.

Then his male comrade was hurried from behind, caught and flung forward by a burst of fire.

The girl nearly made it down the beach. He kept a stream of aimed shots right beside her. Either she was hit from behind or she jinked into his line of fire.

He opened up the engine, trying to work out who had hit her. The outboard spluttered, flooded and stopped.

There were people all around him, ordinary people. He lashed out with the Armalite. Someone caught his ankles.

Women mostly.

He became a red mess in the water.

9.

A man has charge of his mind but not his body.

Dov at the door again. "All over."

Barel's knee was trembling, and his instep ached. It was an impossible task, a contortionist's task, to bend and slide a finger beneath his foot and anchor the lever. It was spring-loaded and his hands ran with perspiration.

Then when he held it clenched in his palm, there was the problem with the pin.

"You all right in there?"

"Perfect."

The pin too is a spring. When it is pulled out the ends part a little. It is very hard to slide it back.

The whole thing had only to snap open again like a badly loaded mousetrap and that would be that. There was nowhere to throw it.

His prisoner was so important that if he dropped it he would have to lie on it.

Or on his prisoner?

He preferred to lie on the bomb.

"I'm going outside to take a look," Dov called.

"I'll be with you in a second."

Kay was watching him all the time, the way a child watches its mother with the nappy pin and powder.

"You should try snakes, Major. You'd be very good with snakes."

Barel locked the door behind him and went up towards the sunshine.

10.

Matson coughed his coffee up. He'd been bringing a lot back lately, what with alcohol and injury, but the coffee he hawked straight into its cup where it beamed black and neat and odourless as if asking him to drink it again. Then his table trembled so much that the cup tumbled in its saucer, and slopped across the cloth, in a decent alibi of stink.

He was looking at a distant particle of leg. It was stretched into the end of the little road nearest to the square. The road was no wider than an alleyway, and deep in shadow; but his eye picked it out in hideous longshot, like a red-paper fragment in a kaleidoscope. He had no certainty that it was attached to anything. His ears, all that was left of his professionalism, recognised the whuff and slam of a launcher, and he knew what a tank-rocket could do.

Other bodies came to huddle in that tiny time-slot. Brown joints in beach-shorts, fillet steak in blue jeans. Civilian meat looks meatier than military meat. Dolls' faces are rosier, but these were children, as he thought the poet said.

He put his handkerchief to his mouth and stood up. He looked too ill and shocked for the café proprietor to object.

Anything that seems reasonable to shopkeepers is unlikely to disturb a security man. Matson shuffled unchallenged past the four officers of the police patrol who were sealing off the street.

This was unfortunate. He had to find the new town and its seafront. And when he had located the Rehov Hayarkon it would still be a fair way to number 192 and safety.

He hoped the British presence was still there, and not removed in its entirety to Jerusalem.

11.

A civilian army or an army of civilians? There were people milling everywhere, in and out of uniforms. Bodies lay crushed at their feet like wet shadows. Barel counted ten of them and then stopped. There were more than ten dead. He preferred to stop. More than ten was half a platoon. Also there were other factors.

Dr. Lubrani was one of them. Beside him Tadeus lay frothing and wheezing from a lung shot. His eyes were closed tight as if clenched against the sun. When they opened it was to show the whites. His chest still made a noise, but gently.

Dov was gasping dry-eyed. Barel didn't want to concern himself with Dov's problem for a second. He said quietly, "Get some of our people out here, will you? Leave a good guard inside, but I want about a dozen here with carbines."

Dov turned away, trembling. "Some bastard's got to Judi," he mumbled. Then he swung back and said, "Judi's dead."

"Corporal Tamir?" To command he must call her correctly.

"Yes. Corporal Tamir."

Shlomo Barel tried to hug a great calm into himself. A European calm. He felt hollow beneath the ribs, and one small reason for this was the Asiatic sound of women keening.

There were other reasons. He heard cloth being ripped. He cocked and uncocked his pistol.

A young lieutenant was walking excitedly about the square, trying not to flourish his sub-machinegun, but flourishing it all the same. He was high on action. Then there were police arriving, ambivalent, detached, taking things in.

Further away there was a bus burning. It was jammed across an intersection where the alley widened into a street. But that was down the hill. Barel tried not to look that far.

"Lieutenant."

The boy came over.

"Tell me what happened."

"We got the lot of them. I got that one there."

"Which one?"

"That one, that one there."

"The girl who's been stripped?"

"They've all been stripped. That one there. I saw her walking through the shrubbery as arrogant as hell. I got her with a leg shot."

"Why a leg shot?"

"To keep her for interrogation."

"She doesn't look too good now."

"She pulled a gun from her bag, so I decided to take

her out of it. Murderers. They don't even fight in uniform.''

"She was off-duty. She's one of ours.'' He wondered
how he had kept calm so long.

"Well, maybe not her, then,'' the lieutenant said. "I
probably got the bitch with the launcher.'' He gestured
vaguely towards the girl's body that hung naked against a
palm tree by its ankles.

"Were they all dead—when the crowd got here, I
mean?''

"You know how it is.''

"Not really. Get something and cover them up.''

Barel took off his tunic. He walked over and threaded
it between the legs of the dead Palestinian girl where she
hung upside down. "Get her cut down, will you?''

"This isn't the one you said was ours.''

"This one is the enemy. Deserving of respect. Read
your military code. Cut her down, and then run that flag
down and wrap Corporal Tamir's body properly.''

"If I try to do that with the flag this lot'll riot again.
They think she's a terrorist.''

"Let them riot,'' Barel said. "I'd love them to riot. You
encourage them to riot, Lieutenant, and I'll have my men
kill the lot of them. When a crowd starts tasting blood it's
time it drinks its own. And when it gets to disfiguring
corpses . . .''

He walked away to join Dov. "Yes,'' he said. "You're
right. Some bastard got to her.''

12.

Above the Roman stairwell there were new wooden steps.
They rose through the hardwood floors of the Martello and
into the tower itself. Here there were rooms of grace and
calm built by the rich former owner to nurse his self-
importance. Barel realised he had not had time to come
up here since returning from England.

There were leather chairs, chunky stone-topped tables,
and the kind of carved, light-filtering screens that make
opulence in the Levant look like a film set. The room
needed a Semite profusion of domestic objects to turn it
towards reality or comfort, but its surfaces had been left

uncluttered. He and Dov did not settle. They leant against the thickened glass of the window and looked down into the square.

The police had sealed it off, and their flashlights peppered the shadows. Everything, each body, weapon and cartridge case, was being documented and photographed. Judi Tamir had been brought inside, and the Palestinian girl cut down, as Barel had insisted. Tadeus had been moved with the rest of the nearly alive. The others lay as they'd fallen.

A tall man was negotiating with an Army warrant officer at the far corner of the square. He was waving some kind of pass, something glued into an overlarge cover as big as a child's birthday card.

The warrant officer called for confirmation to someone unseen, someone below the front of the Martello, then surprised Barel by letting the man through. What was even more astonishing was that the man was wearing a kaffiyeh full on his head, and an ornamental robe halfway between a burnous and a caftan. Hardly the dress to earn safe-conduct.

The man planted his sandals fastidiously among the carnage and picked his way across the square.

"It's the Wandering Arab," Dov said. Barel was on his way downstairs.

The visitor had beaten him to it, and was already inside. The young conscript was sitting in the anteroom and Barel heard the man ask him, "And how is your London business?" Then he turned towards Barel before the soldier could reply. "I am sorry I present myself at such a time of trouble. There are, nonetheless, certain words I must bring you."

Barel couldn't bear to be near Judi Tamir's desk. He led the visitor to his own quarters, and Dr. Ibrahim Nuseibeh clucked, tutted and waited while he made and served green tea in tall Arab beakers.

Nuseibeh sipped and said, "I had to alert the Army to all this. Even here in Jaffo-TelAviv I could not connect with your number. However, I foiled this little contretemps for you. The general has already congratulated me."

"You work for me, not the general."

"I could not connect with you. Besides, the greatest news is shouted from the highest mountain."

When an Arab gesticulates he has too many hands, and only one brings the truth. Barel regarded him with distaste, and said, "You are supposed to be in London."

"London is a little difficult for me at the moment."

"It is hard to know why you spare us so much of your time, Nuseibeh."

Again the blur of fingers, but holding a tiny card. "Merely to tell you I have changed the name of my bank here in Tel Aviv. *Here*, Major." He smiled his uncomfortable illusion of chewed leaf before forcing the address on Barel. "And to add the immediate matter that your Mr. Mat*son* is here somewhere. He was on the very boat I—"

Terrible to have your enemy in your hand and be unwilling to squeeze.

"I am not at all useful at anything *direct*, Major. But your own people—"

Barel's voice was cracking with such a fury he had to start again. "Let him go." He swallowed to prevent himself professing the sweetness of his plans for Matson. "Do you suppose his visit is connected with what went on out there?"

"I believe in Fate, Major Barel. Fate makes a different shape from coincidence."

"So you conclude this is not coincidence?"

"I am aware of the man's contacts in London. Indeed, I allowed myself to personalise my curiosity a little."

"You met him for lunch?"

"*And* their Mr. Pomeroy. You see, I *knew* you would discover how well I go about your business. I can have no secrets from you."

They each had their need for the tea.

"What is this Matson?"

"He is not an Englishman. He is Irish. The Irish are all aristocrats at heart. They like influence, intrigue, connection. Then there was their well-known sympathy with the Kaiser's Germany and worse, far worse—the Nazis."

Barel sipped and said nothing.

"You will have heard of Lord Casement, Major? Viscount Casement was merely a romantic—"

"I don't believe he was a viscount."

"Mat*son* is something much worse. He is a snob. Doubtless you know he is the lover of the daughter of this man we mustn't mention?"

A stillness settled over Barel, a stillness so great that the Arab thought he hadn't heard him.

"This young woman the old Nazi kept locked away for love, Major. Well, they all have their many lovers. It is the custom in London. But it is your prisoner who interests me. The British must know he is who you say he is. That is why Mat*son* was sent to rescue him." Nuseibeh rose rustling to his feet before offering his greatest gift. "Your recent sadness in Spain, the person I was privileged to know as Yitzak. The man *directly* responsible is among those who were here today." He made his way to the door. "I have counted, and I do not think that any of them are going back."

He was not going to earn his money so easily. Barel followed him and said, "Isn't Pomeroy the real villain?"

"You can hardly suppose that such events as these are a customary by-product of English diplomacy."

"I'm talking about the death of my agent."

It was a difficult conversation to hold in a corridor, especially one the Arab was trying to escape along. Nuseibeh offered the palms of his hands and exclaimed, "Pomeroy does not arrange *that* sort of thing. How shall I explain him in such a way as to make myself convincing?" He examined Barel's eyes, which were bloodshot and tired. "Marcus Pomeroy simply does not intrigue—he is too fastidious. He is like the women in English novels. He would have his feet amputated rather than put his toes in a dirty sock."

"Himmler used to sniff flowers."

"Himmler was not *English,* Major Barel. He was not even American. There, in my view, you have the end of it."

Dov was barring their way, as Barel had instructed. "Not quite," he beamed. "We've got a little surprise for you."

A tape-recorder was playing, and the voice on it checked Nuseibeh. It sounded so lifelike, so fruity, that he glanced about him as if he was walking into a trap.

He was listening to a recording of Shlomo Barel talking

to a man he knew very well indeed: Shlomo Barel in his thick English, the man in his lofty home-counties Oxbridge.

"This idiot called us up," Dov complained. "Can it really be Matson? He said his name was Matson."

Nuseibeh licked his lip at the major as if still sensing a catch. "That's him," he agreed. "That's very certainly the voice of the man I had lunch with. And now, if you will excuse me, I must test whether or not this same desk clerk we talk of is going to revise his list and let me back into London."

13.

There were soldiers everywhere, particularly near the sea-front; but pink-skinned fair-haired men are not favourite objects of suspicion. Matson followed his bad breath into the British Embassy and said, "I want the consular section."

A young Israeli secretary got within smelling distance, grimaced, and led him into a corridor.

The walls were marbled. Halfway along there was a grill, like the pay-desk in a cinema. The duty clerk sat locked behind it.

"I've had my book stolen."

The man became watchful. "That's not a matter for us. It's for the town police force to look into. Is it a valuable item?"

"I don't think you understand. It's the manuscript of the book I'm writing, and it's been stolen."

The clerk was undoubtedly English, an officer in the consular service, but he had to pull a little printed list from under the blotter as if he were running out of conversational phrases. He studied it and said, "So—ah—you've been and lost your manuscript?"

"My typescript," Matson corrected. "It's been stolen. I shall need someone to write out a description of it in Hebrew. For the town police, as you say."

"I think you'd better wait through here." The clerk touched a bell, and somewhere behind him there was a jangle of keys, a snapping back of dead-locks. A marble panel opened beside the duty grill and Matson found himself looking at an English redcap, in white blanco and creases, for all the world as if he were back in Aldershot doing jankers.

He was led towards a man who was bending over a desk, his face almost hidden by a ball-pen and an orange. There may have been fingers, too, incense even. There was no disguising the bald patch.

"Well, Paddy—what an odd penny you are." He gestured towards a chair covered in phone-books. "Stirring up mayhem and insurrection on sovereign soil? Still, somebody has to do it, so why not us? After all, we Brits are responsible for most of this little town, what with Allenby, Wingate and Charles Clore."

"Not to mention St. George, as your Mr. Nuseibeh was kind enough to remind us all."

"Ah—*him.*" Pomeroy gazed about him, as if looking for a wall with a window in it. There was no window.

Matson did not expect to get in and out of 192 Rehov Hayarkon without Marcus Pomeroy discovering he had been there, but he had hoped to do so before Pomeroy could find out what he was up to. He decided to be angry. "You made a remark about motorboats the other night."

"I don't remember."

"I remember. You said to Quinlan, 'We won't try to rescue him in a motorboat, that's for certain.' "

"I said 'gunboat.' Are you trying to make a connection?"

"Is there one?"

"You'd better ask someone else. Frankly, I don't know. Ours is an imprecise art, as I've said before, a bit like surgery for cancer. I didn't set the thing up, if that's what you mean. The people Nuseibeh spoke to aren't very susceptible to guidance, that's all. You wanted to erase Yitzak. They wanted more."

"Now they've cocked it up."

"They won't see it that way. They put eleven of their people on the rack—that's the way they'll see it. If they could have lifted Kay for us it would have been a coup. As it is, they scrubbed some Israelis. They like scrubbing Israelis."

"They might have lifted Kay and had him killed with

them as they fought their way back to the beach—did you think of that?''

"I play chess."

Matson had already hit him once today.

"Everyone could have sat back then. End of problem. With all of us where we started, self-satisfied and in the right. That's what diplomacy is about," Pomeroy went on.

"Kay would have been dead."

"As I say, an imprecise art." He gave up attempting to eat the orange. "We've got to get you back home, Paddy. That'll be finite enough. Can you swim?''

TWELVE

1.

Brenda greeted him with an old-fashioned kiss on the nose.

Anyone who returns from the Front is a hero, he reflected sourly, even if he has only been there to deliver soup.

The kiss was only partial, in both senses Matson could place on the word. It was broken off for her to say, "Thing keeps on phoning."

"Thing?"

"Tiny Thing Ginevra. Bleeding chats me up as if I was her big sister. And yours."

"Yes?"

"She hopes you're not up to anything risky. For her sake. Good job I know you've had no time to nooky that little bird. You haven't, have you?"

"You're bruising my face."

The phone rang. Brenda ran to answer it.

"I answer the phone here," he said. "It's mine. Remember?"

She listened to it and handed it to him. "It's Ginevra," she said. "She's yours. Remember?"

"It's become all convoluted while you've been away," Ginevra complained. "There's been a raid."

"I know."

"A raid on Daddy."

"I was there," he said modestly.

She sounded impressed. He supposed that was what silence meant.

When he had put the phone down, Brenda said, "I've

arranged your mail by subject on the kitchen table. All except this. I couldn't put it on the pile marked *Love Notes*. Someone's calling you a prat.''

He would tell her off and turn her out later. For the moment the letter took his interest. Its message was neither handwritten nor typed. It was dot-matrixed and unsigned.

> *Don't be a prat. If I can find you, so can they. Stay at home where it's cool. You're as hot as a miner's jock-strap at the moment.*

''I'd better go and see Leonard,'' he said, thoughtfully. ''Still, it's hardly the tablets of stone, is it?''

''Leonard doesn't know words like prat.''

''Leonard is a master of disguises.''

2.

''You should have stuck with Mr. Layt-Joyner, Patrick. As a duo you two would have gone far.''

''There was no harm,'' Matson said sullenly. ''No harm and no danger.''

''Not to this department? If we'd gone under after all my efforts to keep us afloat, I'd have wrung your young neck. You and that lost book code! When did you last use that?''

''When I was in the Thugs. Dammit, Leonard, it was an unforeseen emergency. How could I possibly know that the second I set foot in Tel Aviv someone would start to blow the place up?''

''Which way did you come out?''

''RAF from Cyprus.''

''I imagine that getting to Cyprus was the crafty one?''

''Our embassy in Tel Aviv buys its sherry in bulk from Cyprus.''

''You mean it was your turn in the barrel?''

''Was to have been. Then they made inquiries and it transpired the Israelis were perfectly happy to let me walk out.''

''After what happened to Mr. Yitzak? I find that incredible. Even our own side thinks it was one of us. Quinlan keeps on telling me off for spitting in the gravy.''

"Not my fault, Leonard.''

"Pity you were sitting so near the plate, just the same. And now I have to put up with Pomeroy shopping you.''

"He said we were both to hold our tongues.''

"Stuff!'' Leonard got up to look for some Scotch. "In our business everyone tells tales. Besides, if you will go limping into embassies, you must expect to get your hoofprints on a memorandum somewhere.''

"I'm glad we're so secure.'' Matson saw that Leonard had only taken the one glass, and was now filling it with his own mixture of three fingers Scotch and one of water, just like a French housewife with a vinaigrette. His own exclusion from the drinks ritual was beginning to look terminal.

"Not secure. Inert. They want you to remain inert, Patrick. You drink this muck—I'm the one who has to keep a clear head round here.''

Matson took the glass and decided it was meant to signal the end of his secondment.

"Of course Pomeroy shopped you. The next time his dirty Levantines get up to something, he doesn't want you in a position to discover it. He doesn't even want to discover it himself. He doesn't want anyone to discover it. Modern governments do not collapse because of treachery, skulduggery and intrigue, Patrick. Such things are the staple fare of governance. They collapse because of *discovered* treachery and etcetera—what the unenlightened call 'freedom of information' and fools 'journalistic flair.' If all the covert operators could get together and silence all the big mouths then governments would have a perfect world. That's Pomeroy's philosophy. That's what makes him so good. Pomeroy's a sound man.''

"Thanks for telling me.''

"It's not my own idea. It comes from the White House. I had a Yank in a bespoke suit tell it to me in the Savile Club. It's got gamma minus written all over it.''

"So where does that leave me?''

"Buying lunch, I hope.'' On the way to the lift he added, ''A lot of good men have come badly unstuck simply by allowing themselves to grow suspicious of their own side. Trust people, that's my motto. They rarely set out to deceive this department. Though I must admit that there's one or two people like Marcus Pomeroy who try hard to deceive themselves.''

In the street, Leonard asked, ''So what will you report to your Chislehurst lady?''

''Nothing honest, I'm afraid. I saw the embassy digests.''

''She'd be right not to hope. The Yanks won't help us. We've stressed to them how keen HMG is to repossess itself of her venerable dad, but the message is that the White House has an even greater determination to keep its green fingers on the Land of the Biblical Kings. It is, after all, the *de facto* fifty-first state.''

''*De facto* perhaps. No-one will go with *de jure.*''

''You may well be right. But poor Mr. K is going to find *de facto*'s as fatal as *de jure* when the hangman comes to weigh him for the drop.''

They paused outside their favourite little restaurant.

''You haven't been writing me any threatening letters have you, Leonard?''

''What—on a word-processor? I've sent all of mine to forensic. What was the post-mark?''

Brenda hadn't kept the envelope.

It looked as if Leonard was going to be discreet about the omission. He led him inside and said, ''Mine were from Amsterdam. What the whisperers tell me is that they're death threats. That little lot that Barel used to head, they always sent an enigmatic warning first.''

''It's too bloody melodramatic for words.''

''Remember what they were formed for? To avenge the killings at the Munich Olympics. When you've got a hundred per cent success rate you can let yourself be a bit loud. What'll you start with? I'm staying away from soup myself.''

3.

''I don't much like you today, Matty; but for the purposes of social commerce''—Leonard's lopsided face became momentarily full of sardine—''for the purposes of all that nonsense I'm willing to concede that I dislike you rather less than most of the imbeciles I have to deal with."

"Matty" represented a linguistic thaw.

Leonard speared a fresh sardine. "This is a disgusting little restaurant, a bit like the Costa Brava. Even down to the television set. I drop in here during the summer months, as you know, to catch up on some wickets."

Matson's neck was too bruised to turn. Leonard didn't need to turn his.

"Who's playing what?"

"Us and India. You should keep abreast, Paddy. That's the trouble with being born in Ireland. It's a Minor County. The Israelis don't play at all, of course. Heaven knows why—they've got the weather for it."

Matson decided he was still an invalid. He dripped some wine from the ice-bucket and tilted his chair.

They watched Chandra bowling. He bowled so slowly that the ball seemed to hang up there mouthful after mouthful.

"Giving it the air," Leonard explained.

"Like a grenade."

Suddenly the image split and dissolved. Transmission was being interrupted by a newsflash.

Leonard was chewing wisdom. His face slowed as he recognised the image on the screen and then it stopped. He leapt to turn up the volume. He didn't have the waiter do it. He did it himself.

Even with a battered eye, Matson could recognise the Interrogation Centre in Jaffo. He'd been there only yesterday.

4.

At seven in the evening a Citroen 2CV blocked one of the two walkways leading to the square. Two men and a girl got out. The girl carried a loud-hailer.

The two men lifted her onto their shoulders and she said through the hailer-megaphone: "Do you know who they've got in there? Do you know who it is? Do you know why those animals came here and grenaded those kids on the beach?"

The police should have stopped her, of course. Especially in the second the hailer went wrong and screamed electric noises like an air-raid siren. On the other hand, it's hard to hurry towards a hailer blasting sound, and harder still to push quickly through a crowd.

"We'll tell you who it is."

Also the police were curious. Some of them still knew what the building was, and that made them more curious still to know who it was they'd got in there . . .

"You read it in yesterday's paper. You heard it on the news. You heard the name of the monster they've caught. I bet you kidded yourselves he was locked up in Lod. The Prime Minister told us he was going to the Justice House in Jerusalem. Well, he's not. He's here with us on the coast where his friends come and blitz down innocent folk in the streets . . . Chuck bombs at our kids as they play on the sand."

The hailer went wrong again, building up hysteria like a probe in the pith of a tooth.

"Tonight just minutes ago the Prime Minister said he is here . . . Tell me his name."

The name *"Halder—Ernst Halder"* was quiet after the megaphone, but it moved around the alleys and streets of the Old Town like a forest wind threatening to tear up trees by the roots . . .

"You were told he was at Justice. Let him have his Justice . . ."

The police could not move. The 2CV had blocked one end of the square, which was already over-filled with people.

People pumped up into an instant frenzy.

Two men were pushed closer and closer together.

One said, "They killed the doctor, you know. He was a good man."

The other picked up a bloodstained stone from the lip of the cactus-bed and tossed it against an upstairs window. It did not break the glass.

Stones, shouts, screams were flung into the air. Most bounced back. There were not many windows.

Everything became as disturbed and futile as a dream. The tower and the detention centre were impregnable, save for a few high windows, and these remained unbroken though struck many times. Facing them across the square was the side of a Tabernacle. At either end were the blind ends of houses. People tossed the world in the air and it fell back on their faces. A policeman's cheekbone gaped from a ricocheting fragment. Several people lay moaning among the cactuses.

The military tried to arrive.

In its frustration the crowd began to turn on the soldiers, on the police, and on the two young men and the girl with the loud-hailer.

The last three were trying to get back to their car.

Then a strange thing came to pass, almost biblical in wonder. A light came on in an upstairs room of the tower. It was the window that had first been marked by the stone.

A man stood there in military uniform. He had a bleached bandage round his head, as if he had travelled from the desert. His arm was in a snow-white sling to command respect.

The light was so bright and so dramatic that everybody stopped. They saw him unfasten an inner window, and then throw back an outer shield of bullet-proof glass.

He stood gazing down, a rabbinical figure as majestic as Moses or Abraham.

He said nothing. The length of the dramatic pause was awe-inspiring.

He was waiting while the police arrested the loud-hailer.

Then he said, "It is true. He is here. It is I who brought him back to this place." His Hebrew was simple and cadenced like the words of the prophets. "I brought him back for Justice. Not my Justice. Not your Justice. I brought him back to face the Justice of a People who have been without Justice for two thousand years, and whose needs cry to Heaven."

The whisper came again, and there was no loud-hailer to interrupt it. It was the whisper of throats that have been loud with emotion but are now touched with awe.

"I should like you, dear friends, to make me a promise. Will you make me a promise? I will show you this man, if you promise not to harm him. If you promise not to harm him, then this is my word. I swear to you before God he will hang in Jerusalem."

He waited for a moment, then asked, "Will you make me this promise?"

The air was full of murmurs, full of breath, indecision. A single voice in the crowd called, "No-one says No!"

The soldier gestured with his hand and another figure stood in the light, a figure who trembled and whose hands were manacled before him. His face was ash-grey, but surprisingly young. He wore a soiled white shirt and trousers which did not belong to him.

"I promise you Ernst Halder will hang."

Then the light went out, and the bullet-proof shield was pulled to.

Television cameras had been recording the scene of the raid, and the resulting confusion. They did not get a good shot of the prisoner because of the street lamps and the tops of the palm trees, but his image was nonetheless given to the nation and then to the world in guilt and dejection.

At the foot of the stairs Barel tore off his bandage and his sling. "The art of gaining and keeping attention," he said. He didn't quite grin. The bodies still lay uncollected in the cellars, and their nearness sobered him.

He unfastened Dov's handcuffs as an elaborate afterthought.

5.

Fossit left Matson to pay for lunch, and he took his time over it.

When he got back he found that the department had been busy.

"They put our chap on show," Leonard said. He led Matson into his office and set the video recorder. "This is bad quality magnetic, I'm afraid. We got it from ITN who got it from NBC who bought it from an Israeli independent. There's the line incompatibility, plus the chromatic mismatch—you know the same old complaints. But at least this is from the uncut original."

Matson's head had been changing shape all day. "If it's American you'll oblige me by going soft on the yellow, Leonard. My liver won't stand it."

The usual run-in of blurs, power-flashes and tramlines, just like a bad hangover; then they saw a square full of riot, the jerky zoom on a leaf-obscured window.

"That," said Matson," is our Mr. Barel. Major Shlomo Barel."

"Hurt his paw, I see. Means you got all your sums right, Patrick. And that's Kay."

"I can see half a face, and half a body. Looks fit enough. Can't we get to the original, and have the thing blown up?"

"It can't be done. It was taken on tape, not film, so it's magnetic all the way through the process." He switched it off.

"They didn't let the prisoner speak, I gather?"

"No. I got a translation of Barel, though. Want it word for word?"

"Hardly."

"I thought not. It was a personal promise to hang our man. The Anglo-American agencies have been pretty cool about that, but there's no knowing what might come out of things like *Newsnight* or in tomorrow's papers. The daughter could be in for a shock. Oh, here's something else for you. This is better quality stuff. New item from Israeli National via NBC and BBC." He switched on again. "They're burying some people killed in the raid."

They watched for what seemed some time, though it could not have been longer than the half minute or so of the news item.

"Seems an awful lot of emotion to me," Fossit said.

"It's the dead girl's body, I suppose."

"A coffin, not a body. They can't all be her relatives, can they? I'm glad it's your desk, Matty. Very odd people in the Levant." His eyebrows went up and up, seeking agreement, sympathy.

"It's the women," Matson said, and watched Fossit's eyebrows droop to half-mast. "Different race from men."

"Yes, another minor county. Bury them fast out there. Latest thing is they're trying it with our chap. Rushing his trial right forwards, or that's the buzz."

Matson sat himself down. His buttocks in general did not ache. "That means they haven't got a confession."

"Yes, a tiny glimmer of hope." Fossit brooded while the tape ran out. "You're right, you know. It's those Mediterranean women. Cut your balls off as soon as look at you." He stood behind Matson and dropped a hand on his shoulder—an odd little gesture that sometimes made Matson wonder. "Thank God that television screen is as close as you're ever going to get to it again."

"I was thinking of going to pick up Mr. Layt-Joyner's luggage."

"Your passport won't even be cleared for the Isle of Wight this time. Rest on it, Matty. Not even for Chislehurst."

6.

The major was shaking him awake.

The major and his little bully boy. It took him a long time to come to himself.

Sometimes he woke to the conviction he was someone quite different.

He had read about torture, but only in the colour supplements. What had been conveyed was the sense of worthlessness, guilt, the humiliation. But that was in Greece or South America, where a certain sort of torturer had been recruited: an ignorant man or woman, whose highest expression of culture was a smart set of clothes and a clean lavatory. Show them a human being without clothes or someone deprived of soap and they would conclude that he had deservedly fallen from the hands of the Living God and treat him accordingly. Their victims felt bad because they were fed diminished values by people of excessive brutality.

Here it was different. The brutality was extreme, but not excessive. More, it was clear that Barel and Lieutenant Gorodish were not intrinsically brutal, and hated him for causing them to be so. And as for the girl, it was a pity that the Jews do not have Grace as a philosophical concept; because sometimes she clearly lived by it.

Her guilt had been their point of balance. It was her poor dead guilt and their live hate, which was also guilt, that was beginning to infect him.

He knew he was awake now, because the major was holding him a cup.

He knew he was awake, and he knew who he was. They were forcing him to be the man who bears the Jews' guilt.

He took the cup. They were offering him a little whisky

and a lot of water. He did not drink at once. He wondered how to separate them. He peered into it timidly, and swilled it around, but still did not drink. The major had offered him a cup, and what the cup contained was the total problem.

"You are going to be leaving us," Barel said. "There may not be any more drinks except for the last one."

It wasn't a problem he could solve.

"Halder won't drink with us," Dov said.

"Any German is happy to compete with a bottle." There was no hostility left in Barel. He placed a jug of water near to his prisoner, and left the bottle within reach.

"I am not a German." The importance of the statement left him free to drink.

Barel held out his hand. "I am truly sorry it had to be this way." He thought it was clear he held out his hand in respect.

What a pity the other did not take it.

"The English always shake hands," Dov admonished.

Even now, every proposition was treated by the prisoner to his closed-eyed scrutiny of contempt. "You're confusing us with the French." He did not speak again for a long time, merely drank; and, as with a dying man, his silence took on a kind of power. "It was a bad show about your corporal, Major. I thought she had something to her."

He drank more whisky, and smacked his lips over it. He still could not find a way to separate it from the water.

THIRTEEN

1.

The big helicopter bumped onto the Martello and settled.

David Ben-Yosof acknowledged Barel's salute. General Zefat stood back and grinned while Barel introduced Dov to the Minister, and then the eight-man Guard of Honour grounded arms and dispersed.

"We're a tiny unit here, sir. It's hard to fall-in enough men for the military niceties."

Ben-Yosof seized Barel's hand and held on tight. "Timing is its own nicety, Major. As I was saying to the General on the way over, results are what count. Not cosmetics. The Cabinet was delighted at that brief television exposure last night." He let go and said, "We'll take him from you now. Thanks for all you've done."

"I've done nothing."

"That lot have done it for you, in a sense. They've come ra-raing in to rescue him, and proclaimed to the world that he's our man."

"As the great give, so do they take away."

"Does that follow?"

"The PLO are hardly going to bother with an Englishman now, are they?"

Yigael Zefat stepped forward and said, "I think it makes it certain, the Palestinian connection. It's not the first time they've stuck their necks out for a Nazi."

As they went down the concrete stairs, Barel heard himself say, but quietly, to Zefat, "It defies common sense."

"It's just that their hatred for us is so comprehensive."

They stood in the Mess while Dov took the Minister to wash his hands.

General Zefat said, "He likes what he's got. It's difficult."

Barel still didn't understand.

"Give a Cabinet Minister an easy triumph, and all that sticks in his mind is 'easy.' This one is going to be a difficult triumph, Shlomo. For him and for the Prime Minister. The word they'll remember is 'triumph.' No-one likes an easy lay."

"You make it sound like a whore's game."

"Find me a better image."

Dov came back by himself and obliged them both by laughing.

Then Ben-Yosof returned, relaxed to find them happy. He took several glassfuls quickly. Barel judged the man's sleep had not been easy these last nights.

He flicked his cuffs, but as a pantomime gesture. He was going to be sociable with the troops. He said, "What I'm looking forward to now is the rigour of the game. Every trial is a game. The more important the trial, the higher the stakes, the more elaborate the ritual. But it's still just a game. You should hear the Minister of Justice on this. He was very good in Cabinet. The trial game, the court game, has its own rules, he says. Its rules are not the same as truth, he assured us of that—though in this case it would make no difference if they were. Still, truth has no part of the rules. What is needed is evidence. Lots of irrefutable evidence. And you need a man in the dock. The evidence need have nothing to do with the man in the dock, there's the beauty of it." He drained another glass and said, "Well, we've got the evidence, and I must thank you gentlemen for putting the man in the dock. There's just one thing more—this woman he lives with."

"His daughter, sir. We're pretty clear now that she's his daughter."

"Halder's daughter. Either his mistress or his daughter. I'll accept daughter if you say daughter. The general asked me to put this to you myself. We're a sob nation, Major Barel. Too much heart, too many tears. Some would say too sentimental. I don't want a pretty girl grizzling in the courtroom and drumming up sympathy for that swine."

Yigael Zefat spoke. "We've already contacted Amos Reitel in London, but it'll be hard for him to do anything for us and keep his hands clean. He'll try, of course."

"It's just that your men are acquainted with the necessary bit of London, Major."

"Can't you refuse her a visa for the trial?"

"With the world looking on? I'd sooner she simply stopped breathing. Can we take a look at the prisoner?"

Zefat interrupted. "One more thing, sir. But it has some bearing." He turned to Barel. "Shlomo, what about Yitzak? Have you taken any action?"

The major waited in controlled annoyance before saying, "I have put certain matters in hand." He hadn't wanted Dov to hear this.

"Will they compromise a move towards the girl?"

"What I have initiated will be quite separate."

The Minister, who understood not one word, beamed. "Providing this new operation retains its integrity. Don't forget, Major, that young lady who died here yesterday was someone's daughter, too."

"Yes, sir. I know the parents. Not as well as General Zefat does, but I know them."

On the way out to the prisoner, the general said, "I'm glad you two get along, Shlomo. It's a bad thing about Judi. It'll finish her mother. Sorry the snake-man couldn't be kept alive. Still, politically it won't do any harm. There's American money behind those laboratories."

"He was a good man, sir. We liked him. He offered to appear in Court for the defence."

2.

They didn't stay long in the cell. David Ben-Yosof looked briefly at the prisoner, then needed to wash his hands once again.

The general followed Barel back to the Mess. "You know how it is, Shlomo. You had to buckle his face a bit, and politics isn't about that sort of thing."

Barel was growing less and less amused. "He knows why we did it. We did it because he told us to do it, the bastard."

"*I* told you and you did it."

"Now he tells us we didn't need to do it. Will he say the same about the little girl in Chislehurst?"

"You needed to do it, Shlomo. I needed you to do it. If he had broken down and admitted he was Halder it would have been perfect. It would have been like Eichmann. But he didn't. And it's still marvellous. I work with politicians, Shlomo. They make me look always for the perfect. If I can't find it, then I'll find ways to feed them with the merely marvellous, as I told you."

"He's a bastard."

"Well, well."

"A fastidious bastard."

"Politician is the word."

They heard the Minister's laughter booming in the corridor, perhaps to cover the embarrassment of the lavatory being flushed. Then they heard his voice, as it addressed Dov as if he were the world at large. "They tell me that to resist torture's a bit like trying to fool a lie detector. You give away something, even by your squeak and squirm."

The Minister came in, surprising everyone by refusing any more to drink. "What interests me is how a man like you keeps his cool in face of all that squeak and squirm, Major Barel?"

"I know that when there's shit there'll always be a shovel. And someone to shovel it."

The phone rang behind the bar. An orderly took it, then called Dov.

Dov listened and said, "The prisoner is in the helicopter, sir."

"Is he secure?"

Barel answered, "Yes. He's chained hand and foot and shackled to the seating."

"Then I'll take that last drink. Now listen, gentlemen. We are delighted. We know the man is guilty. We shall prove him guilty a thousand times over. There is no shadow of doubt. Our case is so strong we shall scorch away even the shadows beyond the shadows." He raised his wine ceremoniously, pleasing no-one. "The confession was not for his trial. It was for now; to silence the British and satisfy the Americans. Well, we haven't got it."

''Simply to keep our good name in the world?''

''If you like. If you like. Well, the Americans care only to see a fair trial. And as for the British . . .''

''He still claims he is a British citizen.''

''Who in the world gives a fig for the opinions of the British? Even the British do not care for their own good name. I was a British citizen myself once. I know.''

He was easy to laugh with, easy to hate. Barel followed him and his general upstairs to the helicopter pad, and decided he had done both.

The rotor-turbine began to scream. The two men climbed on board. There had been no hospitality for the pilot and crewmen who had stayed with the plane, and no last words for the prisoner.

As Barel stood with Dov, eyes straight ahead in front of the eight-man Guard of Honour, it struck him that he would never see again the man who so persistently had called himself Kay.

3.

They left the helipad and went back down the spiral stairs and entered the Mess in silence.

''What I could use,'' said Barel, ''is a real drink. And it's on me.''

''That's right. It's on you,'' Dov said. ''You didn't share your little reprisal scheme for Yitzak.''

''It'll stay unshared. And if you push it, you'll do the buying. Forget what I said to the Gods from the Sky. Some of my personal shit I don't spread on other people's tomatoes, including yours. Not even from a command helicopter.''

''Here are your whiskies, gentlemen.'' The orderly served them and placed himself where he had been all day, at a discreet distance.

''One thing you do know. We've got a leaky general. What you learned about squaring Shmuel Shmuel, you learned because he asked me in front of you.''

''I don't think the worse of him for that. He was speaking man to man.''

''In our business there's no man to man. Some things you don't even tell to your pillow.''

"I still don't know what we're actually doing, even so."

"True, but when it's done, you'll be able to say, 'Ah, so we did it.' I want no man to be able to say that to me."

"Even about Halder?"

"Even him. Things are starting to drip like a rusty bucket. Just because the unit achieves something good, I don't expect the politicians to go blowing our cover."

Dov waited until the orderly had again moved away, then sank his voice and said, "Which brings me to the real question, the Irish malt question: when do I go back to London?"

"Ah—the Chislehurst girl? Let's take a walk to the office."

They strolled along the corridor. Somehow the whole place stank. Or it did to Barel. It smelled of the Minister and the general. It was drenched in three days of brutality and funk. But most, it oozed death, even though the dead had been removed overnight. They walked past the storeroom where the men had been laid, and then the little sick room which had housed the two women. There was no stink here. If there were, it would be of the death of love.

They sat themselves in the office and looked at each other sourly.

"That mess-waiter couldn't hear me," said Dov. "He stayed at the end of the bar."

"I invited you here for this." Barel reached into a metal filing cabinet and pulled out a bottle. "It's a Scottish malt. But I bought it a long time ago. And what I've already bought is cheaper than what I haven't." He fumbled some paper cups from the water machine and poured. "As for returning to London, forget it."

Dov relaxed into incredulity. "But *you* can't go. For you it really would be suicide."

"Yes. I'm sure I'm rather high on someone's list for a sack of cement."

"Dental filling, Shlomo. Don't limit yourself." The scotch was very good, but he sipped without interest, wondering how much he should ask. "I don't think I deserve to be left in the dark," he said.

Shlomo poured a giant slug of malt into his own beaker, and topped up Dov's almost untasted drink. "The short answer is that ten minutes ago I proposed to get drunk.

And the long answer, my old friend,''—he punched Dov's shoulder with a twinkle which left his eyes quite empty— ''is that before I am sober, and you if you'll join me, Miss Kay-Halder will be dead. It is just that I need to be very drunk to pull some kinds of murder. And murder is what it will be, when I kill that particular lady.''

He had Dov's attention now, if only by discussing the impossible. ''I am going to empty my mind out for you— some of my mind. And I do seriously suggest you pay that malt the proper degree of respect, because I really need someone to be drunk with by tonight.''

Dov sank half the beaker, and topped it up from the water fountain.

''That's better. Thanks to the dribblers and spewers you learned that Matson and Fossit have a surprise or two coming to them. As it happens, Amos has already had Matson given a hiding . . .''

''A *hiding!*''

''It's not enough, I grant you. Though had I known in time, I might have left it at that and concentrated on Fossit.''

''Our boys?''

''I'm glad to say not. Some lads who, though not exactly kosher, have experienced during infancy the necessary rabbinical attention with the ring and the knife. Americans, I believe, looking for a flight back home—as simple as that.''

''Good for old Amos.''

''Oh, indeed. Shall we just say I have acted towards Fossit and Matson as I believe they acted towards Schmuel—haphazardly? We now come to focus on the lady.''

He walked to the chart-roller and pulled down a street plan.

Dov knew what it was. He had lived with that plan in his mind for a month, before they had switched their attention to trains and stations. It detailed houses and streets around Caves Road, Chislehurst. ''Sometimes I think we should have shown him this,'' he said. ''Shown him this instead of doing what we did. We could have said, 'Your daughter is here.' '' His finger stabbed to the house by the

Common. " 'Now say what we want, and we may let her stay there.' "

"Never, dearest Dov, make a promise for someone else to break. We could have milked him for the price of such a promise, true, but the little prick who came here this morning would have made us break it." Was Barel drunk, or just tired? "We're soldiers, Dov, soldiers after all. Sometimes I think soldiers are the only decent people."

"I'll grant you that, Shlomo."

"Right. Miss Kay-Halder here. You can bet this whole area"—his arm sketched a circle—"is alive with boys and girls with guns up their jumpers and knives behind their ears. If I sent you in, or if I sent me in, then the lady would be dealt with, bet your old mother. We'd get ourselves in, but would we get out?"

"Seriously, I doubt it."

"We turn our attention to the widow's house next door."

"Our key witness."

"Our nark and informant. It's beautiful how easy this stuff is to drink. Let it help you recall the kernel of the plan. We do the rough stuff, we two and Amos. We have Shmuel with a car in case things misfire . . ."

"Like London Underground going on strike."

"Exactly. And Amos has his back-up team inside the widow's house. And there I have him keep them, as soon as it transpires that Shmuel has spilled the slop. And the boys are still next door, being very quiet—how long has it been?"

"Four or five days."

"Getting highly frustrated and starting to grow spiteful. So in a couple of hours I've got to make a phone-call." Barel lifted the internal phone. "Mess? I'll sign for another bottle, please. Bring it down to the office. We seem to have run out of drink." He put the phone back carefully. "Now we have a little code to send. The boys needn't break through any security net; they're already safe inside. All they need do is hit her and run." He picked up the phone and dialled London. "This will take a bit of time on International. I've got to discover a time-window that will let me ring, ring off, ring again, then repeat. You know how it is."

It took no time at all to pass the code.

Ginevra Kay was unlucky.

4.

The Parliamentary Select Committee sat in a wood-panelled darkness. The gloom was only partially dispersed by clusters of those low-powered light bulbs that are on issue in all buildings occupied by the Ministry of Works. They hung in little forty-watt clusters and Fossit decided their rays were about as ineffectual in the brown atmosphere as dollops of butter in a pan of army gravy. He concluded, after some thought, that the low wattage was a concession to antique wiring. One day, in some future made buoyant with North Sea oil, all power cables in all Ministry of Works institutions, including the House of Commons, would be brailed out and replaced by something appropriate to the twentieth century. It would be the twenty-first century by then, of course, but there would be light.

He had had such thoughts many times before, and they were not interrupted by once more having to give his succinct little resumé of the events surrounding Kay's abduction.

He finished, noted a fair degree of professional admiration around the table, and waited for the coughs and shufflings to subside.

"Mr. Fossit—ah, how many people do your people have to—ah—supervise at any one time?"

"How many . . ."

"Men like this . . ." consulting a note ". . . Yitzak and Barel."

"Perhaps twenty to thirty. I'm excluding known espionage agents and, in some cases, mobsters on embassy staffs, trade delegations, and so on. If you count those, the number goes up to nearer two hundred. Perhaps I'd better interpolate here, and say that a great amount of this supervision is carried out by M.I.5, the Special Branch, and by some other agencies."

"What other agencies?"

"I'd prefer them to identify themselves."

"But your main concern is with this migrant twenty to thirty?"

"Indeed."

"And how many men do you have for this?"

"Four officers, sir, and some secretarial back-up. We also have secondments, contract officers if you like, generally from military intelligence or the police. They are all short-term, though." Fossit was always glad to bake some bread.

"Surely this is entirely inadequate?"

"On occasions, yes." He hesitated. "Intelligence is not really a matter of surveillance. If one were to conclude it were, it would be best simply to deny entrance to all the people we suspect—really, that's a political matter for you ladies and gentlemen. We could, indeed we do, supply a register."

"But once we let them in, surely we keep tabs on them?"

A nice "we," Fossit thought. A dear old Tory darling who assumed that "we" were all on the same side, against a common enemy.

"We lack the resources for that degree of surveillance. Although I would like a bigger force, I doubt if total surveillance would be the answer. As a simple logistic, by the way, really good surveillance that would not be politically embarrassing, would need to operate on—at a conservative estimate—an eight-to-one ratio. So, logistically speaking, if I were doing a surveillance job, I'd need about two hundred and forty extra officers."

"Will you explain why you *don't* do a surveillance job?"

"Partly because other agencies do it already, but more because mine is in reality an Intelligence task. We are able to pinpoint likely troublemakers, then assess the likely risk—hence our register."

"This Barel, Gorodish and Yitzak—what does your register say about them?"

"Barel and Gorodish are both Mossad members recruited from a military unit originally called 101—roughly the equivalent of our S.A.S. Yitzak was a hit man, first 101, but then a member of Hand of God and the Hand of God's successor, which candidly we can't put a name to."

"His function?"

"His—and its—function was to put an end to active enemies of Israel."

" 'Put an end to'?"

"Assassinate."

"By what means?"

"This is all on open record, sir. Originally by shooting. The Hand of God were experts with a specially developed .22 machine pistol. More recently the Israeli hit teams have gone over to other methods without pattern, including telephone bombing, car bombing and letter bombing. But their hit activities are scaled down, now their Intelligence is so advanced. Their intelligence people have, for example, several times persuaded Arabs to assassinate other Arabs for them."

"On the continent of Europe, or in Africa and Asia?"

"Everywhere. But certainly in Paris."

"And in London?"

"In our view, yes."

"What do you people do about it?"

"It's a political matter, as I have already indicated. And one that involves embassy staff. So one *could* ask what do *you* do about it. That being said, we are not a secret service. Except for those rare occasions when we stray out of our depth, we supply information not just to Home Office and Government, but to this Committee and all Members of Parliament at large."

"To the Press?"

"I give briefings. It's an open office."

"Is this one of those occasions when you are out of your depth?"

Not a Jewish member, but one of the much smaller Arab lobby. He was cross-cut by a son of the saw and shovel who growled, "Isn't it true that all the nation's intelligence and security services are run by some effete little Oxbridge quango or other?"

"My office is responsible to this Committee, and I have never heard you gentlemen so described." Fossit smiled to enhance their laughter, then returned to the real question. "If you are asking me why none of our agencies foresaw the abduction of a British national by an Israeli team I must once again stress that there was no reason to suppose Israel had any interest in such a man."

"Yet these thugs were here."

Fossit was always unhappy with hyperbole. "The likely Arab targets were all protected. The men themselves, or two of them, were supposed to be at a function at their national embassy, where they were perfectly entitled to be. The members of this Committee know all this.''

"Are you suggesting a degree of ambassadorial duplicity?" Again the pro-Arab questioner. "I have put this question to Mr. Pomeroy, because, strictly speaking, embassies are the concern of the Foreign Office. He assures me that while that is undoubtedly true, your people are the experts on embassy personnel.''

"I'd prefer not to speculate about individuals, insofar as none of us knows what goes on in other people's embassies. The current ambassador has the reputation of being a bit of an anglophile. That being said, most embassies engage in social camouflage without the ambassador knowing exactly ·what they are being asked to camouflage.''

"That is slightly more than we obtained from Pomeroy.''

"I must stress that there are a dozen embassies that do more of this sort of thing than the current Israelis. The Russians, of course, do it one hundred per cent of the time with one hundred percent of their staff.''

"They're all spies?''

"They're all out to confuse us.''

The Arabist intended to persist. "Given that we have this friend at 2 Palace Green and given the weight of our own briefing, why can't we persuade these people that they have made a mistake?''

"Because we are dealing with what we believe to be an honest case of mistaken identity. The Israelis are being quite frank about this at diplomatic level. Unfortunately our usual allies are taking their superficially persuasive line that an Israeli court of law will be the best place to sift the conflicting evidence.''

The Zionist lobby woke up. "You're suggesting, Mr. Fossit, that an Israeli court, rooted as it is in the Anglo-American legal tradition, you are suggesting such a court is an inappropriate place to seek the truth.''

"I am suggesting that all courts are inappropriate places. I can think of no court whose pursuit of the truth is as many-sided as a Parliamentary Committee's, for example.''

Again there was laughter. Leonard Fossit was doing his usual good job.

"So this Kay would have a fair hearing, here?"

"In my view."

"Even if he were Ernst Halder? I am sorry to press this, but many of us feel it inconceivable that the Israelis could be wrong on such a point."

"On any point?"

"On such a point. It is, after all, one on which their history makes them expert."

The chairman decided to move matters on. "Your man is to be congratulated, Mr. Fossit. We don't, I think, need to ask him any questions, so perhaps you will let him know of our pleasure. The Committee's main concern must be what it always was, however: that he was doing no more than bar the stable door after the horse had bolted."

"Surely that is all that any successful act of detection ever achieves? But it meant we could tell the Israelis, rather than have them tell us. More to the point, it meant that I could tell Sir Terence Quinlan and there could be a statement in both Houses before it was the subject of Press report and public speculation."

"And this tiny swallow is supposed to make my summer?" the saw and shovel asked sourly.

Fossit had spent too long at the mark. His polite irritability was beginning to breed a headache.

Even so, the Arabist was not yet finished. "Can you assure us there is no such Israeli team in place in Britain today?"

"Not on diplomatic accreditation."

"They weren't so accredited last time, were they?"

"That is correct."

"You are clear that there is no-one of the sort who abducted Charles Kay in London at this moment?"

Fossit's headache was now on the outside of his smile. "You really must address that question to the appropriate agencies."

"So far as you know?"

"As far as I am aware, there is no such group of people."

5.

Matson stood with his knees against the rim of the lavatory and watched his horrible face in the mirror. Its stitches were weeping and two days' sunshine had made his bruises yellower than the original iodine.

Brenda came and stood behind him. "Leonard bollock you?"

"He rummaged inside my scrotum with bloody hands."

"No damage to be done there."

"He's now doing penance in front of some Parliamentary Committee or other."

"I been reviewing the Matson shelf."

"I thought we'd eat out."

"Your books, not your larder." She waved some poems in his face. "Most people I worked with have third-class degrees from Oxford and think they know about Art, or first-class degrees at the London School of Pyorrhoea and think they know about Life. You rightly think you know nothing, and so you read. Having trouble with your zip?"

He left his private moment and went to the fridge. All the beer was gone. Two can live more irritably than one, he decided. He had been trained to expect order. Without it, he always felt close to disaster.

"What I found on your shelf was Shelley." She was exhibiting the large-format Standard Edition as if it contained some special source of excitement. "You want to stay away from that Ginevra. She is marked with the kiss of Cain. She is signed with death. You want a girl like me, with the life-force in her, one that will bite you by the ear."

He did not want to be bitten. He wanted the social decorum of Chislehurst.

"Percy Bysshe wrote a poem called *Ginevra* in 1821. You don't need to snatch at the book: I'm going to read it to you. It's only three hundred lines. As I indicated, she dies a melancholy death."

"So will you, if you steal my beer."

"The poem begins with a description of my beloved Patrick." She sat cross-legged on the floor and began to flaunt her missing consonants:

" *'Wild, pale, and wonder-stricken, even as one*
Who staggers forth into the air and sun
From the dark chambers of a mortal fever
Bewildered and incapable . . .'

"Like you just now in the loo, dearest heart—

" *'And I am dead, or shall be soon—my knell*
Will mix its music with that merry bell . . .' "

Matson's telephone rang, rang off before he could reach it, rang again.

She didn't share his sense of bad magic, but broke off to smile. "Answer that merry bell, lover." She went on reading aloud.

It was Dixon. "Paddy, Kay's daughter may need you. If she's still in one piece. We've intercepted a code-call that can only mean there's an Israeli stay-behind in the house next door to her."

"The old lady who's away?"

"It's Israel she's away to. Did you know that? My people are already in place. So are the Terror Squad. But we'll need someone who knows the situation in there to sweep up. I'm hideously scared that's all that's going to be left for us, Thump. Got your car?"

"Twenty minutes."

He hung up to hear Brenda read:

" *'They found Ginevra dead, if it be death*
To be without motion, or pulse or breath,
With waxen cheeks and limbs which, stiff and white . . .' "

then break off to say, "Where do you think you're going?"

"Chislehurst. Come on. Don't bother with your face."

She wanted to bother with her face, so he left her behind.

6.

Matson could see he was too late. They were all too late, perhaps only by minutes, but too late.

There were several police cars with beacons at the top of the road. An ambulance pulled round the corner, just behind him.

Uniformed flat-hats with rifles stood barring the way, looking wide and cumbersome in their flak jackets, like kids with their pockets stuffed with chocolate.

Matson showed his identity and led the ambulance past them.

He drove down slowly towards the house. The street lamps were out and everywhere was dark. He glimpsed people peering from front porches, one or two in their gardens.

He stopped opposite the phonebox and dowsed his lights. The ambulance stayed behind him.

His last image was of her front door blown out and the hallway smoking as if making up its mind to burn.

He jumped from the car and started to run. It was a warm night but his nostrils felt chilly like they did after a strike of lightning.

There were men crouched this side of the shrubbery; others standing hunched over in the street.

Dixon came up to him.

"Call came in the early evening, Thump. This happened a couple of minutes ago. We put some of the Heavy Mob in place, then began to talk them out. Thought we held all the high cards, but overlooked their determination to press on. We were actually ringing the bell when the lights went out, street lamps, house circuits, the lot. Must have wired it up days ago. Meanwhile her door fell in with a bang and the shooting started. Hairy as hell for a second or two. We couldn't tell who was which and where were the friendlies."

"What's inside?"

"You haven't got a couple of dozen ampoules of the appropriate snake anti-venom in your handbag, Thump; or even an Australian polyvalent? I must say I left mine at home with Anne on the grand piano. Meanwhile, I can tell you this much. They didn't get more than a pace or two through the front door. Then back they came running. They'd used stun grenades on her daddy's windows, you see. Shrapnel even."

"Sir! Sir!" Someone was calling from the side of the Common.

Matson grabbed Dixon's arm. "You mean the Taipan's out?"

"I took a peep, yes. Her bloody serpent's escaped. By which I mean its case is shattered. But whether inside the house or outside the house . . ."

"The girl?"

"We don't know."

He knew he ought to look, but doubted if even Adam could have been so bold with a Taipan loose in the Garden.

"Over here, sir!"

They went over.

The man was lying on the Common about twenty yards away. He was on his back, with his shirt up and his belly pecked with blood. He was straining for breath and he was in spasm. He was dribbling, or losing lymph, or just simply being sick.

"That's the Taipan's doing," Matson said. "I watched it bite a rat a few days ago. Is this fellow one of them?"

"I've got his gun," a civilian in a flak jacket said.

Dixon examined it. "Twenty-two machine pistol. It's the old toy."

"Snakes don't move far," Matson said. "Give me a decent torch and I'll take a look for it."

Dixon held out his torch. "Leonard said you were fast becoming the family expert."

"I'm always alpha at theory."

He was looking for a live snake and a dead girl. Impossible to suppose the snake would not have lashed out at her, or whatever the grenades had left of her. That was where she sat, next to its tank, night after night in Daddy's den right near his telephone, the girl who was manning the palisades for him. Matson could understand the police reluctance to put their heavies in against a reptile they'd never seen, couldn't picture, and whose bite would be almost immediately fatal to a considerable number of them.

"How dangerous *is* the thing?" Dixon followed him onto the Common. He was the kind of man who earns his marmalade.

"If it's the one I think it is, its venom is forty times as potent as a King Cobra's."

"Jesus."

"If it's the one it *might* be," Matson treading and speaking with the slowness of acute fear, "the recently uncovered rarer one, then it's about two hundred times as powerful.''

''There it is.'' Neither knew which one had spoken. They saw restless coils and a blue shirt humped behind tufts of grass.

''I think it's brought another one of their chaps down in the bushes behind it. Good old Timmy. Well, we can go indoors and look for Miss Kay now we know it's outside.''

The snake was wide-mouthed. It darted at the torch-beam, still hyperactive. The night was too hot for it to lie up.

Matson had already spent too much of his life watching Timmy. He switched off the light and followed Dixon back to the house, trying to prepare himself. He had seen what the Taipan could do; he had seen what grenades can do many times, with a recent reminder in Jaffo.

The ambulance had moved down and was receiving some of its cargo. A second ambulance was waiting at the top of the road. There were lights on in Number Forty-two now.

Ginevra Kay stood in the front garden. A young man huddled against her, a young man so young that Matson would think of him ever afterwards as a boy. They both had that look, which is indefinable, of being only recently dressed.

''We heard this frightful bang,'' she was explaining. ''We were—we were just upstairs, and in all the circum-stances—'' She caught sight of Matson, and it was the first time he had seen her embarrassed.

He did not enjoy the revelation. He turned away.

Some of the Heavy Mob would have what he wanted. He went towards one of the flak-jackets and flashed his ID. ''What are you wearing?'' he asked, tapping the constable's shot-gun.

The man grinned. ''It's a nice medium-grain pump. Have it and welcome. Not much scatter.''

Someone was running anxiously behind him. It was Gi-nevra.

''You'll try to find Timmy for me? Peter says he'll help in the morning.''

''Tell him to bring his butterfly net.''

"It's so important for Daddy."

"Mr. Dixon will want to talk to you both. You remember the nice Oxbridge one?" He hoped his teeth looked as white as hers in the lamplight.

He walked back carefully onto the Common, spearing his torch through the shadows.

The snake had disappeared.

His skin nettled.

Blue-shirt was still lying behind the frieze of spear grass. He wore a pair of grenades fastened by their levers to his belt. His eyes were as dead and egglike as his grenades. Pimpled like grenades, too. As if dissolving in blisters.

Matson swung the torch slowly, holding the gun crooked back under his right elbow for a quick shot.

He heard it breathe, a dry suck of breath like an old man dying.

Timmy wasn't dying. Timmy was being noisy just ten feet away. Timmy, who was four yards long, was rasping the air through a nearly closed mouth, her head held back over side-looped coils.

Matson knew all about Timmy. He'd read all about Timmy. Timmy was sportingly and decently making her threat display in the blob of torch-light.

It was just like being in the snake-house at the zoo, save in this case there was nothing between him and those ever-ready fangs but the clear glass of night.

Timmy the tom who laid eggs.

Matson adjusted his grip on the gun, coming up slowly to the aim with the torch held straight along the stock.

The Taipan lacks mortal beauty in its daylight coils. It is patterned for the eye of the Gods. It looks its most lovely in a strong beam.

Timmy by torchlight looked at her loveliest.

As she was most lovely in any kind of light.

"Goodbye, Timmy!" Goodbye, Ginevra.

He shot Daddy's snake.

FOURTEEN

1.

The military hospital lay left of the road beyond the fork to Bet Shemesh. Aaron Kaplan had driven from Jerusalem by the scenic route, but he was still early.

The sentry pointed out a parking spot just inside the main gate, then called, "Come here."

Kaplan locked his car before walking back.

"Let's see that pass again." The man looked at it unhurriedly then lifted the telephone hanging in the gate-box. "I've got a Mr. Aaron I. Kaplan here—*Kaplan*—attorney-at-law. You're expecting him? Well, somebody has to do the job, I suppose." He returned Kaplan's pass and said, "I read we got people queuing up to train as hangman. It's a lost art, they say. I bet you'll get paid more money for your bit, though."

"I expect I will."

"I had grandmothers die in those camps."

"I can't have had enough grandmothers. Which way is it?"

"Oh. Over to the glass door there. Glad to talk to you, Mr. Kaplan. No-one's going to drive off in your car, except you if we let you out."

Inside the door, he was stopped and told to take off his jacket. Two sergeants of infantry made him turn out his pockets, then empty his briefcase. One of them felt his legs, the sides of his shirt, tested him under the arms, went back to his cuffs and shoes.

"I hope this isn't harassment of the defence?"

"It's harassment of everyone who comes here, Mr. Kaplan. Thank you for your cooperation."

They handed him back his possessions one by one with deliberate patience. One of them wiped his briefcase with a cloth.

"Everyone? I thought this was a military hospital."

" 'Was' is the word, sir."

"Mr. Kaplan?"

He turned and saw a man in a white lab coat. He was the first person not to be wearing sidearms.

"You're still a few minutes early, but we have a room set aside. Today you'll see the prisoner in his own—er—quarters. If that arrangement seems wrong to you we can try something else for next time."

"Thank you. I'll see."

"He has already had a visitor this morning, and that person would like to speak to you."

"Who's that?"

"I'd prefer not to compromise anybody's right of access or refusal."

Kaplan turned the sentence over in his mind and decided not to make a joke about it. He stepped into a small room that had brown plastic easy chairs and a table with a very large vase.

A man wearing a flame-coloured tie and a crumpled lightweight suit already sat there. He sprang up and held out his hand. "Marcus Pomeroy, from Rehov Hayarkon."

"The British Embassy?"

The man did a little bow to reveal that he had not been in Israel long. The bald patch on his crown was sun-basted to the same absurd colour as his tie.

"I'm not sure it is appropriate to talk to you until I have seen my client."

"When you've seen your client you may well wonder just what *is* appropriate."

"In any event, I'm certain this isn't the place."

"That vase may be unsightly, but it's safe. I've checked it."

Kaplan sank himself reluctantly onto a chair and gazed at the man's plastic smile.

"Most important thing. Can I have a lift back to civilisation? I came by taxi. Costly mistake."

Kaplan tutted his annoyance, and said sharply, "The most important thing is for me to establish whether or not you think this man is British."

"I don't know that. I really don't know." Something cataclysmic was happening to his eyebrows. "He's certainly English. We're not one of your instant nations. Nothing ersatz. It takes a couple of generations to produce a passable imitation of an ordinary Englishman. And this one's not ordinary. He's a mint-fresh monomanic lunatic."

It takes one to know one. Kaplan felt heartened.

"Definitely in the Ark." Pomeroy showed his teeth in friendship. "Even if he didn't fetch up on Ararat with your lot. I showed him a couple of volumes of *Wisden*, you know. He turned to the Dulwich season of 1929 and started to cry. I'd have taken the fellow a cricket bat if only his keepers had let me. You don't want to forget cricket when they've got him in the dock, counsellor."

"What's Wisdom?"

The face grew lofty with disdain. "It's what represents the difference. It's as good as a birthmark. He's going to need a bit of building up, you know. They've been telling him he's not his little girl's father."

"Who is, nowadays?"

Pomeroy looked uncertain. He began to rub his bald spot reflectively, as if making sure God's finger still rested on him, before saying, "Not one of our Nosey Parkers thinks this man is other than he says he is. No-one could have invented him. We have so much documentation, so many photographs that prove beyond any shadow of doubt that he is Charles Henry Kay, a lifelong citizen of the United Kingdom. All the Prosecution will have is that he now bears an uncanny resemblance to Halder all those years ago."

Kaplan felt sorry for him. "There you misinterpret the situation, believe me. What the Prosecution will have against him is all the stuff they have against Ernst Halder, and that's enough to overload a data-bank."

"Something else." Pomeroy seemed frightened to hear himself. "Your client must not know this, but a few days ago an attempt was made on his daughter's life. Two of the agents died in the attempt, accidentally as it happens, but that's beside the point. One of them was an Israeli national. We have a prisoner, awaiting trial. Also an Israeli. It is for you to judge whether you can make use of any of this.''

"I can't. It intrigues me, but it will be of no interest to the House of Justice in Jerusalem.''

"Our main worry is that this jeopardises Miss Kay's involvement in your case. I'll be frank, even if it gives offence.'' Pomeroy was clearly offended himself at having to be frank, but he bit more air with his next statement. "The reputation of one of the finest and most autonomous Intelligence Services in the world is at stake here. Whatever Israel or its Justices may say in all sincerity, I very much doubt if you can absolutely guarantee Miss Kay's safety against your own people.''

"I can't comment on that. What I do know is that she must be here. Her testimony will be crucial.''

"We are still considering. She may be able to give evidence. But only that. I'm a cynical man, Mr. Kaplan. I can't help seeing how much more you may require of her in and out of court. Even if you rule out anything as vulgar, and in this case provoking, as trial-by-camera—and she's a pretty piece—even so, your cause could benefit psychologically if Ginevra Kay could be in the Courtroom or at least in Jerusalem throughout the proceedings.''

"Not my cause. The defendant's.''

"Her Majesty's Government does not, currently, feel that such a course would be expedient.''

There was a knock on the door.

"The prisoner is available now, Mr. Kaplan.''

Kaplan stood, then turned back towards Pomeroy, who was holding out his hand to say goodbye. "If you wait here, Pomeroy, I'll give you that lift. I need to persuade Her Majesty to change her mind.''

2.

The makeshift cell was furnished well, like a bed-sitting room in a student hostel. There were guards at the door and the door was open. Once Kaplan entered, the door was closed.

The prisoner sat on his divan studying some odd-shaped

pieces of paper, none of which appeared to have anything written on them.

Kaplan made an encouraging noise in his throat, but the man went on placing his pieces of paper in a semicircle behind him on the bed. He was wearing a new denim shirt, new jeans and slippers, and they all looked too big for him. He looked like a tortoise in the winter hills, not quite awake enough to poke its neck out.

Kaplan sat opposite him, spread his briefcase and said, "I am Aaron Isaac Kaplan. I have the permission of the House of Justice to defend you. I hope I have your permission too. Indeed, more than that, I *want* to defend you, and although you do not have a great deal of choice in the matter, I should like to think *you* want me to defend you."

"You speak very good English."

"My mother is a Scot, from Edinburgh. I studied in London and in the States. I come to London, for family reasons, once or twice each year."

"My daughter lives in Chislehurst. Do you know Chislehurst?"

"I think I've been there."

"You'll like her."

"Yes, I'm sure. Before we get down to the substance of your case—and believe me, we don't have much time, this thing is being rushed—is there anything you would like to tell me?"

"Yes, I am very comfortable here."

"That's reassuring news."

"They kept me in Jaffo, you know, and used electricity on me and sometimes smacked my head, but I'm better now. I had an erection this morning. They let me drink water whenever I want to."

"Good."

"Sometimes I go to the desert, but I've never been as thirsty as I was in Jaffo. All they let me drink was my tears. They made me drink cups of them in Jaffo."

Kaplan needed to talk to someone, anyone, Pomeroy even. Madness is hard on compassion. He looked for an exit. "What do they call you?"

"They call me Ernst. That's not my name."

"I mean what do your friends call you? What does your daughter call you?"

"She hasn't spoken to me."

"What do your friends call you?"

"Charles, some of them. Or Harry."

"What may I call you? May I call you Charles?"

"Kay. That's my name. Charles Henry Kay. C.H. Kay. You'll have seen it on my books. I'm really quite well known."

"Charles, I'm going to go away now and look through your papers. I'll be back first thing in the morning. Make a note of anything you feel we ought to discuss."

"I'll drink lots of water. The taps make lovely water here."

The door was not locked. Aaron Kaplan opened it and walked into the corridor. The two soldiers still stood there, and they left the door open so they could watch the prisoner shuffling his pieces of paper. Kaplan now knew the pieces of paper would remain empty, virgin as mountain snow, just like his client's mind. He walked along to a cubicle and desk at the end of the corridor. "Where's the Chief Medical Officer, or the doctor in charge?"

"I'll do."

"I'm Aaron Kaplan, the prisoner's lawyer. He's clearly unfit to plead."

"He's got a very slight heart murmur. If anything it's been diminishing since his arrival. We've found nothing else. Oh—occasional diverticular diarrhoea. No infection."

"I'm talking about his mental state."

"He's calm enough, very composed. On the other hand, I wouldn't say he's withdrawn or recessive."

"Do you speak English?"

"Very little. But everyone here is fluent in German. We were specially picked."

"Does he speak any German?"

"A little's coming back to him, but very very slowly."

"That man never spoke German in his life."

"Ernst Halder *is* a German. We make him ask for his food in German."

"And water?"

"That, yes. And the lavatory."

"But he's slow?"

"Yes."

"So if he *is* a German, he's ga-ga?"

"I'm not interested in his mental state."

"He's certainly ga-ga in English. In either case he's unfit to plead."

"We all know what's going to happen to him."

3.

Ginevra Kay changed colour: luminous green transposed to radiant blue, then an impossible fluorescence that steepened through yellow to white. She was fondling her boyfriend Peter and explaining why he couldn't play hunt-the-snake. The Taipan was out in the room somewhere, slithering about them. Or perhaps its eggs were beginning to explode.

Matson's eye opened fully, and there on the pillow was the snake book, with Brenda's red fingernail stopped at the Banded Krait. "Darling Paddy," she whispered, "at least you won't need to study this any more. You were really quite into it, weren't you? Snake kink." She shaded his eye with her hair. "Perhaps I must learn to fuck you like a snake."

"You want to learn to fuck like a woman first."

"Poor old Broken Ribs. How would you like your sausages? Grilled on both sides?"

"Just the inside will do. For a change."

His hard ramming against her bottom and damaging the tissue of her Denmark Hill ego.

"You're still drunk," she said. "When you're awake and compos, I want the whole Chislehurst story. You've been hiding it from me for days. Ralph Dixon says you behaved like a screaming hero. I told you you fancied that Ginny."

"Never mind her. I'm halfway to Denmark Hill."

"Get out of my bum and change trains."

Her kiss was beautifully intended, but the alarm-clock was shrill with daylight. Ten past seven.

"You'd better make love to me properly."

"Demanding little thing."

What a pity the phone tinkled, ringing on, then off, in the usual signal.

"Keep it where it's at," she said.

"Some calls are private." He eased her from bed.

It was the night exchange which they shared with the Ministry of Defence, telling him to stand by for a linked call. He heard Brenda flushing the loo, then padding along the hallway to fetch the post.

"Someone's mailed you some sweeties," she called.

"Wash your hands, if you're going to open my mail," he hissed. "I hope that's no-one from the office." Fossit's voice in his ear, as if from the next room and not somewhere in Sutton.

"I'm talking to the dog."

"Amsterdam sent me a parcel bomb this morning. I told you that biffing wasn't Barel's sort of work."

Matson was halfway out of bed and shouting, but the explosion seemed to begin a long while ago, at the beginning of time. It was just that the heat and the pressure took so long to get out of the hallway. And before it and after it the light. The raw glow of embers. He was looking at a girl with flames in her eyesockets, her hands, her chest. A black girl. Then the blood came.

FIFTEEN

1.

The man who called himself Kay looked around brightly, noting the details of the room. This was where the trial was to be held, *his* trial. It was a fine clinical room, benched almost like a laboratory. He was on his own ground here. Here, at last, he would be able to rise and point his finger at his accusers, and say in measured tones just what they had done to him.

Meanwhile he asked for a glass of water and fell fast asleep.

He awoke to find himself tremblingly on his feet. He was being helped up by the elbows, no—*held* up by the elbows.

The Judges entered.

Little Aaron Kaplan had risen to address them, and someone else was trying to stop Aaron Kaplan from opening his mouth.

Aaron Kaplan was his friend. He played chess with him often. He understood the game with the pieces of white paper. He had seen in an instant that they were aboriginal maps of the desert and the swamps, which as such showed nothing except the pathways of the Snake.

Aaron Kaplan won and was allowed to address the Judges. Kay noticed Aaron Kaplan held a piece of white paper.

"Sirs, I am grateful for this opportunity to address you before the indictment as detailed by your Most Learned Selves. I have two points of procedure for your considerations. Not to put them now would imperil the defence. They are these:

"The prosecution seeks to prove that the accused is a man called Halder. Or rather, the assumption is implicit in its case. The Accused insists that his name is Kay. That is the thrust of the prosecution, the counter-thrust of the defence. Clearly it is intolerable to the accused to be called Halder, whether in evidence, or in cross-examination or in preliminary statement or in summing up. It is obviously essential we call him something else, something neutral to both positions."

The Presiding Judge leant forward. "Let us agree to call him the Accused."

"I believe that will favour the Prosecution."

"I see nothing else to offer."

"Thank you. Then that I must accept. Sirs, my second point is this:

"There is only, by the terms of this Court, which is the House of Justice, the highest of our land, sirs, there is only one precedent for the Trial which very shortly shall begin to unfold. It is the *State of Israel* versus *Adolph Eichmann*, 1962. We regard that precedent as exemplary, but not, I submit, in this case. What rightly unfolded there, in sequels of evidence-in-chief, was a catalogue of Adolph Eichmann's crimes. Sirs, we have studied the preliminaries in this case, and have reason to anticipate such evidence as may be brought. It will consist, we anticipate, of recitals of the undoubted crimes of the Nazi Ernst Halder with an inferential gloss that the accused is that man."

"Counsel, these witnesses will relate to the man as well as to his crimes."

"Sirs, in view of the case for the defence, which I already make plain to you, we submit that witnesses should first be called upon to testify to the identity of the Accused. And then, and only *if* yourselves are so impressed—"

"Mr. Kaplan, it seems to all of us here you are asking for two trials. One as to identity, one as to guilt."

"Sirs, indeed I am."

"We continue our position. This trial has one integrity, relating to both matters which in our minds are indivisible. You cannot compel a witness to subdivide the evidence without seeming to encourage that witness to modify the oath.''

"Sirs, a trial in Israel is not as another trial. We are not as another people, nor like another race. What we accept as evidence in such a case will not be like the evidence we accept in another case. Sirs, we are confronted by the assumption that the Jewish—not the Israeli—the *Jewish* victim's recognition of his oppressor is somehow holy, akin to a wife's instinctive recognition of her husband after a long separation: it proceeds from a conviction that does not quite transcend common sense, but which is more common than sense.''

"Mr. Kaplan, you have been eloquent, and you begin to develop an interesting point. We shall be mindful of it. In plain terms, no evidence which is not coupled with evidence of recognition will be allowed. Thank you for addressing us on this point.''

Kaplan bowed and returned to his seat. He muttered to his junior, "So far we've done quite well. We've stripped him of some of his witnesses.''

"Do you really think so? They've all come thousands of miles just to sing their piece. They're not going to have it thrown out on some silly point of procedure.''

"You mean they'll stick to a lie?''

"They'll say he's their man. They are bound to say he's their oppressor, or their afflictions will lack a frame. I do wish the old boy wouldn't keep on falling asleep.''

The defendant was already an embarrassment.

2.

The days did not seem important to the Accused. Nobody bothered overmuch about his nights.

Witness after witness spoke in many tongues to add to his confusion. Sometimes they were understood. Sometimes only the earphones could explain their interminable accusations.

Often he did not listen. Once he wept.

There was a kind of coherence, even at the Tower of Babel. The lawyers spoke Hebrew, but the Accused did not understand Hebrew. He slept through more and more.

Then he was awake. "That's Coloma,'' he said.

It can take a long time to recognise a person out of
context, especially after so much; but here were definitely
the teeth, the malevolence and the plastic gums of his Little Girl's mother, all the way from Caves Road.

He watched old Cobra Head with attention. "She lives
next door. She'll tell them who I am."

She had given evidence all day yesterday but he had
failed to notice her.

The Chief Prosecutor rose and said, "Yesterday you told
us, of your own knowledge, a very considerable amount
about the activities of the Accused. You told us, right at
the beginning of your evidence, of the two different periods in your life—correct me if I am wrong—the two different periods in your life when you had the opportunity
to observe this man very closely indeed."

"Correct."

"Now we want to continue with the first period of time,
because that is the period that is crucial. He will not, I
think, seek to deny anything about the second period, the
time lived in England.

"You said something right at the end of yesterday's proceedings which I would like you to—not to repeat, because
that would be wrong of me to suggest to you—but to assure the Most Learned Judges that you still remember
clearly. You said, did you not, that in common with other
young European women in the 1940s you had a particular
reason for remembering the Accused?"

"Yes. He forced his attentions upon me, as I said."

"He made you have sex with him?"

"Yes. Many times. He raped me. He made me stay with
him overnight. Yes, I could recognise him all right."

"That's a lie. I only had sex with her daughter." The
translation had worked its way through to Kay. He at last
understood what his charming old neighbour was saying.

"Many times."

"Only twice," Kay corrected.

The interruption had a limited effect on the courtroom,
as not everyone spoke English.

The Prosecutor hitched at his gown and said, "You
mentioned the four little girls?"

"Yes."

"Will you take your time and tell the Learned Judges, please."

"He picked out three or four girls—it was usual."

"For what purpose?"

"Obviously. To have sex with them. It was well known."

"You mean all of the high ranking . . ."

"No. I mean Halder was well known for certain practices."

"He forced himself upon four very young girls."

"Not young. Not in this case. They were merely little."

"He wanted these 'little people' for sexual purposes?"

"That among other things."

"He was a man of large appetites?"

"He was a man of bestial appetites. He was a beast. Some of the things he did . . ."

His deeds and misdeeds again began to filter through the earphones of the night. Kay was once more asleep.

As she detailed what he did, with whom, and how certainly, and how, it became clear through the recoiling horror of the recital that this was no Eichmann, no Himmler, no Speer. He was not a Book-keeper of Death, not even Death's Engineer or one of Death's Principal Architects.

He was Death's Jester.

The catalogue was not only grisly, it was various. It served to tell the world why the Jewish people so much needed to apprehend Halder, how absolute was the conviction that he was this man Kay.

At some stage Kay woke to hear Kaplan say to Coloma: "Are you really asking the Judges to believe that this man—whoever he was—would play his own procurer in such a loathly process?"

"Yes."

"Surely such a man—and it is our contention that this is not the man—would have sent hirelings?"

"No. It was as we heard."

"As you *heard?*"

"As we heard so did we see."

Other witnesses took the old woman's place in the dream. They all told the old woman's story. It was, alas, only too possible to hear the dreadful shrieks of execution, and to flinch at the appalling flames.

Yet, at such a distance, there was also a sense in which the uninvolved could also detect a certain sinister bonhomie in the activities of the Accused.

In Halder, for example, selecting three little sisters, the oldest of them twelve, with this remark, preceded by huge shouts of glee from his fellow devils, ''The Third Reich wastes nothing, gentlemen, nothing.''

He was going to hang.

It has always been so down the ages, the Joker and the Fool always get to hang, even in a pack of cards.

He sat there, shuffling his papers.

3.

Kaplan was clever. After every witness had consigned Ernst Halder to the fires of Hell, Kaplan would advance and jiggle photographs. Kay had not always been like Kay.

No-one would suppose that he had been.

So he couldn't always have been like Halder, could he?

''Do you recognise this man, and this man here?''

''Yes, they are all Halder.''

''That is Herman Goering as a very young man, and that one is Hess.''

Oh, he was clever, that Kaplan. Too clever by far for a Jury, but here there was no Jury. He was making the Judges think.

''And where is this man, Halder?''

''He is there,'' pointing behind, where they all had pointed.

But Halder wasn't there. Kay wasn't there.

The man had fainted long since on the floor. The prisoner was away having his ribs massaged.

''Identification by geography,'' Kaplan observed. ''Local geography.''

Kay was carried back and went to sleep.

When he woke up, Kaplan had produced a dentist. The dentist had proved for a most extensive dream that the mouth in the head that now hung before them was not Ernst Halder's but different altogether.

They had Ernst Halder's dental records.

And here they had the head of the man who called himself Kay.

The mouth if not the brains.

The Prosecutor roared and said, "Of course a man of such eminence would have his past prepared in depth. A mouth can be altered."

"Not in my experience it can't be. Or not to this extent."

The cross-examination finished with an aside. "As for that dentist, well, he practices in Jerusalem."

Was that some kind of in-joke, or simply a blight on the man's future livelihood?

4.

Once he had been friends with a man who worked at the conservation of rivers. He used to show off his collection of snakes, and be invited to look at all manner of beautiful things in return: waterbirds, game fish, subaquatic vegetation, sewers.

The sewers were a love-gift. They smelled of carbolic and chlorination. They were impeccable on the nose. But above and below and most certainly beyond these additives and their subtractions there was another smell. There was shit. Shit at the beginning of the tunnel, shit at the end. The shit of an entire city, the poison of half a nation.

No matter how much was treated today, it would all be there to do tomorrow. Then there were the rats, jolly brown rats, perking and sploshing about in the pipes by the hundred. It was like being inside an enormous python. His friend was showing him the arse of the world.

He never felt clean again.

After all the scrubbing and the rubbing, something still clung to him under the skin. His friend had handed him an irredeemable neurosis. He could wash again and again, but the thought would be there in the morning; and tomorrow it would return. Only in the desert was he free. But his snakes brought him back.

The Prosecutor was taking him to the same place, to the arse of the world. Only this time there was no carbolic and no chlorine. They couldn't bear him to wash it away, and even if he did, it would all be there to do tomorrow.

He looked at the man's face. He saw all their faces. They wanted to hiss and bite and butt and pump and never let go. Suppose he died from it? Suppose he went frothing and jerking about, just like poor Bosie? Their need could never be assuaged, any more than a snake can be permanently milked of venom. You could milk it today, but it would all be there to do tomorrow.

The scale of their outrage could not be lessened by his atonement, not by his death, nor by a million such.

He knew now why he had been unlucky with his little girl. Coloma would have said nothing, or his little girl would have faced him with the accusation of her tribe. What Coloma had done was envenom him with her massive antipathy, a poison he had not sensed until now. He thought he had been nibbling cakes with her. He had been draining her nipples of hate, milking her sacs.

He wanted his little girl. He wanted Ginevra. He wanted her mother.

All he had was Coloma, venomous, looking at him one-eyed, just like a cobra. And the witnesses, the Prosecutor, and the Judges, they were all looking at him, wanting him to die. When they had killed him, they would search for someone else, and it would all be there to do tomorrow.

He began to go to sleep, to wonder if he had ever been awake. Even asleep he had to listen to them, be conditioned by the filth they threw at him. Their voices went on and on like a radio he was too tired to reach out a hand and switch off.

5.

He was becoming aware of the problem. It was inching into the open and fixing him with its intelligent eye.

They needed to shift the blame. For two thousand years they had borne a tremendous guilt and now they must pass it on.

Unfortunately there weren't enough people to pass it to.

He woke from his best sleep to feel hands on his shoulders. They were gentle hands, perhaps even kind hands, but they were also extremely nervous, as if deprecating his bad form. He thought perhaps that he was about to be sentenced, and tried to stand up; but they didn't want him to stand up, merely to pay attention.

One of the Judges was speaking. ''We have heard a

great volume of testimony, as well as the opening speeches. Now this is a High Court, but it also functions as a Tribunal of Enquiry in a case like this. My Learned Fellow Judges and myself have decided that it is time to hear from the Accused. We have taken account of arguments from the defence as to the appropriateness or otherwise of this procedure, and we wish to make it plain that the Accused is free to make a statement now or later, if he so wishes, or simply to answer such questions as are put to him by ourselves or by counsel. He may, of course, decline to answer any question or indeed every question; but he must be produced.''

He stood and bowed to the Court.

"Do you wish to make a statement?''

"I shall deal with matters as they are put to me.'' He sat down, settled back on his chair, began to kneel into himself. Then his hand took possession of his head-set, began to massage it attentively against his ears.

The Prosecutor rose and said, "What is your name?''

"Charles Henry Kay.''

"Has it always been so?''

"For sixty-eight years.''

"Strange. In your depositions, and in other documents I have before me, you give your age as sixty-seven. Now what are we to deduce from that? Are we to assume that you are not quite so well acquainted with yourself as you would have us to believe, Ernst Halder?''

"You are quite simply to deduce that I have just had a birthday. It is not an anniversary I shall look back upon with pleasure.''

"You would have preferred other company?''

"The question is fatuous.''

"I think not. I have been observing you here in this Court of Justice. The Learned Judges have been watching you also. It is not an exaggeration to say that for much of the time in this place you have been under the world's eye. And what has the world seen in you?''

"It has seen a man who has been intolerably wronged.''

"Hardly. I put it to you, that what the world has seen is a creature so insensitive to human dignity and natural feeling—not to mention contemptuous of the House of Justice of the State of Israel—a creature so base as to yawn, and gawp and snore while a succession of people have told of the hideous evils that have been visited upon them at your hands or by your instruction. Now what is the world to think of you?"

"I cannot answer for the world."

"What are the Learned Judges to think?"

"I cannot answer for them, either. If they think I am this man Halder they are extremely stupid."

"Isn't it true to say, on all the evidence of your own behaviour, that you despise Jews?"

"Certainly not. Many of my friends, and a great number of my scientific colleagues, are Jews."

"All the Nazis said that."

"I don't understand you."

"I am saying that you have just treated this Court to a standard piece of Nazi sophistry."

"That is not a question, and I don't see that I am bound to respond to it, save to say this. The word Nazi is more frequently used, and more inaccurately, in this state than in any other. In the Knesset, for example, it is a common form of abuse. You really cannot expect a scientist to descend to the vituperation common among politicians, even when he is being questioned against his will by an imbecile."

"I think that makes my point very adequately. You despise Israelis. You despise Jews."

"It is silly to talk about Israel in the same breath as you draw when you accuse me of being this man Halder. When he was committing his crimes, Israel did not exist."

"That argument has been used before, Herr Halder."

"I am not Halder."

"That argument was used in the case of Adolph Eichmann. So you object to being called Halder, or a Nazi, and you think it foolish for me to say you are contemptuous of Jews?"

"Yes and yes. And yes. All men are Jews. It is only the Jews who indulge the fact. And to a biologist they are talking nonsense."

"Isn't that racist, to deny us our race?"

"It would be racist to do anything else. I reject all eugenic arguments, all those philosophies according to which members of your religion were persecuted. Such notions make no sense to me. I'm a herpetologist.''

''A man who studies snakes?''

''Certain species of poisonous snakes, yes. And you identify snakes by counting their scales.''

''And how do you identify human beings?''

''By nothing as precise, I fancy. There's too much hybridisation. But as I understand racial types—and it's not my discipline—by skin, and hair, and skull—then a Jew must be all of these peoples. What I am saying is that my view of you is very different from the views of your oppressors. Diametrically opposed, you might say.''

''As unlike as are the two prevailing totalitarianisms?''

''I think it is for you to decide whether you wish to cross-examine me or hold a debate. If you want a debate I really must decline. My brain is just not up to it, especially after some of the treatment I have been subjected to these last weeks.''

''I shall pass on to matters of fact in a moment. Your overall frame of mind is of interest to the Court, though. After all, you are accused of monstrous crimes. I'll just ask you this, Herr Halder. Do you prefer the company of snakes to being with human beings?''

For some reason the translator did not relay the words ''Herr Halder,'' and the Accused himself did not pick them up. He thought for a moment, then said, ''I certainly prefer the company of snakes to that of some of the human beings I have been with these last weeks.''

''Snakes are superior to Jews?''

''In small ways, yes.'' The man was quite mad again. ''Superior to all of us. They have two penises for a start. And for a man who has known the magneto—''

The Prosecutor decided not to let this gabble pass the translator. He said quickly, ''I put these questions to you in Hebrew because Hebrew is the official language of the State and of its Courts, Herr Halder. I should like you to comment on the fact that to my ears, and therefore I suspect to the ears of others, your English does seem a little stilted.''

Some people had understood his English well enough, and they laughed.

''I am not this man Halder.'' He lapsed, fell into distant

staring, then drooped his eyelids before saying, "I have
not been where English is spoken these last weeks. At
other times, I have been alone with the trees and the stones
in places where I have no words for them."

"You have no English for trees and stones?"

"They are not my discipline."

"Only for snakes?"

"Snakes talk Latin." There was more laughter, so he
said, "I think I have put up with more than enough. May
all this please finish now?"

The Presiding Judge leant forward and smiled kindly.
"Mr. Kaplan, I wonder if you will be so good as to impress upon the Accused that it is in his best interests to
take his pace from the House of Justice, and not to expect
the House of Justice to adapt itself to him. We appreciate
his frankness so far, and accept that the learned Prosecutor
has exceeded certain of the proprieties of examination.
That is why I have motioned for you to be still. There are
matters here which are plainly inadmissible, but the
Learned Judges will not need to be reminded of this every
other minute. The problems of translation and transcrip-
tion make things difficult enough as it is." He smiled
again. But the smiles of Presiding Judges are never warm.
"Unless there are medical reasons, or signs of manifest
stress, I shall expect the Accused to give testimony, answer questions from the Learned Judges, or otherwise be
available until the proper times of recess. There are many
days to go, and it is in everyone's interest to move forward."

The translation of this took some time. Kay held his
hand to his ear, and before it was finished asked quietly,
"What's the major saying? Isn't the bastard going to let
me sleep? Tell them I'm guilty." He stood up and shouted,
"Let's say I'm guilty. Let's see how far that moves things
forward."

The Court came slowly to a halt. Journalists jostled,
then sat back. The Israelis could afford to go now and
collect a quick headline. The foreigners decided to wait
for what would happen.

Counsel moved to the front, then waited for Kaplan.

He thought over the ground for a second or two, then
said, "Learned Judges, I made it clear in letters to the

Officers of the House of Justice, and then in my opening submissions, and in discussions with yourselves, that my client was unfit to plead, either because of his habitual clinical state, or because of incipient senility, or because of what has been done to him since his arrival in the State of Israel.''

"He was very vigorous earlier."

"But he cannot and does not last, sir."

"Mr. Kaplan, are you asking for time for you to discuss a changed plea with the Accused?"

"I am asking for what he asked for—a recess on humanitarian grounds."

"I must oppose that," the Prosecutor said. "If he wishes to change his plea, that's one thing. But here we have a man of sound mind professing his guilt, and in a way that is most disrespectful of this House. He really cannot be allowed a private consultation with his legal advisers every time he makes a mess of his evidence. He takes advice. He gives his testimony. He can be re-examined if his lawyers think he has presented himself in an unfair light."

"Mr. Kaplan?"

"If today's hearing cannot be recessed on the terms sought by the Accused, then I suggest they go on. I have no intention of seeking instruction for a formal plea of guilty. I believe that the defence's position will be vindicated in a very few minutes if the prosecution continues on its present course."

The lawyers took their places again. The Prosecutor turned towards the Accused and said, "Do you understand what the Learned Judges have decided?"

They woke him up.

"Yes, the major said I have to go on answering questions without a drink of water."

"You say you are guilty?"

"Yes."

"You are guilty of some or all of the charges as laid?"

"I am guilty in all the ways the State of Israel wants me to be guilty. For myself, I should just like to say I am guilty of letting it happen."

"Do you say you are Ernst Halder?"

"Certainly not. The man was a monster. I am a monster, too. I spent all of the war in Australia catching snakes.''

''Just now you said you were guilty.''

''Of course. I have been imprisoned among you, and you are contagious with guilt. The major up there is guilty, and that poor little girl of a corporal who was so nice to me, she was most guilty of all. It's your women who are the worst, Coloma for example. You should keep me away from your women. Men bear guilt, but women carry blame. It's the same thing, you see. It's the same thing turned inside out.''

''You shouted out that you were guilty. You shouted it out in open court immediately after you had been giving coherent and unflustered evidence.''

''Agreed.''

''Why?''

''I would do anything to stop this witless parade of woe. I would even have you hang me now.''

''You acknowledge the Nation's agony?''

''I think the Nation wallows in it. Or no, not quite that. I think there are people who wallow in pain. Some of them call themselves Jews. There are Jews who do no such thing, of course. There is also a state called Israel. Israel is a virile place. She mustn't soak up the problems of the world, even the problems of world Jewry. It is both arrogant of her and unproductive. Her dry places are likely to become soggy with tears. Occasions like this are very wet.''

''You think you have a right to say all this, and in contempt of this Court?''

''I am on trial for my life, remember? I think that allows me every contempt, unless you propose to scourge me before I carry my gallows up the hill. As to rights, I love—loved—Israel. I have been here many times. Later my attorney will show you my passport, and you will see how many times I came here catching your snakes and discussing them with your professors. Why wasn't I arrested then for being this man the whole Nation recognises? I'll tell you why. I wasn't arrested because the State of Israel wasn't in a mood to discover me. It was doing important things in the world. It was making itself. Not wasting its energies, not turning itself into a blotting paper of woe by hunting other men's enemies and sometimes their doubles.''

''I insist you return to—''

''The major said I could address the Court if I wanted to. I should like to ask it what good it thought it was doing by attempting to murder my daughter in London last week? I shall not forgive you for that, nor for the collapse you have occasioned in my ideals. I am not saying that you Jews are any worse than anyone else. Jews *are* no worse than anyone else. The tragedy is they've become nearly as bad. Was that something to aspire to?''

He stood up again. ''One more thing, and then I shall say nothing more.'' Standing was such an intolerable effort for this tanned, once fit man, that for a brief second of illusion he seemed to join the ranks of the oppressed. ''I am going to treat you to your favourite word. I am going to call you Nazis. That is what you are, the new Nazis. There are others, no doubt; but you have elected to swell their ranks.''

He swayed for a moment, and his guards tried to hold him, hoping he was done. He shook himself free, and took off his jacket. ''I have read the history of this war I stayed away from. The Nazis are repugnant to me. They made— you have heard testimony here—they made Jewish males drop their trousers, so they could shame and mock them. I should like the Learned Judges, and the world, to see what has been done to me, not here, but in another place a few miles away.''

He unfastened his trousers.

''Abducting me was an illegal act. It could only seem right if I were Ernst Halder. I am not. So I had to be made . . .'' Here, or a few phrases back, he became incoherent with tears, so much so that Kaplan lusted to see the transcript. The translation had stopped in confusion.

Kaplan's junior was American. ''We should have let him defend himself.''

''I'm beginning to wonder. One thing is sure. We can confidently expect his daughter. Not even the British will suspect any harm dare come to her after that little outburst.''

SIXTEEN

1.

The funeral was on her and Ginevra's side of the river, in a cemetery full of high-rise working-class headstones foreshortening the residential towers beyond a new motorway spur. Behind the grave the scene became tangled in chainlink and convolvulus, and then there were allotments.

Matson stood in the background with one of Dixon's antibodies and tried to see nothing while his companion spied on all. It turned out she had a mum and a man the mum called Dad, and that they both blamed him in full. If he had left her alone in her own nice little flat instead of always having her round to take dictation at his place none of this need have happened. His own head would have been blown off. He agreed without feeling any better.

She was C of E, of course, so nobody knew the parson. He buried her with the New English Prayer Book, which was even worse than Matson's own, and he didn't stop for train-noises or the nearby crematorium bell.

It was as well that the Resurrection and the Life were becoming stylistically mangled. The cosmetic face in its coffin can smile at you from Heaven. Bombs aren't like that. Bombs aren't cosmetic. When you see the red meat you know that it stays dead.

Matson left her in the clay, refused a lift from Dixon's official onlooker, and found his way back to the station. The carriage was littered with noon editions. Apparently there had been a dissolution. Quinlan's lot weren't any worse than any other lot, but they were ragged and demoralised and everyone thought they would go when the votes were counted. Kay's last chance of a sensible political gesture was fading. New governments are never in a hurry to solve their predecessors' ephemera.

At Victoria his need was no longer professional. He hurried to the lavatory. The turnstile was still there. Everything else was being dismantled behind hardboard and hessian. He was almost unzipped when a woman came out, pointing a haughty finger. The sign, in Asiatic whitewash, said it was temporarily a woman's loo. He dashed away to find his Sikhs.

They were at the far side of the station, on stilts. The men were being accommodated in a large Portakabin, up three iron steps. In spite of the transitory nature of the place, the pissoire was backed by an expansive sheet of metal they kept polished so it shed more light than it received. It was a stainless mirror that reflected every droop-headed downfalling detail. "Very well," thought Matson. "The world no longer has any secrets." He watched the Sikhs watching him with interest.

Poor bloody Asians: they worked in restaurants and lavatories, and always dealt with the White Eyes at their least presentable.

"Did your friend recover?"

"He's in a pretty bad way," Matson told the Old Sikh. "But he's still in there swinging."

He had to have a coffee after that, at the end of the railway that took him to funerals and Ginevra. He wondered how she'd fed the snake, whether that boyfriend had done it for her with his limp moustache; and then he realised that the snake was dead.

Somehow she belonged to the snake. The snake was her presence.

Without the snake, what was she? A girl with a father, her father's daughter. He ought to pack his bags, leave his desk and go and study psychology at some soppy university. Perhaps he would learn from it why it was the girl without the snake was not very much. Perhaps because with it her innocence had also been seen to go out of the garden.

No: it wasn't that. It was because she was only a silly little pretence and the real girl was dead.

Dead or not, it was time to go home to find her.

2.

She'd had a tough little body, mean as her origins, which were just like his own. But beautiful. And to touch her was amazing, like finding an ocean beneath a stone.

He stood in his hallway and wept.

They had done a very decent job, the Home Office handymen. Quick dabs of plaster. New lights. New window. A double coat of paint.

The carpet was brand new and better than his other one. There were three expensive inserts in the parquet. It had not been damaged, but in matters like this a person is left to lie a long time and the stains had not been pleasant.

He worked for a firm that looked after its own. For instance, here in the fridge was a new case of beer.

He walked into the living room again and found Shelley open on the floor. *Oxford Larger Standard Authors*, page 649.

He bent to pick it up and spilled a tiny red insert he knew for her fingernail. She was always breaking fingernails. One day they were broken for her.

The phone rang. He couldn't stand noise. The bruising still jarred on cheekbone and ribs.

"Ginevra Kay."

"Just why would that be?"

"The Foreign Office have phoned. They are taking me to Jerusalem. To Daddy's trial."

"Am I the best person to talk to?"

"When it comes to Daddy, yes, I think you are. I don't have many friends."

Only a lout would have mentioned a name or two. He needed to be a lout, but he couldn't remember any names.

"I'll be there in time for coffee." Peter—that was the name. He recalled it as he put the phone down. Then he thought of his wider obligations and checked in with the new girl at the office to tell her where he was going.

3.

Ginevra's place was still broken. The Home Office plasterers were not for her. She had tidied up and someone had screwed a door on, something inappropriate and hideous in unprimed unpainted deal.

He stood awkwardly in the pitted ruin of Daddy's den and looked for something to say. He knew it wouldn't be easy. They were both of them, for the moment, just a tiny bit mad.

She had some news for him. "You'll be pleased to know they're incubating Timmy's eggs."

"I'm very pleased."

"Daddy is going to be given a pair of little ones, if the incubation is successful."

"Brother and sister?"

"Yes."

"Isn't that incest?"

"I wish you wouldn't talk like that. Anyway, snakes are genetically self-protective. I read in the newspaper the other day that you lost your girl-friend."

"Nothing is genetically self-protective."

"I was talking about your girl-friend."

"Yes. I lost her."

"It was a letter bomb?"

"Something like that."

"Because of what's happening to Daddy?"

"Because of Daddy."

"Daddy had a girl-friend."

"What became of her?"

"She lives round the corner."

"That's a fate."

"She's married with two adorable babies. How could you do what you did to me if you had a girl-friend waiting?"

"How could I do it to you?"

"Yes. How could you do it to me?"

"Not to you. With you. I wanted to."

"That's disgusting."

"Bad taste merely. I don't want to do it again. Nor do you."

"Why do you say that?"

"Because I feel it."

"I'm still here in Chislehurst. Daddy's trial is going to last for months. You've got reasons to visit here when I come back. Official reasons."

"Sometimes you come to fancy people, not a lot but a little."

"That's what I'm saying."

"When she was alive I fancied her a little. Now it's a lot."

"I see."

He sat down by the broken snake tank and looked at the flaked walls. He smiled but he couldn't look at her, even though for days he had wanted no-one else.

"Would you like some coffee in one of my dirty cups?"

"In any kind of cup."

"I don't know how Peter got me to go upstairs. You'll think I'm being silly when I say . . ."

"There's no need to talk about it. You were going to tell me about going to Jerusalem."

"The Foreign Office people were wonderful. Mr. Pomeroy's been very thorough."

Her eyes were shining, but with an opaque glitter, like Timmy's in the torchlight. He wondered if she wore contact lenses.

"I have a letter from Mr. Kaplan," she said. "He confirms how thorough they've been, but he asks for certain crucial cuttings Daddy mentions."

Matson wondered about her eyes, wasn't listening.

"Well, I did."

"Well I never!"

"You remember I spoke of Daddy's leg? It happened in 1938. Look: I've found the actual newspapers."

Matson found himself gazing at some clippings so old they were the colour of thick tea. One was in Afrikaans, one was in English, The *Johannesburg Mail*.

He didn't understand.

"Oh, yes," she said. "Daddy is Daddy. There's no doubt about it. Not even a very clever lawyer could say otherwise. Look at him there with his snake sticks. You've heard the term Divine Idiot?" She was in a kind of ecstasy.

"My department deports them."

"Daddy is more of a picaresque saint."

Those we shoot at sight, he thought. Aloud he said, "I'm old and slow. You'll have to explain."

"Puff adders," she grinned. "This is the proof. Everyone told me how clever the Israelis would say the Germans were at copying scars, burying fingerprints."

"Fingerprints," he picked up. "There are no documents with Halder's—"

"Nor with Daddy's," she said, still as bright as a bean. "No surgeon could fake what a puff adder does, nor risk repeating it with venom. But even if they could, I've got the Old Daddy here in 1938. You should see the mess his leg was in. No-one could pretend this was Halder, not in 1938. They'd not even started to win, let alone lose. Look at the poor dear. He's lost so much muscle."

"Sloughing?"

"That's the word."

The newspaper photographs were very clear. Kay's lower leg looked like a rotten tree, a tree struck by lightning, peeled back, exposing the bone.

"I mean, he's grown some tissue, but not enough. It looks hideous, even now, even after all these years. You see why I must give evidence?"

"I'm sure Mr. Kaplan would be glad of these pictures."

"I won't let them out of my hand."

She would have to go, wouldn't she? There was a chance that the appearance of the girl, hysterical over the newspaper clippings, might just do it. The clippings would convert the court, the hysteria might galvanise the people who convince the politicians. Matson had always been sure of the truth of Kay's case. Until now he had never felt that the truth would be loud enough.

He was about to say these things when the phone rang.

"I was talking about Peter," she said. "He disgusted me, you know. Just as you disgusted me. Men seem to disgust me. Otherwise they're quite nice, really."

To say them, if not with Irish charm, at least with grace and wit.

"Hadn't you better answer that?"

She went into the hallway, picked up the phone and listened anxiously. "He'd like to speak to you," she said. "Says his name's Fossit."

"From the office." He knew his news made him grow in her sight. "Will you be offended if I close the door?"

"I'll be in the kitchen."

He put the phone gingerly to his still-bruised ear and heard Leonard say, "Good old Matty—you do keep at it, don't you? I must say I'm damned glad you're there. Are you all right? Are you feeling better?"

"I wouldn't mind meeting you for dinner this evening, if that answers your question."

"Anything that helps. We'll do it on petty cash. Fact is, I'm going to ask you to do a bit of the ticklish. You where you can't be overheard?"

The girl came into the room behind him, setting a coffee tray on the splintered table.

"Tell me what you need to tell me, and tell me till the end."

"Our man is dead. Pomeroy's just been on direct. Then Quinlan. Every bugger. Pardon the diplomatic language. He died during the morning recess. Israel claims it's from natural causes, but it's highly unlikely we'll get to see the corpse. Apparently he showed signs of myocarditis during his detention—inflammation of the heart-muscle. Electricity does that. So do certain drugs. So does old age. We'll make a lot of fuss, but our last lot of fussing didn't do much good. Tell her, if it's appropriate to tell, that Pomeroy's working for recovery of the body: or, failing that, family and diplomatic representation at the funeral. Whoever tells her that today is likely to have to disappoint her tomorrow. Now answer me yes, or answer me no. Are you feeling whole enough to help stir a little Foreign Office manure?"

"I have an ongoing commitment."

"Pomeroy wouldn't mind the whole package being presented to her in a way that'll get her hopping mad—I don't mean at once; I mean as part of the total strategy, and before the Press arrive. Those little bastards have made a mistake, but our man has died, and that lets them off scot free. What we have now is not merely diplomatic abduction, but international kidnap culminating in death. Their own court proceedings stop with death, so Pomeroy's quite hopeful there. The Foreign Office lawyers are working on ways that Miss Kay can bring a case against them either internationally or, failing that, in Israel. Got that?''

''Very thoughtful of them.''

''I'll see you at seven. Same place. Same table. I can watch some telly while I'm waiting.''

The phone went dead. He didn't want Leonard to ring off. There was no way he could bear to tell her.

He turned back towards her, sitting with the coffee against her pushed-together knees.

She gave him the most natural smile he'd ever had from her. ''That took a long time. Beakers,'' she said, ''not cups.''

He bent over her quickly and lifted her up. Even Ginevra would sense all the things his kiss was lacking. ''Oh my poor darling,'' he said.

4.

She lay underneath the counterpane in her blouse and tights making the bad breath of anguish. She had asked him to help her into bed as if she were an eighty-year-old invalid, and suddenly she was. She had no mother, no sister.

She had only removed her shoes and skirt as an afterthought. In a few days for him, and a few moments for herself, they had moved an eternity beyond the possibility of being lovers. He was now her nurse, her brother, her friend.

''Say something,'' she said.

He had already said everything that occurred to him, about his mother's death, Brenda's death, the death in action of several close friends.

''I'll say something,'' she said. ''I don't feel pain, not now. Only anger. If Coloma comes back, I'll kill her.''

''Shall I get you her daughter—I mean your father's—your friend?''

''I'll kill her,'' she said. ''If I had the men here, here in this house, the men who took my father, I'd give them to Timmy.''

''Yes.''

''Timmy's laid some eggs.''

''You told me. That's the best news yet.''

''What were their names?''

"I don't think I should. Though, in fact, come to think of it, the Israeli press has—"

"*Newsnight*," she said. "I saw *Newsnight*. It's just my memory just now."

"Excuse me a second." He offered the lying smile one always gives to invalids. His briefcase was downstairs, wasn't it?

He went to the loo. Bladders, he thought wonderingly, they're like hour-glasses. His mouth tasted as if it was full of sand.

He found the kitchen, made more coffee, dried the tray. There were no scars in the kitchen.

Upstairs again he showed her the photograph he should have shown her weeks ago.

She confirmed what he already knew. "Yes," she said. "That's him."

"The one with the trolley?"

"That's him."

"There are those who say revenge never helps."

"Oh yes it does. Do you ever read their Bible?"

"I only read mine."

"A tooth for a tooth, it says. An eye for an eye."

"That's what it says in mine. I used to know a priest in my old mother's day: he said that real revenge would be more like an eye for a tooth."

"That's it." There was a religious glow on her face.

"I can't quite do that for you, Ginevra." He took hold of her hand. "But, with a little luck, I might manage a tooth for an eye." He kissed her carefully, not on the mouth.

5.

The phonebox was hotter than ever. It still seemed listless with his and the old lady's air.

He dialled Euston and asked for his Inspector C.I.D. "About Julia Keppleman," he wondered aloud.

"The one with a lid on. I hate that one. Do you know she's still not released for burial? Think what that does to a Jewish family."

"Are you on for a little unofficial revenge?"

"Never, but I could make an exception," the man growled. "I saw what he did to the body."

"I can't quite get you Yitzak." He left out that Yitzak was dead, in case it blunted the inspector's ardour. "But I can point out the little sod who put him up to it."

"Doesn't he belong to some embassy?"

"He'll pull his diplomatic plonker all over us. But we'll get him on his gun. All those Israelis carry a gun nowadays, and I can assure you the Home Office doesn't like it."

"Suppose it's not on my patch?"

"It's a murder enquiry. It's a hot tip. You can blame me. Everybody does."

"Shall my chaps come armed?"

"Just you and me," Matson said. "For myself, I don't trust me with a gun these days." He liked saying that. He liked not trusting himself.

He rang off and dialled Ralph Dixon.

Dixon dutifully gave him the three addresses, then said, "Sorry about the no-score draw in Jerusalem, Thump. But it means we've got him watched tonight. He's been holed up all day at the one round the corner from you."

"Perfect for Euston C.I.D."

"And he's got both sisters with him. I mean, one's *in situ*, the other's dropped round. Sorting out their family problem, is what the bidet says."

"If there's any aggravation, he'll leave before I get there."

"I doubt it. He's good with aggravation. They both give him that, but he's a diplomat. He sees it as practice."

One more call to Euston and Matson was on his way.

6.

Matson didn't call home for a gun. The trouble with guns was he only knew how to use them to kill people.

Sister Number Two lived in Camden Higher Rented, just like Matson. A gritty concrete stair with a prominent fuse-box, a capacious mob-size landing.

Matson's inspector turned out to be disconcertingly youthful, a kind of toughened-up Peter. He had brought two uniformed constables with him, one with a long-handled axe. They looked like men who were about to enjoy themselves.

There was a morally satisfying aroma of hash seeping under the lady's door. They all relaxed into smiles.

"Puts me in mind of Confucius," the inspector said. "The hunter after excuses can always come up with a better one." He rapped on the woodwork and called, "Police. Euston C.I.D. Open up!"

The silence became thicker. The smell of hash went away, licked its lips and came back again. There was no whispered consultation or instruction behind the door; just, right against their ear, the thud of a bolt.

Since the door did not open, they could only conclude it was being latched tight.

The Inspector drew back and motioned to the constable with the axe.

The constable swung the axe over his shoulder in an arc from the ground and hit the upper part of the door with it.

It wedged in the panel, so he shook it.

The panel came away from its frame, showing haze and soft light and empty walls.

The other constable reached in and opened the frame, then stepped to one side so his Inspector could enter. His Inspector was elbowed aside by Matson.

Matson knew the lay-out of the flat, so like his own. The first and second alcoves led to bedrooms, the third door was a cupboard. There was nobody there. That left the kitchen, the bathroom, the lyceum-like parquet of the lounge.

The parquet was slippery with Indian rugs and two naked girls. They were just wrapping their legs in some modesty, possibly the rugs; but they weren't as well covered as the parquet, and Matson could see most of that.

"An experiment in existential living?" he wondered aloud. If he weren't numb with death he would be jealous.

Reitel had moved quickly. He was perfecting tricks that diplomats and lechers learn early. He already wore his shirt, his trousers and his shoes; but not his socks or underpants. Not one sock at least. There was an agreeable amount of orgiastic litter. None of this detracted from the chill authority of the small Astra pistol he held with a steadiness of hand that went well beyond the norm for Second Secretaries with special responsibilities for Trade and Tractor Parts.

"That's an inferior Spanish gun," Matson advised him. "Astra do a damned good magnum, just the same." Stress leads to social exchanges, even with a man who may be about to kill you. "I'd be pretty miffed myself," he went on, "if I got to be interrupted in the middle of all this."

"Are you Amos Reitel? Are you Celia—"

"Skin it!" Amos already had, and it didn't affect his colloquialisms a bit.

"I am an officer in the Metropolitan Police and I have warrants—"

"And I am a diplomat." Not enough of one to make him lower his gun. "I shall, of course, claim the usual immunities. I do not propose to follow you anywhere until I am accompanied by at least two people from my Embassy. You say you are a police officer, but you are in plain-clothes. Anyone can fabricate a warrant or a warrant-card, or any other document. Two of you are wearing what may or may not be authentic uniform, but one of you is carrying an axe. I have no intention of being found in some alley with it stuck in the back of my head. You are led by a man I believe to be a murderer and know to be a clown. In his more usual capacity he is well up to borrowing, or stealing, a pair of theatrical costumes."

One of the women tittered.

"I must warn you—"

"I am well aware that people who ignore a properly drawn warrant are punishable at law, even if they can show they believe the warrant to be false. But I am not available to your courts, nor to your police-station unless I choose to accompany you there. And I don't. This gun will keep me here. Matson knows about guns. Ask him and he will tell you it holds seven shots. I don't propose to miss with more than three of them." His eye and his gun were directed towards Matson now, both with a nasty glitter. "Shooting you," he said, "you in particular, in these circumstances, is not going to harm my career one bit. Not in *my* country. For reasons you very well know."

There was no more tittering, no more breath, just a gentle shuffling to be somewhere else.

The inspector lightened his throat and said, "Mr. Reitel. For the last—"

Amos fired. It had taken him time to react, perhaps half a second, but the bloody little Astra got off the promised three, all of them at Matson and not all misses.

Matson was fed up with Amos's calm, his sexual abundance, and if the sod had managed to put his jacket on he would also have loathed his suit. At the back of him were Kay and Ginevra, his own long-distance spanking; up front a raw swell of rage for the girl who had risen from his bed and been reduced in an instant to a shriek of eyeless meat. He may even have shouted her name.

His elbow-roll lacked practice, he was light years away from his time in the Thugs; as he somersaulted in beneath the horizontal snout of the gun he skidded on rugs, parquet, flesh and felt pain score his buttock; but he had covered the required twelve feet to sweep pistol and gun-arm aside then unwind upwards into a chin jab, the hard heel of his palm collapsing Reitel's face.

Women shouted. There seemed more than two, but two women can be a lot. He staggered upright with blood running down into his shoe. He knew he had been more than nicked, and he hated their home-counties voices.

"You've killed him," the inspector said.

Amos was flat on his back, his mouth tongue-thick with liquid.

"You've broken the wanker's neck."

"It's only unhooked his jaw." Matson kicked the gun away and watched Reitel twitch and spasm like a girl at the peak of love, and tried not to shudder. "Turn him over before he drowns."

Someone found a phone in a pile of cushions. They waited for ambulances and two more cars, the women with their wrists cuffed, still draped in rugs. The policemen eyed their naked mouthings without interest. One constable held a plastic sack full of ashtrays; the other leant contentedly on his axe. This was the bit they were used to.

The inspector had bagged the Astra in a small polythene pouch. He was thumbing it through the latex to jam the safety on hard.

7.

The Ambassador did not think he would be leaving London after all. Or not yet, if not never. Not until it was time to go to Washington or at least to the United Nations in New York.

It was a pity Amos had pulled out a gun. Even more of a pity he had fired it. A great amount of tact would be necessary if the Embassy was to register a complaint about the ruin of his jaw, his severed collar-bone. That English security man had been hit, though hardly in a manner his superiors would be glad to advertise. He had dealt Amos terrible damage in return.

Amos would have to be sent home, of course. Leonard Fossit would see to it that quite a number of others went home as well. Marcus Pomeroy could block all of Leonard's nonsense if he had a mind to; but Pomeroy had grown strange of late. Pomeroy was turning into a bit of a Nazi.

That was on the negative side.

On the positive was the happy circumstance that the agent Yitzak had never once set foot in the Embassy, not even to carry the Minister's case. Nor had the wilder sections of the Press—and in the business with Amos as well as poor Julia the Press had been united in wildness—nor had they got hold of Yitzak's name in connection with her death, nor the full extent of the national involvement. His conscience could be quite clear tomorrow when it would be his unpleasant duty to stand close to August and Olga Keppleman at their daughter's funeral, her body at cruel last having been released for burial.

When he was old, when he began to babble after the last drink, he would probably tell intimates that it had served her right for not staying for the champagne he had summoned for her, for being so perversely argumentative, for not wearing more sedate clothes to an Embassy function, for not . . .

The sun was not planted yesterday, he thought. Nor will its leaf lend shade.

Then he thought: the young are their own murderers. If not, there are enough of us to help them.